Cathy Lane & Angus Carlyle

Sound arts now

Uniformbooks

First published 2021
Copyright © Cathy Lane, Angus Carlyle, interviewees
ISBN 978-1-910010-26-6

Uniformbooks
7 Hillhead Terrace, Axminster, Devon EX13 5JL
uniformbooks.co.uk

Trade distribution in the UK by Central Books
centralbooks.com

Printed and bound by T J Books, Padstow, Cornwall

Fore-
words

A written record of the origins of this book can be found in a trail that threads through files in folders on desktops and in shared dropboxes, pages in notebooks, txt messages and email exchanges, the earliest of which date back to 2014. These documents scope out potential structures, suggest possible interviewees, consider different emphases that might be adopted, echo conversations that took place between ourselves, and between us and our publisher. If the evidence of these files and folders amounts to the immediate backdrop behind this account of contemporary sound arts practices, a more substantial setting for this work is older still, arising out of a collaboration that began in 1998, when we first taught together at what was then the London College of Printing.

This collaborative context has involved, alongside many friends and colleagues, a history of developing curricula and courses; establishing the CRiSAP research centre, which has been broadening and deepening the disciplinary field of sound arts since 2006; organising the 'Sound Gender Feminism Activism' series of research events (among many other academic symposia); and publishing *On Listening* and writing *In the Field*. In a sense, it is from *In the Field*—which explores field recording as a creative practice—that much of the impetus for this current publication derives, in part because the format of an extended interview which focused on the complexities of practice seemed to resonate with readers, in part because we both sought an opportunity to situate sound arts in wider horizons, in terms of practices and practitioners.

For us, a desire to enlarge the perceived dimensions of sound arts practices is, in part, what has characterised the collaboration as a whole. With the BTEC, HND, BA, MA and PhD programmes we designed and worked on together, overcoming narrowness in bibliographic, artistic and other referenced resources was as much a spur to transformation as broadening the scope of the visiting practitioners invited to exchange their ideas with students. Successive iterations of 'Sound Gender Feminism Activism' made this motivation explicit in a stated commitment "to develop and expand upon dialogues and discourses related to feminism and sound as well as to form an international network of researchers, artists and practitioners working in these areas", and this language echoes the ambitions expressed in the administrative proposal through which CRiSAP was formally instituted as a research centre by the University of the Arts London.

The collection of interviews in this book has been determined by a mix of individual and joint discussion, design and circumstance. Over the time that we have been thinking about this book, we have made many wishlists of artists we would like to interview and many of those are represented here. For various reasons it proved impossible to interview them all, but we hope some future encounters will feature in later volumes. The fact that this book exists at all is largely due to our ability to enthuse each other about new possibilities and, conversely, our joint amnesia about how long anything takes and how much work is involved. Apart from all the conversations about what kind of book we wanted to write and the initial research into potential subjects, each interview required extensive research and preparation—listening, watching and reading—followed by communication with the artist concerned and more listening, watching and reading. This research is of course generally enjoyable, often involving us taking time out to travel to performances and exhibitions, and has enriched our teaching and other writings.

Many of our discussions revolved around various canonical formations within sound arts. We felt that the main points of reference that had been primarily open to us for the last two decades had been predominantly white men from the global north. Whilst we do not want to formulate a new or alternative canon we have been, as already mentioned, motivated by the desire to talk to and explore the work of younger artists at early or mid-points in their artistic 'careers' from a wider range of practices, geographical locations and experiences.

We each wanted, as far as we were able, to interview people whose work interested us individually and who, when put together, might offer differing practices, approaches and ideas. Distribution and dissemination systems determine that it is often difficult to find out about artists and works without them being widely exhibited in one's own country or written or talked about. Over the long gestation of our research, many of the artists interviewed have become more prominent, and most recently a number of books highlighting less explored sound arts practices with a wider geographical and cultural reach have been published. We aim to encourage artists and curators to talk about their work and working lives putting the unheard voice of the maker back at the centre of the discourse. While, for this book at least, we are hampered by our linguistic Anglocentrism, we hope in future to be able to include more artists who speak other languages. We appreciate the conversations that we have had with artists who are expressing themselves in English as their second or third language and are aware that this might have been a different conversation had it been in their first language.

There was less discussion between us about the interviews and how they would be conducted. For *In the Field*, we had asked all interviewees pretty much the same questions; this time we left this much more open. The majority of Cathy's interviews were conducted in-person in cafes, restaurants, university campuses, gallery spaces, private houses and parks in Berlin, Taipei, Hong Kong, Bangalore, Calcutta and Beirut, places that she was lucky enough to be invited to during this period. As a result, they meander and unfold in a very leisurely manner, are conversational and often had to be very severely edited! By contrast, if Angus's interviewees occupied a similar range of locations to Cathy's, they were, with two exceptions, addressed remotely through the technologies that Covid has made more familiar. This arrangement was further distinguished by shorter, more focused, dialogues and a greater reliance on predetermined questions. We talk more about the consequences of other differences between our approaches in a postscript to the texts of our conversations.

With Angus's transcribing his own interviews, much of his less severe editing was done on the fly rather than after the whole shape of the discussion had been revealed. All of our twenty interviewees were encouraged to suggest amendments to the edited transcripts; some of the proposed changes corrected errors that had crept in during processes of transcription and editing, some involved clarifying names and titles, dates and details. Further corrections and clarifications were introduced by our copy editor and proof reader, John Bevis, and publisher, Colin Sackett. Though almost all interviewees took the opportunity to further develop themes inspired by the original conversation, and these additions may be legible to the reader, what is not accessible are passages that were removed. An element of what was taken out after negotiation related to material that was thought, on reflection, to simply be less relevant, but other sections were withdrawn because they were thought too sensitive in terms of what they said about others, or too personal in their revelations.

We have been driven by a genuine desire to explore what might be called 'sound arts' at this present historical moment. This has encompassed artistic practices and formats, theoretical concerns, education, details of working life, the availability of opportunity and the barriers encountered. Each of our twenty interviews has a short introduction which focuses on why we were interested in talking to that person, followed by the interview itself. The volume ends with a transcribed discussion between the two of us about what we have learned through the interviews. This is not by any means a definitive survey of sound arts now, but we hope it offers some different pathways, frames of reference and ways of thinking about the discipline.

Inter-views

Adam Basanta 11
AM Kanngieser 24
Budhaditya Chattopadhyay 35
Caroline Devine 47
Elsa M'bala 59
Evan Ifekoya 69
Hanna Tuulikki 81
Hong-Kai Wang 91
Jau-Lan Guo 102
Jennifer Walshe 110
Khaled Kaddal 121
Lawrence Abu Hamdan 131
Lina Lapelyte 141
Maria Chavez 150
Mark Peter Wright 162
Mikel R. Nieto 171
Mikhail Karikis 182
Samson Young 191
Yang Yeung 202
Yashas Shetty 212

Locations 221
Afterwords 222
Search index 235

Adam Basanta

Adam Basanta first entered my radar a decade or so ago. We met at a conference where his presentation of a spoken word work grabbed my interest. I was surprised (as it turned out so was he!) and delighted to encounter a very different kind of work when he was part of a rare London sound art exhibition, at the now defunct Carroll / Fletcher Gallery in London with Mikhail Karikis and Christine Sun Kim. Since these encounters I have been aware of his work and growing reputation. In summer 2019, I took advantage of the fact that we were both in Berlin to interview him. I had watched him steadily build up an international career over the previous decade and was interested to find out more. I wish I had seen the installation *A Large Inscription, A Great Noise* in person, I find the video thrilling in terms of its simplicity and elegance and every time the large heavy concrete block drops, it makes me smile at the ambition and daring that it evidences. I am interested in how Adam has moved from the small-scale installations shown at Carroll / Fletcher in 2015 to this celebration of material noise and power in 2019. Adam is a generous interview subject, ready to share his ideas and to discuss all aspects of his creative labour in detail. I appreciate how honest he is, and how much he is able to open up about developing his career and his work so far.

What got you into working with sound in the first place?

My background was as a guitar player, I played rock and jazz in bands in Vancouver. I had a four-track and was recording my own bands and writing songs and then doing these teenager-in-a-basement experimental things.

Who were you listening to at that time?

Oh, it was rock music 100%, Nirvana, Radiohead, that kind of thing. After high school, I did a recording engineering one-year programme, so I was recording other bands and I could record my own music without paying an arm and a leg and I was doing these experimental things, again on a computer, almost like little ventures into electronic music or experimental electronica—field recording with some beats and synths. But I was not listening to experimental music. I had no idea that it was a thing. I was starting to get into free improvisation, more 'new music' improv than free jazz, as an instrumentalist, and I had a brief flirtation with that, and then, there was just a coincidence of things. I was feeling a little… stuck. Somebody suggested Simon Fraser University's weird experimental music programme. I was really not into the idea of going to study in a university at all, but then I saw that there was one course using MaxMSP and I had found out that you could use it to do video so I thought I'd take this one course and do live video projections for my band. It was all revolving around this idea. They wouldn't let me take one course; you had to enrol in the programme. My plan was to take one semester, then, all of a sudden, this world of experimental sound stuff opened up and it was mind-blowing, you know? I took a class with Barry Truax and it was like—electroacoustic music—whoa, I'd been doing this and I had no idea that anybody else was doing it. So I did my Bachelor's there.

What you've just described is quite a classic route in my experience. When you think back on it, what are the things you take away from that course?

Oh, everything that I didn't think was important at the time! The programme was amazing for me. I went to university when I was twenty-one and the idea that there was a physical space where people came in to preserve old knowledge and create new knowledge was intoxicating. It's a very idealistic way of looking at academia, of course, but that's how I saw it at the time.

The programme was interesting and unique. You had to take some acoustic instrumental composition courses, although it was a very experimental school and the electroacoustic part was very strong. In hindsight it was important that it was not an acousmatic composition programme. Barry would provide a theoretical perspective with the acoustic ecology research and other topics that weren't purely to do with the aesthetics of sonic material.

In the world of electroacoustic composition there are few people who engage with the world outside apart from with 'real-world' sound and 'real-world' listening or have ever thought about sociocultural contexts or subjectivities.

I remember it was the first time—probably one of the only times, actually, that I heard the term 'the political economy of music'. Being able to look at music from a wider cultural perspective and how it intersects with economy, politics and culture are what I appreciate more and more since I graduated. The resonances occurred years after.

You went on to do an MA—obviously academia had got you by then!

Yeah, I was convinced that this was the route I wanted to take but I knew that I didn't want to do a Masters in Music. I wanted to combine theoretical research with music-making and something else. Someone suggested that I should talk to Sandeep Bhagwati at Concordia so I decided to try and enrol in the independent studies Master's programme there. The application process was very rigorous. You had to prepare your own interdisciplinary course of study, sign up three supervisors in different departments and get their approval. It was basically a test to see if can you work in a self-directed manner for two years.

Had you proposed moving into a more sculptural practice?

No, I proposed combining theoretical ecological psychology perspectives with a sound-based practice, which would have been mostly electro-acoustic music with the vague notion of electroacoustic music not in a concert but as an installation. The idea was still very rooted in music.

Who works in that area?

In ecological psychology? I know there's Luke Windsor who studied with Eric Clarke who wrote *Ways of Listening: An Ecological Approach To The Perception Of Musical Meaning.*

They were both at City when I was doing my PhD there.

I remember looking at Luke Windsor's PhD and thinking that it was an interesting subject and that I would take it some steps further.

What about Bernie Krauss and niche theory?

Yeah, he's like this soundscape, field-recording stuff, right?

Was it anything to do with any of that?

No, I was aware of that through studying with Barry: that was part of the course material. It was more trying to understand how people listen and grasp meaning through listening. My electroacoustic music at that time always used a combination of abstract and 'real-world' material, and I felt if I could just crack the code of how people listen to these combinations, that could guide the way that I composed. In the first year, I was pursuing this direction, and then I just became less interested in it!

I think there is an intrinsic dead end in that.

Absolutely, that's what I think now. Thinking about listening is very interesting, but to synthesise something utilitarian out of that is very uninteresting to me now—it's a little bit embarrassing!

    The first time that I saw people who were in electroacoustic music doing things that were not electroacoustic music any more was in Montreal. I'm thinking of Nicolas Bernier, I think it was before he went to study in England, he had these performances with Martin Messier—they're both still active in Montreal—integrating cineography. Audio-visual performance was still very new, and I managed to shift my project to composing with materials that are not sonic.

    I did a lot of research on perception, and realised that sound is not this separate sense—there's a lot of interaction between the senses. I was thinking about how can sound and light be used and how I could apply my knowledge and skills as a composer to compose sound and light in tandem in a non-concert context. That became the focus of the thesis, and I made an installation with sound and lightbulbs. It's on Vimeo, it was called *Room Dynamics*.

You had the technical background?

Yeah, I had to learn some stuff, there was a lot of educating myself and getting into media art.

Whose works were you looking at?

Xenakis' *Polytopes* was the oldest work, and Hans Peter Kuhn's work was super-important. There was also Artificiel, a collective in Montreal who did a piece with light bulbs,

So this was around 2012. Were you then, or are you now, aware of the work of Haroon Mirza?

I remember seeing his work for the first time, probably just after I finished my Master's, in New York, at the big survey sound art show. I would have still considered myself a composer then, not a sound artist or a media artist or whatever. I remember his piece very vividly and thinking, "Why do I love this?" It was almost the opposite, from the approach that I had been working in, which was still very composerly "working with the materials". In this, the sound was not pretty but it was great. It wasn't complex and yet there was so much there.

At that show I was quite unimpressed with a lot of the works that I thought I would like. The other piece I liked was by Richard Garrett, a New York sound artist, it was very well-received. It was a turntable sitting on an amplifier, and there's a marble on the turntable and a microphone, and the vinyl is turning and the marble stays in one place and you just hear the grit, just live amplifying the whole—I remember loving that work and not knowing why. I wasn't really into that kind of work, but I just thought it was really different, you know?

You hadn't actually been exposed to that kind of sculptural work, it's very visibly and audibly material.

It's sound art from the visual art perspective. I'd always kind of not liked that, actually, I always felt that it was just an idea done badly. So that was very much where I was coming from. I'd seen works in Montreal that were more DIY electronics, but in Montreal, at least, a lot of the people that were doing that weren't calling it sound art, but maybe media or kinetic art.

Since then you have been successful making the move from electroacoustic composition to being a gallery artist. Did you have an awareness that you needed to change the way that you were thinking about yourself?

I had a very strong awareness that I wanted to make a different kind of work from what I was making, and from the opportunities that I was getting, which were in music. I was doing fairly well. I finished my Master's and I was able to freelance and get a few little commissions and of course you're so happy to do that. I wasn't financing myself completely, but between grants and commissions once in a while and concerts, I was doing well for myself in that world. But I had a growing dissatisfaction with the work that I was making, the presentation opportunities and with music (or the concert) as a presentation medium. I was trying to find ways out of it and using light was one way.

Around 2011, my Master's supervisor gave me *Musicking* by Christopher Small. This radically changed the way that I looked at music and it occurred to me that it was ridiculous that I was defining every microthing of the sonic gesture (and we're talking about zooming in into a five-second window with twenty sounds in it and a cue on each one) but I was never thinking about the situational aspects of presenting the music. There's probably a lot more impact to whether or not your piece is first or last in the concert and what comes before and after, than there is to working on that five-second part. I felt like I needed to step into a different world in order to explore these ideas.

So, at first, light and sound was the way out, but in a performance context. I had a group with two close friends, Max and Julian Stein—they're twins. We had a project called *Music for Lamps*. We had a load of the kind of lamps that you might find in your grandmother's house, we would put transducers inside and control the light and do audio-visual performances. We always tried to set things up differently, responding to the space, so that the stage was not so front-centric. We did a small Canadian tour and played a lot in Montreal and in a few other cities in North America.

It sounds brilliant.

It was a really fun project, and probably the first project of mine that people outside of music liked—but it was still situated in the experimental music world. Then I did an installation with Julian Stein. I was starting to experiment with feedback, and he was also interested in it, so we ended up collaborating on a work called *Invisible Lines*. We did a few presentations, mostly in music contexts, like music festivals that wanted an installation.

Did someone invite you to do that installation?

No, it was my initiative in the sense of sending out applications. One of the applications we sent to Germany was for a Media Art award, and we won! So we came to Germany and did the installation at the Edith-Russ-Haus in Oldenburg, a small town with an amazing institution for media art which has scholarships every year.

I didn't have any gallery contacts, because I had gone to music school. I didn't know people who will end up starting spaces or curating or telling somebody about it, so I was completely disconnected from that. I had all these contacts in music, so I could be the weird thing in the music festival but I couldn't be the weird thing in the visual art gallery. There were no human points of contact. So the only thing that I could do is send out applications. In 2014, I think I sent forty or fifty applications, all over the world to everything—shows, festivals, galleries, open calls, awards, scholarships, just carpet-bombing. That was my strategy.

With the same projects or different projects all the time?

Instead of always writing a grant application for a deadline I would develop ideas, write a description, and then when I saw the deadline, I could move very quickly.

Did that feel depressing?

So depressing! You're almost only getting rejections. Then I got one acceptance, in Montreal, in an artist-run centre called Galerie B312. I had wanted to make some more sound sculpture feedback pieces. I had a grant for a music project, and I siphoned funding away for materials and I even hired somebody to help me with construction. I put 100% in hoping that I could get documentation which would make it easier to maybe get another show in the future.

I tried to make it the best show that I thought I could make, documented it and put it all online, and a blog picked it up then another blog picked it up and around 50,000 people saw it, then all of a sudden there were less rejections and more invitations. *The Sound of Empty Space* at Carroll / Fletcher gallery in London came from a blog post about it and I got an email. I thought it was junk mail! That was maybe my fourth show.

It sounds like you were very lucky and also quite canny in lots of ways.

It's a complete combination of the two. I mean, there's luck, absolutely, but I was thinking statistically—there was a kind of strategy as much as you can say that sending something to anywhere, even if doesn't fit, is a strategy, and I would say yes to everything no matter how little it paid or what the conditions were. In that first year I would be doing something somewhere nearly every month which is crazy.

Was that the Carroll / Fletcher year?

Yes. A lot came as a windfall from that. A lot of people saw the work there, and I was still applying to things and I was still pushing, you know, adding people on Facebook and sometimes just emailing people out of the blue. I had an idea of what I thought was interesting and there was something I wanted to say with these tools and these materials, and maybe, because I was so blissfully unaware of what was going on in visual arts, it was incredibly freeing, coming from music.

But there was never even an inkling of suspicion that people would be interested in feedback sound sculptures. So the idea was to work with the same material in the different ways that I couldn't explore in music, related to the production of sound. The idea of using feedback as material is a way of placing the tools that I had used for sound production for years, in the forefront, and to explore their materiality, as opposed to just making them a vehicle to capture or transmit sound. In one piece, *Pirouette*, a microphone rotated over speakers and created a feedback melody as it passed by every speaker. It was one of the first times that I thought, I'm not going to write music for this. The whole piece had the visual analogy of a music-box ballerina, so then I thought that I should have music from 'Swan Lake' as the melody. So it created a relationship to texts outside of the work—it was a nice experience to work with that as a material.

Because I knew that I didn't know how to make sculptures, I put a lot of attention into how I made them! It ended up looking really good because I was just so scared. Of course there are many people working with feedback, but I don't think there are many who've made it tonal and delicate.

So The Sound of Empty Space *was the three sound sculptures that you developed for the Montreal show—did the same exhibition go to Carroll / Fletcher?*

Two of the three and another piece. The one that I described, *Pirouette*, was not in the Carroll / Fletcher show. At Carroll / Fletcher, there were two container pieces, 'Vessel', a small jar with a kinetic feedback thing inside; and 'The loudest sound in the room experienced very quietly', one of my favourite pieces. It's a sound-proof aquarium with 120 decibels feedback inside it that you can barely hear because you 'hear' the empty space; the quietness of the feedback is in a sense you hearing the air between two closed spaces which is dampening the original sound. The third piece at Carroll / Fletcher was *A Room Listening to Itself* a feedback piece with microphones and speakers hanging that you can walk through. Because of that show and because I was applying so much, there were more things in Europe. I did that one show in Montreal, but I was completely unknown there.

A lot of your work has this very pared-down aesthetic. Is that minimalist aesthetic something you're exploring?

Yes and no. I think paring things down and emphasising what is important and getting rid of the clutter, is something that I've always admired about certain composers. I mean that in a very different way from the minimalist aesthetic. You probably know Yves Daoust, his music is not minimalist or fetishising the minimal, but he is able to shed the things that are cluttering, and let the idea be very clear.

This is something that I think about when I'm developing a work. It's usually coming from a visual, sonic or conceptual idea and I'm thinking about how I can stretch and play with the idea, manifest it in different ways and create a multiplicity of layers, but in a way where it's still focused. When the idea relates to sound production and to the vocabulary of these tools—microphones, speakers, etc. I'm using these things as ready-mades, they are already sculptural and so sometimes you don't need to add much around it. I never really set out to make something minimal and I'm afraid of fetishising the object in the work.

Was A Large Inscription, A Great Noise *made for a particular space? How did it come about?*

I had the idea and applied to a few places, I do a lot less applications than I used to! But still for shows in Montreal in artist-run spaces, it's an application process. I started working with a commercial gallery in Montreal (Ellephant) that represents me—which is great—but there is certain work that makes sense to show there, and work that doesn't make sense to show there! The work I show there is still experimental but neither one of us gets paid if it doesn't sell.

I'm presuming that most of the work needs to be slightly smaller-scale.

It's sculptural work. I'm doing a second solo show there in September which will be mostly photographic, primarily digital prints. The first solo show, *All We'd Ever Need Is One Another*, also didn't involve sound, it involved the ideas that are in the sound installations—it's like an art factory that makes images in real time, using scanners, which is similar to the microphones with feedback.

So you've kind of adapted your practice for the art market.

Yeah, you need to know your audience and be a bit smart about it. Different work fits in different corners of the art world, some can fit (barely) in the commercial art world and others fit in the 'non-profit' / experimental / artist-run sphere. But I think attempting to do something that you find genuinely interesting and could also (in theory) seem 'saleable' is a worthy creative challenge—taken in the right mindset it's very stimulating. The other thing is that after a few years of working with sound and feedback in a focused way there was a bit of an end to that cycle of work, and simultaneously, for the first time, I felt confident to make work that didn't involve sound.

But for example, a non-commercial work like *A Large Inscription*, was thought up probably two years ago, and then I sent that application around to a few places and I was accepted for a solo show at Optica centre d'art contemporain in Montreal, and so then I was making it for the show, with a grant from their programme and funding from the Canada Council that I had also applied for. The process and time-line is a bit different, given that you will not see any money from it, aside from subsistence, while making the work (and that too, thanks to the grace of public funding, or on very rare occasions, a private collector).

It looked like an expensive piece to make.

It wasn't the most expensive piece to make, but it was an extremely difficult, physically demanding piece to make!

The ambition and scale of it! In the video it starts and you've no idea what the scale is.

Like with *A Great Noise*, the piece where the block falls, it's obviously the ground floor of the building! There's five metres of cement and a parking lot downstairs. I was sure they wouldn't let me do this, but they were OK with it. There's a lot of testing that goes into these pieces, but you never really know what it's going to be like, until it's there, and when that thing falls, you feel this in the room! It's an incredibly tense, visceral experience.

One thing that strikes me about that work is that, compared with minute-by-minute manipulation of material that you were doing as an electroacoustic composer, you presumably have to do a huge amount of sort of administration: logistics, buying of gravel chips, making things, getting other people to make things, testing, etc., before you actually get any sort of sound pay-off. How do you feel about that, emotionally and professionally rather than physically?

I find this way of working more interesting. It's not always fun! But it is very rewarding when it all comes together.

The moment of it coming together must be a huge buzz.

It's wonderful. But there's a lot of frustrating parts of the research. If I need to do a building-sized projection I can go online and look up information about projectors and find out what the best way to do it is. With these pieces there is no answer, because, even if it is based on something which has some utility in another sphere of life outside of art, the combination of things is such that you have to find two different answers and then kind of put them together and hope that they work. For example, lifting the block and dropping the block are two very different things. Combining these things is an interesting challenge, and can take a long time and a lot of uncertainty. You're going on a gut feeling.

Do you do all that stuff yourself? Surely there must have been fabricators, designers or engineers involved in the process.

I will do the design and go to a fabricator I've worked with before and he will source the metal and do the welding and maybe we will adapt the design. I love working with fabricators, and learning the way that they solve problems. I come to the fabricator with all the materials, meaning that I have the motor, the driver, the microprocessor, the hardware, the bearings and that stuff, and a design in 3D software that's more or less the dimensions and we go over it and modify it maybe. It's possible to hire somebody to do the whole thing, but it costs more money and it's hard to find somebody to do everything because it's a lot of different skills. When somebody really has all those skills, they either have a better job than freelancing for an artist like me or they're working for an artist who's on another level. I can't learn every skill but I like to be very hands-on.

From initial idea to the exhibition opening, how long do you think that period was for this project?

I'd say a year to a year and a half. But in terms of intense production period maybe four months.

Have you got a studio?

I have a big shared studio space.

Is it big enough to put gravel all over your floor?

No, the size is not so much the problem as the kind of space that it is, it's more like a dentist's office from the 1970s, but it's 1,000 square feet. There were a lot of really physical, dirty parts to this show but other pieces, like the piece with the scanners, you need to install in a clean space. So my studio is in between, clean enough that I can do electronics works and I can do some dirty work there.

Presumably it's quite difficult to come up with the idea unless you've had some previous experimentation with materials somewhere.

There's definitely a progression. That couldn't have been the first installation I made. Mechanically, I had made things that rotate before, so I already knew how to do that more or less. Of course, the first ones I made were a lot smaller. I'd done some casts with cement, again, small, the first time I worked with it I hired somebody to help me make the moulds. I was their unpaid assistant during this process, and so you get more comfortable about doing it on a larger scale. I knew that I couldn't make this work in my studio, but I had already done enough so that I could strategise accordingly.

That's a key point!

I do think it's key. I have nothing else to do every day, other than the email management stuff, so I go to my studio and try to work. I need to generate money so I try to work on four to five projects at the same time, in different phases, so I always have one that's in production. Then there's also pre-production research and experimentation, making maquettes, writing proposals, and thinking about what's next long term, even pre-writing a description or just thinking about it and researching a bit. I'm balancing something that's going to happen this month, in three months, in six months and in a year and a half, all at the same time. It's very different from writing music.

I really appreciate the way that you're explaining what happens for you. I think that people have got no idea that that's really how you have to work!

I do think everybody is different, people work in different ways and some people like to have long-term projects that they're investing in, and for some people, it's very good to have a part-time job that they go to then go to the studio three days a week. It's a personality thing. I like the intensity of always working on different projects and always having something germinating and something ready to present. That coincides with economic reality—I can't concentrate all my resources on something and then show it. I still need to live the next month!

Do you actually make working maquettes?

I can't draw well, but I might start with a sketch in a book then do something in Google SketchUp that I send with the application. I never make a small version but I would look at some motors and other parts to get some sort of proof of concept. You're trying to imagine what the problems will be and solve them as much as you can.

A Great Noise does achieve a certain minimalism in terms of concept, but I can imagine the visceral pleasure—it made me laugh with pleasure when the concrete block came down. I recognised a crazy ambition—'What would it sound like if I just dropped a concrete block and it was amplified?'

I think in some way these pieces are more related to performance art. At the opening, it was like people were watching it as a performance.

Have you got any idea how long people will stay in the installation?

That's the big unknown with this kind of thing. I've heard from the people at the gallery that some people come in and they stay for two drops, but it really depends, they told me there was a group of teenagers who were there for forty-five minutes. You need to spend more time than looking at a photograph, and sound plays a very important role. There are also ways in which you can lure people into more time: for instance, in *A Large Inscription* it does one turn in about two minutes, and there's EQs and filters that are changing, with resonators mixed in as an effects loop. It's changing very slowly, and once you start noticing that it's changing, maybe you stay a bit longer.

Is the microphone sound processed by a Max patch?

Yes, it's a Max patch. I did ten pre-sets of different resonant frequencies, so, in theory, if you stayed there for an hour, you would hear resonant harmonies that are changing,

Your electroacoustic roots are showing! The holy grail of the electroacoustic world is to get a sound source that's got natural occurring internal change.

I'm remembering the original question was also about this relationship to sound, you were saying there's so much logistics and how much time is spent on the sound is something that I found very frustrating when I started making installations, because I care about the sound and now it's 'How come half an hour before the opening, you start working on the sound?'

My experience has been that you spend your whole time up a bloody ladder!

Yes. This project is a product of experience, because now I know that that's the case. I had the luxury of a long set-up period at the gallery and I'd come prepared, with the Max patch and I kept coding on top of that. I had three or four days of trying things out, and then settling on something and tuning that to be exactly the way that I wanted in terms of the resonant frequencies. But that was after months of thinking about how it should sound. There was a kind of sonic dialogue between the two pieces and the concept, visuals and sound need to relate to one another materially. The texture needs to be continuously evolving at a very slow pace and then *A Great Noise* is punctuating it. A lot of work goes into the relationship I want to articulate.

You are talking still very much like a composer.

I am still a composer, that's the only thing I know how to do in any official capacity! One of the things that I find fun about making this kind of work is that it can be appreciated in different ways; an electroacoustic composer can still like it because they feel like it's been cared for in a way that they understand; a visual artist can also appreciate the visual elements; somebody else can read the text and think about it from a conceptual point of view. Hopefully, in a good piece, all of these levels are in dialogue with one another.

This work that I'm doing now feels like it's mine in a way that I've never felt before. I feel ownership of it. Maybe that's just like an age thing, maybe if I'd studied this, I would feel that it's not the case, but I feel like there is this shift from music to sound art—or art in general where it's allowed me to come up with ideas and develop ideas in my own way, without the weight of the giants of other centuries on my shoulder. I feel like I have a freedom that I didn't feel in music. The last piece of music that I wrote, 'Only, Only, Only, Only' was, however, also the first one that I can say is really mine.

I was wondering if that was something you wrote in between more sculptural things, for sort of fun?

I realise now that I didn't listen to music. We don't think about it when we're working in music, but we don't listen to it, because it's so professionalised and we're dealing with sound, and just want silence. Working in what I'd call visual art means that I can have the radio on or I can put an album on, and I've learned to enjoy music again and to not listen analytically. Now I write music if I feel like it, and it's completely changed my relationship to music.

That's a very good exposition on the subject. I know exactly what you mean.

But in terms of future directions, I don't know. The last couple of years have been super-great because I feel like now, there is a sense of freedom, because I know more, so something mechanical doesn't scare me like it used to five years ago, but also because there's less expectation of what am I going to do. The feedback piece was a very defined language and then I intentionally tried to do other things—making the first installation with no sound was a big thing, and now I feel like there's very little expectation for me to be working in one style or genre. The future goal is to keep that kind of freedom and do things on a bigger scale, and a bigger platform or something like that.

You're going for The Armory!

That's too small! No, no, it's funny, but it really depends on the project. Each piece is an opportunity to try something. When I was in electroacoustic music, I really loved it, and then one day I realised that I had painted myself into a very small corner of a very small world, and I don't want to be in that position ever again. So it's always about expanding the territory in which I can navigate.

I don't have career aspirations in terms of very clear benchmarks. I want to be allowed to do what I'm doing and I'm making a living off of it, and it would be nice to make a slightly better living, of course! But it's not like I need The Armory! Of course I want things to develop, but I'm never really thinking too far into the future. It feels good to be at a point where sound is a tool, a material and a theme but I'm not obliged to make sound work, or to deal with sound in a particular way.

AM Kanngieser

That AM Kanngieser was one of only two interviewees who I met face-to-face for this book represents a twofold irony, perhaps. Firstly, since what originally drew me to them was their early research on radical radio, in part a medium where, technically and aesthetically, distance is collapsed; and, secondly, because they are someone who I had previously met on several occasions, so we already had the kinds of connection that supposedly can only be provided by the metaphysics of a present encounter. Two years after the first 'Sound Gender Feminism Activism' conference that I co-organised with Cathy Lane and Holly Ingelton and at which AM presented, we were both at the 'Invisible Places, Sounding Cities' conference in Viseu, and went on to speak together on a number of subsequent occasions, including at the memorial for a mutual friend.

AM's analytical approach to writing, audible in their 2011 *A Sonic Geography of Voice*, 2015 *Geopolitics and the Anthropocene*, and 2019 *Sound as Violence*, reverberates with their inventive, co-productive and multiform field research practices adopted in investigations of environmental stresses among Pasifika. Both the analytical writing and the innovative field research make, in their turn, resonant circuits with such broadcasts as *And Then The Sea Came Back* and such recent contributions to exhibitions as *Mining The Deep* at the Queensland Art Gallery, and *Tawara Night Song* at the Museum of Modern Art, Warsaw. A sonic ethnographer by admission, AM's creative criticality / critical creativity makes for an engaging discussion about the political economies of sound practices.

....

I wanted first to ask about what might be described as the sonic turn in the humanities and to invite you to consider whether you think it is a real phenomenon, or whether there's something more rhetorical at stake. Ultimately, I guess, this question involves wondering whether those disciplines that are seeking to incorporate the sonic as part of a broader sensory turn are themselves being changed by that encounter.

It's a really interesting question because there is actually no accepted consensus, within my discipline of cultural geography at least, on what sound is, or how a sonic turn might be constituted or what working with sound actually entails. I think there are so many different disciplines—

and not just in the humanities, either, but equally in the sciences—that work with some level of sonic engagement.

By sonic engagement I also mean work with listening, obviously, and this is present even in the social sciences, and in social work, in medicine, psychology, all the way to physicists working with radio waves. So, from my perspective, sound, variations of sound, sonic methods, are integrated in all disciplines in some way or another. As such it is problematic to speak in terms of a sonic turn since it feels as if those practices have been within those disciplines for a long time—and interwoven into those disciplines as a very integral approach. I can only really speak about sound within geography because across the humanities I have less of an idea. Here in the UK, it is similar to Australia, we don't really have a discipline of sound studies as they do in the US. By sound studies I mean a kind of analytical discipline around sound and sonic histories which is simultaneously tied in with literature and the humanities. But I think even from what I've seen in geography, where the sonic emphasis is very much bound up in the so-called cultural turn in geography—which has been linked to a wider kind of sensory and I suppose embodied approach that derives very much from feminist philosophies—even within that, there is no consensus of what sound is: is it an onto-epistemological approach to sound? is it a physics-oriented, scientific approach to sound? is it an ethnographic approach to sound? A political analysis of sound? What is it even?

And I feel like that makes it a very disparate phenomenon, because it sometimes feels like people are talking at cross purposes to one another, talking around this thing called sound for which there is no definition, just as there is no definition of listening. Instead, it's just people tapping into the sonic and going with it—as such it is almost always, then, like a carrier for some other, greater, argument. And I really like that, actually, because for me, personally, I'm not interested in pinning down what sound means. I mean, I know the definition of sound as a physical, material phenomenon just as I know what significance sound and music has in a kind of ethnographic sense. But I think to pin down sound's definition would be to do it a disservice and besides, it would be impossible to achieve.

There's been such a dominance of the visual, especially in geography, for such a long time, particularly when thinking about landscape and space and place, which has been very much through a visual lens, you know. A lot of geographers are also very interested in photography and film, maps and cartography, all of these things are, again, very visual ways of engaging with space and place. And I think that the way sound has entered into this is through having been presented as an all-new approach: I do wonder if that's sustainable or even sustained.

Despite this growing interest in sound—because of its ephemerality, in a sense—while geography is open to interdisciplinarity, I think it feels a bit too hard, since it means going into disciplines that are not close to geography. Sometimes there is a tendency to just utilise sound or listening in a very metaphorical sense, as sonic analogies, that serve particular kinds of purposes. But a more intensified engagement with sound? I don't know that that's really happening or indeed will happen.

Does this connect to questions of the non-representational or more-than-representational? Has geography reached the disciplinary point where it is able to constitute the non-textual as an entity, as an active agent in discourse? Or do these always need to be supplemented and anchored by a textual dimension?

I mean geography is about writing, isn't it? And it is always going to be, I think, about writing. The non-representational has been a very contested term.

The ways that we approach sounds are themselves representational —we represent sound in particular forms, we analyse sound, we make it make meaning. And I don't think that geography as a discipline is equipped to adequately mobilise sound. I also believe that there is such a strong political economy within geography that leads to the tendency to ask such questions as: What is making this sound? Where is this thing coming from? What does this sound mean? And to whom? How is this sound being instrumentalised in a certain way? How is it being used to do something else?

That leads me smoothly towards the next question on my list which is to invite you to consider the corollary of the sonic turn in geography, namely the geographic turn within sound? Where is that? Where is 'our' humanities turn?

Personally, sound is always inherently geographical, always placed. Even acousmatic sound is placed, always a product of its environment, in a sense; sound is always resonating off matter, moving in a particular way. I'm sure philosophically this claim can be refuted—and I'm equally conscious that it is a claim that is influenced by my disciplinary background as a geographer—but sound and geography are bound together. I think there is a really strong fascination for sound artists with space and place and how sound works in particular spaces and places, from the gallery through wherever sounds are recorded, to the ways we process sounds and what kinds of spatialities they express in how they're played back and how they're communicated. This might especially apply in terms of those sound artists doing field recordings who are more aware of their social, political, economic environments, for which it becomes more critical to contextualise and identify where this was recorded, how, why and what the circumstances were.

Sound creates spaces, sound creates worlds, sound creates environments, environments create sound, and there does feel to me a growing interest in the importance of looking at the way in which environments create sound, and what those sounds then come to mean.

Are there examples where the geographic is revealed yet other contexts are occluded, obscured?

I think this is where I would deviate quite strongly from sound art and reach for one of my greatest criticisms of the aestheticisation of geography. Within the discipline itself, geographers need to contextualise the spaces that they are researching within the political, ethical, economic relationships which that space is creating and is created through. And I think within sound art that contextualisation can get lost and it can become an aesthetic moment which doesn't actually reflect on its own construction, on the conditions of production or on the potential impacts it might have in terms of producing particular kinds of perceptions around things.

Especially when dealing with highly politicised themes, themes which have very strong impacts on the people and/or on the animal and plant species who are living in those places there is a particular ethics that needs to be addressed, and as, a community, sound arts needs to hold itself to account for this. The other position that I have heard is that not everything needs to be 'political'. But for me, in purely personal terms, my art does need to be political in the sense that it needs to attend to its own ethics; those things need to be reckoned with, especially when sound is being mobilised like in highly politicised, highly vulnerable and highly violent situations.

I'm now moving between my written questions to try and keep the flow going. I had a question about the ethical, which was about whether there's enough discussion about the ethical in relation to sound and to listening...

<interrupting> No!

...for if we look at something like photojournalism, there is, successful or not, a professional, almost technical, understanding of ethics that attaches to the moment of capture but is also extended to aesthetics and history. And some counterpart of this ethics is also available to those many constituencies who consume photojournalism. I wonder if the equivalent needs ethical amplification in sound art, particularly in field recording practices.

There's a tendency to see sound as benign, a tendency to see recording an environment as a benign act and these tendencies maybe derive from the ephemerality of sound or from sound's position outside the dominance of vision. But eavesdropping, hidden recorders, failing to ask permission, failing to respect boundaries and refusals—these are charged activities and they change a lot when you are in a location where there is a keen emphasis on sound such as the work that I've been doing in the Pacific where there's a very strong oral tradition around voice, storytelling and listening. Realising that an environment derives from particular kinds of relationships and particular understandings of kinship means that recording environments is not a benign act at all and there certainly are environments that cannot and should not be recorded.

And actually, this is a side note, but one thing that I've spoken about with a Wiradjuri curator and archivist in Australia is what does it mean to repatriate sound: not in terms of repatriating recorded songs, but repatriating field recordings? I don't want to say that it is a theft in the same way as taking an ancestral artefact is, but, without permission, it is a theft. And I don't think sound recording gets talked about in that way at all, because of this assumption that it is something benign. There is no discussion of power dynamics, of who it is that is doing the recording, the conditions that enabled them to undertake that process, of what it means to capture particular environments at a certain moment in time, to intervene in those environments as well. This is particularly crucial in terms of thinking about the broader context of global climate crisis, and how we understand how field recordings function as archival objects, as documents of a 'soon-to-become extinct' environment.

<shows the notebook with written questions> Just to prove to you that I'm not making it up as I go along, here I've written my next question inviting you to think about how we hear environmental change. I don't want to hold up the visual as an exemplar—and especially not photojournalism—but the practice of what is called re-photography allows us to, for example, visualise where a glacier has been in the past and, through a pictorial archive, have a sense of what has been lost, or at least altered. Without an equivalent archive of sonic history, how can we hear change?

One comment that I got from people while I was doing my work across the Pacific was, "It's so funny white people always need to document everything to believe that it's real". And it's very true. Recording sounds is documenting in the same way that taking photos is documenting; it is an ethnographic practice, a capturing of an environment in order to say that this exists because we can't exclusively believe our own imagination. And then the question around environmental change and recording environmental change is interesting sitting here in the British Library, which has a massive sound archive. Working with people where those changes have been happening for a long time already—and where change is very, very noticeable—has really made me question the value of this kind of documentation, especially a documentation that's done without speaking to people who are experiencing it. If the documentation elides the broader impacts on people and people's relationships to those places that are changing, you lose a lot. It tells one particular kind of story. And I think that for me feeds very much into a particular kind of ontological positioning of the natural, the natural as something outside of the human, as something that is changing in ways that we are abstracted from and not implicated within. And I really think that this is a very dangerous position to hold. Extensive engagement with arguments from disciplines like geography and political ecology situates the Anglo-European construction of the natural and the processes through which the natural became distanced from the human in such processes as colonisation, enslavement, the dispossession and displacement of people from land and mass agriculture. If, despite all those arguments, we continue to record environments without acknowledgement and engagement, we just end up reiterating those divisions and distances and dynamics uncritically. Which is not to say that there isn't a really important place for bioacoustics as a scientific method but without those contextualisations I don't really know what it is that we're listening to and why.

Does the logic of what you are saying suggest that we should be building a circuit between this current emphasis on documentation and a fuller impetus for actual intervention and change?

I would say there are parallels with images of icebergs melting or starving polar bears with some forms of sound documentation: you hear something and think, "Oh, that's terrible, that's sad." You have had an emotional reaction and then you walk away. I want to believe that sound can be utilised for interventional purposes, even though environmental sound art is largely a white American-European movement that is quite exclusionary to a lot of people who are making music around environmental change that does connect very directly to local struggles and struggles that people are going through. I think there needs to be more attention paid to who is visible in environmental sound art and why, and from there it is worth broadening what constitutes the sonic arts.

Are the exclusionary aspects of sound art derived in part from the kinds of devices and the technical apparatuses that we've invested in historically?

In terms of cost, most likely. Gear can be very expensive, travel is expensive, who is able to make a career as a sound artist is entirely racialised and economic. But in terms of who uses the technologies themselves? No. A lot of musicians and artists use field recordings, use sound design, use compositions derived from 'found sound'. It is easy now to record and integrate sound from environments around us. But there is a very strong European tradition around sonic arts that is exclusive, with what falls into that category therefore being very narrow and what falls outside being seen, instead, as pop culture, as somehow not niche. You know, sound art is very niche.

So I guess one question is around whether it's useful to continue to hold on to a definition as exclusionary and as non-diverse as sound art?

Maybe the term sound art doesn't have to do everything? I think there are a whole host of other practices to serve our different purposes. The problem is when particular artistic forms feel compelled to do work that they're not capable of doing, when people feel pressured into undertaking work in response to the imperatives of funders, or to a cultural shift around the form. Particular mediums are useful for certain things, and given sound art's history, its boundaries and its parameters, it doesn't have to do everything all the time.

One of the things that might be interesting to pursue, then, would be to consider the methods which might be said to have originated within sound arts practices—such as those that might be attributed to acoustic ecology like sound mapping and sound walking, which have at least a chance of repeatability, of being sharp enough as modes of inquiry.

I would identify what I do as sonic ethnography and one of the first things that I have to do when I'm working with people is to develop an attenuation to sound and for this, sound mapping, sound walking, deep listening, these are valuable methods to use. As a social scientist, however, they constitute a starting point: they are not an endpoint in themselves, rather they are ways towards a shift in comportment or disposition to one that's more experiential. I think they're very valuable tactics but because I come from a social science background, I'm always going to have a different approach to what sound can do to someone else coming from an artistic approach. There's an agenda for me. Sound works to a particular kind of agenda.

So does that mean that the strategies—deep listening, sound walking, sound mapping—have a kind of a neutrality?!

<laughing> No, no, not at all. What I find most interesting about those three methods is that they show how different people's listening actually is. And that's why I appreciate them. Not because they homogenise nor because they make everyone experience the world in the same way, but precisely because they show that people do not experience the world in the same way.

That moves me to a set of questions that I have to ask you around collaboration: about skills and resources, about remoteness and proximity, and about labour.

Go for it!

What are the ways you can negotiate collaboration through sound when you are working with people who may have a diverse range of skills, resources, levels of health, mobility? Are there ways to think of sound as helping those kinds of collaborations operate with justice?

The first thing to think about with collaboration is the principle of each according to their capacities, each according to their needs. It took me a long time to accept the fact that I can't do everything. At first, I wanted to be as technically proficient as I was ethnographically proficient, as

I was textually proficient. But it is not possible to do all of that, and to be honest, my ideas only exist in relationship and in conversation with what other people are doing. I think collaboration through sound for me is interesting because the range of opportunities and of motivations are vast: it can encompass someone reciting their own poem, someone doing an interview, a recording of a conversation, a very formal co-authored composition.

One of the things that is very important for me, especially working with people who have got differential access to resources, is the just distribution of money. I think that it's really important for people to be paid, and paid well in a way that they ask for, especially considering that in my own role I have often had a salary. This aspect of collaboration itself can be manifest in many different ways. For instance, the situation where I'm working with someone in a very technical role, where I say, "Can you make it sound like this?" and they're paid a technical wage. Or where we all work together and talk about what we're going to do and how that's going to come together, and it's treated as a co-commission. None of these forms of collaboration are smooth processes, they are always in some ways fraught, there's always friction, but that's what I love about collaboration, because you always negotiate those differences. In one of the pieces I did relating to Fiji, we wanted to use the sound of a bell, and the person who was working as a sound designer got the sound of a bell from a Catholic church. When they heard this, the people who I was collaborating with in Fiji reacted with "No, we don't have bells like that! You can't use that bell with our poetry." So all navigations reveal assumptions and contradictions that can best be approached through collaborative relationships.

Is there a possibility for a remote collaboration, a collaboration which might avoid some of the carbon cost of travel, but allows for a local proximate engagement. Does sound allow this distance or do we need to hear the bell you described close up?

When working with anybody from anywhere there need to be relationships of trust in place. I am a white academic, a European first generation Australian. It doesn't work to presume that I can collaborate with someone from somewhere where there is ongoing imperialism, research extraction and very unequal dynamics between researchers and communities. I would not feel comfortable asking anyone to collaborate with me without having had a previous relationship with them or people that they know or being invited by them into the collaboration.

However, technologically speaking, the possibilities for remote collaboration are absolutely there: it's very easy to share sound files from recordings on phones, to have conversations with people online. But I would prefer to have an established relationship that enabled very upfront conversations about the power dynamics and the economic dynamics of that collaboration, about how people will be credited, how they will be attributed.

So collaboration becomes a kind of co-authorship?

Absolutely.

Is there anything about sound that makes these kinds of co-authorial collaboration distinctive?

Yes, for me that distinctiveness comes from other people's voices. I love hearing people narrate their experiences or read their poetry and their stories in their own voice and in their own words: that's what is important for me, sound lets me hear what people are thinking about when they're speaking, hear them changing tack, stumbling, or pausing. This articulates a whole other narrative that is only captured through sound.

This sounds like I am changing tack now, but I've noticed that since you reorganised your website, you've jumbled things together: the textual, the creative, the artistic, the academic. And this is a really interesting move for me since it cuts against its converse, the trajectory elsewhere always to demarcate things, to separate them out in order to assign them an institutional legitimacy.

Well, in my discipline of geography, on a very bureaucratic level my artistic works do not get counted towards research excellence, they cannot be accommodated within my discipline (I know that this is possible within the arts and within some humanities subjects). It took me over a decade to arrive at a point where I can declare that this is my research practice, working with sound is an inextricable part of my work, an integral part of my analytical work (for want of a better word). I want to be believe that the artistic will be recognised as a legitimate form of research within the social sciences, especially since there is so much lip service given to alternative forms of output and an emphasis on impact and public engagement.

I had a colleague who got very excited about the possibilities of sonic geography. After they had been out with the recording device, they wrote to me to say: everything I did sounds so crap! I can't use this, it's awful! But I think there is a really strong push for social scientists to take up creative methods without any kind of acknowledgement that these are practices, these are skills that are learned and honed over time, like any other skill.

Where does what you on your website call 'non-academic'...

...non-REFable!

...'non-academic' writing fit in to you moving between the fields of the academic, the artistic and the activist?

For me personally, I don't know how to be an academic who doesn't communicate in non-academic ways. I'm the first in my family to go to university and I'm constantly under pressure from my family and friends to tell them what I'm doing. I can hardly give them an academic publication and say, "This is what I do. Have fun".

But I'm also very cautious about following this line of argument because I do know, at least in Australia, there is an increasing focus on impact and increasing focus on a specific form of linkage, to industry linkages. Non-academic publications are being enfolded in that process. So, obviously writing for a major national newspaper is seen as a very positive thing, whereas somebody maintaining a blog for ten years about their research practices is seen as irrelevant.

I wonder whether those issues of institutionality are something that needs to be opened up in terms of sound practices. It seems to me that sound arts projects remain unexpectedly beholden to particular kinds of institutions, particular kinds of galleries, publishers, radio stations, particular kinds of networks and environments who themselves are steeped in quite problematic histories—commercial, industrial, military, eco-destructive and colonial histories. Are balances of power replicated rather than disturbed?

Sound art without institutions doesn't exist and this is foundational to its inaccessibility. It's not like music that can be played on a stereo and everyone's gonna dance! It's oftentimes quite obscure and as I said before quite niche but also only exists within the institutional spaces in which it is transmitted. As I start to work with sonification, one of the issues I am struck by is whether it is even possible to work ethically with a form that was developed through research and development from military, government and commercial interests. I would like to see far more investigation into the technologies that we use and the spaces in which we work—an institutional critique, so to speak. That would be fantastic within sound arts.

Ah, the willingness to use Google API!

Absolutely, absolutely. We've spoken to each other about this before, but even the unquestioned use of maps, without the critique that geography has of colonial cartography, needs to be addressed. Going back to what we were talking about at the start of our conversation, the way that geography is taken up in sound is that all of these huge issues that are tied to social, economic and political critique are absorbed but without the criticality. Take sound walking: Who is allowed to participate in a sound walk? Who can walk through space unharassed? Who can loiter in what kinds of spaces? What racialization goes on through that kind of listening? Whose body can move in what way? Who does aural hearing exclude?

It's not just sound art, though, that shrugs criticality?

It does feel that sound art needs to engage with these issues, to have a real reckoning with itself.

Okay, one more question. Why is there not more grief in sound arts? Why is there not more anger?

Sound is an incredibly powerful register for communicating grief and anger and fear. What happens when that translates into artistic practice? I think this relates back to what I was saying about listening. I'm going to generalise, but I wonder what do white, middle class and well-educated audiences want to listen to? That's a large demographic for sound art, what do these people want to listen to? And what becomes too uncomfortable to hear because it asks you to question your spectatorship and yourself as someone who is consuming particular kinds of sounds, and is then able to leave them behind.

Sound artists have worked with sound on the level of sonic discomfort in, you know, pitch, tone, volume, all these kinds of registers, but have they actually thought about what those things mean for other people who aren't us sitting in that room listening? What happens when something is too hard to hear or too uncomfortable to hear or calls your own responsibility and accountability into question? I think these issues get missed out in a lot of sonic art practice. Or artistic practice goes in the other direction—which I think is equally as dangerous—which is a voyeurism of trauma and suffering. Both responses are a silencing, since they involve a time for listening that is then left behind, forgotten.

This, for me at least, is the really important question to ask of artistic practice, especially around issues like climate crisis: how can sonic arts enfold social, political and economic contexts and be mobilised in those directions and still be experimental and playful and open?

Budhaditya Chattopadhyay

I have known Budhaditya for several years, in fact I interviewed him in 2012 for *In the Field* (2013). At that time he was living in Denmark and studying for a PhD. Since then I have watched both his artistic and scholarly work flourish and his career develop. We met in person first in Calcutta, and then finished the interview off in Beirut where he was a visiting researcher. I always find his work engaging and I am particularly interested in the emergence of the broad field of sound art in India and from artists based in or from India. I wanted to know what initially attracted him to working with sound and to investigate those early geographical, radiophonic and family listening experiences, and the gradual developing and launching of himself as a sound artist through a series of fortuitous encounters with films, film school and in Europe. I was interested to discuss his thoughts on the tradition of orality and improvisation and the subsequent development of India's relationship to recorded sound, as well as the specific traditions of sound in Indian cinema. His passion for film has been a significant driving force in his life, as have his own experiences of liminality: socially, academically and geographically. At the moment Budhaditya has a number of works and projects in the pipeline, some of which will result in publications in the next few years. I anticipate that, when they come to fruition, they will offer a significant and potentially transformational contribution to thinking about sound arts and associated practices.

How did you get into working with sound?

I got a cassette recorder when I was eight. I was already quite sensitive to the sonic environment I was living in at the time, and as you know, around the Santiniketan area, it's quiet and in the evening there were tribal drums and ritual-like performances.

From your house, you could hear tribal people's drumming?

Yes, every evening, after coming back from the field or from the factory nearby, they used to make music and from my window I could hear that.

Does that still happen?

No. My 2018 work *Decomposing Landscape* captures some of the sound elements that I grew up with during my childhood. They have all gone, industrialisation in West Bengal is partly responsible for eating out many of those sounds.

Which tribal people were they?

Santhals.

Are they still in the area but don't drum any more, or are they not in the area any more?

They're Bengalised. Their culture is so informed by Bengali elements, Bengali sounds and visuals, that they have lost the idea of how to sing or to make their instruments sound. Their culture is so endangered and many of them speak in Bengali, which, even forty years ago, they didn't know.

Has there been a Bengal state programme to integrate tribal people through schooling?

I don't think it's integration but exploitation to produce profit for the Bengali people, who came to that area as outsiders and economically and culturally displaced the aboriginals. It happens all over the world—in Australia, America, and also Bengal.

So the distant drumming is one of the sounds that you remember hearing as a child?

Yeah, distant drumming, and women's voices singing collectively. The tribal people used to sing together, maybe six girls would be singing on the way home after the evening's work, it was unbelievable, the poetic fading out of the voices as they walk away. It's not in my tangible memory, but in my heart, you know? Radio was another element which was strongly present within my childhood. My generation was living by the BBC World Service and American radio. The BBC was the most-frequented channel, because of the BBC Proms, a Sunday night concert of classical music. When I got a cassette player, I started buying classical music cassettes. Every weekend, I used to go and search for the new classical music cassettes in the Subarnarekha Bookstore in Santiniketan. I also listened to classical music from the large collection of the Indian sculptor and music collector Sarbari Roy Chowdhury, who was married to my cousin sister, and living in Santiniketan.

Who were your favourite composers then?

I started with Schubert, the first piece of classical music I heard was 'Unfinished Symphony, Symphony No.8'! And then I heard 'Symphony No.6' by Beethoven, which I consider is his weakest, but at that time I found it wonderful.

How old were you then?

Nine?

You must have been a very serious little boy!

Well, I was, because of my father. He had a huge library, and he used to read whenever he was not teaching. My father used to read and discuss literature, philosophy—Sartre, Schopenhauer, Nietzsche—and films, with his friends, such as the writer Sandipan Chattopadhyay. It was amazing. When I was six my father took me to a film festival and I saw Sergei Eisenstein's unfinished film, *Qui Viva Mexico!* which completely blew my mind. That was the first film I ever saw in my life. Indian classical music was also around. My mother learned classical music, and was a music director for a local group who used to do regular live performances of dance dramas, especially Tagore's 'Rabindra Sangeet'. My mother and my sisters used to sing. But I learned about Western classical music, through media: first cassettes, and then records.

You originally went to engineering college, was that was how you first got interested in sound? At what point did you move from being an avid consumer of sound and music to being a maker or creator?

The cassette player changed my life because then I could record. I had been a consumer of sound, but I understood that there was a process of mediation whenever you recorded a sound. As soon as you detach the sound object and listen to it in another place, there is a reconfiguration of its objecthood. I didn't theorise that at that time, but I understood that the sound was changing through being rooted somewhere and being uprooted to somewhere else. This experience of schizophonia started when I got the cassette player, but what struck me at that time was not the schizophonic element of recording, but the mediation, the change of texture and tone, and the specificity of the particular recording medium. I understood later, when I got a minidisc recorder, that the quality of sound is so different. I also started to understand the spatiality of sound, that space can be manipulated through the recording distance between me and the object. Texture, mediation and the change of the texture through mediation and spatiality: those two ideas are still the basis of my sound practice.

Did you ever feel that this interest in sound was more than a hobby? What made you feel that you could do something with this?

During film school, I was given a Nagra recording machine, one of the finest and asked to record sound for a film, and the experience made me revolt against the power structure of film-making and, as a kind of rebellion, I started recording outside of the film. That was the start of my field recording practice.

Did you go to film college to study film sound specifically?

I chose the sound department for two reasons. The first was my musical taste and interest from having a cassette player. The second was the flooding in the year 2000 when many of our cassettes, records, and books were destroyed. I was in Kolkata but came back the next day and I saw the devastation. I started salvaging some of the recordings, and learned how to restore them. I didn't have Internet then, but I found a manual and made some ingenious processes of how to salvage damaged recordings. For three years, I was salvaging cassettes and some of the records, transferring and cleaning them and a bit of archiving. So the reasons that I came to the sound department was to learn engineering in order to restore my collections.

You weren't seeing yourself as an artist then?

I had a sense of becoming, but no outcome in my mind. When the flood happened, I was a student of electrical engineering at Javadpur University. I absolutely hated my engineering course. I was hanging around film festivals, and in 2001, seven of Tarkovsky's films came out on celluloid with English subtitles. I entered a film auditorium one fine morning and Tarkovsky's *Nostalgia* blew my mind. A few students from SRFTI [Satyajit Ray Film and Television Institute] came to our college and that made me realise that I wanted to study at film school. In 2002, I graduated from engineering, got a job for a short time, earned some money, and applied to the film school. In 2003 I got accepted into the sound department and a new life started. For next four years, my life turned upside-down. I could do whatever I wanted to. I could record anything I liked. I had a sound studio where I was restoring all the materials I had. I could see seven films a day, any films I liked, from the archive, from the collection, from festivals all for free. It was like a dream for four years.

Did you specialise in sound for four years?

Yes. In the first year every student learns everything: photography, cinematography and editing, then at the end of the first year, you make your first ten-minute film.

I didn't know a thing about field recording, but, as we have discussed, I did know about the process of recording and what kind of changes it makes to the texture and tone of the sound. I think my first recording, without being directed to make it for a film, was of in the evening from the rooftops. I recorded the evening as if it was an object, on Nagra. I was very interested in the film shooting, but then I was disillusioned a bit with the way that sound guys and the sound are treated. This process of disillusionment from the first year to the fourth year pushed me to work independently with sound. I wanted to come out of the clutches of a storytelling process and of pre-prescribed narrative. I understood that the sound loses many of its possibilities and charms boxed in by doing sound for a particular visual situation. There are thousands of other interpretations and possibilities of sound outside of that visual reference.

At that time, whose work in sound did you admire?

Nobody in particular. Now there are many, but at that time, I was not exposed to sound art, nor knew that sound art existed. I only knew my own experience of sound being marginal in film school. I also knew alternative rock music, electronic music, and contemporary classical music, such as Ligeti, Boulez, Penderecki, Stockhausen, Xenakis.

Most people I've talked to come to sound with no awareness of a canon or that what they're doing could be called sound art. They're just doing stuff with sound, and they often have very similar stories to you. In some ways, you were lucky that SRIFTI was opening then, that it opened in Kolkata, so many things.

Yes very lucky. At that time, in the film school, my gurus were Tarkovsky, Satyajit Ray, Kieślowski, Antonioni, Fellini, Sergei Parajanov, David Lynch. I already knew their names, but I got to know their films. Every evening there were archival screening at 6pm, It was such a world! I was recording. I was listening to music of different kinds from morning to night. I was very into classical music, I collected many, many CDs and I also got into rock music <laughs>—gothic rock, acid rock, metal rock, alternative music, some folk music. I don't listen to music now, I'm so invested in sound of the environment. My colleagues from film school used to gather in my room or in Sukanta's [Majumdar] room and we used to listen to Indian classical music, starting at midnight and finishing at 4am when we went out for our first tea at the tea shop which opened in the early morning. It was a very nice life.

What was the first sound project that you made at SRFTI? How did you come to sound art?

In 2007, my girlfriend, who was a photographer, came to India to do her diploma project. We went to a similar area to where I grew up in Bengal, where I learned the intricacy of field recording. My first field recordings were graphic, like snapshots of an atmosphere. I started to follow her photographic exploration of a place. We also visited Benares—which is sonically so amazing. My first finished piece was from Benares and I sent it to the Berlinale [Berlin International Film Festival], they selected it and funded my travel to Berlinale. On the same evening in December 2005, I got two email acceptances, one from the Berlinale and one from Sarai in New Delhi where I had applied for a fellowship. I screamed in the computer room! For the Sarai project I went to the Berlin Phonogram Archive, to find wax cylinder recordings of a particular Bengali Dhrupad music tradition from Bishnupur, in West Bengal.

Who were those recordings made by?

Arnold Baké.

He was very influential. Is he the only person that recorded in India?

Deben Bhattacharya made some recordings in the 1930s. He was an amateur recorder and folk collector, like Alan Lomax. Also of course Moushumi Bhowmik is doing that now for *The Travelling Archive*.

So you went to the Sarai fellowship, with the Berlin wax cylinder recordings?

I gathered recordings from various sources, from private collections, from the All India Radio archive, then I went to Bishnupur a number of times and recorded the few people who were still singing in that tradition. So it was a collection of archival materials and contemporary soundscapes of Bishnupur.

How did you show the work?

Before I get to that, I must tell you that when I got the email confirmation for the Berlinale, I started looking for people working with sound, and got to know about both Gruenrekorder [a German organisation which promotes sound works and phonography] and Derek Holzer who was running SoundTransit. When I got to Berlin I had already a series of meetings that I had arranged from Kolkata. Derek Holzer invited me to perform in an evening concert that he was curating. I went with my first laptop and I did a performance of the train stations piece that I had recorded from all the stations in Kolkata, which was recorded directly onto a disc and sold for ten euros! Then I played the Benares piece in Frankfurt with Gruenrekorder.

A lot of strokes of luck and good things happening.

But initiative as well! <laughs> and the interest in finding peers.

I suppose you'd learnt all the software at film school, and had access to that.

Technologically, I was very well-trained. I had the best software available. I was a spoiled brat in terms of sound technology! I started with a Nagra, you know!

Did any sort of network exist in India then?

No there was no network working creatively in sound.

Do you think there's anything now?

There is an emerging network of people from various practices, including electronic music, film sound and off-shoots of film sound, some amateur nature recordists, and some people from fine arts who are trying to integrate sound in their installation work like Shilpa Gupta and Sanchayan

Ghosh and also Raqs Media Collective. Sound is a strong component at CEMA, the Experimental Media Lab at Srishti Institute of Arts, Design and Technology in Bangalore and Yashas Shetty, who I met in 2009, is one of the people contributing to that. Now he has developed ISRO, the Indian Sonic Research Organisation, so Bangalore is a fertile place for sound practices and there is some Indian sound research.

So there are pockets of activity?

I don't think there is a network in Kolkata, but in Delhi there is Sound Reasons run by Ish Less.

What about in Mumbai?

In Mumbai, there is a very strong network of people working with film sound. I met many of them because from 2012 to 2017 I recorded thirty-two interviews with sound practitioners from all over India for my PhD. I'm working on a book from those interviews. [*Between the Headphones: Listening to the Sound Practitioner*, due out 2021]

Are they all men?

No, there are four women! Gissy Michael is from Kerala, Amala Popuri comes from Hyderabad but she's based in Mumbai, Sneha Khanwalkar, and Surabhi Saraf are to be interviewed.

Was that the main bit of your PhD project?

My PhD has three different threads. One is my own creative practice, then the interviews are looking at other people's practice in film sound and establish a manifesto for a better practice. The third and the most important element is the theoretical aspect—I'm redefining the idea of ambience or of what I call mise-en-sonoré or auditory setting.

So you're going to publish that as a book in English?

I have plans for publishing three books from my PhD.

One on the interviews, one on your theoretical construct, and the third?

The third is a history of sound practice in India in audio-visual media. I think I need five years to finish all the books.

So do you think you're going to be founding a sound art department in a university or art centre in India?

Who knows? Right now, there is no such department, but in future, maybe in ten, twenty years' time.

Contemporary Indian media and installation art seems to be very socially and politically engaged, do you see engagement with those issues or any other commonalities of theme and interest in sound arts practice in India?

I am curious about the cultural and political implications of recording as an aesthetic practice. Because the Indian mind is not open to recording or registration. The tradition of orality is that it is open for constant multiple transmissions from one ear to another, from one mouth to another, from one speaker to another. It doesn't like to get registered as an object. Recording technology first came to India in 1900. When the first recording was made in 1901 by Fred Gaisberg, there was a strong resistance among the Indian music practitioners and intelligentsia who felt that in two-and-a-half minutes the improvisational quality of Indian performing arts is killed and becomes fixed. The improvisational quality is something very important—every performance, stage drama or musical, will keep its improvisational structure open in terms of duration. Many people immediately dismissed recording as a technological intervention in musical production and practice, then, slowly, cinema embraced recording technology.

However, in contemporary India, recordings are everywhere.

Everywhere!

And you can buy them in the market by the gigabyte.

Yes, but I don't think there will be a strong tradition of field recording in India because people don't know what to do with it. Sound practitioners are not very aware of the political, social, religious or site-specific, the transcendental approach in sound is prevalent and this is manifested in film sound, for example, the song and dance sequences as interruption and the lack of ambience in Indian cinema—it's a wiping out of site-specificity. Ambience is not a predominant aesthetic in Indian thinking.

Is that what your book is about?

Yes. Audible absence.

In India, which is so incredibly full of sound, especially urban India, maybe audible absence is a psychological necessity?

It's a kind of escapism from the here and now which is embedded in Indian thinking. The idea of here and now must be transcended immediately, and that is manifested in musical practices, through improvisation and through lack of recording.

Can we talk about your project Exile and Other Syndromes? *Could you describe it?*

I was in Europe from 2007 to 2009, then I came back for my PhD in Copenhagen in 2011. From 2011 my encounters with spaces, people, institutions and the built environment of Europe was a kind of a coming of age. I wanted to respond to that experience in my sound work. Europe was also changing, it was becoming protectionist, more racially aware, and post-9/11, it was almost a trauma to be somebody who looks and sounds different. I felt exiled, left out or on the periphery. This sense of exile comes into my work again and again from 2011/12 onwards. *Exile and Other Syndromes* is a response to my struggling to cope with being exiled.

After you were in Europe, you went back to live in India for a while. Did you feel also exiled there?

Yes, in India there is a different kind of exile. In the last ten years, I didn't get any invitations from art organisations or research universities. They don't recognise me, because I left India and distanced myself from traditional media and artistic production. I work with sound art. India is still grappling with how sound art is made or conceived, although a few artists like Shilpa Gupta or Ish are working with it. But my work was not fitting into that kind of methodology. I was using text, video, various intermedia formats and my work was not entertaining, in the sense that I was not producing beats and electronic ambient music which one can play in a club. Another rupture in India was social. I was getting established as a researcher and as an artist, around 2014/15, so people got, to be frank, a bit jealous. I don't have many friends in India any more. So India does not seem like the place for me. But after ten years, just recently, I got an invitation from Serendipity Arts Festival in Goa. So I'm going to show *Exile and Other Syndromes*!

Yes! What sort of space are you doing it in?

It's an abandoned building which Serendipity have taken over. There are five or six artists and it's curated by Sneha Khanwalkar who is a very interesting composer working in mainstream Indian cinema.

Would you like to be in India?

I would like to go back and settle in India, but there would have to be a context—an institutional framework or a family. I know a few people who go and live the life of an ascetic or go to the mountains or travel around. I don't know if there is really a context for me there, I like to be associated with an institution, because I need support, you know?

I interviewed you for In The Field *in 2012 in Copenhagen at the beginning of your PhD. It feels like you've been on a journey since then and you have emerged stronger.*

Exactly! *Exile and Other Syndromes* starts from there, responding to that sense of being exiled, an outsider.

Did you experience overt racism?

I was never verbally attacked in the street, but it was the little things. I was also feeling racially discriminated against within the institution.

Danish students were writing in Danish on Danish subjects. I was writing on Indian cinema and felt a kind of discrimination within the institution. I always feel that I'm not quite integrated in social situations. This was very pronounced in Denmark, Germany, and Austria, but a little less in the south of Europe.

How is it here in Lebanon?

Lebanon has a hangover from the French Mandate, people consider themselves European. There is a strange stereotypical view that South Asians only work in the kitchen or the textile industry. They think that everybody's from Bangladesh. Every time I enter the university the security people ask for my card, they're not asking the cards of white people, so they are profiling me in a particular way. It's different from Europe. Europe is not so explicit.

Daily microaggressions! Tell me more about Exile and Other Syndromes. *What do we hear, what do we see? What is its physical and material set-up?*

From 2012 to 2016, I was recording wherever I was travelling in Europe. I was travelling between conferences, festivals, coming to Berlin, going to the Netherlands, going to Austria for a residency, and I was recording what Marc Augé calls "non-places"; I think of them as dehumanising spaces like airports, large-scale car sheds, basements, electrical generating plants, sometimes the large train stations, where my existence is not even registered apart from by the surveillance system. Places where my individuality means nothing, where I am no one and I experience a dehumanising sensation. I recorded these dehumanising spaces with their subtle vibrations. Immediately after or during recording, I was also taking notes which are very personal and poetic. Those writings are coming out soon as a book called *The Nomadic Listener* [Errant Bodies Press, Berlin, 2020] and those texts are part of the visual material. I use the software program *Processing* to modulate them according to the sound, so the sound is changing the visual. There are no visuals when there is no sound. And the live visuals are modulated text patterns, some words you can read, some you can't. There is a semantic rupture I wanted to incorporate.

It was premiered at Screen City Biennial in Norway in October 2017 at the Rogaland Kunstsenter in Stavanger. I used the entire ground floor to project onto six screens, attached to three iMacs projecting three versions of the work. The final version will be four-channel video and sixteen-channel sound. I did a sixty-four channel beta version of the work at the Institute of Electronic Music and Acoustics, a multidisciplinary research centre within the University of Music and Performing Arts, Graz. They have a sixty-four channel sound projection system, it's amazing. I spent six months there. *Exile and Other Syndromes* has a kind of contrapuntal relationship with *Audible Absence*, my PhD project. They are parallel projects.

I get the impression that you work on each of your projects for quite a long time. Do you do other things at the same time? Or do you just generally sit with one project for quite a few years?

I cannot work with one project for long. For five minutes I work on a project, and for the next five minutes I work on another. I'm trying to be more concentrated because then I feel I'm more productive. Also all my projects are on-going. None of them are ever finished. It's like responding to a problem or an enquiry, which is never finished.

Have you started a new enquiry?

Yes, in the meantime, I have started *Connecting Resonances*, another big project which addresses concerns about an unfair social divide in contemporary sound studies and media art history, and the curating and showcasing of sound and media art. This divide is practiced often by a lack of critical engagement with the artists from South Asia, Middle-East, and Africa, broadly known as parts of the Global South, and through ignoring, under-representing or referencing, pigeonholing, or appropriating 'non-Western' scholarly perspectives in a globally canonising body of work in the field. One of the arguments of this project is that a non-Western perspective in sound art can be found in the work of non-Western artists, but not as a pure form, there is always a confluence of Eastern and Western ideas. I'm looking at Chinese, Indian and Middle Eastern artists and how they're dealing with Western cultural imperialism, including recording.

Are you looking into a history of recording in those places?

Yes, I am looking at various artists' work. There are three specific areas. One is how perspective is negotiated in non-Western sound or media art. The second is duration, because in any improvisational mode of presenting Indian classical music, time is a fluid but in Western thinking, time is durational, with a beginning and end, so these are negotiated constantly and these negotiations, in my understanding, are a kind of resistance against cultural imperialism of the West; resistance against recording, documenting, or keeping a register of everything. Orality is far more human, open-ended and based on transmission from generation to generation, without keeping a fixed record. The third is subjectivity.

So is that the post-doc you're working on here in Beirut?

I'm just starting, I think it will take ten years.

That's an example of that kind of non-durational time!

All my projects become life questions. I think that the intensity of *Exile and Other Syndromes* will slowly be replaced by *Connecting Resonances*, which has become my life now.

Is the sound in Exile and Other Syndromes *fixed and composed?*

The sound is fixed. It's composed but it uses live processing. I did the basic programming, but for the final version, I worked with a collaborator because I am not trained to that level. I also design my work, but then someone else adds the finishing touches.

Does it have a duration?

It's a variable duration. It's a generative work, there is no beginning and there is no end. I think what I'm trying to communicate and maybe sublimate is the trauma of being a stranger in any given social situation through transcendental potential of writing, listening and sound. It's one of the most personal projects I've ever done, because it's coming from a deep sense being left out or of being out in the world without having a base—that kind of insecurity. These texts are responding to that as a mode of transcendence, of coping, or of assimilating and coming out with a response which again make me reconnect.

How have people received it so far?

In Norway, people liked it, I think. They were a little intrigued by why someone is working in text and sound and why the texts are not readable? For me this ambivalence between readability and intelligibility is like my positioning and my reading of Europe, something ruptured, strange, and uncanny.

The sound, from what I've heard, does feel like a lot of noise in your head that sometimes sounds OK and sometimes just sounds overwhelming and alienating.

Alienating. <laughs> It's all coming from months of trauma!

It will be interesting to see how it's received in India.

Yeah, I'm talking about Europe in India. You mentioned that you thought that I had changed. I think it's something to do with getting my PhD from Leiden University. If there is any achievement in my life so far, it's getting the PhD degree.

PhDs are a very hard-won thing, I can understand that. It gives you a sense of some sort of validation at least.

I felt that at last I belonged to a community which I always aspired to be part of.

It will happen more, after your books come out. Hopefully you will never feel that again, it will be all about connecting.

That's my next twenty years!

Caroline Devine

Caroline Devine is unique among the people that I have interviewed for this edition, in that her work remains largely sound-based, often multi-channel and site- or sometimes theme-specific. I went to meet her at the MK Gallery, an iconic, publicly funded contemporary arts space in Milton Keynes, where her work *City of Things* was generously installed in a glorious large upstairs room. As the listener is immersed in sound they can gaze out of the huge windows looking out onto the cycle paths and green spaces, imagining the life and layers of history that informed and provided the material for the work. We listen together for the best part of an hour, occasionally talking about parts of the work, then we walk to the shopping centre where the work was originally installed, and around some of the sites that feature in it. I am interested to find out how much Caroline's work, over the last decade, has been inspired and seemingly cultivated by her relationship with Milton Keynes, the medium-sized modernist new town around an hour north-west of London where she also lives, as well as the relationships she has built with people and other institutions in the area. Our conversation ranges around the arc of her work and how it has evolved, and explores the variety of public commissions that she has won in London and elsewhere.

How did you get into working with sound?

Initially it was through learning guitar and then starting a band. I did that for maybe seven or eight years—making records, song writing, playing, performing, touring, and I became more and more interested in the studio. We were going into studios and working with producers, but I really wanted to be able to do it myself. I saw it as a vehicle for autonomy, a democratic way to make your own sound and record it—it looked like something I could use.

What era are we talking about?

I recorded two LPs with Linoleum. The first was recorded to tape in Boston over December 1996 and January '97, and the second in 1999, and, that was when I probably first saw Pro Tools. Prior to that, I had always used a four-track recorder for song writing. I think that I got the four-track after the band got a deal and some money. Before that, in the early

1990s, I had a friend who had an old reel-to-reel tape machine that we used to play around on.

Around 1998, I started to set up a little recording thing for myself with an Atari computer and a Tascam four-track and a thing called a Unitor box. I can still remember that moment when I pressed play on the four-track and the computer started working, it was so exciting!

That sounds quite sophisticated!

I had started a part-time course called 'Composition and Synchronisation for Film and Television', I was still in the band, and quite a few of our songs had been used in film and TV. I really loved it when the music was in that kind of context and created experiences. I thought that I wanted to do more of that so that's when I got the Atari set-up.

Was there anything particular that you were interested in exploring that you hadn't been able to when someone else was in control of the means of production?

Just being more experimental with sonic material I guess. Often the studio was being used in quite a standard kind of way, and I liked the idea of being able to use it as a compositional tool or an instrument where you could make any sound for yourself.

And were you making any sound at that point, or were you still thinking primarily musically?

I was thinking musically, but I did want to—I wanted to explore sound more generally, particularly the boundaries between music and sound.

And were there people whose work you were interested in at that time?

Well, I don't think I was too concerned about what might be considered sound art whilst I was part of a band, I had always loved feedback and guitars and the use of silence too. I was interested in bands that used alternative tunings and textures, such as Sonic Youth, and Fripp and Eno's tape manipulations of guitar or Lou Reed's *Metal Machine Music*. I also admired Laurie Anderson—her work with voice and personas, and the way she used technology to create experiences. I began to develop an interest in the idea that composition didn't need to be presented on a stage or within a concert space. Around then, I visited Tony Oursler's *Influence Machine* in Soho Square, London, and I was really taken by the complete transformation of space through sound and the way that the work embedded thought, time and memory into the site. I gradually became more interested in site-specific practice and eventually that was where I wanted to go.

When you got that set-up, what did you start to do?

Well, initially, because I was doing a course, I did some sound tracks.

I don't know if I was being particularly experimental, except that I was combining lots of different sounds all of a sudden, which was quite experimental in itself. The idea that I could then use any sound, and combine it with the guitar, was where I sort of started out. I'm still doing that now.

At the moment, you use a lot of field and interview recordings in your work. Were you using any of that then? Did you have a portable recorder or the ability to record anything like that?

Initially, I didn't. I was thinking about instrumentation, even being able to work with strings or horn sections was very new to me—but I did use my own voice quite a lot as it was one of the instruments I had to hand and I was used to using it in the band. I used it in a more abstract way though now, more to make sounds, textures and atmospheres or fragments of speech, rather than words or lyrics.

How did that develop?

I did some film sound tracks for student films. I remember I used a lot of slide guitar and some voice—I was just using whatever I had. The band was still going and we were doing a bit of touring. I also started working as a news monitor and after a while, I got a job at the BBC World Service in Bush House, London. This is when the really intensive listening started to develop. I worked in the Actuality Department, where all sound comes in from the various news agencies like Reuters, and sometimes a reporter would dial in as well to phone in their report. It still used old reel-to-reel tape machines and it was just around-the-clock listening. I loved it!

So you were sitting in a room?

Ha, yes! I was sitting in a room!—a small, stuffy, room with lots of machinery, sometimes with one other person. It was shift work, so quite often I worked through the night. It was quite a solitary sort of existence.

I can see this room and things are coming in different formats, from different places, at different times.

Yes, yes, yes.

Which actually really relates to the work that we spent the morning listening to!

It's interesting, I don't usually think of it very much! But yeah, it's true. I did used to be fascinated by the things you could hear in the background behind the foreground voice. I also really liked editing; all the stuff would come in and you'd have to prepare clips for the news bulletin. So you might get a story in and you would have to pull out the key elements of what was being said. I got quite good at that. Then you would make a few clips available, and the editor would decide what they wanted to use.

What was your job title?

Actuality Assistant. So a bit like a librarian or something. So the actuality is the audio that's coming in. Actual audio, I suppose.

Were you still continuing your own experiments?

Yeah, I remember taking time off work to go and see the London Film Festival because I had a track in a film, so I was still doing that. I left the World Service to have a child and then I saw an advert in *The Wire* magazine for a BA in Sound Arts at London College of Communication and about a year after finishing at the World Service I started the course.

What did you you want to learn or develop?

I knew what path I was on, and I wasn't going to deflect from it. That course combined aspects of sound that I was interested in and it looked quite challenging.

Up to that point, most of your work had been quite applied. Did you see yourself developing as an artist?

In hindsight, my work developed a lot at that time. I began working with voice a lot more, recording other voices as well as my own. Directing an actor, for example, to achieve a specific performance was quite a step up from using my own voice. I was interested in working with sound in different spaces—that might be a radio space, architectural or physical space. I liked the idea of altering space through sound, even in the band, I was very aware of that. Also, through working in the studio and always thinking in terms of channels I developed a multichannel practice, which combined with this alteration of space.

I also worked in recording studios before I started making my own work and I think that experience is also why I started to think about multichannel. My training was much more in electroacoustic composition and diffusion, but prior to that, I'd been a studio engineer and producer.

Yes, you're always soloing and combining—there's something about that.

And creating that idea of space in the recorded image. So at that point, you were already living in Milton Keynes, weren't you? You have forged a good relationship with both the local gallery and the local community since you have been here. Can you talk a bit about that?

Yes, when I moved to Milton Keynes from Kings Cross in London, I was already in the habit of recording all the time—I was finishing the BA course, and I started to look around for what was here. I knew that I was close to Bletchley Park, the English country house and estate near Milton Keynes that had been the principal centre of Allied code-breaking during the Second World War, and that was instantly something that I was interested in. So my first forays into recording were probably there—at that point, it was still an abandoned place full of flapping tarpaulin. It really was ghostly.

The Museum of Computing's there now, isn't it?

It is. Since then, Bletchley Park has undergone a big transformation. When I first arrived, you felt like you were walking into the past just as it had been left. Now it's all been done up and recreated. Initially I did a tour to learn some more about it and discovered things like the exact patch of ground where the Colossus, a significant early computer, had been invented, now just in the middle of a field, so I did things like record in that field. At some point, I got a Very Low Frequency (VLF) receiver, and I began recording radio signals in those areas, just thinking about what's in the air in response to everything that had been developed there and these kind of aerial radio technologies. So I just started making a lot of recordings of the abandoned feel of it and the way the sound felt quite abandoned, as well.

Had you got any output in mind?

No, I was just gathering material at that point, and I also began evening classes at Bletchley Park to get my amateur radio licence. I knew a woman, WREN Madeleine McDonald, who had worked at the Park, and I asked to record her story and that was amazing. We did a long oral history. Between 1942 and 1945, she had worked on the Bombe, the famous electro-mechanical device which had been used by the British cryptologists to help decipher German Enigma-machine-encrypted secret messages during World War II. It was rebuilt down at the Park, and I had a recording of it in action, and half-way through the interview I played Madeleine the sound of the Bombe. When she worked there she would have listened to it all day long, but she hadn't heard it since 1945. She recognised it instantly. First of all she laughed, and then she said, "Oh, I seem to remember it smelt quite oily" so her olfactory sense was being triggered, at the same time. Part of that oral history—which I must have done in 2010 or something—is in *City of Things*, the work that we heard today. Initially what I did with that interview was to put it onto a CD and give it to Madeleine, who gave it to some of her relations because, of course, she hadn't told them much about it as it was all under the Official Secrets Act.

    I was doing other stuff, I started working with a theatre company and by then, I had made contact with MK Gallery. It's quite funny because I just wondered how likely was there to be any interest in sound art in Milton Keynes, and I remember doing a Google search and finding that the gallery had just started a sound art scratch night and were looking for sound artists just down the road!

    The first installation I made was a multichannel piece called *Phishing* based on spam emails, that explored female voice and identity. I installed it in the gallery for a scratch night. There was an international festival going so there were quite a lot of people who hadn't been to a pitch dark room to hear sound before, so that was all quite exciting. It felt quite experimental.

That's so lucky that anyone was asking for sound art works, let alone locally! It seems like your relationship with the gallery has been moderately consistent since then.

Yeah, I've been quite closely connected with them. They're generally interested in sound. The first large-scale work that I made, *Recording Contract Recordings* was for their Cube Gallery. I had wanted to make it for a long time, based on the experience of being in the band which started out being just about music and ending up being pretty much about business. I put my recording contract—which was a massive, thick, horrible bit of text—onto a record. I got an actor to speak out the text, so the record was defining itself with phrases from the contract, like "Record means all forms of reproductions" and "Territory shall mean the Universe, excluding the United Kingdom", these things that are in a contract are quite ridiculous. I felt like I needed to make this piece and expose all of that because, ultimately, that is what I had come away from it all with.

Was that something you proposed to the gallery or something that they invited you to do?

The gallery invited me to exhibit and asked me what I wanted to show so I proposed the work. I had won a local artist support bursary and the eight finalists were invited to show at the gallery. For my application I made a record. You had to do a fifteen-minute presentation of your work so I took some of the Bletchley Park work, some of the stuff I'd done with the theatre company and my own voice, and I pressed it onto a fifteen-minute dub plate so all I had to do was just go in and put the record on.

What an incredible opportunity!

Yeah I suppose it was—I was thinking about copyright and ownership, and I wanted to expose the legal background to the music industry which contrasts so much with the romantic ideas of song and music. *Recording Contract Recordings* was fourteen channels that extended throughout the gallery and spilled out into the public square outside—I thought of it as a kind of exploded vinyl record. At the centre of the Cube Gallery, on the turntable, was a vinyl disc on repeat that endlessly described itself in dry legal terms from the contract. Around that, I diffused room resonances and test tones and other fragments of material such as the "left, right, left, right," that is used to test speakers, backing vocals, and more legal jargon. Vinyl cracks and pops moved around the room, as though the record was revolving around the listener, and occasional piano fragments animated the spaces. Increasingly my works have become about being able to step inside a sound or a concept and I was experimenting with ideas of being at the centre of this record, the recording process and a legal framework. I was also thinking about muzak and systems and methods for the distribution of music—the sound moved all around the gallery, including through speakers I had installed in the loos, so that it was inescapable.

That is a big jump in both ambition and scale, from your previous work. Did you feel you were waiting for that chance?

I think I was, yeah! It was amazing; it was a great opportunity and it was also quite cathartic—before *Recording Contract Recordings*, I had been trying to distance myself from the whole 'being in a band' thing. In some way that work represented a line in the sand, enabling me to move forward and embark upon bigger ideas.

It also sounds quite technically complex. Did you work with people to design the distribution system or did you do that yourself?

No, I did that myself. I think at that time, to do that 'officially' would have probably cost a fortune! It was just my usual DIY way of working—I housed a computer in a cupboard, and I just built up the system for diffusion myself and then the gallery's installation technicians made it all look professional.

We've been listening to City of Things *this morning which is also a large-scale multichannel piece in the same gallery. Can you just tell me about that?*

So, before the fiftieth anniversary of Milton Keynes in 2017 there was an open call. I had already made two big works here, *On Air*, a multichannel outdoor work for the Open University Campus, that was short-listed for a Sonic Arts BASCA Composer Award, and *5 Minute Oscillations of the Sun*, an eight-channel work exploring VLF radio signals and frequency data from the Sun; a version of this was later exhibited in Temple Contemporary in Philadelphia, USA.

Who did that open call come from?

It was from a combination of several heritage partners, including Bletchley Park, the Cowper and Newton Museum, the Open University, MK Gallery and the Living Archive. It was quite a lengthy application process. So anyway, eventually, I was awarded what was, for me, a really big commission. By then I'd done the commission for the Open University and a couple of Arts Council projects, and learning how to manage these things is all part of it, isn't it? I did find the responsibility incredibly stressful!

Can you tell us what the actual proposal was for?

I proposed a sonic portrait of Milton Keynes that would open the city up to the ears. I felt that people had certain ideas about what Milton Keynes looked like but I had never heard anyone discuss what the city sounded like and it had such a particular soundscape. Having moved there from London, I was very aware of the fact that its planning and design had made it very different sonically from other older cities.

So it was a sixty-channel, site-specific sound piece for a series of windows at the bottom of the shopping centre.

Yeah. The shopping centre was built in the 1970s, very minimalist, it's quite an elegant glass structure, and it has all these wonderful palms inside and lots of Travertine floors. It's highly reflective and reverberant, and there was this particular spot in there where it was very untouched by commerce; it was just about the architecture, and so much of the city is about its architecture, and an architectural vision. I wanted to bring the people and the nature in to populate that spot, because that shopping centre building is actually a key aspect of the city and, in a way, at its heart.

How long were you working on this piece for?

I was planning and working on the proposal for some months. But the actual recording started with the bells on New Year's Day 2017, and continued throughout that year. I went to loads of events and gathered masses and masses of sound, so although the piece is two hours, it's actually quite a small percentage of what I recorded.

I'd been experimenting with resonators for a while—transducers that can be attached to glass or other resonant surfaces. Sound is sent through the resonator and micro-vibrations cause the surface to act like a giant speaker. When I began imagining a piece for Milton Keynes, I wanted to embed the sounds of the city into its architecture and I thought the resonators would be great for that. I proposed diffusing sound across the huge large glass windows of the shopping centre building—effectively turning it into a musical instrument. I was able to do lots of testing early on and develop the entire composition with the acoustics of the glass as well as the space more generally in mind. The long reverberation time meant that choirs sounded particularly good and I built the choral material up in multiple channels so there were literally thousands of voices.

You hadn't used the transducers before this?

Only experimenting with them in the studio, though I've used them for a number of works since.

What we listened to today was installed in the upstairs of the gallery. How many channels was that?

It was a sixteen-channel version of the original work with eight resonators on the windows, six spot speakers and two bigger speakers.

So we hear a lot of sort of natural sound and recorded traffic—the key sounds of the city, but we also hear a lot of people. Can you talk a little bit about some of the groups you interacted with?

Yeah. I started initially looking at the William Cowper collection—which is housed in the Cowper and Newton Museum in Olney, close to Milton Keynes. William Cowper was an eighteenth century poet, forerunner of the Romantic poets, who struggled with depression and had moved to Olney to get away from the stresses of London life. He wrote poems and letters that provide documentation of the local landscape and the soundscape nearly three hundred years ago—countryside that was later to become the city of Milton Keynes. Cowper was particularly sensitive to sound. His poem 'The Winter Walk at Noon' begins "There is in souls a sympathy with sounds, and as the mind is pitch'd the ear is pleased". Cowper's writing was a rich resource for me, because I was thinking about R. Murray Schafer and acoustic ecology, and what was here before Milton Keynes was built in 1967. The city is only fifty years old but of course the spot is millennia old! So I was trying to trace what we have about sound and how far back it goes. The words of the song 'Amazing Grace' are attributed to John Newton, a friend of Cowper's, who also lived in Olney at that time. I found a local Gospel choir—Joy Community Choir—and worked with them on an arrangement of 'Amazing Grace'. That was the first choir I had ever worked with.

Did you record them in a studio?

I recorded them at the Open University studios. I went on to record a number of choirs including a Japanese choir that I found at a festival, as well as seven choirs performing Thomas Tallis's 'Spem in Alium', and from that I met another choir, so I met all of these choirs one from each other, in a way.

    I did lots of field recording. I did a course at the beginning of the year on identifying birdsong, and through that, I met quite a few naturalists, so I went out with some of them sometimes. I recorded the dawn chorus in particular with one birdwatcher, we went to a wood at three or four in the morning and recorded the whole dawn chorus, so that's quite prevalent in the work. I recorded binaurally. It was the first time I had gone out to a wood and listened to the dawn chorus. It was an amazing experience. I went to the football stadium and recorded the crowd there. I invited the poet, performer and broadcaster, Murray Lachlan Young, initially to do a recording of William Cowper's 'The Poplar Field' and a number of Cowper's other site-specific poems. I was excited by the fact you could go down and stand by the River Ouse, where Cowper wrote it, and it's still the same! Part of the project involved making a sound map and I asked Murray if he would also write some poems for it. I took him to six sites that I had chosen, where Murray took notes and I made field recordings. He then went away and wrote the poetry that is woven throughout the piece. So there are poetic responses that span three hundred years from Cowper's response to Murray's modern, contemporary response. I interviewed residents, and there's also some archival sound material from one the architects of Milton Keynes which I was able to use in the building that he had designed—like we were saying earlier, the city just came from the imagination and then it was realised. It was a giant project!

Did you do all your mixing here or did you rent a studio in that time?

I worked a lot in the space, as soon as I was awarded the commission, literally the next day, I was in there. I tested lots of different types of speaker there as well as demos, but most of the composition was done in my own studio.

Did you have any assistance with the production or managing the budget?

I had an installation technician, Lee Farmer, who helped me throughout. There was no way I could have done what I would normally do, which would be everything. Bletchley Park held the funds and did the procurement for me so I didn't have the worry of that sort of stuff and dealing with all the paperwork.

You must have made so many friends!

Really, and it was so rewarding to make it. You know, it was stressful and it was a huge challenge but it felt a privilege to work with the community in that way. Also, because it's a 'new' city, it's writing its own history and that's exciting, and it meant that I could go to the shopping centre and ask them to use the tannoy as part of the diffusion system, for example, because for me it was about embedding the work into the building. It would be hard to do that in some places.

I think it would be hard to do that in a lot of places. The fact that it was produced, commissioned, supported, and eventually exhibited locally is really quite unusual, and as you say, a privilege. How did you follow that up?

Well, the next project that I did was *Resonant Bodies*, the piece for the Victoria and Albert Museum, which was also a new thing for me because it was working in response to objects—bringing the sounds of a case of nineteenth century classical Indian instruments to life on the surface of the glass.

You used the transducers again for that?

Yeah. Again, it was about drawing out sound, this time from the instruments, where previously it had been from the city. I'm interested in sonification of museum collections and drawing secrets or stories out of objects that otherwise can just sit there, silently, and you just read about them. So that was an exciting piece to make after *City of Things*, and felt like a step forward in my practice as well.

So what's next?

I've been working on a new site-specific piece for Greenham Common. I've tracked down four women who lived at the Peace Camp in the 1980s, and I plan to record their oral histories and take their voices and memories back to the site. I've devised a three-layered soundscape using bone conduction headphones and speakers hidden in the bushes of Greenham Common, so that the underscore emerges like a threat from the landscape itself. The women of the Peace Camp had a unique relationship with the landscape of Greenham Common and their voices have significant stories to tell.

Over time, I've realised my practice is about exploring voices, sounds and signals that are ordinarily unheard or in some way absent. For example, the secrecy and silence at the heart of Bletchley Park, the resonances of derelict buildings, the voices of nature, the overtone structure of a star, the orbit of an exoplanet. Through sonification, transformation or transposition, I'm scaling signals for the human ear and presenting them as a sensory experience—like a kind of sonic landscape that can be inhabited or walked around in. Really it comes from thinking about ways to understand the world through sound.

I'm now going back and revisiting my work on stellar resonances, which I started in 2012. I'd been thinking about Very Low Frequency radio back in 2011, and listening to live streams on the Web. Then I got a receiver and started listening live—you can hear signals called whistlers and aurora that are the result of solar activity. Around that time, I got some really long wires and I was thinking about these two ways of listening using wires as antennas but also as acoustic sound sources. I started wondering, if I could hear VLF radio emissions from the Sun, maybe there was an acoustic component as well. I found that helioseismologists study the natural acoustic resonances of the Sun and contacted a research team at the University of Birmingham, and asked whether they would share their data. I then sonified the data for *5 Minute Oscillations of the Sun*, a microtonal composition that allows us to hear the natural resonances of the Sun as music.

From there I did a Leverhulme residency in the School of Physics and Astronomy in Birmingham, and made *Poetics of (Outer) Space*, this time with NASA Kepler data. It's quite a small department in Birmingham, but they were working on the NASA Kepler Mission and discovering exoplanets, planets outside of the Solar System, which felt significant at the time. For *Poetics of (Outer) Space*, I sonified frequencies from stars and the orbits of exoplanets. I've been wanting to get back to it. There's another mission—the NASA TESS Mission—to map the whole night sky in the Southern and then the Northern Hemisphere, they're collecting the data now so I'm working on that.

You can do a thousand million channel sound piece!

Yes, exactly! When I first knew stellar resonance existed, I thought of it as feedback. I wanted to be able to walk into this unfolding palette of tones that I knew to be the overtone structure of the Sun. *Resonant Bodies*, the piece I made with the instruments, was also about the overtone structure so maybe it all goes back to the guitars!

Elsa M'bala

I had heard of Elsa M'bala as one of the few African female sound artists and the only artist working in sound in Cameroon. I was intrigued—how do you become a sound artist in a country where no-one else is? How did it happen? I was lucky enough to see Elsa perform in London as part of Art Night 2017, the first of a now annual event, when galleries and other spaces opened through the night. Curated by Christine Eyene at Yamamoto Keiko Rochaix, it was publicised as a sound art performance. It was twelve days after the Grenfell Tower fire, the appalling tragedy of negligence in which seventy-two people lost their lives in a tower block in Kensington and Chelsea, a rich borough of West London. Many of those who died in Grenfell Tower were the borough's poorer, mainly ethnic-minority residents. Elsa's semi-improvised performance was a mixture of poetry, song and electronic music, and a moving tribute to those who had lost their lives. I was affected and impressed by its directly emotional and political nature. Over a year later I was curating a series of concerts by women in London, and invited Elsa to perform. Elsa travelled from Berlin with her baby daughter, Maeko, who was calmly happy through the concert, the meal after, and the interview the next day. I was interested to talk to Elsa about how she had come to working in sound and about the openness and improvisatory quality of her work as well as her inspirations and working methods.

You grew up in Cameroon and moved to Germany when you were ten years old. Did you stay in Germany?

Yeah, I lived in Germany for approximately eight years, and then I lived in Canada, then Jamaica… and then I moved to Cameroon for five years. I just returned to Berlin two years ago.

How long were you in Canada for?

I was Toronto and Montreal in for almost six months, and then winter came and I left! <laughs> I have family members there, and I guess I wanted the home vibe that I missed in Germany. In Toronto the winter was just awful. A good friend was living in Jamaica at the time, and I spent almost a year there, mostly in Kingston, but also in Oracabessa, a small village, well, everything besides Kingston is village basically. Back then I was in a band, a singer-songwriter, playing the guitar, and doing poetry.

When did you first learn the guitar or discover that you could sing?

That was in Germany. I think I got the guitar from my mum when I was about fifteen. I was supposed to start with the church band. I wanted to play the bass, but the guy from the church said, "Ladies don't play bass". Yeah, dreadful, right? So he told my mum to get me an acoustic guitar. I didn't touch it for a few years because I wanted to play bass and it was just too mellow! I wanted that heavy sound, but then I started a band with a friend, I knew three or four chords on the guitar, and from then on I learned more and got into it. I found that writing poetry was a good way for me to express myself, and the guitar came in to accompany and to smooth it out a bit.

Were there any artists or musicians in your family?

Richard Bona is a far-off relative. I never met him, but he's a super-icon. He's a bass guitarist but he also sings very well in Duala, one of the many languages of Cameroon, he's very talented. He lives in New York now and has a jazz café there.

Who were you into when you wanted to learn the bass?

I guess I just thought that the bass was cool—so heavy and demanding attention. I liked Prince but I wasn't drawn to any specific artist. At the church, there was a bass player and I felt like that was my instrument more than the drum or the singing. If you are female, you have to go into singing, but I was drawn to playing an instrument.

Did you just start writing poetry?

I guess so. I have always liked literature and I'm very blessed with languages. I speak six languages and pick them up very easily. I always felt very intrigued with the way that people express themselves. You realise this when you learn a language and specific words don't exist in that language. People tend to not have the vocabulary to express certain emotions if they don't have the word. So it also really shapes people.

Do you feel you're a different person in some of the languages that you speak?

Yes, totally. Now I'm trying to shape all those persons into one, but at the beginning it was really hard for me. When I express myself in a particular language I tend to use one part of my being. German was definitely the brain, a very heavy brain; French is for the heart, probably because I have been speaking it since childhood. It's funny, I spent a little bit of time analysing that because I realised that sometimes type of blockages were happening, especially when I was performing, when the language that I used to write the poem kind of shaped the person that I was presenting myself to be.

So which is your favourite language to perform or write in?

The one that I have been using a lot is English, because it connects a lot of people.

Do you feel you have an English persona?

Yes. It was definitely that pan-Africanist type of persona. Coming from Germany, where I didn't see a lot of black people, just my mum and my two older brothers in this little village, I felt a type of loneliness. I moved there when I was ten years old, so I knew Cameroon and I knew the life and the loudness of the continent already, and then this German village was so quiet. I remember, they even sent the police to our home on Christmas Eve one time because we were being too loud! I was around twelve years old. That's stayed with me, because you could feel that even the police were ashamed. It was so awkward because we were having a family dinner and laughing and being a happy family. But if your happiness disturbs other people you should be less happy!

That's a terrible story.

A lot of my youth in Germany was like that. Be happy but don't overdo it! It's a strange concept. How can you control happiness?

Maybe that's why you wanted to play the bass!

Yes, I think that shaped my whole youth. I was playing the guitar which was kind of acceptable, and, not trying to be arrogant or anything, I was good at it. I could write nice songs and people liked them. But, when I got to Cameroon, I just felt it was all too quiet! So I needed something heavy and that's when the synthesiser came.

Was that your first electronic instrument? You could have gone for an electric guitar.

Yes, I could have and I thought about it for a bit, but I felt it was too melodic. I was also a little bit tired of the song format, and the repetition of always having to perform it similarly. I was trying to escape it and thinking about our expectations of how sound and music are structured. What is music at the end of the day? It's a concept and, like all concepts, it can be broken. So Cameroon really freed me from a lot of concepts.

When you went to Cameroon were you in touch with many musicians or people working in sound?

When I got to Cameroon, I had time and space. I think I was more grounded, in who I am. My going back to Cameroon was not regarded very well by my family. They felt that they had "got me out of the gutter" and now I was going back—so it was a fight. But looking back it felt like my destiny. I got there and discovered that my mum actually had a house that she had never told us about! So I was able to live there rent free, which is a huge benefit as an artist! That freed me a lot also in terms of what I allowed myself to buy and how I shaped my art.

So she was the person that sponsored you...?

She definitely did. She bought me my guitar and she also bought me my first recording devices. My mum played a big, big role in whatever career I'm having now. Looking back, being in Cameroon and free from financial strain was huge. I was lucky. I have a German passport, I was renting out one room in the apartment and I was also working on different projects with mainly German institutions, so I could really move in and out those spaces. At the same time I was at home in Cameroon, I was very free and I was able to grow immensely.

What sort of synthesiser did you buy?

I bought the small Arturia, because I have a lot of equipment, and I need to be able to carry it. It's really great.

What sort of work were you doing in Germany, was it sound or music related?

Yeah, sometimes. I studied education in Germany, and was doing arts-related projects. I was also working at the local university, with children and with young people, introducing movies to them and pulling out their history.

What did you train in, what was your specialism?

Children and young people.

What was the first work you made or performed with the synthesiser?

It's called *Die Grenze* in German, that means *The Border*. There was all this polemic about too many immigrant people travelling to Europe, but at the time, I was going the other way round and leaving Europe to come back to Cameroon, so it struck a nerve. I was leaving Europe because I didn't feel well there and going to Cameroon, hoping to feel well there, and I didn't, which was also interesting. I had changed, of course. I grew up in Germany, but in my head, it was going back home, yet it wasn't really home, it was still different. I was trying to deal with that and the concept of borders. The synthesiser was very helpful in managing that anger.

Do you think that most of your work and your words come from a very personal place?

Yes, for the longest time it was a big issue for me—it got a little bit too personal at one point and as an artist you need to let go of certain issues.

It's just a performance at the end of the day and not so much about your life, you know?

Was Die Grenze *made as a performance piece?*

Not really. I was working from home and then posting on my SoundCloud. The piece is basically a reporter's voice talking about the whole immigrant problem happening in Europe, people arriving in Lampedusa and everything. I cut up the voice and the waves come and then get bigger and bigger, like a tsunami, just loading up one on top of another, and then you have this little girl's voice that's kind of swallowed by this reporter's loop.

I can really hear from the way you've just described it how it offered you a different vocabulary from the guitar and song format! How did you know how to use the synthesiser?

A lot of YouTube tutorials! The internet was a blessing and like I said, I had time, I was at home in Cameroon, so I was just really watching a lot of things. There's Ableton tutorials, I took a Berkeley Music School class, so I learned a lot of things alone—there's a lot of places you can go and have people teach you.

Did you know many people that played synthesiser, either in Germany or in Cameroon?

Not really. The way that the synthesiser is used in Cameroon is very harmonic or as a substitute for other instruments. I was interested in really playing with the sound itself.

What a great thing to be able to do!

It was amazing. I felt like I was trying to shape myself into something. When I was able to perform it at the Institute Francais for the first time, I was very nervous, because up to then it had just been me in that little room, YouTubing and then SoundClouding into the world, with nobody judging, and you couldn't see me… and then I had to perform it! The reaction was so amazing, people were really like, "Wow, I never saw something like that".

In Cameroon, who would have been at that performance?

There's a specific crowd of arty, Francophile people and people from the scene, which means a lot, because they were intrigued, meaning they have never seen something like that. I think that's where I knew that whatever I was doing could work. Because I was really insecure— it was the first time I had performed like that and I knew what expectation of musical and synthesiser performance would be, and I was not even close to that expectation. Before that, I had given a concert with my guitar and people knew that I could play guitar and sing well, but this time I wasn't singing, I was talking, reading poems, making noise, tearing papers and looping that!

Were you using a loop station on your guitar before?

Yes, exactly, that's the first electronic device that I got and that's how I realised that I could actually manipulate the sound itself, so that slowly introduced me to the synth,.

Is there a conceptual or experimental art scene in Cameroon?

Yes, mainly in the visual arts. There are quite a few big names from visual contemporary art like Barthélémy Toguo.

What is the government in Cameroon?

We have had the same president for thirty-seven years now. He has just been re-elected and the next election is in seven years, he's almost ninety years old. The country became independent in 1960, like most African countries. This current president was the prime minister of the former president, who was put there by the French. He kicked him out and took power, and has been there ever since.

I'm guessing there's certainly little or no tradition of working with sound outside music, film or the radio? But your work has been put on in Cameroon and in other African countries, like Senegal, do you think this means that there is a growing appreciation of sound art?

I think that sound art is getting time and space. What I love about sound is that it sucks you into a world, even maybe into your own imaginative world, which is pretty powerful. I think people want to engage differently with art.

It's like a little space where you're allowed to just go off somewhere.

Yes, exactly, exactly. Which is beautiful.

What about being an African woman working with sound?

I'm black, African and a woman, living outside of Africa—all of those things play to my advantage and to my disadvantage. It all comes into my work, of course, because they're all part of who I am, and that must attract people as well, but I think that if I was living only in Cameroon, my work would be totally different. I have grown up being able to navigate cultures. If I had never left Cameroon, my concept of the art world would be pretty different.

It seems that in most non-European countries often the people that succeed, even in their own country, are often the people that get educated outside the country.

It does, it does. And you cannot even be mad at that, because you're just richer in that sense, because you have the local things and you have the outside things. I used to want to be Cameroonian, and then I realised that what I had was not a loss of home but something more. However, I only realised that because I went to Cameroon, I got grounded into my multi-ethnicity by being in Cameroon.

Have you met any people working with sound in a more experimental way in or from any other African countries?

Yes. There's quite a few… well, only men, but Nigeria has Emeka Ogboh, who is very big, he's in Berlin. I met and worked with African artists working with sound, including some that were working visually, but with sounds as well, on the Dakar Biennale. There was Nyakallo Maleke from South Africa who is also a young artist, she's 24 or something, she's currently doing a residency in Switzerland. She was the only female besides me, the rest were male. So there's not a lot. It's also the financial thing, right? No one is buying sound art.

What made you decide to come back to Germany?

Security.

Did it feel really unsafe?

Things were getting mad. There were demonstrations, the internet being cut off, huge accidents—at one time a road literally split in two and the train derailed. I was supposed to travel to a coding workshop that night and didn't go because I had a bad headache but I was aware that I could have just died. I was trying to get into Raspberry Pi, and that was the only place to learn, but I felt that if I was in Germany then I wouldn't need to travel miles and miles for a coding workshop. I didn't own a TV, and my whole family just started calling me, worriedly wondering where I was, it was just very crazy. After that, my mum also got very sick, and even though I loved the situation and it was very beneficial to my art and my mental health, I just had to let it go, and go back to Germany.

So that's when you moved to Berlin?

Yes, I couldn't go back Kahlsruhe. My mum still lives there, but I need to breathe, not just be stared at! So Berlin was the perfect option. There are just a lot of weirdos in Berlin, people are coming from outside looking for that weirdo vibe, although it's becoming more and more expensive. A lot of people from my generation feel that Berlin could be the place where they can feel like themselves, and I also felt like that.

How do you think the work that you've made in Berlin is different from the work that you made in Cameroon?

In Cameroon I was just starting, I didn't even know what sound art was, I was just experimenting. I was drawn to certain instruments and to a different way of working with sound and I managed to kind of create my own musical vibe. Now I think that I am a sound artist, I do experimental music.

You call yourself a sound artist?

I call myself an artist that works with sound but I'm not solely dealing with sound.

When you start to work on a piece, are you usually coming from a sonic or thematic place?

Thematic, definitely. A lot of my work is political. I think that everything is political—what we eat, what we listen to and the way that we are programmed.

Does that mean you usually start with words?

Yes, with words and a vibe.

Do you feel or hear that vibe?

I feel it. Which can be intense, it's not your life you're supposed to portray on stage, it's just a vibe, right?

Will you have written the words totally and then accompany them, or is it more iterative than that?

It's more iterative. Sometimes I just create something and then the meaning comes out from singing it at the end, as if from engaging with it I realise what I am trying to say.

Last night you performed Sounds like Re-birth *in a concert at London College of Communication. Were they your words that you used in the work?*

No, the words are from that *Hurakan & Other Short Stories* by Boitumelo Moroka which Tomimo Mohoko, a friend from from South Africa, gave me and I really loved. The book is basically talking about conservation, the universe and the rebirth of a star. When I first read it I was pregnant with Maeko, my daughter, so I thought it was fitting, at the beginning of the piece you can hear a recording of her heartbeat. I whisper the words in the audio track, and then yesterday I also spoke them in the performance.

It was really nice, people liked it, you know?

I got really nice feedback. I was very happy.

Recently there seem to be more young black women working in what we might broadly call the sound arts—is this something that you have noticed?

Sound art is getting more attention, and people want to find different ways of communicating through art. I think we carry a lot of images and material in us, and collect more because of the film images and emotions via our phones, and sound art can just trigger it to come out much more than, say, ten years ago. When you think of sound art, you think of all those white men. But I guess black women are looking for a different way to engage, not being your clichéd black woman on stage. It's like me not being allowed to play bass because that is not woman-like, and trying to free myself from that. I'm still a woman, I just don't need to play soft tones for you to be acknowledged as a woman.

Have you ever made a piece without your voice in it?

Yes, *Die Grenze*, the first one, had no voice in it. I have a deep voice, I was told it's like a radio voice, calming and low which works very well on radio apparently. Of course, as a girl, you want to sound like a girl, you want to sound pretty: but what does pretty sound like? What a girl is supposed to sound like? I guess we all grow up with that knowledge, and then you question that. I think that's also kind of got me to sound art basically.

Can you tell me about the piece that you're doing for Dakar?

Absolutely no idea yet it's still one year away!

So your next exhibition is at the IFA?

Yes—Institut fur Auslandsbeziehungen on the 8th of March, International Women's Day by a wonderful coincidence. It will be a Women's Day type of topic, it's the first time that it will be a vacation in Berlin. My new approach is taking heavy political topics and chopping them up live into musical pieces, with instruments, with my voice—reading, and looping and sampling. I am using audio by Spanish-speaking indigeneous activists, mainly women or non-binary people, and connecting our need to heal ourselves and the collective via nature and rituals.

So some of it will be in the voice of the original speaker and some of it will be in your voice?

Yes, exactly. I will have some recordings of people talking, I will read some words and at the end I will live edit, chop and loop some parts and turn that into musical pieces.

Will it have an installation life as well?

Yes. I'm working with Zoey Vero, she's a visual artist, a VJ basically, and we are collaborating on a thirty-minute video that will stay in the space. It is actually quite intense, I'm supposed to do something for a whole evening, I still have to write the whole text. I'm really looking forward to it, I think it's going to be good. Who knows what will come out of it?

I was listening to that track Gatherings, *is that a Cameroonian track?*

Yes. *Gatherings* was the piece that I performed at Dak'Art, the African

Biennale in Dakar, Senegal last year (2018) and it was a mix of a recordings from Cameroon and from Halim El-Dabh, an Egyptian composer. The curator, Bonaventure Soh Bejeng Ndikung, who has a space in Berlin called SAVVY, invited a group of African artists working with sound to create work responding to Halim's work.

Evan Ifekoya

I met Evan Ifekoya in their studio in South London in the same Gasworks Gallery where, two summers before, they had exhibited the complexity of currents and energy flows that was *Ritual Without Belief*. To enter that installation was to be submerged in multichannelled and shifting volumes of words and sounds, was to be almost enveloped in a vinyl sea rising to a wave whose frothing crest was formed by coloured helium balloons. In 2019, I made repeated visits to two other Ifekoya installations, both part of the Transformer exhibition, each distinguished, as we discuss, by parallel processes of sensory embedding that offer succour—beanbags at Gasworks, cushions at Transformer—as much as challenge.

If an individual Ifekoya work is itself constituted as a syncretic layering of different dimensions, the range of their work revels in a similar breadth, since it can crystallise in installations, as prints, as radio art, in writing of all kinds of registers, in film and as performance. This range is equally applicable to the kinds of contexts that Ifekoya sets in motion and pluralises. One context that appears as compelling as it is consistent is that of club culture, there as a reference in those balloons at Gasworks, there as *Disco Breakdown* in the first performance of Ifekoya's I saw in 2014, there in a mixtape of theirs that was published a year later by Verso, the "largest independent, radical publishing house in the English-speaking world".

One of the things that really excites me about your work is imagining the process you undertake in order to create and, specifically, whether when you're creating, you are creating with a listener's modality in mind. You produce film work, radio work, sculptural interventions, all kinds of different approaches: within each of those projects, as you are developing them, how soon does the idea of a listener enter the creative process?

I would place the position of the listener right at the forefront. For me, and I know some people find this a little controversial, music comes first, comes before art. You know, I would much rather be at a live show or in a club than go to an art gallery! I would say that I am way more driven by music and sound. I don't know how I've ended up in the field of art although I guess that is because I've come at sound from this conceptual angle. Having said that, the experience of what it is to listen, of what it is to be a listener, to be in a space, to be in a live environment, to be within a club—these are always the positions that I'm thinking about. Alongside that, creating spaces where there is a level of comfort within them is really important to me—even when there is a level of discomfort in what is being discussed or put forward. There's a certain kind of space that I want to cultivate, to physically construct, and that's where the sculptural / installation element comes into things.

And did you think that this recognition and respect for the powers that sound has over the human body is partly a reflection of that relationship with club culture that you've talked about eloquently in the past—such as in your Frieze article where you create an autobiographical journey between different tracks? A lot of your work seems to have this sense of an appreciation of the powers of sound and I wonder if you come to that musically?

The second video piece I made—I don't know if you seen it?—was called *Hybrid Vigor*, a work from 2010 where I created a collage from found footage evoking different kinds of cultural references. As well as the visual element, there is a soundtrack which draws on music. Some of the music is there because I find it really enjoyable and resonant, too, because of its political affiliations, because it mentions various aspects of queerness—an example would be the band Le Tigre. At the same time, the music for that video draws on very different sources like Toto's 'Africa'. I've always been interested in music's ability to kind of create spaces of community, to connect me with people.

On the one hand, there is the lyrical aspect of music which I use to create such emotions as humour, and different works that I have made engage with lyrics as a key part of them. On the other hand, I like dancing, I want there to be a flow from the music, I want there to be a rhythm, for there to be a way that the work is able to hold people's attention. *Hybrid Vigor*, with its processes of speeding up and slowing down and chopping and re-mixing, was the beginning for me towards an understanding of how music could be used as a tool to make those kinds of explorations.

You made a distinction between the lyrics and the rhythmic component; another dimension to music or sound might be the vibratory, certainly that was a component I responded to in one of your installations at 180 The Strand in London, the multichannel work ranged along the corridor called Prophetic Map.

That work was called *Prophetic Map I: Toju Ba Farabale*. For *Transformer* at 180 The Strand, I showed two works, one in the corridor space and one in the interior of the exhibition. I also showed another part of the work in Venice called *Prophetic Map II: Oceanic Sage*. Both the Venice and London works happened concurrently. I worked with a number of collaborators on the audio aspect of these works—Josh Anio Grigg on sound design,

Petal (Golden Paradise Music) and Tobi Adebajo on vocals and Kiera Coward-Deyell on the mixing and mastering. Sorry… what was your question?

The question responded to Prophetic Map I *and was about how sound has something other than the lyrical and rhythmic available for bodies in its vibratory qualities. In that work I heard mantras, chants and the other knowledges that it feels like you are exploring at different points and at different times across your works—I perceived that piece as an opening up of the body to something different, installation as portal, gateway.*

Yeah. For me, there's something about a physical response to sound and to music that I am really pulled by. With this work in particular, I was thinking about different things. I have a meditation practice, meditation is a big part of my daily life, and there was something about that moment in time—in winter 2019—that made me feel the necessity of bringing a kind of more meditative moment to public space. In *Prophetic Map I*, there is the mantra, affirmations, phrases that repeat, which connect to my interest in processes whereby through repetition something can integrate with the subconscious mind. On another layer, I was also working with Solfeggio frequencies, frequencies which form part of an ancient scale and represent tones that can help balance mind, body and spirit. This, for me, amplifies sound's ability to physically reconfigure the cells of the body. The installation in the corridor space uses a tone set to 432 Hz, the installation in the interior of the exhibition uses a tone of 536 Hz [and another frequency] and these are part of an exploration of the potential of frequencies to contribute to healing and to a kind of physical transformation within the body.

And those cellular resonances—those vibrations that we might think about as a kind of visual analogue to the orgonite that you have included in the sculptural work Prophetic Map I: Toju Ba Farabale *in the interior of the exhibition—prompt me to ask a couple of things. One question is: do you think that people pick up that one of the substances is orgonite or recognise the Solfeggio frequencies?*

I don't think it is a binary of either/or, for both things can happen at the same time. Of course, it could be great if a visitor came to the installation and said, "Yeah, that's orgonite!" and understood that the orgonites were different colours that referred to different chakra points. I commissioned the orgonite from a great craftsperson based in London—Orgonise Yourself— so that within each piece of orgonite there is a separate crystal.

Nice.

The one which is at the crown of the structure is purple, an amethyst. The one that is red for the room is carnelian. I wanted the stones and crystals to be imbued physically with healing and transformative properties—perhaps to be recognised for what they are or perhaps to contribute something to another part of the audience without them realising at all, except in so far as they might leave the space of the installation in the gallery feeling a sense of uplift or transformation—without being conscious of why. I'm always excited by the potential of repeat experiences: for me, it's actually in the coming back that you really begin to feel the effects of something. I can't control whether somebody recognises orgonite or the specific crystals and connects them to an understanding of their supposed benefits. I guess none of these things can be proved, but nevertheless it's a really interesting story.

Do these reparative, restorative effects of voice, rhythm, crystal, constitute a conscious project on your part to step outside a kind of Western, white, straight cosmos, which has particular ideas about how the world works, how causality works, how sound even works, and to embrace some more queer, mixed, pluralised forms of knowledge?

Yeah, it's all of that. Those things are definitely in the mix but, actually, I think it's very much led by my practice in the world: the way that I'm moving, practising and ritualising becomes part of my creative practice. The way that I was working with sound in those days when I produced *Hybrid Vigor* was very much based on how I was relating to people. At that moment, I felt like there was a degree of representation, of visibility, that didn't exist and so I wanted to put that into the world through sound, through video. Whereas now I feel differently, I realise visibility is actually a trap. Ultimately, there's a lot of trauma that has not yet been dealt with and has still to be resolved, and another part of my research is around epigenetics and inherited trauma and this explains where my attention to healing frequencies and crystals comes in. It was an investigation into what are the non-conventional, the non-Western ways, those outside of logical thinking, that enable us to start thinking about the reparative potential of sound.

Is there a point at which audibility can equally be a trap?

Well, I suspect everything has the potential to be a trap. As a subject who is racialised, who is gendered, I have these labels put on me. It is because of my visuality that these things become easier to compartmentalise, to be reduced. To centre the audible means to create a tension around legibility. For me it is about disrupting legibility. My experience was that when I was so focused on the visual, it was easy to reduce, to compartmentalise. By contrast, there's something about sound's ability to disrupt legibility that has me really excited.

You work with visual archives, such as in She Was A Full Body Speaker. *Don't they reveal that there is a strength in the visual, in making things visible?*

For sure, and the visual is, to a degree, still important to me. But even with as apparently a visual work as *She Was A Full Body Speaker* there are still strategies employed that draw on sound—such as the loop. In the film there is a cycle of repetition that is not necessarily revealed unless you spend some time with it as part of the audience. There's a cycle where a part repeats but then something always shifts: so there will be a thing that remains consistent, but then there will also be a thing that always changes. Structurally, even when something is visual, I'm thinking about it in more sonic terms, thinking about it as a song, you know, that there should be a verse, a chorus.

And does that mean that the sonic gives you access to different temporalities and dimensions? Your work Ritual Without *Belief has a six-hour duration, doesn't it? And although there have been video works that long, it feels that such temporalities can only really be achieved by something that's sonically attuned.*

Definitely. I have to say that part of me does wonder what would it mean to make a six-hour moving image piece, but working through that sonically made more sense. With *Ritual Without Belief* I was thinking about the archives that I spend time with, the music that I spend time with, the conversations that I'm having, and how to kind of catalogue those, how to categorise those. I call the methodology a black queer algorithm across generations. I was also thinking how to create a system from all of these conversations, all of these dialogues are happening concurrently, simultaneously. But again, even with that work, on each hour a refrain is repeated that lets the audience know that an hour has passed. Such strategies are what I employ to create a structure and framing for a work.

And does that structure and framing also have a home in your compositional technique? Do you like to think structurally not just in terms of how you organise material—the algorithm and the taxonomy—but how you manipulate and manage it?

I would say so. Within that particular work, for example, there are the layers in the base track from which I tend to build a work. *Ritual Without Belief* was when I first started to compose with healing frequencies. I made this element more explicit with the *Transformer: A Rebirth of Wonder* show which, in a sense, took those sections of *Ritual Without Belief* where there are mantras, where there are healing frequencies, where there is meditation, and then made those into a whole installation. It just brought that element more to the forefront. I tend to create these base tracks, which might involve using healing frequencies, or might come from some of the underwater recordings I do, the hydrophone recordings of different spaces that I spent a lot of time with during the research phase of the work. These base tracks ground the work, they create an atmospheric texture.

Ah! So, they are the kind of weather systems which are evolving and help create a kind of pressure?

Exactly. They weave in and out to create moments where the work becomes denser, with a lot of things happening simultaneously, and moments where things become more spacious, when the base track itself comes more into focus.

And we are sitting in your studio, there is a lot of equipment around us and what you are describing is a process that involves a lot of technical skills. Is that part of how you see who you are as an artist, someone who's comfortable using these technological resources?

It's funny because I wouldn't say that I'm a hugely technical person, but I am somebody who likes to try out and test things. With the Gasworks installation Ritual ~~Without~~ Belief, some of the sound parts are just me jamming in my studio, the vocal stuff is just me improvising by putting the voice through my Korg Kaoss Pad KP3+.

There is no software processing?

No, no, no, some of it is literally me with the KP3+ or whatever bits of equipment I have in my studio. There's a comparison with the sound system: I've never built a sound system, but I saw that it was something that we really needed within my community. Often, we would be organising parties in spaces where the sound systems just were not very good. So when the opportunity came up for me to do the show here at Gasworks and I knew I wanted sound to be the driving force, it just made sense for this to be the moment for the sound system to come into existence.

So I just reached out to say "I want to build a Sound System, do you know anyone that's built one before?" And then I found the people that had done, we then came together, we started to plan, people then brought bits of systems that they had built before, we designed something new and invited people who we thought would want to be part of the process. That is just how I am, I'm up for pushing myself, for finding new ways to work, to operate by trial and error. I am conscious that there is the idea that unless you have trained for years or unless you have a certain piece of technology or unless you possess a particular craft, you shouldn't have access. I believe that frequently as marginal subjects we are not allowed entry into certain ways of working or being and for me, through sound, through music, I've enabled myself to push beyond. That drum kit over there, that's just something I've played since I was a kid, it is not necessarily my work, rather it's there when I want to vent, or just have a little play around.

I wanted to ask you about science fiction and your interest in that genre and to wonder whether science fiction—for you—can be as much a resource as listening to techno, or working with computers and learning new software?

Of course, through techno music there has been a whole scene around Afrofuturism and Sci-Fi. There are a few books there <points to shelves in studio>. Octavia E. Butler, for example, is somebody who has really inspired my thinking, and just before *Ritual Without Belief* I went to Los Angeles and spent two and a half weeks in her archives.

Oh wow!

Yeah, I did. And actually some of the recordings used are from a beach in Los Angeles. How I work is often to start with an archival investigation and a few months before the Gasworks show, I was in Octavia E. Butler's archive and came across a lot of these affirmation cards that she would write to herself: statements of encouragement, telling herself to keep going, because when she was writing it was a real challenge to make the kind of work she did. So, on the one hand, you know, her published books have really inspired my thinking, especially the *Parable* series, which very much became a stimulation for my radio work that is set in different moments of simultaneous time. On the other hand, there is the stuff around her books, those cards, her journals, the way she wrote to herself. The cards, the journals and her letters are all in the archive. Science fiction encourages me to speculate, to demand more of the present moment.

I'm very grounded in the present and that is why the sound system we talked about earlier—which is called the Black Obsidian Sound System (B.O.S.S)—exists: it responds to the demand to think about what can be brought into the world right now. By contrast, my interest in science fiction allows me to imagine, to speculate more. Interestingly, a few years before B.O.S.S came about, I was doing a lot of research into Black women-led clubs and social centres in the '80s and '90s, research that led me to discover that actually people did run sound systems. For example, there was one called Sistamatic run by a group of Black queer women. Having this historical knowledge led me to a realization: "Why don't we have that now? This stuff can totally exist!" In a way, there is equal importance in my work for archival investigations into the past, drawing on science fiction to look forward to possible futures, and bringing things into the present world.

I've heard you use this expression 'affective encounter' and wonder if, by extension, it means that, inspired by the SF of Butler, Delaney and others, speculation is also aspiration?

Well, one of the questions that led me to *Ritual Without Belief* was: what would it mean to start from a place of abundance rather than from one of scarcity or lack? Marginal subjects might be thought to often start from a place of deficit. This science fiction, this speculative thinking is about saying, 'We have everything'; the issue then becomes one of how do we bring together all of these resources and push for something more. This idea of bringing together one's pleasure and politics has always been at the centre of what I do, and I think that is where the interest in music comes in, as well as club spaces and social spaces.

Speaking of spaces, are you someone who grew up with access to the internet?

I'm in my early thirties, so I can just remember a period before the internet was ubiquitous, but by the time I was a teenager, music was present on the internet. From a very young age, you know, I was really active on Napster, Limewire. I am such a music geek that through MSN, chat rooms and LiveJournal, I had pen pals like across the world who I exchanged mixtapes with. By the time I was eleven or twelve, I was finding out about music through this whole huge network—and the music was digitally distributed but also took physical form. Those experiences also influenced the way that I think of access.

And have those early encounters also influenced how you view the contemporary art scene? Is there ever a point when you wonder why what we have now is not as amazing as what you called the "whole huge network?" Maybe you don't experience this, but I wonder if the contemporary scene is more guarded, if it is a place where people hold on to their resources a bit more?

Perhaps it is partly that. It could be that people are more guarded, but equally the art world right now is so market-driven, so concerned with the objectification and monetization of the art work. As a project, B.O.S.S—the Black Obsidian Sound System—completely goes against that closed, objectifying ethos because I didn't make it to be an art object to live in somebody's house. I do use art to come to money but for me B.O.S.S is a community resource, made manifest, as far as I'm concerned, through redistributing resources from the art world to in particular, benefit the QTIBIPOC [queer, trans intersex black indigenous people of colour] community. And that is really fundamental to how I work: it's about how resources get redistributed. Even with the 180 Strand exhibition *Transformer*, it was high production art world work but at the same time, critically, I wanted to create meditations through works inside and outside the exhibition that my communities could spend time with.

I like that idea of making community a plural like you did just there, it suggests an openness.

As I said earlier, I practice meditation, I go to Buddhist retreats and that is another community—not necessarily the community that I run the sound system with or go to art spaces with, but I want them to be able to access the work just as much. For me, it is communities in the plural, it has to spiral outwards, it has to have multiple points of entry.

With the voice and vocality, with the manipulation of the voice and the voice's relation to text, are those central to what makes your work possess the ability to move between communities?

I've always said that my voice is my primary material. It comes before video or any of these other things—it's the voice through which I'm able to express and communicate. The voice is the root of my power in a way. When I'm writing, I'm always thinking about what it would mean for the words to be uttered, for it to be spoken? The spoken word is very much a part of the way that I work, the way that I write. It's fundamental. I'm always thinking about what would it mean to be expressed.

And does that cut both ways? When you're working with these archive materials, is part of the speculative or imaginative encounter with the Octavia Butler archive or the archival materials that you used for She Was A Full Body Speaker, the investigation of the texture of the voice you discover and the need to bring elements of it back with you?

I would say that exploration of archive material came around most concretely in 2016 with a work that I made while investigating queer, female-led social centres in London and the women's library in Glasgow. I was coming across different flyers, listings, magazines and I became aware of the issue of how to talk about what once happened in a moment in historical time without just reproducing it? How do I make it something that can reverberate outwards and have some kind of impact in the present? For what became the radio play *The Catalogue of Poses* (2016), I created three different narratives, which were rooted in my research but didn't just reproduce what I came across; instead, I used artistic licence to draw on real experiences, on anecdotes, and on imagination. My research unearthed photographs depicting people and these people became the figures in the play and they allowed me to invent stories about their portraits, who they were, what kind of life they lived, and also what kind of life they might have gone on to live. So returning to your question, it is ways like that that the speculative and the imaginative come into my work.

Audre Lorde developed the concept of biomythography—the idea of mythologising one's biography. Lorde does it around like her specific life, but I'm interested in applying it to the lives of the people that I come across in archives or who have otherwise really inspired my work. This is the notion of taking moments past and thinking of what role they might continue to play, how we might strategise or live better in the present. Not necessarily live better but live differently. This is a fundamental part of my practice.

If you speculate differently, if you imagine another world, and commit yourself to understanding some forms of marginality as an abundance rather than scarcity—and this seems an incredibly powerful strategy—are you logically stopped from being able to continue to think about the negative pressures of marginality?

No! It is not that all of the problems miraculously disappear. It's closer to something that Octavia Butler said along the lines of what you pay attention to grows. By focusing on and turning towards what feels nourishing and reparative, you might then be better resourced to deal with the more oppressive forces that come into play. To constantly focus on the negative makes things feel hopeless; it feels impossible to navigate. For me, it's that re-orientation, about being fortified, strengthened; by focusing on what feels nourishing, I can better deal with the shit that comes my way.

Does that parallel a self-care that then helps other people?

Hmm. I feel like self-care is such a contentious term, so loaded, over-used to the point of being empty. I went to a talk by Stephano Harney—who wrote *The Undercommons* with Fred Moten—and Harney spoke of the idea of militant rest and that idea really captured me. He hasn't formally written about militant rest and when it came to the Q&A, I asked him about how that concept might relate to self-care, and he discussed how militant rest emerges when self-care becomes a collective endeavour. For me, my healing, my transforming, my growth is completely tied up in yours, in hers, in everybody else's. It has to be a collective endeavour. That's where I believe that self-care falls short: it's become completely commodified, but also presumes that all I have to do is take care of myself and then everything will be okay. The desire for becoming a collective endeavour is fundamental, which is why I'm so invested in bringing things into the public spaces that I can access, such as art spaces.

When you're thinking about these collectivities, these communities, these different zones that you travel through and live in, we've talked a lot about the people in the past who have inspired you, but are there parallel inspirations for you today?

You know, I really wish that I could say that there was. There are people that I see as mentors for my practice, and yet their work is not in a direct alignment with mine. Lubaina Himid, Ingrid Pollard and others are artists who have really grounded my work, who I can draw on and can draw from and who really inspire what I do. There are also definitely newer artists out there making and doing who I'm really excited by; but in terms of being able to locate people doing similar things to me, I'm less sure that there is a community of that kind.

They don't need to be very similar. My question was one that acknowledged how expansive your work has been; sound seems always to have been important for you, even during your undergraduate degree in Media Arts, but how do you see yourself in sound arts?

<laughing>: I don't know if I do see myself connected to sound arts! Someone whose work I like is Hannah Catherine Jones, who occupies this weird territory, like me, of being an artist who also very much works in sound. I feel like these disciplines are a little arbitrary. Of course, I under-

stand that there is a history, a lineage, but to be honest, it's a lineage that, up until this point, I have felt excluded from, so I don't know how I fit into the legacies of sound art. Another person who comes to mind is Christine Sun Kim but again I'd see her as within the realm of art. I do think there's a big shift happening, you know, within sound art with people like Ain Bailey now coming to prominence, and I think that's why you're here today. Previously quite gate-kept disciplines are realising that the conversations are shifting, widening out, and that maybe at the same time, the criteria have also shifted.

This is really interesting to hear. Of course, it is also very dispiriting to learn again of these experiences of sound art as exclusionary. A lot of my undergraduates think of you as a significant node in what they see as a constellation of sound arts practices and, as you know, one of my students devoted some of their PhD to an analysis of your work. But that is maybe me being defensive, I think it is important to be transparent here about how a field is operating.

I know, I know. It is tricky, though, because even if we were to think of the queer, black elders in music and sound, I can't… I can't grasp them easily. I don't know if that's because they don't exist; I want to believe that they are out there as part of the canon but they are not visible. Where are they? Even in the Her Noise Archive, where I did some research a few years ago, it is amazing but it is very white. I was a bit "What's going on here?"

If our discussion was about music rather than sound art, would you be saying the same thing?

No, it is different for sure, in terms of DJs, in terms of producers, there is much more of a legacy. There is something about the art / sound space in particular that is a problem. There may well have been people within that lineage but maybe they died really young or didn't have any attention paid to them, even if their work was amazing. So, yeah, that's the moment we're in. We are in a moment where a lot of reparative work has to be done. I think Julius Eastman is a good example of where people didn't hold on to the talent, didn't nurture the talent when it was out here.

I'm in a really fortunate position that from fairly early on people paid attention to what I did, and in turn I was able to be resourced. That is why I do projects like the Black Obsidian Sound System, to make sure that I can, where possible, provide resources for my community. But out here, it's not easy for people, and statistically speaking, we are a lot less likely to commit to being an artist because, as you know, it's hard. It's tough out here.

That's where your speculative futurism and your idea of echo as an affective encounter might be able to empower…

...the next gen. Yeah, we'll see. I really hope that the landscape widens, I hope that things become more available, more accessible. I would love that. You know, there is still work that we can do. There are still ways that we can contribute.

Hanna Tuulikki

The artists we interviewed for this book might each seem to occupy a different niche within the broad spectrum of sound arts practices (indeed, representing those differences has been an impetus behind our wider approach). However, one quality that many interviewees appear to share in common is—perhaps paradoxically—their inclination to work through plural, parallel, processes. This was palpable in a performance lecture that Hanna Tuulikki gave, where I and the rest of the audience could hear how one specific, focused, project—*Away With The Birds*—could take on all these other dimensions simultaneously, dimensions which subsequently burgeoned first when I started to explore that work further on my own, and then multiplied again when we had our discussion.

Although she explores much else besides, one of the particular differences that excites me about Tuulikki's practice is its engagement with the audible aspects of animality, which she articulates in a language, echoing Donna Haraway, of how critters might be become-with, and of how generative oddkin might be made. Tuulikki is an attentive listener to and enthusiastic learner from the entanglements in which diverse cultures bind themselves to the human and to the more-than-human, just as she hears keenly the ways in which those knots are to be found located in places within the morphologies of landscape and of language. If these connections sound densely drawn, the very opposite is the case: Tuulikki finds the beauties as well as the difficulties in the sonorous.

How are things?

It is difficult to know when you're in the midst of something, isn't it? We are in a strange rift between past and future. I keep returning to the image of being on one of those warped funfair rides where there is nothing to grab hold of when the floor keeps shifting and with it your perspective of the horizon.

Some of the thematic concerns that you engage with in your work are not entirely distant from times of heightened tension—Deer Dancer, for example, could be said to articulate several overlapping crises—so it is not as if I'm talking to you as someone whose work is completely separate from political and ecological concerns.

Before the pandemic kicked off in the UK, I had been reading about Timothy Morton's 'hyperobjects' and it really does feel as if his ideas are being laid out in real time. In terms of the pandemic, not only is it revealing an X-Ray of prejudices but it's also showing that certain communities will suffer the most because they are vulnerable. In a way, we have experienced Covid-19 like a sped-up version of the climate emergency.

I am sure we will return to those deeper themes later, but one preliminary question that I wanted to ask concerns the journey that you have taken to become the artist that you are. I've read interviews with you, of course, but I wonder whether this is somewhere that you imagined you would be?

Well, I have sung ever since I was a child and also danced from a young age. I actually wanted to be a dancer but ended up going to art school. While I was there, I started playing in bands, improvising with other musicians, and was exposed to loads of weird and wonderful music. In a sense, I gave myself permission to work with the voice within an 'arts practice'—in inverted commas—and in my third year at art school, I started doing performances, such as singing in the dark, and singing with geese, through which I began to explore the edges of the human and more-than-human, and the interactions between both human-and-human and human-and-more-than-human. I remember a really incredible Pauline Oliveros workshop on listening, at the Instal Festival in Glasgow, having a profound impact on me. I don't think I ever really knew exactly what I wanted to be, other than a general sense of being an artist, since I've always navigated the world through creative practice.

In one of your interviews, you talked about the Copper Family of folk singers, whose former house in Rottingdean I occasionally walk pass. I quite like the idea of you being somewhere between the Copper Family, Pauline Oliveros and fine arts practice!

When I saw the Copper Family perform, I was in my late teens—it was before art school. I found it incredibly moving, especially when Bob Copper put his hand on his son's knee during the performance. There was so much love in the room, it was very powerful. When I moved to Glasgow, I started a more serious investigation of traditional music, also listening to music from around the world. As a consequence, I became interested in vernacular culture and the tacit knowledges that are embodied in tradition.

I guess that leads me to the question about where for you those knowledges, if they are tacit, actually reside, especially in terms of the voice. I am thinking about how your vocal approach explores the lexical and the non-lexical, the semantic sound of speech as utterance simultaneous with the beauty of the sonorous.

When I talk about tacit knowledge, I mean the kind of embodied knowledge that is carried along what Hamish Henderson called the "carrying stream", from teacher to novice, from one tradition-bearer to the next—traditional songs that are learned not by reading notation, but acquired through the experience of listening and learning directly. In terms of my explorations, I wasn't born into any particular tradition, so I have sought out those that are willing to be my guides, or mentors. My learning so far has been quite a hotch-potch! I am curious about traditions where the voice is used as an instrument—what does the song communicate or express beyond words, beyond lyrical meaning? Or what about songs that have no actual words? In Scottish Gaelic, for example, vocables (non-lexical sounds) often make up a refrain or a chorus—sometimes these sounds are thought to be magical, sometimes they imitate sounds of the more-than-human world—and in the collection of songs that underpin *Away with the Birds*, it is these vocable sounds that are often mimetic of birds. What does it mean to learn these songs in parallel to studying the birds they imitate?

But as well as tradition, I'm also interested in experimental and contemporary, vocal and eco-poetic work too—you're probably right in saying I exist somewhere in between! There are two things I particularly remember doing at art school: one was continuing to work with Pauline Oliveros's slow walk and slow singing exercise and feeling language dissolve in a space with other participants; the other, slightly romantic memory I have, involved my wanting to lose my 'human-ness', while also recognising how impossible that was, through attempting to find a common ground where my vocal tone might meet a goose's vocal tone. Around that time, I started performing outside a lot and became interested in wider processes of listening. There was a David Dunn essay that was inspiring in thinking about the latter. I don't remember the exact quotation but Dunn argued that our ears deceive us in the way our eyes don't, an implication of this being that we can mistake the wind in the trees for the sound of waves in the sea. I started to think that the voice might constitute a meeting point between self and the world—how could my breathing connect to the sound of the sea?

At that point, were you consciously listening to things like yoiking and other traditions involving singing outside and placing the voice in relation to the sounded environment?

Absolutely, yes. I was thirsty for listening to all sorts of music from around the world. I wasn't articulating it as such at the time but I now see these musics as kinds of vernacular knowledge. I was very aware while listening that when cultures had an intimate connection with the land, the music seemed to grow out of that intimacy. That was the kind of beginning point for me to search out traditions closer to home—although since then I've also been fortunate enough to go and study traditions from further away.

I wanted to ask you about those studies of yours with reference to Deer Dancer. *Maybe we could talk about it now?*

Well, for *Deer Dancer*, I turned my attention to dances that are mimetic of deer—the Abbots Bromley Horn Dance from Staffordshire, the Scottish Highland Fling, and the Yaqui Deer Dance from Arizona/Mexico. I was lucky to be able to attend the various seasonal rituals and to learn directly from tradition bearers. I researched the dances' connection to hunting practices, going stalking at Trees for Life [conservation project, Findhorn, Forres], and observed deer in their habitats. I discovered that all three dances' movements imitate the male deer—their behaviour and gesture, from the frolicking of the fawn and the alertness of the adult male, to the bravado, display and aggression of the rutting stag. Another feature is that they are, or were, traditionally performed by men and, with their displays of strength and athletic endurance, they're all thought to have their origins in (or associations with) hunting ritual practices. By conjuring the antlered male deer, the dances evoke images of wild nature, but I realised that for various reasons, from appropriation and romanticisation of the deer to the effects of climate breakdown, there is a disconnect between what is encoded in the dance movements and the reality of local damaged ecologies. I was also acutely aware of the striking relationship between our cultural perceptions of 'wilderness' and ideas of 'masculinity'. Drawing on multiple layers of this research, I created a film—a story of an imaginary 'wilderness world' where I play five hybrid deer-men who stalk each other to the death. But, of course, because I was following the deer and their seasonal patterns closely, this work took quite a long time...

A lot of your work seems to involve long periods of percolating, developmental research. How long was the gestation for Away With The Birds, *for example?*

I started working on *Away With The Birds* in 2010 with the performances taking place on the island of Canna in 2014. I was digging deep into archives, working with living tradition bearers, and beginning to practice with two other vocalists, going back and forth between these different processes—which is what I do: research, research, research, and then begin to distil in order to find a methodology or a framework of questions that I want to explore.

Forgive me, this question is coming from a place of ignorance because I don't use my voice in the way that you do, but does part of your process of research involve relearning the relationship between your body, your breath, your voice and the new context you are exploring?

Yeah. Going back to this idea of tacit knowledge, I'm interested in getting deep into the material and learning aspects of the tradition that I'm particularly paying attention to. What can I learn by doing as opposed to simply watching or listening? You know, I could collage together audio from archives, I could assemble a montage of historical film footage, but instead I want to see what is possible to learn through doing—which includes learning how these traditions relate to the ecologies that they speak of or embody.

Earlier this morning, I was listening to examples of your vocal improvisations as part of the Outlandia project in Glen Nevis in Scotland. Outside of their contacts to the traditions you have discussed, one of the things that interests me about sound and voice is precisely those relationships to ecologies, to the morphology of the landscape. This also feels like a very important part of what you do as an artist and what you bring to your audiences.

Thinking of *Cloud-Cuckoo-Island* and its reimagining of the tale of the Irish King Sweeney, or of *Women of The Hill* which revolves around the past matriarchal culture of an Iron Age site, both those works had their origins in me singing out loud in the places which their narratives connect to—the Isle of Eigg and the Isle of Skye, respectively. My process began by singing in those places, and connecting with different knowledges embedded in those sites—the archaeology, history and folklore, but always from the perspective of how voice connects with place. With both of those pieces, they animate the echo from the surrounding hill or cliff—and with *Cloud-Cuckoo-Island*, the echo took on another form with the cuckoo bird responding directly to my singing.

Is that the same cuckoo from the valley on Eigg that you talk about in your online diary? If so, this leads me to a next question about the kind of the opportunities your work discovers for the human and the more-than-human to encounter each other.

Well, in my practice, I keep coming back to a sense of exploring meeting points. It has been really useful over the past year or so, to reflect on these meetings, between human and more-than-human, but also other meeting-points such as between male and female, either in my own body or in the voice. As an illustration, my work *SING SIGN: A Close Duet* for the Edinburgh Art Festival, is a hocket between a male and female vocalist—

<interrupting>—a hocket? what is that?

Sorry! A hocket is a mediaeval musical device where the melody is split between two or more voices or instruments. In *SING SIGN*, in order to make the hocket work, Daniel Padden—my collaborator—and I, had to find common ground in our pitch range; I had to reach into my really low notes and he had to reach into his high notes, otherwise the difference would be too pronounced and there wouldn't be the same thread running through the melody. The work, then, became about this meeting point and compromise between us. I'm also interested in other meeting points in that work, such as those between the ancient and the contemporary.

Going back to what you asked about the human and more-than-human, I keep returning to the idea of mimesis, a term that I borrow not from theatre, but from ethnomusicology, specifically from the writings of Ted Levin who has spent a lot of time with people in Tuva and Sakha in Siberia. Levin talks about how in the sound-making practices of these nomadic people, there are no single words for music and sound, they are always articulated together, in a spectrum of sound mimesis from something that is iconic and directly imitative to something that is stylised or metaphorical.

Nice.

This, for me, has become such an underpinning for my work: I am interested in this spectrum in the voice, but also in the body, and why these aspects of mimesis reside in our traditions. Originally, I was focusing on mimesis in terms of language evolution and music evolution, and whether these developed through our listening to the more-than-human. Now I'm engaging a different kind of criticality so, for example, in *Deer Dancer*, I'm beginning to question the rituals and the structures that surround mimesis, including considering how it is that these mimetic practices continue?; what are the cultures that have maintained those practices?; and how might they reinforce both problematic normative behaviours and problematic constructions of naturecultures?

Do these meeting points relate to thresholds, too?

Yes, I want to know what happens to my edges when I engage with 'others'—what happens to our sense of boundaries and thresholds, and whether these can be transgressed in ways that are responsible and sensitive?

That Cloud-Cuckoo-Island diary entry of yours that you published online which I mentioned earlier was tinged with an expression of an ethics of listening and sounding, of responsibilities and sensitivities.

Well, I'm a big fan girl of Donna Haraway! So, I have the sense that it might be possible to make oddkin through my creative practices, and 'become-with other', whether that other is a human being encountered in a performance space or a theatre, or whether it is the cuckoo encountered on an island. I also ask myself, how can technology augment my voice into male deer pitch range, or extend my ears by slowing down the sound of birds to hear something of their way of hearing.

With your works SOURCEMOUTH: LIQUIDBODY and Deer Dancer, is part of your approach to investigate other culture's perspectives on oddkinship, on becoming-with and finding in those practices different kinds of encounter?

Well, *SOURCEMOUTH: LIQUIDBODY* was a response to a commission to make a place-responsive work for the Kochi-Muziris Biennale in India.

This was after *Away With The Birds*, *SING SIGN* and *Women of the Hill* and the curator was particularly interested in *SING SIGN* where I was beginning to look at the relationship between gesture and the voice. The curator put me in touch with Kapila Venu, who is a formidable practitioner of Kutiyattam, a form of Sanskrit drama told through gestures of eyes and hands. I was thinking about the context of Kochi and the Biennale and the importance of water, and while I was talking with Kapila, she demonstrated a series of gestures that embody the formation of a river. We really clicked as people, and I was drawn to consider how this gestural embodiment of the river might have similarities with the vocal embodiment of birds in the Scottish Gaelic tradition. In terms of your question, I don't think I consciously sought out 'exotic' cultural traditions, it just happens that a process unfolded on the basis of invitations from curators, conversations I've had with people and... accidents.

But I am trying to understand more what I mean by mimesis and meeting points, so whether that will involve me studying further with traditional bearers from other places, I don't know yet—or even whether the current climate will allow that.

Although our discussion so far has concentrated on sound and processes of sounding, one of the dimensions of SOURCEMOUTH *that looks striking in the documentation I've seen of it, is its emphatically multi-sensorial approach to the world: there is costume, movement in space, visual scores, and these flow through your other works.*

SOURCEMOUTH was the first time I included visual scores in the final installation, and in that piece, I was also consciously giving myself permission to explore movement and, dare I say it, dance. I am interested in cross-modality and synesthesia and I don't believe that you can box each sense off from another. In *Away With The Birds*, for example, the songs that I was studying are mimetic not only of the sounds of birds, but also of their movements and of the motion of waves. So, just as listening is intimately connected with other senses, so gesturing is related to drawing, in ways that perhaps take us back to Meredith Monk's "singing body" and "dancing voice".

Drawing was something that was part of your project in Cromarty on the North West coast of Scotland, where you portrayed the inhabitants of the town and connected their breath to the crash of waves.

Drawing runs through my practice. Drawing helps me think—it frees me to think—and it's how I develop a visual language or a visual score. And then the drawings that I share with an audience become keys to unlock meaning in the work.

Speaking of audiences, in Away With the Birds, *it feels like it meets the audiences in a number of different w—*

—but works can allow audiences to meet themselves, too, and that was definitely the case with *Away With The Birds*, where, because it was on an island that took a three-hour ferry to get to, people ended up camping overnight. Scientists met with arts practitioners and some of the conversations that began there are ones that are continuing today as collaborations. That is so exciting.

I am interested in re-animating bodies of knowledge, whatever those entanglements might be within the work. For outdoor performance works like *Away With The Birds*, I am also creating a space for audience to tune into a continuum between human and more-than-human—sometimes a vocal performance is really just an opportunity to frame the listening. At the end of that performance, we (the vocalists) walked through the audience, so they no longer watched the ten women performers, only listened to our singing which created a kind of intimacy. When we stopped singing this became an invitation to listen. A lot of people said to me afterwards that they started hearing everything as music. And that was just a beautiful outcome for that work. I hope I can continue to make work like that in the future.

Although the composition sits at the heart of the work, I see the other elements as satellites. Going back to my drawings, they are very precise and very illustrative of the birds as they appear imitated in traditional song and again in my score. Working with field recordist Geoff Sample and with the tradition bearer Mary Smith we spent time unpacking the relationship between traditional song and the sounds of birds and I learned so much through that process. But I also learned a lot through drawing the birds.

As well as offering the chances for people to be present in the outdoor spaces, you also pay attention to an online presence for your compositions, giving us access to all kinds of other related materials, such as the bird drawings, texts, archive resources, scores.

I think this aspect comes back to responsibility. I am exploring traditions with tradition bearers and therefore I have a responsibility to share what I'm learning in a sensitive way. I felt it was important to be transparent about Kapila Venu's role as my Kutiyattam mentor and to share some of the underpinnings to her practice. But at the same time, I am committed to the story-telling around the work—as Donna Haraway says, we tell stories through other stories. Those digital spaces allow stories to be told with a vast reach, creating conversations across cultures and disciplines.

One of the ways I imagine you telling stories through stories is by giving them a modern inflection. In Cloud-Cuckoo-Island, *the Gaelic stories of King Sweeney become stories of gender heard with contemporary ears.*

Yes! I am asking "Where are the resonances?", in the multiple meanings of that word.

Do you have to be as responsible with stories like Sweeney's or can you give yourself more liberty?

I think I'd have to reflect on that. Not working directly with a living tradition bearer is perhaps freeing in some ways, but I'm also sensitive to Sweeney as a character and to his vulnerabilities. By queering this figure, I am asking what is revealed about culture's normative ideas of gender. There is a different process of unearthing, I guess, a different process of archaeology. One more thing I am really aware of is another meeting point, that between science and sentiment. I was really struck with Sweeney by the fact that although he is a mythological character in a mediaeval text, although he took on avian form, growing feathers on his skin and sleeping in thorn trees, his condition speaks to us now: the way he carries himself through the world might be weighted down by memories of some of the battles he was in. Might this be an ancient story of a what today calls Post-Traumatic Stress Disorder?

Of course, what is also important is the relationship between a text and the folklore, the archaeology, the geography of a particular place, what I call 'mnemonic topographies', which are like living libraries of tradition. How can I, as an artist, animate these entanglements over time in a particular place, in a way that is sensitive?

When you are unearthing these mnemonic topographies, do you have site visits, look at maps, take photographs?

Yes, but it is not formulaic, each project carries its own set of questions, its own particular framework, its own particular temporalities. However, there is always that question about the relationship between a place, its ecology and its human cultures. Think of the Gaelic place names for the meeting point between sea and land and how these will become submerged over the years. I have an increasing sense of urgency and I find that it is not enough for me at this current moment in time to create a space for an audience to only experience something beautiful. I'm beginning to think more about our mythologies, traditions and impacts on real ecologies and how I might engage with these connections. When *Away With The Birds* was made, the summer of 2014 was incredible in Scotland, with the referendum for independence; there was such an energy about a possible reshaping of futures. It felt like anything was possible, that we could make positive change and this project was part of that energy, an energy that could be felt on the island where the performance happened.

Can I just ask you one more thing? In my notebook where I've gathered my questions for you, I've written the phrase "magico-religious" and nothing else. Is that something that you've said or something that someone else is saying about you?

<laughing> I'm sure I've used those words! In *Away With The Birds*, as well as being mimetic of avian sound and movement, the songs and poems also carry with them their social and cultural meanings. And some have magico-religious symbolism. For example, the redshank is imitated in a keening song to sing the departed safely over to the spirit world. The oystercatcher song is a lullaby and oystercatcher in Scottish Gaelic is 'gille-brighde', which means 'servant of St. Bride' who, before she was a saint, was the Celtic goddess Bride. There are layers to these songs just as there are layers to the landscape, just as within mimesis there is an element of magic, as humans have sought to become-with other critters.

I guess a lot of my work has an element of ritual within it, but I am interested in the creation of rituals that can help us navigate the places that we find ourselves in now. *Deer Dancer* felt very much like a life crisis ritual for a damaged planet, connecting the ecological crisis with the crisis of masculinity. Hopefully I'll be developing this as a live work with other performers. Mostly, it all comes back to navigations, to senses of meeting points and boundaries, transgressing and questioning, and to liminal spaces like coastlines, hillsides, dawns and dusks, and also to the theatre space as a space of ritual, as a space where all the arts resided.

Hong-Kai Wang

I didn't know anything at all about Hong-Kai Wang when she contacted me out of the blue and we meet up in a café in Dalston, a perfect spot, in East London, to talk about gentrification. She was a PhD candidate at the University of Vienna and she was interested in spaces of commoning. A year or so later Hong-Kai, along with two fellow students, invited me to collaborate with them on designing a workshop for their PhD cohort about de-colonised listening. The two-day event turned out to be highly contentious and a bonding experience for the four of us. In the few years following, I heard bits and pieces from Hong-Kai and saw that her work was being shown in various places and that she had moved back to Taiwan. I was delighted to spend the day with her in Taipei consulting fortune tellers at the temple, and sampling various of her favourite restaurants around town. Yet, despite these small but intense and very enjoyable encounters, I barely knew anything about her. It was great to get to know her better through the interview and to understand more about how her current practice has developed from working with sound into something extremely situational and relational. I am interested in her concentration on different forms of labour, and her collaborations with groups and investigations into what holds them together. I enjoy her humour and I admire the fact that she maintains collaborative relationships over a long period, and the pacing and originality of her work.

You did an undergraduate degree in political science, is that right?

Yes, at National Taiwan University. After that I worked as a television journalist, off camera, interviewing, editing and script writing, so I was working with audio-visual equipment a little.

You left to go to the USA?

I first visited New York in 1995 and I had a gut feeling that I must live there, and I just followed that feeling. The easiest way for Taiwanese people to live in the US is to get a student visa, so I got into a Masters programme in Media Studies at the New School. I met my mentor, Chris Mann, the Australian poet, there. He was teaching sound production.

Did you start making your own work then?

Yes, but I don't remember what! Audio work, maybe using field recordings and interviews, it might have been to do with immigration or alienation. I remember being very excited by Janet Cardiff's work and have a vivid memory of her retrospective at PS1 maybe in 2000. After the New School I worked in a used record store in Manhattan for half a year, and got to meet a lot of music nerds and that's where I was exposed to jazz, experimental music and new music. Then I got a job as assistant to the Chinese artist, Cai Guo-Qiang, who works with fireworks and gunpowder. I did that for three years.

What was your job there?

Administration, co-ordination and logistics. At that time, I think he had three assistants in the New York office.

Is he still based in New York?

Yes, I think he owns three or four properties in Manhattan and a big ranch in New Jersey.

That must have given you such a good insight into aspects of the art world.

Yes, but only the upper tiers.

Were you still making your own work when you were working with him?

Very, very rarely. It was not possible, because it was 200% dedication. The degree of commitment goes with the territory. I quit in 2004 to pursue my own practice. I was working on a big show curated by him in Taiwan. It was a really large-scale group show, using bunkers and an exhibition site on a formerly militarised island called Kinmen. While working on the show, I befriended the artist Su-Mei Tse from Luxembourg. After the show opened, we were having tea and I was telling her that I couldn't find time to do anything that I wanted to do, and she said, "Then just quit," just like that. You need someone to tell you. As soon as I returned to New York, I told him that I was leaving.

Did you have a plan?

No! <laughs> I don't wait to move on until I have a plan, because we can be very easily paralysed by our dependence on security. I was working for some other artists, and in the meantime, I came across this open call—'Art in Odd Places'—and my proposal to make a sound installation at a friend's dumpling restaurant in East Village got accepted. So that's my very first solo work. It was called *Listening With the Dumplings*! <laughs> It was really tongue in cheek.

What sort of sounds did you use?

I recorded sounds generated in the restaurant and composed a soundscape, and then played it back there. It was not very audible, because the restaurant was always noisy and busy, but it was that work that got me invited by Dan Cameron for the Taipei Biennial in 2006.

That is amazing.

I was really, really lucky, I literally didn't know what I was doing—I was just exploring and trying to figure out my direction. The work that I ended up doing at the Taipei Biennial was not very good, I don't even talk about it anymore. I was mainly collecting the sounds of labour, as with the dumpling restaurant, but this time it was the sounds from museum staff including those who worked as security guards, giftshop clerks, janitors, volunteers etc.—art labour. That seems to have been a very consistent concern of mine.

Had the curator heard the dumpling piece?

No. I met him at Cai Guo-Qiang's studio, before I quit, and when he knew that I was from Taiwan, he asked me to send him something. At that time, I only had one piece, so I sent him that. He wrote to me maybe three months prior to the opening of the Taipei Biennial, and told me that he was listening to my work, and that the more he listened the more he liked it, and so he decided to invite me.

Is it predominantly Taiwanese artists?

No, it's international. I think there were only four Taiwanese artists out of about thirty that year, and the four of us were relatively unknown, both within Taiwan and outside.

So the work was about the labour of the gallery workers, how was it displayed?

There were maybe eight speakers inside a courtyard, again it was difficult to hear it properly, because it was a public space. At that time, I was really drawn to transitory public spaces.

Re-inserting invisible labour into those spaces.

Yeah. So after that, I went back to New York and the next year I was invited back to Taiwan by an old friend who was actually running a big culinary corporation and was opening an organic hot pots restaurant in Taipei. She read about my participation in the Taipei Biennial and she commissioned me to make a sound installation for her restaurant! She wanted me to record the sound from her organic farms, and insert it back into the restaurant, so the customers can have the food and hear the sound of the ingredients.

I think I have been pretty lucky, I've had a project commissioned about every year since 2005 or so. In 2007, I made an outdoor sound installation in Madrid, invited by David Caballero, an artist himself and a good friend of mine, who was curating a section for the White Night Festival

(La Noche en Blanco) in Madrid. He wanted me to do something at the private garden of an insurance company that would be open to the public during the festival. At the same time I had been invited by a film-maker, J. L. Aronson from New York, to do sound design for his film about Coney Island, where the Astroland Amusement Park was about to be dismantled. Aronson introduced me to the owner of the Park and I got access to all the rides with contact microphones and a field recording mic, so I had lots and lots of amazing sounds. For the Madrid project, I decided to create a sonic amusement park in the garden using lots of hidden speakers and turn it into a public space. That was a shift for me as that's the first time that I didn't use the sound produced on the site and re-insert it back. Actually it's probably also the first project that I really liked. I got the best compliment on the opening night, in the middle of the night a middle-aged man approached me and he said that he was very moved by my piece, then revealed that he was the gardener of that garden. I think that's the best compliment I could ever get!

You must have been building up your compositional skills...

Yes, it's all coming back—after I stopped working for the artists, I was freelancing, making audio guides for museums in New York. Most of my work was cut and splice, I didn't know anything about sound processing.

So, within a few years of starting to work as a freelance sound artist, you had received commissions in three different countries.

I know, I was very fortunate! I had built a connection with Madrid and the next year, 2008, I got invited back to be part of the In-Presentable performance festival by the Spanish choreographer Juan Dominguez. There was no Chinatown in Madrid but there was a huge Chinese population. So, I started to approach the Chinese shop owners and commercial businesses and to create a sonic Chinatown. The Chinese in Madrid are not invisible, but they are also not audible and people don't really pay attention to them.

That's interesting. Were you recording the sounds of work again?

Yes, and because I speak Mandarin Chinese I could talk to them and record that, so I also made my voice present. The curator suggested that I could accentuate my presence in my working process, because he could see that the way I worked was very performative, in an everyday way, and I thought that I could make the traces my encounters with people and spaces more present. I think that is when these performative elements started to take on more prominence as in my later projects. I saw it as a social performativity, when they are working, when they have to work with their body and their labour, out of necessity to survive and to live.

So you've these themes of labour and performativity, and you've also started to bring a little of your identity as a Mandarin-speaking person of Chinese descendent in.

Yes. That can give me access to a world that a lot of other people don't necessarily have access to. For example, one of the store owners took me to a huge Chinese compound outside Madrid, which was like a Chinese colony where people work in the same factory and eat at the same communal kitchen. It was pretty astonishing! As far as I was told, most of the Chinese in Madrid probably migrated there in the 1990s, they were economic migrants, different from the earlier Chinese migration to London or Manhattan. They'd got capital, and my Spanish friends would say that they arrived with lots of cash and bought up properties. When I asked them why they chose Spain, not London or New York, they said that Europe was cheaper in terms of broker fees, getting paperwork and all the legal work sorted out etc.. I even remember one owner complained to me that they have become lazy here, because Spanish people take so much time off!

That sounds like quite a kind of significant work for you.

The next thing is also very interesting. A friend of mine overheard a woman, in a restaurant in New York, talking about curating a show in Korea. He approached her and told her that he had a friend who did amazing work and gave her my email. I emailed her, we did a studio visit, and she, Thalia Vrachopoulos, invited me, just like that. Luck again!

It's luck, but you also knew how to approach things—what was your studio at that time?

I didn't have a studio, just my apartment. I learnt a lot from working for Cai Guo-Qiang.

So you were invited to do something in Korea?

Yes for the Incheon Women Artists' Biennial, I think it only happened once? I did a performance. I posed as a Taiwanese woman who was running an unidentifiable campaign in the streets of Incheon, where the biennial was. In both South Korea and Taiwan, a campaign truck is a very commonplace campaign tool, it drives round outfitted with a banner with a photo of the candidate and their slogan, and a big megaphone blasting out the campaign speech often accompanied with catchy pop music. I pre-recorded a speech in very broken Korean about how we conceive of change—I was asking a lot of questions instead of making statements and the piece went on, driving around for three days. That was my very first performance.

It sounds like quite a big conceptual jump from the piece before.

Yes. I just didn't want to make another sound installation!

Fair enough. And this issue of translation and pronunciation?

It really took me a long time to get comfortable with English during the first several years of my New York phase. I couldn't understand 70% of what people said. I often talk about this in artists' talks, I think that my interest in sound comes out of this language alienation. I started to develop this habit of listening to a lot of non-linguistic sound and trying to understand what is really going on around me.

It sounds like a great piece of work. Were you pleased with it?

It was really, really well-received. I think that was the piece that helped me to get a grant from Art Matters in New York, it's given to artists with a social practice. At that time, I was invited by the Taipei Women's Rescue Foundation to do something for the comfort women survivors. They're a non-profit organisation so there is no budget or anything. I proposed an adaptation of *Dust*, the Robert Ashley opera, in Taiwanese, for the comfort women. So, instead of working with them to re-present their experiences, I wanted to make a piece for them to watch. I had seen an iteration of *Dust* at La MaMa Theatre in Manhattan, and I was very moved and on the verge of tears throughout the piece. It's about six homeless people reminiscing to one another about their lives and histories. My friend and mentor, the late Australian poet Chris Mann, introduced me to the late composer Robert Ashley who gave me permission to translate the script into Chinese and Taiwanese, but he told me that the music is scripted tightly with the text, so I would have to recreate it. So I came back to Taiwan and reached out to my old network who have all become directors, composers and artists, and they all came on board, and I got a sponsorship, space at an avant-garde theatre, and a small grant to cover the production costs and the performers' fees. It was a big job for more than a year.

It sounds primarily administrative and less about you going out recording and then working with the materials.

Yes. I have a very good friend who is a clairvoyant and around 2009, he called me and he said, "Hong-Kai, I can see that in three years from now you will do less and less recording yourself, and become more and more the producer and organiser".

Are you happy about that? I think a lot of people don't want to let go of that kind of their own manipulation of material.

Yes, it feels right. There are pros and cons about this kind of way of working.

How many performances did the Robert Ashley opera have?

Five. But only one comfort woman A-ma (meaning grandma in Taiwanese) survivor came to the show. Most of them were too old and frail at the time. It was 2010, and I am afraid that by then they had probably all gone.

How big was the team?

Five performers, a director, a composer, and a sound artist who did acoustic design, and also two administrators. I did the translation and mainly worked as the producer. That piece didn't really turn out the way I would have hoped for. In retrospect, I regret that it was too much like a conventional theatre piece, whereas Robert Ashley's work is musical and the music is rooted in the language and its delivery. There were definitely creative conflicts among the team. The composer Bo-Wei Chen who I collaborated with at the time was an old friend whom I met when I was eighteen. We have been collaborating since 2010. The sound designer Fujui Wang is one of the most generous and coolest people in Taiwan. He also did the acoustic design for my other work, *Music While We Work*.

So you've worked with the same people for a long time.

Yes. While I was developing *Dust*, I had already received the commission for the Taiwan Pavilion in Venice. I went back to my home town, where my parents still live, and started to work with the retired sugar factory workers. I invited them to make recordings in the sugar factory, one of only two sugar factories still in operation in Taiwan. In the heyday of the sugar industry, there were up to fifty. After Taiwan became a member of the World Trade Organisation in 1995, imported sugar took over the local market and the industry declined very rapidly. My home town, Huwei, used to be called the Sugar Capital during the Japanese colonial rule before the Second World War.

Did you work with the sugar workers, getting them to record sound?

I invited the composer Bo-Wei Chen to facilitate three workshops with the sugar factory workers and their wives, where we talked about our sonic memories of their workplace. It was Chen who reminded me to invite the wives, because reproductive labour is equally crucial to keep the sugar community running. I totally agree, I look at my grandma and see how important family is for the workers. Both of my grandparents worked in the sugar factory. My grandpa was on the shop floor and my grandma was selling tobacco to the workers in the compound, and housekeeping for the Japanese management.

You have had a long relationship with this factory! How did you first go about making the contact as an artist?

I just asked my father to make the call. He worked in management before his retirement. I met the director of the factory and he really appreciated my proposal and asked the whole factory to help me. He saw me as part of the community because of my father and of my own history with the community. I see myself as a director of that project. Then my father's former colleague, Mr. Huang, kindly brought together five retired workers who were interested in working with me and four of their spouses also came on board. After the workshops, we went back to the factory during the harvest season and they made recordings while we followed and videoed them. The resulting work consists of five chapters on two screens. The sound track was made from their field recordings. That was part of the group show in the Taiwan Pavilion at the Venice Biennale in 2011. I knew that work was just the start. On a very personal level, I'm trying to sort out my complex relationship with my home town.

Why did you start a PhD?

In 2013 I was kind of frustrated with myself. After Venice, I allowed myself to get into a bad space and I knew that I would not be happy to just be an artist. I have always want to do lots and lots of different things, and I was following my instinct. I wanted to be more critical in my work and I think the PhD really transformed me.

Let's talk about the work you're making now, and maybe reflect about how the Vienna experience has been transformative. How many pieces of work have you produced related to the sugar factory?

A number, but most of them are not really museum-exhibitable works but experiments with workshop methodology—I think that's my way of trying to sharpen my practice.

Tell me about some of those workshops.

In 2013, I started working with two different groups of people in Hökarängen, a suburb of Stockholm. I was on a LASPIS residency, and part of a group show titled Augmented Spatiality. It was an invitation from the Spanish curator María Andueza whom I recently worked with on a radio project for the Reina Sofía Museum. We have been in dialogue ever since. One group that I worked with was The Great Learning Orchestra inspired by Cornelius Cardew's Scratch Orchestra, and another group was a choir named as Konsensus Kören from a commune in the same suburb. We were exploring the idea of 'consensus', as you can guess from the name of the choir. I wanted to connect these two musically different groups, one professional, the other amateur, and see if it was possible for them to work together. I gave them a very short script, written by Chris Mann, and asked them to respond to this text. It was a very difficult process. I was working with each group on and off for more than half a year and video-documenting it, but the first and only time that they met was on the day of the performance.

So, on the day, the process was they had to get together and they had to reach a consensus on how they were going to make a performance?

Yeah.

And you videoed that?

Yeah.

And have you ever shown that as a piece?

No. I haven't had an opportunity and it's very difficult for a non-Swedish-speaker to understand.

The performance and the negotiation was in front of an audience?

Yes. A French guy came up to me afterwards and said thank you very much and that he was really scared because he had no idea what was going on!

How many workshops of that kind have you done in situations which are not familiar to you?

Many.

So the methodology you gathered from these workshops is more like a toolkit or something?

Something like that. I am very surprised—most people seem to respond to it positively, despite the fact that it is often a bit difficult and demanding.

What would you call your artistic practice at the moment? It's not sound art— what is it?

This is not an easy question! Hopefully my practice is always changing and going somewhere. Perhaps I'd call my practice a sort of moving and navigation or making through listening, asking, thinking and forging.

The things that you're describing all have some area of risk or confrontation.

Yes, with people on multiple sides of a situation or a practice.

What did you do with the village women in Italy?

It was a commission by a sound art festival, Limineria, in southern Italy in 2015, curated by Leandro Pisano. The festival was held in a small, beautiful village called Baselice, about two hours by train from Napoli. It was based on the transcription of conversation that I had with a composer friend, who is a clairvoyant, about various forms of rituals in ancestral worship and mourning for the dead in Taiwan. I invited a group of village women, mostly middle-aged and elderly, to read and to discuss it together. It was all in Italian, but Eleonora, a young girl, was simultaneously translating the whole conversation in my ear. Afterwards a video presentation was made out of the workshop. I asked three younger women if they were willing to make a summary, like a lecture of the workshop, and the next day, we got together and had a camera rolling and they had a discussion about what had happened in the workshop, and we videotaped it. No editing: it's just one take. It was really interesting. They live in a small village where they all know each other, but somehow, the workshop brought out memories that they hadn't even shared before. For instance, one lady in her eighties was talking about her grandpa, who emigrated to the United States years back. After he passed, his family in the United States cremated his body and sent the ashes back to the village, and his family in Italy didn't realise it was his ashes, they thought it was black pepper! So they cooked food with it <laughs>. It was fantastic! I still vividly remember the sound of the group's gasps of shock!

How did you get the women to agree to be at the workshop?

In every village there's always some women or men who know everybody and are very good at mobilising, and Leandro got one of them to arrange the occasion. Allegedly, one of the ladies, her name is Maria, was still practicing witchcraft at the time, according to the translator!

So what sort of workshop practices have you been putting into place at the project 'Southern Clairaudience'?

The only material we work with over the series of workshops are the lyrics of a protest song, 'Sugarcane Song'. It was written in 1925 by a sugarcane workers' union in Japan-colonised Taiwan to mobilise a strike against an unfair harvest management policy in Erlin. Erlin is a small town in south-central Taiwan, about twenty-seven kilometres from my hometown. This grassroots protest was unprecedented at the time. It was class-conscious, anti-colonial and self-organised without any leader. Many historians nowadays argue that it might have been the very first agrarian uprising in the recorded history of Taiwan. However, due to many reasons (too complicated to elaborate here), this incident didn't exist in any form of written record until 2001. In other words, it lived in the memories of those who participated in it, witnessed it or heard about it. I stumbled across this incident, including the song, when I was researching radical agrarian histories around my hometown. I was immediately drawn to the song, because there is no record of its melody. The lyrics survive but the tune does not. For some unknown reasons, the sounds of the song eluded the oral transmission.

There is a lot more to say about this project. But to make a long story short, except for the lyrics, there isn't any sort of protocol or methodology used in the workshops, regardless who and where. The only aim is to make and sound out a new melody collaboratively, in whichever way imaginable, no matter how messy the process gets. Each interpretation of what the song might sound like is so different from one to another. I am writing my long overdue PhD dissertation on this project.

Have you exhibited it?

Yes, in various configurations, for instance, as a live performance at The Lab, San Francisco; as a sound installation at the Sculpture Centre, New York; and a sound piece at the Documenta 14's radio program.

Jau-Lan Guo

I only met Jau-Lan Guo for a day or so before I interviewed her but it was quite an eventful day involving both communal meals and massages. She had invited me to Taiwan to perform and speak in 'Witness, Listener and the Involved on the Move' along with Hong-Kai Wang, Viv Corringham and Douglas Barrett. Jau-Lan is a curator and academic with a background in Western art history, currently part of the New Media Art MFA programme based in the Graduate Institute of Trans-disciplinary Arts at Taipei National University of Arts. She has curated in Taiwan and internationally, including exhibitions of sound art. I want to try to gain some kind of overview about what is happened in Taiwan, and Jau-Lan seems like a great place to start. I am interested in how her sound art curation developed and her primary concerns, as well as the relationship between Taiwanese and international sound arts practices. Jau-Lan has brought catalogues and posters, traces of her curatorial practice, for us to look at together during the interview. She is a generous subject with a wide-ranging and deep knowledge of contemporary art practices. I am particularly attracted to *Harsh Landscape: Sonic Cartography*, which she curated for the Hong Kong Arts Centre in 2016, and which I find elegantly minimal, highly relational and thought provoking. Through the interview we discuss various manifestations of her work, and I am delighted to be introduced to a number of artists who I was previously unaware of.

How did you first become interested in sound art?

Great. Whenever I talk in public about why I am interested in sound art, I tell the same story. In 2006 I curated a show, *Polyphonic Mosaic: Co6 Avant-Garde Documenta* at the National Taiwan Museum of Arts. I'd just got my PhD and I was invited to apply in collaboration with one of my friends who was doing noise music in a bar. There was an open call for the Co6 series, a new grant from the government to support very young local artists, to counter the fact that some of them felt that the Taipei Biennial was all about international art. This third version was an open call for curators. At the time, I didn't think of myself as a curator, I had no idea about curating, but we invited some noise artists, some young graduate students in fine arts and some artists who make use of sound to show their work. That's it. I wasn't happy with this exhibition because when the noise guys were invited to show in a white cube they started to make installations, and the younger generation from the academy were using sound as an element in interactive art. This made me think about how sound is treated as a newcomer or a 'foreign' element in visual art and thus loses its own distinctive identity.

So when the noise artists were invited into a gallery they changed their practice and did something different?

Yes. When they performed outside the white cube, they had a strong relationship with the audience, but in the gallery they just made an installation. This made me realise that sound practices were something to be discussed. I started to think about sound and space in the contexts of bars or the white cube, as well as the problem of white cube as an institution.

Yes, does it demand or maybe suggest a certain response?

Suggests—yeah. The noise artists just thought "I want to show" they didn't think, "OK so I can perform every day in the museum".

It's a problem across all time-based art forms, I think.

Exactly. It's all about timing because if you perform there is a specific time duration. I found thinking about this very inspiring, and wanted to see how different institutions and different artists had thought about occupying time in the white cube.

At that time, had there been a sound art show in Taipei or Taiwan? Had anybody exhibited sound art in a gallery before that exhibition?

I don't think so. But there is a second thing I'd like to mention. In 2001, the National Taiwan University of the Arts started a graduate programme in new media art, and the first sound artist was invited to teach there. The BIAS International Sound Art Exhibition and Sound Art Prize for the Digital Art Awards Taipei were also launched, so sound art began to gain some sort of recognition. However, because it was part of new media art it focused on works using electronic sound.

That is a real problem, isn't it? That's why you need a dedicated sound arts department! If you're in a visual art department you might only focus on the conceptual; if you're in a music department, you might only focus on the musical aspects of sound, and in the new media department on the technical aspects. Where it is situated is problematic? Who was that sound artist?

He is Wang Fu-Jui one of the first-generation noise artists in Taipei. Partly because of him, there are several government funded sound art festivals in Taipei, and sound art is becoming more and more popular.

But you were the first to bring it into the gallery?

I think that show might have been the first show related to sound but at that time we didn't call it sound art. Actually Wang Fu-Jui might have been the first to show their work in a gallery.

I feel that in many countries, the very first aspect of sound art is often noise performance. Do you have any thoughts about this?

As far as I know part of it maybe might be Japanese influence.

Interesting! So, after that show, did you do anything else with sound?

My background is art history, not sound, but after *Polyphonic Mosaic: Co6 Avant-Garde Documenta*, I started to curate, but I didn't focus on sound art. In 2011, I went to New York for a residential programme in ISCP and met Samson Young. He had composed a score for chamber ensemble that would make the violinists very, very busy and tired. I asked him the questions that had come out of my first curatorial practice: "Why, when some artists are invited to show in white cubes, do they always make installations?"; "Is it possible to deal with sound issues in the white cube?" and "Is sound art international or global—do you think Hong Kong sound art has its own local issues?". These discussions with Samson were very important to me. The sound artists in Taiwan were not interested in these questions, but he understood why I was asking them. In 2012, Samson asked me to write an article for his new project about sound on the Hong Kong border. I think he was responding to my question about sound art relating to the local issues (which I did not believe it could). Samson's work wasn't just using sound as a medium but also as a method and was very definitely located in Hong Kong. After that, in 2014, I curated Samson's solo show in Taipei. I picked three of his works and put them into a conversation, and finally got the opportunity to discuss how sound is related to contemporary and visual art. The exhibition also dealt with the local situation in Hong Kong. So finally, I could deal with the everything that I had been thinking about. For me this was not only conceptual, it also pleased the ear. In my first show in 2006, I think I did sacrifice the sound.

I know only a little of sound art in Hong Kong, China and Taiwan so far but I think I can detect some commonalities of approach. What do you think?

I'm thinking that anything ignored in modernism will be focused on in contemporary art. Bonami was the curator of the 2006 Venice Biennale, and he invited six or seven independent curators to curate parts of it. Hou Hanru curated *Z.O.U Zone of Urgency* and that show was very noisy—it contained a lot of art work from Asia—Japan, Korea and China—but it wasn't about sound art, I'm talking about the sonic quality or sonic atmosphere of the exhibition which tried to give an impression of Asian society. Both Asia and sound have been ignored by modernism. I think that Asian, Taiwanese or Hong Kong contemporary artists somehow seek to make local issues transferable to international platform.

Are there artists working in sound in Taiwan whose work you feel is really interesting and who aren't maybe so well known outside Taiwan?

There is Dawang Huang—he is a kind of DIY artist. He performs other people's songs in his own way. He studied in Japan and during that time spent a lot of time listening to noise and going to noise performances. In *Harsh Landscape: Sonic Cartography*, I'm showing his sketchbook of that time in Japan. He is very hard to put in any category, he makes songs, improvisations, and does a kind of karaoke performance. It's very weird but he is the guy that I would say is the most interesting at the moment.

So maybe that's a good time to talk about your 2016 exhibition Harsh Landscape: Sonic Cartography?

I was invited to curate this at Hong Kong Art Centre. I decided to focus on sound, but, because there was very little budget, to show only work on paper. So, the poster is also the catalogue. There are three artists in the exhibition, all of whom grew up in Asia in the 1980s. The first is Ayoung Kim from Korea, do you know her? I first came across her work, *Zepheth, Whale Oil from the Hanging Gardens to You, Shell 3* at the Venice Biennale. When you entered the room, you heard good, maybe eight-channel speakers, singing songs very hard, not harmonically, but very harshly. During the oil crisis, the Koreans sent some officials to the Middle East, her father was sent by the government and in the work she is trying to follow her father's story. She collected archives including charts of the changing oil prices and newspaper pictures, and invited a computer programmer friend to make a score from these materials. When you entered her space, you saw this image and heard eight-channels of voices—it's very sonic—my ear was pleased! <laughter>. This picture in my exhibition shows how the score was translated. Then she invited a chorus to sing the song. I'm interested in the process of how she translates the picture into a score. It was made automatically by an algorithm, so the song is not harmonious and it sounds very weird. I like the fact that history and the archive become audible. So I showed this art work, but because of the space available I only showed the video of the chorus, and had this poster to remind the audience that the score was made in this way.

There has been a lot of co-operation in contemporary art between Taiwan and Korea—I think the Taiwanese Government is trying to copy the way that the Korean Government supports contemporary art.

So another artist in your show was Dawang Huang?

I showed one of the many sketchbooks of when he was in Japan and went to a noise performance almost every day, and a video of his live show. I wanted to show how, at that time, he was planning to become a DIY punk.

So it's like him gathering his influences and working out where he was going?

I don't think people call him a 'sound artist', but I think we should find a new way to define sound art. Chao-Ming Teng's work is also a kind of notation based on his research into 'Rainy Night Flower', a famous song composed during the Japanese colonial period and banned during Chiang Kai-shek's regime. During Taiwanese democratisation, this song became a symbol of independence. Chao-Ming Teng researched the history of the song, wrote down many, many sentences about it, made them into a square and then cut out all the words except the names—so you only see hundreds of names.

The names of people?

Yeah. Many politicians, including the Taiwanese president, liked to sing this song in public. Each of these three artists grew up in the 1980s but they are all trying to react to the history of their surroundings.

That sounds like an interesting show and also very sonic but maybe not pleasing to the ears!

This show is not very pleasing to the ears!

Was this the last gallery show that you curated?

No—in the same year, I was one of three invited to curate a show from the collection of the Taipei Fine Art Museum—the other two were an architect and an artist. It wasn't about sound but… I do think it was a great show! <laughs> Each of us was invited to curate our own show from the museum collection. I didn't show any art work from the collection but I tried to deal with the collection as a system. I invited a video artist to film the storage of the collection. I also invited Dawang Huang to collaborate with me. He is a hoarder and I went into his spare room and 'dug', pile by pile, and documented each pile giving each of them a title, for example, 'The CD on the left side of the bed', or 'The box on the left side of the bed', implying to the audience that all the organisation was according to the typology of the space of his room. So, I'm working as kind of an explorer or archaeologist.

A domestic archaeologist!

Exactly! I divided the whole space into forty-eight grids, and then the space was measured out so that the audience had a comfortable space to walk around the piles. I tried to ask them to think about the relationship between the public collection and the personal collection. There was also a room named 'Brain' where I showed two artists' works. One artist collects garbage at the seaside, and the objects were shown in a lovely case to try and show how the museological exhibition can offer a way for an object to be transformed, in fact the museum or collection is where the object is transformed. The second work in this Brain space was a video. In 2012 there was a big scandal at the Taipei Fine Art Museum, because there were so many popular, commercial shows of French Impressionists like Monet in Taipei. Some artists and art critics protested in front of the museum during the exhibition, so this art work becomes a history of the museum, but will it be collected by the museum? I think the collection is about history.

And how you make the history?

Yes. There was one more artist who—oh, this is kind of sound art maybe —performed like a radio DJ. He interviewed the oldest art historian in the Fine Art Museum, and asked her about the history of her work in the collections department, then he re-edited the interview into a script and asked voice performers to read it out every day into the white space.

It sounds like a great exhibition. Thank you.

It was called *Amnesia and Malevich's Pharmacy*. During the Russian Revolution a lot of antique paintings were damaged and some people said "We need to protect the antiques of Russia", and Malevich said "Don't worry about the antiques, if the antique paintings are burned into powder, we can put the powder inside a bottle, then we will have a pharmacy of that history". I think he meant that what we need is the idea, so if we don't have a Rubens artwork anymore, we will imagine what a Rubens artwork might have been like.

I think sound works like that.

Really?

Because I feel that if you listen to a recording of something, what you imagine will never be as concrete as a visual image, so sound itself is like the pharmacy or maybe many sounds are like a pharmacy—each sound is like Malevich's powder. Every person might imagine it differently, when they hear it, maybe?

I like that idea.

So we are talking about a materiality of sound?

We're talking about the reception.

Reception, the reception of sound.

If I put that cup on that table and you then listen to a recording of it, you wouldn't know that I'd put that particular cup on that particular table. If sixty people listened to that recording, each one would imagine that a different thing had happened. So in a way, it's like the powder of the Rubens painting which everyone imagines it in a different way. <laughs> Anyway—what do you think are the limits or the limitations of sound art?

Yeah, this is a very crucial question, and I need to think about it. I would rather answer your question tomorrow!

That's fair enough. I haven't thought about that question that much, but, for a long time in the UK, sound art has been called "an emergent area of practice", and now I wonder if it has emerged—and therefore if it is fixed or still changing and developing? I'm also interested in how it's developed slightly differently in different cultures or countries. Although this is of course an over-generalisation, I would suggest that certain concerns or tendencies have developed—for example, German sound art with materials; Scandinavian sound art with remoteness and 'nature'; Canadian sound art has maybe a socio-geographical bias and in Japan, again, there's a concern with material.

There is Mono-ha in Japanese visual art, an objective school. In fact, I think the word 'object' means 'material'.

In some countries, maybe those with a history of colonialism, there is a re-thinking of the past, of the boundaries and the histories—of what was banned, for example the songs.

I think there is a kind of the tension between local contemporary art circles and how they try to relate to the global. There was an exhibition with an exotic flavour in Taiwan last year focusing on the past and the local. It was called 'Kaupue' in English, which means to build up a relationship or a kind of a brotherhood between different people. I don't think this show was for international market. But the first three shows (1997–99) in the Taiwanese pavilion in the Venice Biennale were very exotic... I think they were thinking about how to show Taiwan-ness and this show was the same.

And was this a very successful show?

Yeah, I think so, and the curator has been successful, but to show this kind of exoticism is a problem.

Maybe it's something that has to happen! Has traditional or classical Taiwanese art been pulled apart and re-formed and pulled apart and re-formed in the same way that the European classical tradition has?

No. I do think we have a kind of tension between what we can call a regional vision and a global vision at the moment. I don't think we do have a modern avant-garde, like abstract painting, in Taiwan, and that's the problem. There is a generation who paint abstract painting, like American abstract expressionism, but I don't think that they are fighting with Western tradition. Also, because of the relationship between Taiwan and America, abstract painting was welcomed by the government. We even had an American art and culture centre, the Taipei American Culture Centre, which was the only place where young artists could show their work. Most of the artists of the 1980s were trained in New York.

You did all your training in Taiwan, didn't you? Is that unusual? Do people often leave to study in America or Europe?

I think yes.

In Taiwan, is it possible to actually make a living as an artist without teaching?

It's difficult. I think most artists need to get another job to survive. I would like to add something to what we were discussing before—normally, if an artist had got their BA locally and their MA internationally that would be better. There are a lot of young, emerging artists who have done this. But in 1998, there was the Taipei Biennial and the Taipei Contemporary Art Awards, and the Taipei Fine Art Museum started to put one young artist in the Taiwanese Pavilion at the Venice Bienniale every year—that's the way that Taiwan supports young artists.

So the government or the Ministry of Culture is proactive?

Yes, in Taiwan and Korea. It's not the same in China, because China has a different art market; but the art market here is very bad and is not so friendly to contemporary art, so it has been about 80% supported by government. This offers an alternative career path to the local BA and the international MA route.

Jennifer Walshe

I have been trying to remember when it was that I came across Jennifer Walshe's work. An article in *The Wire* magazine from a while back could be a contender, but equally persuasive candidates might be made of a promotional review coming into my inbox as a Boomkat circular, a friend telling me about a premiere at the Huddersfield Contemporary Music Festival, or a retweet of one of Walshe's posts appearing on my own timeline. Scrolling up and down the many pages of works listed on her Wikipedia page, and then searching the web for details of her live shows, suggests my first encounter was at 'Colour Out of Space' in my home town of Brighton, nearly a decade ago. A friend confirms that I was at the festival but I have no recollection of Walshe's performance. Given the impact on me of her live shows that I have been to, I must have been watching another act on a different stage at the time.

During the year that we have been researching and writing this book, I was definitely in the audience for two more of her performances, both referred to in our conversation: the complex opera extravaganza *Time Time Time*, commissioned by the Serpentine Gallery in collaboration with London Contemporary Music Festival, and a concert in a field at Wysing Arts Centre cramped in a structure that memory makes resemble Baba Yaga's Hut. These performances embodied (or embrained) the oxymoron 'serious play' which—however prone that terminology may be to slide into the idioms of start-up speak—encapsulates something powerful in Walshe's energy to combine meticulous research, conceptual alertness and virtuosic delivery, with a gregarious and lively attention to every part of culture.

One of the first questions which I have concerns the breadth of your work: compositions, text scores, graphic scores, performance-based practice, film, music theatre, works that exist entirely in the digital domain. Is this range something that has been more easily understood in the world of music or in the world of contemporary fine art?

Within the music world there is no clear model: if you make a project that is digital, where does *that* exist? Or if you make a film how does that exist? The artists who I was influenced by when I was young, and then later the people who became inspiring to me as I was developing, were all people who worked in this way, with this range. An example would be Tony Conrad—who was a very close friend of mine, a very close collaborator—he would do stuff in the art world and then do stuff in the music world. What he cared about first and foremost was the idea and executing the idea. The idea was something that bit him like a bug, that made him want to explore. So that has always been my model.

I should also say that I come from a family who—if I were to say that they are artists, it makes things sound terribly middle class and that's not really an accurate description. They were just always doing their own little weird projects, and that created an environment where it seemed totally normal that somebody would say, "Oh, I'm saving all these newspapers for x", or "Look, I found this in a charity shop". The Catholic school-educated part of me would say, "Well, if you are going to do it, you better do it good. Because you can't just make a film and toss it off and think you can get away with it because you're a composer". If you are going to make a film, you want your film school friends to think it's good, and you want to ask them for advice and try and learn. The only thing about it is that you're always on your toes, you're always learning new skills, but in the long run I enjoy it; even though, within the music world, there is the idea that you should not work way beyond those historically-established bounds.

Within the conservatoires there is such an emphasis on a very specific craft, on a very particular approach to composing, that itself has a very defined way of being written down. Especially in the UK there is a proscribed pathway: you're going to go into the Royal Academy or the Royal College and then hopefully get funnelled into a BBC commission; there's no room there for the kid who says, "Well, I want to make a film", or "I wrote a book this term".

If you go to art school, you're fine since the teachers will just go, "Okay, grand. How are you going to go about doing that?" Even if you've decided that you're focusing on book art and are spending your time washing stones, the teachers might ask, "Can you actually make a connection?" but you could probably just take photographs of the stones you washed and then make them into the book: there's always a way around in art education.

Do you think that your training as a composer, your training as a musician, offers you a kind of passport that you can show at a barrier in order to be waved through?

I don't know if there's a passport. I would say that there's a rigour which comes from the conservatoire tradition because from a young age you are pretty disciplined, you're in a room practising, you have to be self-motivated. When I come to doing projects in other disciplines, there is a part of me that is motivated to try and do as well as I can, to learn as much about it as I can, to read that history. Certainly, I was very lucky with the teachers I had when I was younger, especially with Amnon Wollman, where the expectation was that I would be well-read, that I would be interested in film, in visual art. Wollman was the person who introduced me to the idea that you could do feminist musicology, that you could apply Queer Studies to music, should always be stretching yourself. If you were a little Irish kid from a Catholic school who has imposter syndrome, you are just going to read everything you can get your hands on, see everything you can possibly see.

Some of my students will say, "I just want to get into the art world", and I will reply, "Well, that's really good but it is also like having a whole lot of dollars and expecting a shop in Europe to take them!" The art and music worlds do have different currencies, have different ways to value things. I say to my students in the conservatoire, you can have some of the best drawings that anybody has ever done, but if you drew them as a composer, the art world just won't care, because they're not interested in the simple fact that they are great drawings.

Can sound art then function to convert from one currency to the other or—maybe better—to be a bridge between the fine art world and the classical compositional world?

It's a really tricky one to define what sound art is. I feel like there's a whole realm of commissioning and structuring that is cordoned off from sound artists. There's so much money funnelled into the young composers, since they are carrying on a 'grand tradition', but nowhere near the same amount is channelled towards sound arts students—they don't get those goodies or such nice treatment. I went on a residency to Schloss Solitude in 2003 and Max Neuhaus was the juror. It was very interesting being around Max, since he is regarded as one of the early sound artists and yet his background was being a percussionist, he played feedback performances in John Cage's work. I realised that Max was a constellation of many different elements, such as that percussion background and the feedback performance, such as living in New York in the sixties, such as his ability to be in Times Square at four o'clock in the morning and bribe the guy from a phone company, "Can you just hook me up to the power under this grill for my installation? I'll give you two hundred bucks".

Sound art is still a contested area. Its students tend to be much better read and much more aware of philosophy, of contemporary and critical thinking, than a lot of composers; but sometimes, not always, there can be the issue of students judging their output primarily in terms of its political, its philosophical validity. When I mentor at art schools or even down at London College of Communication, where you work, I keep reminding the students that this sound is really amazing, keep telling them not to forget how incredible that sound is. But it's always the same with students: composition students have their own trends and their own approved aesthetics.

One of your projects that I'd like to explore fits—in a certain way—with what we've been discussing. I'm going to mispronounce it, but it—

<interjecting>: You mean Aisteach?

Yes, sorry. It feels as if, in its miraculation of a previously marginalised Irish avant garde, Aisteach resonates with some of the earlier themes of our conversation—there are aspects of Joseph Beuys, for one thing, then the oscillation between fine art and contemporary music, and there is the range of components—the book, CD, live performances, its online life, and the nebula of reviews and other elements that have attached to it. It has a lightness, but at the same time, looked at from the outside, it feels very serious.

That project, it's not a joke. It's not just "Ha, ha, you thought it was true!" It is playful but at the same time a very serious attempt at trying to imagine a parallel history, a history where colonisation didn't happen, where the country wasn't as poor, where the Catholic Church didn't have as much power. It didn't make sense for me to imagine it on my own, it had to be a collaborative union. It is full of gags, even in the most obscure corners of *Aisteach*, there are weird jokes that only me, the sound engineer and one musician know about. Simon O'Connor, the graphic designer for the project, had all sorts of wacky fun when he made the website, because he was the Director of the Little Museum of Dublin at the time and had access to all this ephemera, and he went crazy with that. At the same time, *Aisteach* is very serious because as a project it concerns itself with legacies of colonisation and colonialism, with experiences of growing up and coming to terms with who you are when there was still the idea of a "correct" national identity, one that was developed in opposition to another identity that was itself historically imposed on the country. There are layers and layers to negotiate and attempt to understand what, in this case, is Irish identity.

With this being a communal thought experiment in the way that the disclaimer on the website has it, do you know of any cases where people were taken in?

Yes, of course, there were many times when people looked at it and thought it was all true. I received emails telling me to "Keep up the good work" and offering to volunteer to help with data entry for the archive. I would write back and say "That would be completely amazing. Do you want to read the disclaimer and then get back to me" and they would read that 'thought experiment' disclaimer you mentioned in your question but always reply with a "Yeah, I'm happy". It's not about "Ha, ha, you were fools", I don't want anybody to feel excluded or laughed at. Even people who know it's all fake talk about it as if it is all real.

Yes, there were *Guinness Dadaists.*

There has to have been, even if it were just in their heads.

I wonder if I can push you a bit further on this question, about the elaboration of fictions. When I saw you perform at Wysing last summer, it was an astonishing afternoon. The two parts to your performance that I've thought about a lot afterwards were the Gwyneth Paltrow piece and the James Brown / Britney Spears work. Both gave off a heady affective quality in that relatively small and crowded space. Perhaps I was late and missed something at the start but I went back to my tent utterly convinced that you had learned your performances from the instructions of an AI. I did feel a bit disappointed when, as I gather it, the AI's contribution is slightly different. I want to talk about Ultrachunk *later, but am I right in thinking that with the Britney Spears / James Brown work the process of learning is more human than a machine?*

You are completely correct. The way that I think about AI and the projects that I'm doing in the AI space—a phrase that makes me sound like *that* Silicon Valley start-up guy—is that, on the one hand, I do projects working with AI that are completely legitimate, solid and expensive and require collaboration either with those who have already made the software, or with others who can code it from scratch; and, on the other hand, I do projects which are speculative, which are a form of thinking through AI, which are, in essence, science fiction

The project *Ultrachunk* that I worked on with artist and technologist Memo Akten—that was real AI. I was nose to the grindstone on it, improvising into the webcam on my laptop for over a year. Those videos were then all tidied up by my assistant Ragnar Árni Olafsson who edited out things like footage of me leaning in to switch the camera off. Ragnar also synced the sound from the Zoom recorder (that I used when I was travelling) to the moving image material, massaged the resulting videos into the specific format that Memo required. Memo then coded a conglomeration of six different neural networks, all working in tandem. These networks listen to me as I perform, and they generate, frame by frame, sample by sample, a video version of me singing. It's incredibly complex. One network, for example, has the sole responsibility of ensuring that the eyes as the focal points of my face are in the same part of the screen from frame to frame so that my face doesn't jerk around. Memo designs and codes the overall network, I provide the dataset, the network is trained in the Cloud. We were very lucky to have funding from Somerset House Studios and the Case Foundation.

The reason I'm going into this level of detail is to identify the huge amount of work at every single stage, not just the human labour but also the carbon footprint involved in all that training. I just read *Uncanny Valley*, Anna Wiener's great memoir of her time in Silicon Valley, and at the very beginning she says, we talk about the Cloud but the Cloud is actually a server in Cork or Bavaria, it is something on the surface of the earth, a server farm that is operated by people. Out of all of this comes

Ultrachunk, a system that can listen to me and generate its response live, a response that is not processed, is not sampled—video of about 20 frames per second, audio at 44,000 samples a second. Every step of the way involves incredible amounts of work, massive amounts of data, and immense amounts of labour.

Going back to your question, I also want to make projects about AI where I don't feel the need to make them real in the way *Ultrachunk* is real. Of course, it would be lovely if I could train everything myself, but I've done so much research into machine learning over the last few years—watching talks, reading DeepMind papers, so many different books and articles—that I have a decent idea of what it would sound like, of the sounds the James Brown slash Britney AI would make. In the piece *Is It Cool To Try Hard Now* there are parts where I'm creating sounds I learned to make by listening to the examples from the 2016 DeepMind paper about WaveNet, where I imitate the imagined outputs with my own voice.

With the Gwyneth Paltrow part of the work that you heard in Wysing, I did a lot of research, such as devouring that amazing *New York Times* profile of her by Taffy Brodesser-Akner, and such as scraping the newsletters of Paltrow's lifestyle brand Goop and dumping them in text files. But it would be wasteful in terms of human labour and carbon cost to train a neural network when I already have a 90% accurate idea of the output. Instead of real AI, I call this part of my work speculative AI. It's to try and bring the audience's attention to what is happening.

It's really interesting that you mention the human labour involved in Ultrachunk*. One take on Garry Kasparov's defeat by Deep Blue was that it was not so much human vs. machine, rather a collective enterprise of many human beings against one solitary egotist. There are a lot of references in the work that you do, whether these are speculative invented ones which constitute a communal fiction, or whether they attach to that amazing Drew Daniel comment in the liner notes for your LP* ALL THE MANY PEOPLS *where he says that you have "found contemporary culture's search history". Who do you expect to get these references? Even Dwarfs Started Small and KRS-ONE? Really?*

I don't expect everybody to get all the references in the lyrics. It's totally fine with me that people don't get them. I have no problem with that. I put the references in because that's the way I move through the world, picking stuff up, like the huge ball of chewing gum rolling down the street in *Katamari Damacy*. It's the way the world operates, full of a plethora of different materials every which way you turn. Surf any website for three minutes, and you're seeing a surfeit of information.

I'm a Professor in Stuttgart at the State University of Music and Performing Arts, and in October 2019, Rebecca Coleman from Goldsmiths came to give a talk about different types of temporalities for our lecture series called The Short Now. She was talking about the Welsh Marxist theorist, Raymond Williams and his idea of structures of feeling. I hadn't known Williams's work prior to this, and I was very excited, because it was one of those times when someone describes perfectly something that you've always known but haven't had the right words for. Williams's "structures of feeling" are what gives our moment a particular feeling, a particular texture; the ways of thinking, the art and fashion that we can't quite articulate, yet will come to define the time we live in. Like a contemporary colour palette that feels very fresh, that screams now, like a certain shade of green, a really pale mint, that captures a period of time. I am talking about colour here because it struck me recently... for my new cassette—another AI project—*A Late Anthology of Early Music*, the inlay card is being printed using a risograph by Page Masters down in Bermondsey. I went to visit and they were showing me their colour swatches – their super-fresh colour swatches, with all these pastels and neons, I suppose the feeling I got looking at those colour swatches—

<interrupting>: *Like* Miami Vice *in the '80s?*

Well, yes, like the echo of that today, but knowing it's an echo and a comment and something contemporary. So, when there are references, it's a way of me letting in those structures of feeling, or maybe trying to think them through by playing with all these references. I'm very open about it, that it's a massive quilt. I always love it when you see Donna Haraway give a talk because she's one of the contemporary philosophers who actually references lots of people. "This is from Bruno Latour and this is from someone else". You get the sense from Donna Haraway's talks that philosophy is a beautiful community...

Really it is just me trying to play with what it's like to move through the world. I understand that most people won't get everything, but I should say that there are definitely people out there who get every single tiny reference. Wobbly aka Jon Leidecker is an extremely close listener. And I was so happy that Drew Daniel from Matmos did the liner notes for ALL THE MANY PEOPLS because when I first met him, he came to a performance and then grilled me in the bar, forensically, about the piece.

Another track on the ALL THE MANY PEOPLS *album is the one where you have this iterative recombination of objects and placements, so it goes...*

That's *Watt* by Samuel Beckett! I just use his structure but I substitute all the furniture words: instead of, you know, wardrobe and chair and bed, in my version it is rainbow, celebrity dog, unicorn, XBOX. My position is that Beckett invented process composition.

Some of the references in your work are very unexpected, though, if I may say. I know you created a work that has a loose connection to Dungeons and Dragons. Is it called the Park Service?

Ah, no, what you are referring to is called *The Legend of the Fornar Resistance*. That project came out of a bigger work, *Grúpat*, which had nine different alter egos, and which was when I first started working with imaginary narratives. One of the alter egos was Dermot Fitzpatrick, aka the Park Service, whose backstory had him and his brothers growing up in Glenasmole Valley just south of Dublin.

When I was young in Dublin, we only had aerials for TV reception. If the weather was very good, we had a shot of getting BBC, but if you lived down in Cork, you had no chance. The conceit for the alter ego has Dermot growing up in a valley with terrible television reception, forced with his brothers to invent an extremely elaborate D&D-style game to keep themselves occupied. I loved working on it because I played a bit of D&D and some Middle Earth role playing systems—or MERP—when I was a teenager. There's a famous Irish myth called the Bruidhean Da Dearga which is set in Glensamole where the brothers are supposed to live, and which has an unusual structure. The first part of the myth is devoted to a big preamble about how there is going to be a fight; the middle 80% of the story is taken up by a guy looking in the windows of Da Dearga's Hostel describing the terrible monsters and warriors he sees; the final, very short, portion is dedicated to the fight itself. I thought the structure resembled how D&D worked: you have the *Dungeon Master's Guide*, the *Monster Manual*—

The Fiend Folio *as well!*

—and I worked with my sister Caroline, who is an artist, to create the brilliant drawings, following that particular kid-down-the-back-of-the-class, ballpoint-pen-on-lined-paper aesthetic. I did a lot of research on depictions of Ireland in comic books and in Sci-Fi. The work has been exhibited several times, always in a little shed with woodchip, a musty smell, and with the visitors armed with a regular torch and a UV torch. When they shine the UV torch they can see the secret information, the different portals and how you travel between different zones. It's just like a weird clubhouse. At one exhibition, I invited the comic book shop owners from Dublin who I'd interviewed during the project research; one of them came in and asked the invigilator, "Who did that?" The rule was that if an invigilator was asked a direct question they had to respond truthfully and so they pointed to me. The comic bookshop owner said, "There's no *way* a woman would do that". He didn't mean it a negative way either. My sister Caro and I were so happy, "We nailed it!"

I wanted to move on from that work to asking more generally about the role of science fiction / SF in your work.

I love Sci-Fi, and have done so for a long time. As I am massively into science, so science fiction is a way to like talk about science and art without it either being didactic or an exercise in 'outreach'. The importance of Sci-Fi is not just in terms of reading it, but in terms of offering technical models for how to talk about some of these things that excite me. When I'm giving talks, I constantly quote William Gibson from the great interview he gave in the *Atlantic* where he says, "Whenever I read a contemporary literary novel that describes the world we're living in, I wait for the science fiction tools to come out. Because they have to—the material demands it. Global warming demands it, and the global AIDS epidemic and 9/11 and everything else—all these things that didn't exist thirty years ago require that toolkit to handle. You need science fiction oven mitts to handle the hot casserole that is 2010".

Gibson's *Pattern Recognition* very much influenced me. I've given it to so many people as gifts, especially female, younger, students, because it was one of the first books that I read that had a female character—Cayce Pollard—that felt utterly contemporary who I could relate to. Quite a few women artists, writers and composers of my age have all had a similar experience with that book. *Pattern Recognition* is not set in some Sci-Fi future, it is occurring in what is basically now; Gibson was already working on it when 9/11 happened and then he tore up the 150 pages he had and started again. The world seems so bizarre and strange today—and part of the reason for that is technology—and science fiction writers have long been developing techniques to talk about this.

Aisteach and *Grúpat* are speculative projects and owe a huge amount to Edgar Allan Poe, to Ursula K. Le Guin, to *Sans Soleil* and Borges. With speculative AI, my way forward is to treat it as a form of science fiction. Instead of having to spend hours and hours of human time and training time to make something of which I already have a rough idea, I would rather spend that time thinking about it as if I were writing a science fiction story.

I am conscious of the clock ticking and there is an area I really want to discuss, especially in the light of seeing your work Time Time Time, *and that is performance and your performing voice.*

If I'm in a taxi and the driver asks why I'm going to the airport, I just tell them I'm a musician, and I think this is a reaction to the idea of the performer being split off into a separate category, which is something that comes from how composition programmes are structured at third level. By contrast, if you went to rock school, it wouldn't be separated, everybody would be writing and playing, helping each other out by performing on their tracks.

I was dead lucky that I played the trumpet as a kid, in the Irish Youth Orchestra. Because you don't play all the time, you are in a position to watch things, to listen and learn, to follow the score and understand how the sounds are made. Because I was the only girl in the brass section, that could be difficult at times. You became very aware of the fact that you were not a neutral human body in that sort of context. I enjoyed it, I got through it, but when I switched to composition, I sort of put the trumpet under my bed, which is quite weird, because it had been such a huge part of my life for so long, and now it's under the bed. And then I had this amazing teacher, Amnon Wollman, who's still a very dear friend of mine, and in the very first lesson he said, "Every week, I'm going to tell you a composer and I want you to go to the library and listen to everything you can get your hands on". The first composer with Meredith Monk. Then there was Laurie Anderson, Diamanda Galás, Pauline Oliveros… it was the first time anybody had ever recommended that I listen to any female composers. When I listened to Meredith Monk's *Our Lady of Late*, something just clicked in my brain where I thought, "This is it. You do it, you do it yourself, you can make the whole thing yourself". I know I don't sound anything at all like Meredith Monk, but at that moment in the library, it was like a light had been turned on for me; and when I found out she also made films and did choreography that was even more inspiring.

The other significant moment was when I started to learn free improvisation and develop that part of things, it was phenomenal. I didn't ever use text when I was improvising because I was never around any singers who did; if I had questioned myself about it, I would probably say there was something of a taboo around text. When I worked with Tony Conrad, he said to me, "I don't understand why you aren't using text all the time when you're doing free improvisation. It doesn't make any sense". Gradually I started to use text and that opened the door, ending up in all of my pieces, because I'm really interested in language, in the sound of language from other people's mouths. I'm one of those people who writes things down in restaurants, I'm constantly making little recordings on my phone that I learn to reproduce, stopping the TV to replay a turn of phrase that I've heard.

Do you know Svetlana Alexievich?

I've never read her but I know who you're referring to—she creates massive oral history-based narratives, like one on the Chernobyl reactor disaster, right?

In the beginning of one of her books, *The Unwomanly Face of War*, Alexievich talks about texts, I'm paraphrasing it badly, but something amazing along the lines of "Texts, texts, all around me are texts and I need to get them down". That's how I feel about voices. I was always writing things down in notebooks, and one of the first machine-learning projects I wanted to do was to explore these deeply personal text archives that date back to my teens: a sentence here, a joke my friend told me there, a poem that I wrote, a quote from an article in *The Face* magazine. Now if I want a weird turn of phrase, I just open up the Google search bar and I just begin to type and I get ten batshit things that previous people have entered into the query bar and that's even before I get to YouTube or Reddit. So, now my digital eavesdropping is completely enabled by the internet: I can get turns of phrase that I would never make, that somebody else has made, sound files alongside text; and I never feel on top of it, a massive slippery pile that I'm trying to get my footing on, at times I'm completely overwhelmed and stressed out and panicked by it all but I'm just trying to make pieces out of the scraps.

I remember reading an interview with you, which was talking about the process through which you wrote This is Why People OD on Pills / And Jump From The Golden Gate Bridge. *During your conversation, you mentioned you were reading the Iain Borden's book about the city and skateboarding and I was interested to know whether you are constantly immersing yourself in the world of ideas?*

I am constantly reading and trying to learn, and some of it makes sense in terms of the work I do and some of it doesn't. Reading books, looking at movies, and since *Time Time Time*, I've become really obsessed with natural history museums. Here in London, while I was working on the piece, I was going to the Natural History Museum over and over and over again to see the same two dinosaurs—Sophie the Stegosaurus and the Iguanodon—or to visit the Hall of Gems. I have a restless imagination and just try and keep learning. When I'm looking at like projects like *Time Time Time*, being able to do all that research was like developing a weird form of documentary, but not didactic, as I was saying earlier, and not a nice REF project with some knowledge transfer. I just want to keep working like this. With *Time*, I felt like I was constantly learning things; working on that piece genuinely changed the structure of my brain.

I interviewed Paul Barrett, the head palaeontologist at the Natural History Museum, and asked him whether there was one thing about dinosaurs which he wished people understood, and he said that it was deep time, the vast scale of time. When you start thinking about that on a day-to-day basis, it starts to warp your brain a little bit, and then look around at this planet that we live on, this planet the dinosaurs lived on for so much longer than us, and you just really can't help but think "Jesus Christ, it's like we moved in last weekend, we just trashed the place". You know, we're like the most awful students ever who just moved into a beautiful apartment and wrecked it that night.

I know it sounds really cheesy or new age-y but the amount of time that we as humans have existed here on the earth is so insanely, infinitesimally brief. Why would we use that time to be hateful to one another, or to be hateful to the planet, instead of taking that same time to love each other and love the planet and love the universe, love it as hard as we can, seek to understand it and wonder at it. If that meteorite hadn't hit the planet, the dinosaurs would just still be here and we may never have happened. And that is wonder enough for me.

Khaled Kaddal

Much of Khaled's artistic output to date draws on ancient and recent Egyptian ideologies, philosophies and histories. I liked the unique mix of sound, performance, visual material and personal experience that he uses to create immersive performance pieces. I liked how, in turn, these performances have communicated something of his past physical and emotional experiences during times of intense political upheaval in Egypt. I am interested in his contemporary work that, again, seeks to provide experiences devoid of certainties, but located in a past and future time that may or may not be Egyptian. I first met Khaled when he came to London College of Communication to study for Masters in Sound Arts. Although the course attracts students from all over the world, Khaled had been the first from North Africa and proved to be an extremely thoughtful and talented student. I was interested to find out more about the events and influences that had led him to become a sound artist. We met and talked in Berlin where he was living while applying for residency in Europe. His current life has more precarity that many of the other people that I interview, which impacts on his ability to fully make the most of all the opportunities offered him. We chat for quite a few hours punctuated by lunch and our conversation meanders widely—our many diversions and deviations have, for this interview, been omitted.

What attracted you to working with sound?

It developed through my musical practices, as a guitarist and film composer. When I was ten or eleven my parents sent me and my sister to music lessons. My sister picked up the flute and was into Western classical music, and I learned the piano for a while, but I felt that they wanted me to be like my sister, so I resisted. Then, as a teenager, I picked up the guitar in the late '90s, inspired by the new wave of metal and rock in Egypt.

Electric guitar?

Yeah, it started with the classical guitar but then I got an electric one, and later performed in rock and metal tribute bands. I gradually got interested in studying music theory, and then joined a band that played Sufi music, I learned more about researching ethnic music, improvisation, composing and orchestration in that time.

Were you still playing electric guitar at this point?

Yes. The band was called Station and the line-up was an oriental ensemble consisting of Duf, Riq, Tar, Toura and Darbuka; an accordion, locally-customised to play quarter notes; a violin and a six-people percussion ensemble. We also had a three-year project with a Sufi-dervish dancer and Sufi singer from upper-Egypt. Then the revolution happened and we had a political clash about whether we should shift from our focus from Sufism to respond to the political change. I was active in the revolution, but I didn't want to mix my personal experience with this group's activity. So from that time, I stopped performing and I got involved in film-scoring, theatre and choreography.

You must have already been in a position where it was easy for you to move into that?

There were not so many people working on that in Egypt, especially for experimental film. In my city I was the main one composing for independent movies. I wanted to develop my technical skills and aesthetic skills and to diversify my practices.

Presumably it was quite a small arts scene, so you knew people.

Yes, exactly. In Alexandria there wasn't that much happening, there was a small active scene and limited opportunities to search, learn and practice, especially for anyone who was interested in Western avant-garde music.

Can you remember what got you into that?

I was inspired by monotonic music and at the same time learning harmony, melodic structure and improvisation from classical notation to free graphic scores. The process of deconstructing and abstracting canons seemed to be aligned with the political change and activism of general deconstruction during the revolution.

Were there any composers or artists in particular that you were interested in?

At that time I was specifically interested in minimalism.

Reich, Glass?

Exactly, although John Cage was the main introduction. Minimalism spoke to my engineering persona, I studied Computer Engineering originally, and minimalism allowed to make a sensorial connection with computation and design. Later, minimalism introduced me to sound art—I was, and still am, eager to taste and learn new aesthetics.

So what were the conditions for sound art at this time in Alexandria? How come you even thought you could do that? And how did you get the space to do that?

Sound art wasn't established in Alexandria. There were occasional initiatives for artistic experiments, that sometimes included sound as a medium, but never sound art as a discipline. I made two sound-related projects in Egypt: *Sawtyat*, where I installed wind chimes along the seafront, and *Trapped Sounds*, a performance related to trauma and the body, using my heartbeat and breathing sounds. I wasn't intentionally producing sound art, I think my interest in experimenting was intuitive. There were funding programs and institutions that encouraged artistic production. Bodies like the British Council and the Arab Fund for Arts and Culture (AFAC) supported my projects, and spaces like Townhouse Gallery, D-CAF Festival, Goethe Institute, Bibliotheca of Alexandria, and Atelier of Alexandria, welcomed and hosted my performances.

During the revolution there was so much sound and I was recording a lot. I had an archive of my participation in the demonstrations. So I was getting into sound art as art of listening, not as performance. My listening was really enhanced during the rioting, all the time I was aware of the inflections and the intensity of it. That's what I wanted to work on when I came to LCC to do the MA Sound Arts course.

Was there an awareness of sound as art in Egypt at that time?

It is relative. There were no academic studies and very rare curatorial initiatives in sound art. However, there were opportunities and showcases for interdisciplinary experimentation, like the 100 Live Electronic Music Festival, organised by a record label named 100Copies which hosted local and international experimental music performances. There was no focus, however, on sound art as a stand-alone discipline or on the aesthetics of listening, soundscapes or sound studies.

The fact that you were going out and recording suggests that you had some skill?

I learned my skills by practice, researching on the internet and being active in studios.

So were you following particular field recording artists or blogs?

I was following blogs. I had access to Anna Raimondo, she is a friend of a friend, so I was following her work in radio activism on the internet. I always liked watching and following videos, blogs and doing a bit of reading, even thought a lot of it was complicated for me to understand at that time.

So you switched from being interested in rock music to fusion and then to working with real-world sounds, field recording, and making solo work. Can you expand on that process at all?

It's all home-based study. I didn't have any social interaction with any community related to sound art. I used to download the work of Steve

Reich or Philip Glass and study and record it line by line. This is something that the revolution helped with because you got detached and alienated from society—it got too much to participate, so I had a lot of time in the studio working on my stuff, or studying.

Sometimes in Alexandria I used to organise listening sessions at dawn, and see if anyone wanted to join me at the seaside at sunrise to listen in silence. People did join—they didn't know about sound art, but joined as a kind of meditation sunrise thing. It was an opportunity to have a silent time in a loud city.

Who facilitated you making Sawtyat?

At that time, I was working for Gudran for Art and Development, a local organisation with three venues, it's not active anymore as they lost their funding. Through them I learned a lot about how to develop a project, how to write a proposal and to find out about art funds in the Middle East. I applied to the British Council's second round of a grant for young artists. Then *Trapped Sounds*, in which I developed the performance using my body as instrument, was funded by AFAC [Arab Fund for Arts and Culture] based in Beirut.

I'm disturbed, inspired and intrigued by the thought that all over the world people might be studying Philip Glass! Minimalism's got a lot to answer for and it all came from somewhere else in the first place! I'm interested in how people move from being a bedroom musician or sound artist, to actually getting out there.

Yes. Sometimes I think limitation has benefits. My generation are thirsty and want to see and make new things. I wanted to get into new activities and I thought that there was a lot of dryness in Egyptian culture, but when I grew up, I understood that it is very rich. For example, I stumbled across *Akhenaten*, the opera by Philip Glass—it's like a feedback loop— the ancient Egyptian minimalist aesthetic goes through Western composition and then feeds back to me as an Egyptian.

What do you mean by Minimalism in ancient Egyptian aesthetics?

There is very little research on the sonic culture of ancient Egypt, but in the visual arts there's a lot of repetition of motifs, it's not only linear but also inward—symbols within symbols within symbols—with very structured minimal design. Even the way that the statues stand is timeless, or time-still. There is a stillness in time in ancient Egypt that I see as a very minimalist aesthetic.

Does the history and culture of ancient Egypt feel like a heavy weight to carry or something that's difficult to break away from?

Now I would think of it as a light weight to be embraced, without the need to break away from it. It is part of me and my background. Its mystic philosophy is presented and explained through literature, murals, sculpture, architecture and visual aesthetics. The aural culture and practiced rituals in Egypt mirror fragments of its sonic culture. Unfortunately in Egypt, students are being taught a narrow perspective and Western scholars are more active in studying ancient Egyptian histories.

Is that because it's all been done by colonial scholars?

The academic discipline of Egyptology developed out of the work of nineteenth century British, French and German colonial scholars, but there was even research into Egypt's past in medieval and renaissance Europe and before that by Islamic scientists, and before that by the Romans and ancient Greeks. There are even epochs in ancient Egypt that undertook archaeological excavations to study their predecessors.

I noticed that, on your website, you describe yourself as Nubian first and Egyptian second.

I never wanted to identify myself as being from any national background, and being in London gave me the opportunity to transcend my identity and not be defined by it, and I really loved that. But the more active that I was, especially with installation-based work in gallery venues, I felt somehow forced into being identified as an 'Egyptian artist' rather than it just being me and my work. When the High Dam on the Nile was constructed in the 1960s, the Nubian communities were split and partially displaced, some in the North of Sudan and others in Egypt. My background is hybrid and inter-faith. My lineage from my father's side is Nubian, my grandmother is a Catholic Italian whose family emigrated to Alexandria in the nineteenth century. Both of my parents were born and grew up in Alexandria, but as part of different diaspora minorities. I present myself as Nubian-Egyptian, grown up in Alexandria, because the Mediterranean, Arab and African parts of me are all major influences to the development of my artistic language.

So you have just had a solo exhibition, To The Nostrils of Time *at the Overgaden Institut for Samtidskunst in Copenhagen. Can we talk about that exhibition in relation to what you've just been saying? Can you start off by describing it?*

The installation is revisiting a specific healing praise from Ancient-Egyptian literature. The praise says "Rise like Nefertem to the nostrils of Ra and come forth upon the horizon of each day". It wishes that you should be like a new born scent that rises from the morning bloom of the Lotus Flower to the nostrils of the noon-sun, then coming forth and setting with the horizon of the next day. The praise projects a cyclical understanding of time. Its poetic, symbolism and imaginative scenery inspired me to compose a multi-sensory space. The installation is in the form of a landscape or alternative physical reality, composed of different mediums, such as soil, golden film, mirror sculpture and multichannel recording of a hovering screaming falcon. The installation starts by walking in through a black hallway, followed by a sudden glowing golden-space. The space is dominated by a hovering sound of a falcon. Its scream isn't loud, but dramatically painful. It proposes stillness in the space.

When you explain that, you really realise how different it is culturally!

During the development of the work, I was keen to remind myself that it is an alternative reality. After the opening, and engaging with visitors and audiences in Copenhagen, I noticed how culturally different it was.

Does the blue lotus actually exist?

It does exist, but it is not very common in Egypt, due to the changes in the Nile ecosystem. It is known as the blue lotus, but it is actually a water lily that contains a psychoactive substance.

There's one in England called morning glory, it flowers every day, it's a climber and it's also psychoactive but not very strong. And it's a very purply-blue flower, a little bit like a lily, a little trumpet. Are you trying to create a space that puts or brings people to that state to suggest another reality?

I was trying to share a physical reality that proposes an alternative perception of time and the exhibition space. I was inspired by the poetry of the praise and intrigued by the thin differences and divisions between stillness, cyclical time and linear time.

Trapped is a little bit of a theme in your work, isn't it?

I think so—physical, psychological and spatial entrapments. It started explicitly in the *Trapped Sounds* and *Code.20* performances as psychological and political responses to the Egyptian revolution. Now, I am more interest in spiritual dimension of entrapment, in life and its physical end, and how the phenomenon of death shapes our constitution of spatial reality and time.

How do you expect and hope that people in Denmark will relate to that?

Hopefully sensorially. I don't want to explain all the layers, I think they are my engagement with the work in the studio phase. I want people to experience the body and the space. This was my first solo show so I am learning how explicit I can be and where to position myself. I am keen not to impose any expectations, other than me listening to people's experiences. For me, the work is completed by their relationships with what I present.

Are you concerned about the possibility that if your audience don't understand they'll just pop their head in and leave?

My primary concern is developing the conceptual and aesthetic elements of the work. I am more used to performance, where the relationship between audience and work is different, and the fact that it is live allows me to experience the work with audiences. In installation my relation to the work finishes at the opening of the exhibition. People attend and form their own personal attachments. In *To The Nostrils of Time* people stayed inside the exhibition room even if they couldn't make a rational meaning. I was happy with that, because the main difficulty in producing the work was to propose an alternative sense of time that is still. The space intimately absorbs you, and, even if you don't understand the historical narrative, you stay there. The falcon speaks to you, it tells you something and you try to listen and embrace it.

That's nice. I've definitely been in art installations where I haven't wanted to leave and I don't quite know why, just because it's a nice space to be in. Why did you move from performance to installation?

I became interested in experimenting with objects and their inversion, that is, space. Now, I look forward to including the element of space in my performances. It truly allows me to freely reflect my existence.

Are you working on performance pieces at the moment?

I have a few questions and ideas, but I don't want to rush. At the moment I am reflecting on how I'm dealing with works and production.

Does it tend to be that someone invites you and then you make a piece of work, or do you make a piece of work and then try and find a place to show it?

I am at the stage of discovering and I am building my experiences in production along the way. Currently, I work for commissions. I'm kind of in-between these at the moment. When I moved to London, I decided to be active, and go for any opportunity to perform. Now I want to work differently, so rather than being so opportunity-based, it will be more content and project-based. Also my work has somehow drifted from being a sound artist, but for me it comes from sound, and from a listening state, and the visuals comes as a second phase. So am I still a sound artist? I need to figure these things out and to take time to pause a bit and reflect and know how exactly I want to present my work.

How does that equate with the need to earn your living?

I intend to diversify my streams of earnings between tech and cultural commissions. I'm trying to figure out how I'm going to manage my financial life and my art in parallel. Do I really want to make a living out of art? Does it work, really? I can take the psychological intensity of it now but I don't know about later. Now I'm living day by day, project by project, and I'm jumping from one place to another, and between that the discipline of writing proposals, talking to people and socialising: it's a lot.

In terms of the gallery and the visual art economy, most people working with sound who've been relatively successful do have a visual element in their work... is that something that you're taking into account?

In terms of the medium and economic states? To be honest, I've been brainstorming how sound can have an economy anyway, and when I think about it, I don't think as an artist, but I keep thinking about what else could possibly generate finances for sound artists.

So would you call yourself a sound artist?

Sound is definitely a main medium in my work. The practice of listening has an intense impact on the development my work. I perform sound and looking to intertwining it with other mediums and formats. I learned a lot from the discipline of sound art, but I would like to explore its role in multi-sensory experiences. Often, I work with electronic means, but I don't see my practice fitting in the world of electronic music.

Or being part of the economy of electronic music?

The current music industry limits many aesthetical possibilities and ways of ethically engaging with states of listening. I wonder how all of that will evolve? I would like to be part of those future integrations. It's similar to the topic of being identified as Egyptian, because being identified as a sound artist brings more opportunities these days, especially a sound artist from Egypt! But it's destroying the meaning of it and it is definitely colonising. I'm not going to generalise, but many people from the Middle East plug their instrument into a guitar effect, play the same thing as before but with an electronic manipulation, and define themselves as sound artists. I don't want to be judgemental, but I believe that being a sound artist is totally different from that.

At various times, I've had to call myself a sound artist because I am actually trying to define a space, particularly in an academic environment, that isn't visual art or experimental music but one that focuses on sound as a means of communication or as a sensory experience. Obviously, this is very geographical, and time-dependent, but recently more people seem to have got an idea of what sound art could be—what would you say sound art is?

The thing I learned most from sound art is the art of listening not performing. If I make a performance using metal textures or abstract sounds without any rhythm or melody, something more sonically textured or sensorially based, then that comes from my listening ability. I'm introducing you to how I'm listening. So it's all based on listening. I would say there is nothing called 'sound performance', it's a happening, a collective listening session. So am I a sound artist? Everything is based on a state of listening, and from there I start to construct the work.

I think you are! I could say the same—am I a sound artist? My primary medium is sound, but actually, a lot of the stuff that I relate to is about people so am I actually a people artist? I think with those labels, you should change them as and when you see fit. I was thinking about noisy countries like Egypt where you might want to spend your time not listening. Is sound art even a thing that needs to develop there or is it more a listening education of some sort?

I think we have to emphasise sound art in terms of practice, but also in research. Definitely, there is a huge need to discover other ways of interconnecting beyond the excessive visual consumptions, in Egypt, but also everywhere. In the Middle East and African cultures there are still active sonic rituals that need to be revisited. In different Arabic languages there are beautiful terminologies for sound and listening, but globalisation removes local sonic encounters.

Forgotten cultures of listening is a topic that needs research.

It is. When my mother was a child there used to be a weekly family listening session where people would sit and listen to radios or to local musicians in the street. Umm Kulthum, who used to be the main female singer in Arabic classical music at the time of Abdul Nasser, used to perform every Thursday, and families would sit together to listen to her live radio broadcasts. It was used as a political propaganda, in terms of us all gathering together to listen to this 'national voice', but this was built on an already existing practice of shared listening. I would love to include Islamic culture in relation to sound within its aural culture, rituals and architecture. I am interested in the Quran recitation, from a sonic perspective. It is structurally unique in scales and accents. In Islamic science, it is called 'tajweed'. There are seven methodologies or schools for reciting the Quran. They do not only differ in melodic style, but also in sounding the letters and giving texture to the overall sound. The reciter follows a method and develops their own 'tariqa' (style). The tariqa could also be copied or mirrored by others. Of course the sounds and maqams are intertwined with the meanings and contexts of the text.

Non-Western sonic culture is explicitly present in nomadic life, for example the desert Bedouins in northern African countries, and how their everyday culture is at ease with silence.

Is it easier to go on the internet and access all the stuff about the minimalists than to engage with more local traditions?

I feel that the internet is reshaping things both positively and negatively. It feels as if the centralisation of the West and Europe are being de-constructed globally and this is allowing more non-Western initiatives to be present, which is creative and productive. The internet also allows us to share knowledge and influences across, over and under borders. I am not worried about holding on to traditions, they evolve and are shaped by contemporary events and technologies.

Over the last decade, it wasn't easy to be in Egypt politically or artistically. In 2014, I was arrested for making field recordings. But although there are many obstacles, there is also an influx of new and valuable art initiatives and particularly an interest in sound studies. However, the lack of cultural and academic institutional support means that there is little help for cultivating or sustaining alternative voices. In Egypt, most of the cultural scene is in the cities and is supported by the British Council and similar things.

For example, I got invited to a conference about soundscape at the American University of Cairo last year, but it was all musicology, I was the only one who was talking about sound. I met this guy who lives in Aswan, he's totally independent and has the best audio-visual music archive I have ever seen in Egypt. He has rare and beautiful recordings. This guy is doing it out of passion, to save the culture of his village in Upper Egypt. I feel that there needs to be more support for these more local initiatives.

Lawrence Abu Hamdan

Although all our interviews followed sustained periods of preliminary research, with Lawrence Abu Hamdan it felt as if those preparations took on a certain impetus as the publisher's deadline for our materials approached; this despite Hamdan's work having been known to me at least since his first solo show *The Freedom of Speech Itself*, at the Showroom in 2012. My exploration of Hamdan's practice was informed by exhibition visits to four different galleries—Nottingham Contemporary first and then the ICA, the Chisenhale and Tate Modern (the last three all London-based)—and was further bolstered by finally getting around to reading *Forensic Architecture* (in which Hamdan's work is analysed) and by engaging with some of his own writing and with other interviews. This trajectory reached a culmination of sorts when Hamdan conspired with his co-nominees Tai Shani, Helen Cammock and Oscar Murillo, to jointly accept the Turner Prize, an act of collective agency that I took as a signal flourishing of generosity and hope in a grim period of contemporary British history. Others interpreted the situation differently, something that was briefly addressed at the start of our exchange.

That our Skype connection traversed the furthest geographical expanse—at 6,500 miles nearly twice as far as my next most remote conversation—yet still came across as lucid and unequivocal seemed in some measure a reflection of Hamdan's own practice. For his work might be thought to contract, through listening, what would otherwise be kept at a distance (hidden behind official secrets, separated by political barriers to solidarity, abstracted by 'expertise') to the proximate and the intimate.

Is it too late to still say congratulations for your collective response to the Turner Prize?

I'm happy to hear that, it's just that the press were so ridiculously negative. Because the Turner Prize is such a large media event, as soon as you interact on that level, it gives you a weird window into the ways in which people maintain a commitment to forms of power that I think are actually harming the world.

…forms of power that, in a sense, are one of the many dimensions of the

world that you explore through your work.

Yes, forms of power that *all* of us nominees explore.

As someone who has followed your work from the outside, I get the impression that the projects that you commit yourself to are ones that unfold over long periods of time. The projects involve quite extensive prior research but also establishing relationships of trust—a lot seems to have to happen before we get to the gallery or the museum.

On some level, there is a consistency across ten years of work where more or less the same question is being asked, but being asked in different circumstances. I think you'll find a similar situation with many artists, actually: they are asking one or two questions, demanding the answers through different media and forms but with a consistency of inquiry that is stretched over time. One project bleeds into another, certainly, and that helps a lot with protracted periods of research or development in which things can start to evolve simultaneously. Sometimes, a project exists in different forms before it meets the museum or gallery, and those later spaces become where another form of reflection can happen, or where a mediation is possible outside of the confines of specific contexts in which the initial research might have emerged—such as a human rights report or an asylum tribunal.

It's still what happens in museum and gallery space that I'm most committed to because I'm more interested in trying to mediate and negotiate a politics of listening that I can ideologically manifest—that is, not one that already exists and that I am fitting into. And though, of course, there are compromises—indeed deep compromises—within the space of the museum, it is still a place which I have found to be able to develop languages to reflect on practices and to develop a kind of sensorial politics of experience with which things are both felt and understood at the same time.

Dare I ask you what is the question which has animated the last 10 years of your work? Is it that question about the politics of listening?

More or less. The question becomes more clear to me and then more unclear; if I could answer it then I'd probably retire, so I am not going to try. What I would say, however, is that the issue of sonic bleed is important: thinking about sound not only as a medium but as a kind of conceptual tool that allows us to blur thresholds. The case against Ben Deri, the member of the Israeli Border Police who shot and killed two Palestinian teenagers, is a very interesting example of a series of thresholds that get continually blurred. The initial request was to isolate things, to establish which round was a rubber bullet and which was a live bullet, to divide the boundaries between legitimate and illegitimate forms of violence. In fact, in that case, the sound that we were investigating, that had been recorded at the site of the killings, was already a blur because the Israeli soldiers were firing live rounds through rubber bullets, using a suppressor or bullet adapter as a kind of alibi for the use of live ammunition. So immediately you hear the entanglement between supposedly legitimate, less lethal, forms of violence and illegitimate forms of murder. That case that I worked on is just one example. When you look at the ways in which sound physically behaves, you start to understand politically what is at stake in splitting things or breaking them down and how those forms of separation are adept at winning legal arguments. In fact, when you actually take sound for what it is—as a kind of condition of resonance—to comprehend resonant entanglements, to become a witness to the sonic bleed rather than to extractable elements, you start to understand that what is good for winning legal arguments is immediately at odds with the pursuit of justice. The ways in which these things resound are continually fascinating for me, because they start to allow for a spatial political analysis of who's listening, who's regarded as a reliable listener and how we can actually use sound as a kind of medium of inseparability to understand where the boundaries become blurred in any given context. In the context of the example I gave before, instead of a boundary marking a separation between legitimate and illegitimate forms of violence—between human rights and war crimes—what are supposedly two sides start to somehow become similar. There have been parallels within other projects. Another illustration would be the situation where an accent test is used against asylum seekers—something I've been working on for many years—where you see an interesting bleed between free speech (and the ideology of free speech) and the false confession. Once you start to investigate the processes through which those accents are heard and are circulated within the immigration jurisdiction, what you realise is that what is apparently separate is by no means, actually, diametrically opposed.

One of the ways in which Eyal Weizman introduces you in the book Forensic Architecture *is through a job description that defines you as a sound artist and an audio investigator. Are those two processes also very much blurred in the world that you're investigating?*

Exactly. And I think that the blurring we are talking about was never more the case than when I worked with Forensic Architecture and Amnesty International on the Sadynaya investigation exploring the Syrian regime's secret prison. In that context, there was a demand for something beyond the traditional idea of what an expert would do, what an acoustician would do, because what we were dealing with were the ways in which sensory deprivation and other kinds of extreme brutality actually change the conditions by which one hears. What I was asked to do in that investigation was, at times, a form of technical work which could contribute to the audio investigation, we were using the verbal accounts of former prisoners to work out how many doors were in use in a particular wing and then to try to understand how many people were being held inside. At other times, there were ways in which my work as a sound artist, as someone who can help name phenomena that tend not to have a strong vocabulary behind them, enabled me to create language, to use our mouths to mimic sounds, to use sound effects from film, to create language in a consensus between me and the interviewee. That second approach to working tended towards the necessity of listening and the experiences that I had become accustomed to when working with sound for audiences, when working with sound aesthetically as well as technically. In the words themselves, you see that same boundary I spoke of in my last answer, the boundary between, let's say, the analysis of the frequency spectrum and the analysis of political events. Again, it's never one or the other, they are always together and that's why I came up with this idea of the private ear—

<interrupting> Which I think is a deceptively simple expression to describe the complexities of what you do.

Well, it is both stupid enough and smart enough that I like it. It's a stupid kind of joke, in a way, but there's something about the word private pertaining to the ability to operate independently and to deduce independent political analysis that is extremely important to the work I do. It is about both being able to investigate sound for its contexts and also to deduce from them my own reflections, to pull out things that I think are pertinent to the experience. To go back to Sadynaya, the investigation ranged broadly across walls, architecture, the relation of sound to violence, sound's relation to the human voice, to language and to memory. Those dimensions start to emerge from the independent side of the work, the side that does not only seek to establish the violence that's going on in Sadynaya but to try and learn from those people, to find the right format which can mediate their lessons, lessons which changed the way I thought about sound and led me in subsequent art works to invite others to question the way that they think about sound and its relation to the listener.

Continuing to refer to the work that you did with Sadynaya, I understand that you also created acoustic atmospheres intended to help the former inmates contextualise their experiences. Is that right? Were these environmental compositions played to released prisoners alongside the Foley work and library recordings as a way of evoking the prison's spaces?

Yes, that was mostly in an attempt to reconstruct the proximity from which things were heard, the position from which things were heard. Using the stereo field, it was possible to ask, "If you were looking at the door of your cell, where would you hear the metal stairs that lead to the guard's room?" These recordings could be used as a compass with which to start to place things in space. All the prisoners would talk about hearing the main door and the kind of "welcome parties" that would come through that door. Most chillingly, perhaps, they also described what we later understood to be the sounds of mass execution. This was not the sound you might expect it to be: at night, people could be heard having their names called out, being taken from their cells, being loaded into a truck which was driven until no longer audible and then returned after fifteen minutes at which point no prisoners could be heard getting out. That period was too short for the prisoners whose names were called out to have been taken to Damascus or anywhere else, so a series of deductions turned this fifteen-minute silence during which the truck couldn't be heard into the sound of mass executions. It was really about thinking laterally through sound, and often thinking not-so-logically because a lot of the sounds pertained to distortion, pertained to sensory deprivation. It was a strange experience and one that I have learned more from than anything else I've ever done.

One of the things that you've just described very much interests me about your work—at least as far as I interpret it. The complexity of listening that you embark on is one that means there is no such thing as innocence or guilt in the acoustic realm—everything is open. For example, with your Earwitness Inventory *work at the Chisenhale in 2018, we hear discussion of buildings collapsing "like popcorn" or of a gun shooting "like someone dropping a rack of trays". When we looked at the Foley objects in the room, they were innocent-looking things: shoes, bags, a kid's swimming pool, buckets. They are objects imbued with an apparent innocence. The silence of the absent truck you just talked about does not immediately evoke horror or violence, instead it is open to interpretation. And it would seem that we would have to embark on a deep process of listening, not just to sounds but to people's interpretations of sound, to finally understand that what can be heard as innocent can also be heard as cruel, as unjust, as pain.*

Yeah, I think that's a really great observation and it occurs to me that it also contextualises what was said before, in that it is the logics of interpretation that are what dissolve some of those boundaries that we've previously spoke about: fundamentally, they dissolve the boundary between the sonic event and the listener. Whereas an acoustician would have been interested in the sonic event, often I'm more concerned with how that event was heard. If we could get access to Sadynaya prison—and we cannot, of course—and we could measure the sound of those doors or measure the sound of food landing on the ground outside of one of the cells, it would not get us any closer to understanding what the prison sounded like until we understood how the prisoners heard it. It seems very simple, but a lot of the work is trying to listen to the way people listen. Shifting to another project that I've previously mentioned, the one about the killing of the two Palestinian teenagers, Nadeem

Nawara and Mohamad Abu Daher, one of the strongest pieces of evidence that demonstrated that this was not a one-off incident or one rotten apple within the Israeli Border Force but was actually a tactically-adopted practice of cloaking the firing of live ammunition with the use of the rubber bullet adapter, was the analysis of the crowd reaction. Although these people would never testify for political reasons, they are the real experts in this case, in the sense that it could readily be perceived that the crowd responded visibly differently to those two types of gunshot sound. To understand the event involved looking to the way people listened on the ground as more meaningful than the spectrogram analysis of the sound itself; and this distinction speaks to the collective nature of what I called these resonant entanglements in which you no longer separate, for example, expert from victim, just as you don't divide a gunshot from the architectural space in which it resides.

If you are listening to listening or listening to listeners—

—or looking at listeners—

—or looking at listeners, one of the ways we are taught to listen is through the cinema. I wondered about the extent to which when you create a soundtrack or are playing something back, you find that people have had their listening recalibrated by the processes of cinema? When hearing live gunfire for the first time, people are often assumed to say, "I don't recognise that noise since it doesn't sound anything like what I've heard in a film".

That kind of negation was the whole point behind Earwitness Inventory. It was what drove me to become interested in how the production of sound effects is so linked to the way we understand the world acoustically. I was fascinated by alternative or imaginary sound effects, the narratives of how a sound can be reproduced, which are extremely plentiful. I wanted to conjoin notions of cinema sound to the memories that we create of objects that compensate for the lack of an adequate language through which to speak about sound. Those objects that you talked about earlier which populate the *Earwitness Inventory* installation in the Chisenhale stand in for a kind of language we don't yet speak.

You read about these kinds of phenomena in audio culture, but what we are discussing was never more clear to me than from the work I was doing in relation to the Syrian prison Sadynaya, 90% of which involved accounting for a language that we didn't really have, when we weren't able to really speak to those sounds, even though that prison had engendered some of the most acute listeners that I have ever met. I would say that the people who I met who had been incarcerated in Sadynaya had a trained listening acuity relating to that specific prison soundscape that was equivalent in power to that of Dr Peter French, the foremost expert on forensics of speech and acoustics. What I'm trying to say is that it wasn't that we lacked acute listeners, rather the issue was the absence of a vocabulary through which to speak of sound. In that context, I found it fascinating that the sound effect could be deployed to fill that void, with cinema being both a negative and a positive example of the ways we negotiate our memories, our acoustic experiences—specifically in relation to violence. We have acoustic experience of speech, after all, enough to know that not everybody sounds like James Earl Jones, yet many of us don't know what violence sounds like. At the same time, of course, many people do know how violence sounds, as in all the cases that I have been describing. An interesting example occurred with two videos that started circulating in around 2014-2015. In one, a young girl in Syria—three, four years old—could actually identify every one of the different kinds of ammunition that was being fired. In another, a toddler who heard a pressure cooker bomb detonating described it as a thousand pianos dropping to the ground—which might derive from that familiar piano dropping sequence from kids' cartoons.

In your work Earshot—*which came out of the research you have already discussed into the live and rubber bullets fired by the Israeli Border Police—there is a transposition of the acoustic violence into other registers, such as where the sounds of weapons discharging are translated into the visual information of the spectrograph. Voiceprint technology has been used by the FBI, I think, since the '50s and '60s when they borrowed the spectrograph from Bell Labs. If you are the private ear working independently, outside of the state, do you nonetheless end up using the visual strategies of the state such as the voiceprint technologies that have been part of law enforcement, espionage and military analysis?*

In the case of *Earshot*, I couldn't hear the difference—only the people on the ground could hear the difference—I had to see the difference. If you return to this ontology of the bleed I have been speaking about, how boundaries get blurred, this extends to the distinction between sound and image, since deciphering a sonic event allows you to understand other kinds of waves. A lot of the work has been dedicated to grappling with the sonic image: what do images that behave like sounds look like, and what do sounds that behave like images appear like? One example from *Earwitness Inventory* would be the person in court who became fixated on associating a punch with the sound of an egg cracking and could no longer separate the two, they had been filed together in his cognitive taxonomy, with the egg continually appearing every time he wanted to speak about the punch; that conjoining is where the sound behaves like an image. The opposite example would be when the image becomes sound, when we hear an image, when it disintegrates, become viral, spreads and resonates, become sonic. In the work *Conflicted Phonemes*, I had to use an image because it was a situation where people's voices, their accents, were being used as evidence against them in the context of asylum claims. Because the asylum cases were not criminal cases, there was no right to silence, and the burden of proof resided with the applicant and not the state, so the people involved could not not participate in the voice analysis. Using the image of the voice in *Conflicted Phonemes* became a way to produce the silence that they have been stripped of in the immigration process; the image stands in place of the asylum seekers' voices as a kind of political gesture. It is not a spectrograph, it is a sonic image, the logic of sound applied to an image so that it behaves strangely, starting to disintegrate and dismantle and bounce, to cross political space and different kinds of political event. In the end, there is a total inseparability between those voices and the politics those people have lived through, the itinerant lives they have inhabited. In that work, it was important to understand the voice as a network—rather than separated into the accents that the state insisted on—and one way to achieve this was visually, to create a sonic image.

The question you asked about state technology has a very simple answer: what I learned from Eyal Weizman and Forensic Architecture is that these technologies are becoming more and more available and that we should use them to listen back.

Is there ever a worry that those technologies come with a sense of being 'his master's tools'? You talk about bleed but do those technologies bleed their origins into your attempts to re-deploy them against the state?

Well, precisely! And that's why I'm saying that things are not exclusively used in one way. Besides, the most important work was not the manifestation of the spectrograph, although that helped create a legal argument within the language of the state, the language of human rights and the language of the law. The most important thing that spectrograph did politically for me was to undo me as an expert.

In *Conflicted Phonemes*, the politics of the visual, which I described prior, are such that the image we produced is very different from the one the state uses, which is a map that divides Somalia into three places labelled northern dialect, coastal dialect and southern dialect. If you look at my maps, they were extremely different, because the ideology behind them was extremely different. The political arguments that you deduce from those technologies have to be distinct: what is at stake is made manifest in the forms that are at work.

If you are only using the spectrograms, then you are forced to work within the tight confines of what it is possible to claim legally, which is very small, especially in the precedent-based system in the UK and the US. Those narrow limits mean that in almost every legal case in which sound functions prominently, clear perpetrators get away with what they have done. When you have have Darren Wilson [who killed the unarmed eighteen-year-old Michael Brown in Ferguson], George Zimmerman [who killed the unarmed seventeen-year-old Trayvon Martin in Sanford] and Oscar Pistorius [who killed the unarmed thirty-year-old Reeva Steenkamp in Pretoria], there is no denying that they each shot someone dead in cold blood, but when it comes to the question of sound in court, legal gymnastics mean that sound is never understood in terms of its resonant entanglements and instead becomes functional on behalf of the perpetrators. What I'm trying to say is that there is a distinct correlation between a failure to understand sound for what it is—and understand it in its complexities—and failures in the pursuit of justice.

In much of your work sound, directly or indirectly, becomes a kind of conduit for pain and violence. If sound becomes associated with suffering in this way, can you listen outside of these experiences? Is it possible to keep listening with an innocent ear?

Only as much as it's possible to keep looking with an innocent eye!

I imagine that you're someone who worries a lot about how you deliver meaning to an audience in a gallery or in a performance, and I imagine you care about other people's vulnerabilities. But I wonder if you have to offer equal care to yourself when you are listening to other listeners?

To me, it feels inappropriate to think about myself in that context. If you think about what those people in Sadynaya went through it would be inappropriate to make any sort of claim that I was traumatised in anyway whatsoever. But I don't think that's necessarily what you're asking. I do feel that my work over these ten years has taught me to listen in different ways, largely in terms of bringing a political urgency to sound and of learning to hear with a political sonic imagination. Although it is changing a lot, this approach to sound wasn't evident when I first started, it wasn't there in the way that sound art was understood and the way that sound itself was understood. We probably both know the bibliography on that, it's not extensive but it has been increasing. So much of what has to happen is bringing the complexity to sound that we already have when thinking about images. Only three years ago, I was in a show called *Listen!* You couldn't have a show called Look about images—would anyone be interested in going to that? All I'm asking for is that we get to that same point with the sound.

With your work, Recovered Manifesto of Wissam [inaudible] *where you are exploring the Islamic juridical concept of Taqiyya, one of the really telling details is the discovery of the dicataphone tape around the orange tree. This detail lets me think about different sensory modalities and about questions of context (and the sensitivity to context that feels fundamental to your work) and it leads me to ask whether there is a compromise involved in reaching beyond sound itself, to bring, in the case of* Recovered Manifesto, *the trees into the gallery to address the origin of where the tape was discovered?*

Well, I still get asked about this at talks. I think I've already answered about why I think that images are sometimes necessary, and I've also already talked about sonic bleed and how dissolving that boundary is very important for me. Sound doesn't teach you about sound, sound should teach you about other things; it's not about sound itself, for me, it's about a sonic imagination. That work *Recovered Manifesto* is not 'about' sound, it is about lying, about the politics of lying. Maybe it is also unfair to ask me to resolve that comparison because often the works are not sound art as such, but about many other things. In *Recovered Manifesto*, it is about the voice, about expression, about the ways in which we conceal various parts of ourselves, protect them, about the ways in which the voice is an artificial construct. In that work, the voice is specifically argued to be definitely not a register of the self, but something that is created by and for the ears of other people. I think reducing all this to sound alone would be just as problematic, and you would arrive at something that would be extremely directive.

One of the things that you just said distinguished Recovered Manifesto *from a work of sound art and this leads me to ask whether you view yourself within a sound arts context?*

Yes and no. I still think some of the most important experiences I had with contemporary art were those that involved sound, ones that came specifically from a history of sonic imagination. But perhaps you could say that of almost every contemporary artist in the sense that there is this influential genealogy from John Cage. People can tend to essentialise sound art, to see it as a new field, forgetting that ways of thinking in response to music, acoustics and sound are really at the heart of the conceptual practices that the majority of artists now adopt. Listening and sound were ways of conceiving the world in Fluxus and Cage and in others that lead to logics to which we are much more accustomed today.

I'm interested in sound arts as long as they are about expanding what it means to listen and not reducing everything to an essentialist category of the listener. I'm not saying anything radical. A phenomenological reading of sound would be very difficult to make function as springboard from which I could make tangible political claims. The phenomenological reading produces a floating sense of experience that is very much about separating sound from the rest of the world, whereas my work is really about putting sound back into the world.

Lina Lapelyte

I had always wanted to interview Lina Lapelyte for this book: ironically she was the last person that I interviewed, and the only one that I did not meet face to face as her planned talk at DRAF in London was cancelled due to the pandemic. I had loved her performance project *Candy Shop* which transforms and exposes the politics of various well-known hip-hop texts by re-setting them to very different musical backings and performing them in an extremely unemotional and stylised way, often with a group of other women. Then, over the time that we were researching and conducting interviews for the book, Lina was one of the three artists, with Vaiva Grainyte and Rugile Barzdziukaite, who won the Golden Lion at the Venice Biennale in 2019 for the opera performance *Sun & Sea (Marina)* in the Lithuanian Pavilion. It was wonderful to see three women win the prize, particularly for a sound work that was performed live, but more than that, it was exciting to see an ex-student do so very well. As an undergraduate in Sound Arts at LCC, Lina was always enthusiastic and organised. Her talent was obvious, but it has been great to have watched the development of her work since then. I am interested in the mixture of experiences and influences that have led her to develop this very distinctive practice and, having achieved such a high level of artistic recognition at a still young age, where she might go from here. I am also interested in the practicalities of building a performance-based career alongside raising a young family while based between the UK and Lithuania.

You studied the violin originally and then you completed a degree in sound arts in London followed by an MA in Sculpture—can you say how, or what, those three experiences have contributed to your current practice?

It's quite clear to me what each of them meant to me. I grew up with the classical violin—it gave me skills, particularly listening skills, but it also gave me a lot of complexes and discomfort because it only offered one, very old-school, understanding of music, and how it is supposed to be performed and listened to. It was like a museum practice. I have had a strange relationship with that instrument since I was a teenager. I was a good violinist, but it was also good to move away from it. Studying sound art was amazing. I had to unlearn a lot, to rethink the instrument and to widen up my preconceptions. I also started to use my voice. For a long time I felt so vulnerable doing that! Later I chose to study Fine Art at the RCA to widen up my perspectives even more—as studying sound art had started to feel a bit geeky.

Do you have a feeling about when you made a work that was 'right' for you?

It was probably the opera, *Have a Good Day!* that I made together with Rugile Barzdziukaite and Vaiva Grainyte [haveagoodday.lt]. I had to train the singers, which helped me to rediscover my own voice and singing practice. With this work I sort of rebelled against what was, at that time, 'cool' in experimental music circles. The work was not at all experimental in those terms and the singing was very intuitive, almost 'poppy', with a lot of harmonies. Probably, at that point, my practice started to have two different roots, both influenced by each other, but one belonging to this experimental, live, improvised music scene, and the other, more conceptual, involving more people, but also appreciated and understood by a wider circle of people.

Collaboration is a major feature of your work—you're collaborating with performers, writers, librettists, directors and you've collaborated with the writer Vaiva Grainyte and director Rugile Barzdziukaite, your collaborators on Sun & Sea *for the Venice Biennale in 2019 more than once. Can you say something about that process? Let's start with* Have a Good Day! *because it seems like that was quite a break-through for you, and that collaboration has been very strong and has led to fantastic outcomes: how did that come about?*

Have a Good Day! was actually a crisis piece. In 2009 my partner lost his job in London; Jeronimas, my first child, had just been born; and we thought that there was nothing to keep us in London. So we went back to Lithuania. Vaiva, Rugile and I had a short residency together and we worked on a sketch of our first opera. After presenting it, we ended up developing a full-length opera *Have a Good Day!* for ten singing cashiers, supermarket sounds and piano which is set around the inner lives of cashiers in a shopping centre and is based on what lies behind their mechanical "Good afternoon!", "Thank you!", "Have a good day!" and fake smiles.

Did you work closely together or did Vaiva go off and write the words and then you composed the music?

The process was collaborative from the very beginning, the three of us participated in and were part of every element of the work. The text and musical parts all influenced each other. Also a big focus was on the auditioning of the singers—the qualities of their voices and their characters were extremely important to the final work. The same method was applied while working with *Sun & Sea*.

Is there a big leap between working as a solo artist and working on a much bigger staged production with performers?

Yeah, I think so—mentally and physically. The collaborative work allows for a much greater complexity which is not possible when working alone. But both methods feel like a privilege to me—after working in a group it's amazing to make the decisions alone, and after a period of working solo it feels really special to share ideas together. From the production point of view, even these staged, collaborative productions almost never had a big infrastructure behind them—they were mainly created and rehearsed in our living rooms!

Maybe that explains one of the things that I noticed about that work and probably some of the others as well—you use the format of the static row of seats a lot. If you're rehearsing in your living room, that could explain it!

With *Have a Good Day!* the supermarket situation is what influenced the sitting positions.

I also love Candy Shop, *was that after* Have A Good Day!*?*

Yes, I developed it during a year and a half that I was at the Royal College of Art in London.

I've seen the video performance of you performing the initial song on your own, was that what you developed at the RCA originally?

The dirty rap hit, *Candy Shop* by 50 Cent was the starting point. That song came about when I'd just started at RCA and I thought that I would like to do more performative work that involved singing.

So it expanded from your solo performance of the song?

Yeah, I felt that a collective approach would probably have a much stronger impact. Hip hop is very much about the ego and power, the idea was to subvert this and turn it into a collective voice that questioned certain behaviours or amplified specific messages. I invited the people that I really wanted to work with and the idea resonated with all of them!

Were they all your friends already?

I think I had met Sharon Gal during the performance of Pauline Oliveros's work *To Valerie Solanas and Marylin Monroe in Recognition of their Desperation*, as part of *Feminisms and the Sonic* at Tate Modern in 2012. Angharad Davies I also knew from before, we'd played in various situations from time to time. We met Anat Ben David in a Spor festival in Denmark and Rebecca la Horrox at Resonance FM. Heidi Heiderberg and Nouria Bah joined through the public audition, which was also part of the piece. All of them have super strong voices and are amazing people.

It's a great selection of young women performers doing interesting things.

Oh, they're brilliant! It's really good working with this group of women—I love them.

The Candy Shop *lyrics are so hard-core. I was thinking about how you staged it, what you were wearing and how it's all performed in this very deadpan way. If you dropped your neutral personas for a second it would have a totally different meaning I think. Did you think a lot about that?*

Yeah, this was very thought through. Each of us chose a selection of lyrics that grew into songs. Choreography and video elements grew up together with the songs. As for the costumes—we wear men's shirts that have the labels on and we return them to shops afterwards.

What about the composition?

At the beginning, I thought we would do it collaboratively then I realised that it wouldn't work! I felt the composition needed to have continuity. We did quite a few improvisation sessions and some of that became part of the work and then other some parts were added, as well as the video, which is a piece of work all on its own.

When did you last perform it?

In Prague—at the Kunsthalle Praha. We usually perform it once or twice a year somewhere. But there is also a bigger project, including a workshop that I do with teenage kids where they dance slowed-down hip hop movements and then, in Riga at the Sonic Dawn Festival, I played the vinyl record in combination with my own singing of the material. So, it takes on different forms.

I guess it's quite an expensive piece to put on.

As a performance work of this complexity (the latest iteration involves a local men's choir and a marching band) I don't think it's expensive, but as an experimental music gig—it may feel complicated.

Performance is really important to you. Do you do any work that doesn't involve some live performance?

I've done a couple of works like this. Even if there is no performance, there would most likely be sound, but the performative element is very important to me—I like to watch music being done.

That's interesting, personally I quite like sitting in a dark room with my eyes shut! Let's talk about sound sources: I haven't seen one piece of work where you've used the violin.

I do, I even have a duo with Angharad Davies that toured Sweden and Norway last year. We play two violins with a volume pedal, it's very low-fi, but we also do a bit of a choreography of the space while performing.

In most of your performance pieces you're either playing accordion, synth or singing. Oh, actually I remember seeing you perform something for violin, electronics and voice at Café Oto in London.

Yeah, I pressed the buttons with my toes on the keyboard. The synth was programmed in such a way that different keys would bring me particular sounds. I used a surround sound system and samples of my cut-up voice so I was performing with myself and also triggering these different electronic sounds.

So the move into using lyrics has been quite significant for you.

It moved things from the abstract and conceptual to the very concrete.

I have noticed a big compositional difference between the early work and Sun & Sea, *which you're not performing in; it feels like the compositional texture has become more intricate, even more harmonic, actually.*

The bright harmony is part of the overall concept—a brightness that is almost dark! I do perform in *Sun & Sea* sometimes, I can do all the roles! I did it quite a few times in Venice because sometimes someone gets ill or falls asleep on the stage and so I would have to step in.

Did you always have to be in your beach gear?

Yes, we were wearing the beach outfits all the time so that we could be on the beach if needed. Our children were involved and sometimes they would get into fights or they would drop sand into performers' mouths and they would complain, and we would say that they had to tell them off just like on a normal beach! It was very much a performance and a life situation. Compositionally however, *Sun & Sea* is a series of songs. When we were working to construct the piece, we had these blocks of different songs and characters, which we were moving around and getting rid of until the very last minute, until it felt complete. The keyboard accompaniment is also very reduced and very simple.

The harmony writing feels rich. Maybe that's because there are so many people involved, but it feels like there's a lot of quite close harmony going on.

Yeah, I like harmonies and I like togetherness. I like it when a collective of people are in tune, it's not just tuning with each other in the sense of sound, but I believe that if people are in tune in general, then the magical resonance happens—you know? The harmonies are very subtle, the voices are different and the performers come from very different singing backgrounds, so it's a big challenge to combine them all. Classically trained operatic singers, for example, are just not used to singing in choirs, but then it's about how do we do things collectively and it's amazing when we can do it!

It must have been great and quite a big jump in scale from the work that you had been doing. How did it all happen?

Well *Sun & Sea* started before we knew about Venice. So it was not done for Venice but it was the second work of the three *Have A Good Day!* collaborators. We started to work on it in 2015 at a three-month residency at Schloss Solitude. During those three months we developed a sketch, then half a year later we applied for some funding in Lithuania, and in September 2017 we presented the *Sun & Sea* Lithuanian version. The working process was quite similar to what we did for *Have a Good Day!*. There were many different stages, it took us about five years to build a piece from the initial idea because we are all individually practising artists as well. Also, we three are not focused on the quantity of works—we like being slow.

About half a year after we did the Lithuanian version there was an open competition to represent the country at the Venice Biennale. We talked with Lucia Pietroiusti from the Serpentine Gallery and Rasa Antanavičiūtė, director of the Nida Art Colony at the time, and we all delivered a proposal which got selected. We had a year to make it happen, including finding the location, the local singers and raising additional money for it, because it was way too ambitious for the budget that we had!

In the end, was there a huge difference between the Lithuanian version and the Venice version?

No, not such a huge difference. We worked together with the translator to translate it into English. I had to go through the translation and to make it singable then re-write all the music so that it followed the text in a natural way. I believe that the text itself is music and it offers many musical propositions.

I think you did a great job. How many performers were on stage at any time?

So, there are thirteen characters, and usually fifteen people are singing, some only do the choirs and are there in case someone gets ill. Everyone else is volunteering as bodies on the beach.

How long did you rehearse with those people for?

It took about six months to prepare for the Lithuanian version. We had a one-month session with very loose material, and then for every rehearsal we would come up with something else. We were constantly workshopping the material and seeing, with our selected performers, what was good, what worked and what didn't. Then the three of us worked the whole summer to finalise the material and had another month sticking it together and fixing it, learning and being confident with the parts before presenting to the audience. A very big part of the work was the casting and auditioning—the voices and characters of the people inspired a lot of material.

So it's taken up the last five years?

Well, 2015 was the proposal, then the residency, then developing the material... yes, there have been many steps.

So it was incredible for you to win the Golden Lion at the 2019 Venice Biennale. You must have been so utterly delighted. Do you feel it's made any long-term difference to the sort of offers and commissions you've been getting?

We stayed in Venice the whole time and kept working on it, often in the kitchen surrounded by kids. A month after winning, a German journalist came to interview us and he was suggesting that we must be rich and famous now. But actually during that interview we even struggled to pay for the nanny to take care of our kids. After winning we suddenly got so much more attention and work and we didn't want the quality of the work to drop. We had to accommodate the queues and the extra audience. Before that we had thought that we would have maybe thirty people a day and that the singers would be able to just drink tea all day because no one would ever find the pavilion—who would go to the Lithuanian pavilion? Then everything just turned upside-down which meant that we just had to work like crazy to keep it all in place. Of course it's amazing and incredible that we won, but in terms of future work, it's very hard to say. Each of us is working on some individual ideas and commissions and there's a lot of demand for *Sun & Sea*: we have a tour schedule for two years including Brazil, America, Northern Europe and many other places. But now with Covid everything has been cancelled until July, and then we don't know what's going to happen.

Will you tour the same cast every time?

We made the decision to keep the same people touring, otherwise we would just not be able to do anything else, and it's really healthy for all of us to also go back into our own practices.

Have you got lots of work that you're meant to be doing in person in the coming year?

I had a couple of things that have been postponed to the late summer or next year. The nearest event is RIBOCA2—the Riga Biennale where I am working with Mantas Petraitis on a work called *Currents*, a large site-specific sculpture made out of two thousand logs in the river, as well as a sound installation and performance to accompany it. There is one project in Sweden that is going to involve a lot of 'tone deaf' people and hopefully some musicians from London, it's planned for the beginning of 2021 now. After the lockdown—the first thing we did was to go to the countryside and plant seeds—I felt that if everything stops for more than three months then that's it! I'll enjoy not having to fly, but when I don't travel I don't get any income. I'm so very lucky that there is this land that is waiting for the spring!

Do you have any help with producing your work? How do you actually manage to do it all?

I don't know!

You have three young boys—they must be very good and well-trained.

They are amazing! I have always travelled with them. There were a few times when a local festival organiser would organise me a babysitter for the hour that I was performing, or sometimes I would just hand them over to the ticket or cloakroom people for twenty minutes, not for a long time! Then I learned that not all the kids liked that. The first one was completely fine but the third one—I did it once and then never again! I could hear him screaming during the performance and knew that it wasn't going to work! My partner is a freelance architect, so whenever I go for a longer residency, we all travel together and share the childcare duties equally. It's not easy. We don't have an au-pair or a live-in nanny; we actually don't have much help, so we really cope with it as we are.

I only had one child, but I remember that after I had her, I wondered what the hell I used to do with all my time—so with three, you must feel that threefold!

Yeah, but also they ground you. I like to be grounded. I think it's important. They don't ask you if you're tired or if you have the most important thing happening in your life, they just want to eat—it's a way to balance things out and you realise that nothing is more important than to get some food now and that's it!

That's very sobering. You live between Vilnius and London don't you? Do you feel there are advantages to being in Lithuania, is there support for you there? How does it feel compared with being in London?

Lithuania is a very small country, it's less bureaucratic. I'm not a composer writing chorales and symphonies, I'm not a visual artist who has a gallery or makes objects, yet we were still given this opportunity to represent the country in the Venice Biennale! I feel that London had and has a strong influence on me as an artist and as a human being. I feel the support everywhere—I have met amazing people in both places and feel very privileged to be able to belong to both.

Do you feel that you can hear anything of Lithuania in your work?

I'm not sure. Maybe it's the way that I think and do things, or what I appreciate. A lot of people in Lithuania come from the soil, we are forest people, we like foraging and planting. I also grew up with song, singing was present in every celebration, even our independence in 1990 was called the Singing Revolution.

Whose work has been influential or who do you admire?

When I was a teenager there were some Lithuanian publishers who started a journal called *Tango* about experimental music. I started to read it when I was sixteen and it really opened my eyes. I realised that the classical violin could be very different and that I didn't need to stick to the score! It was in Lithuanian, which was important because my English was not so good then. I was reading about La Monte Young, Laurie Anderson and John Cage, and it had a big influence on me then. It was published by people who had a passion for experimental music and who had decided that it was important to share all this knowledge.

When I was looking at some of your work, I was thinking about Meredith Monk and Heiner Goebbels —there aren't that many people who are actually staging experimental music or sound art.

I discovered Meredith Monk much later and I can really relate to her work and her thinking beyond music, also Robert Ashley and Laurie Anderson, the fact that she plays a violin was an important factor. But there isn't anyone in particular, my influences come from a combination of things.

Maria Chavez

I have known of Maria Chavez's art and music for a long time, and yet it is only recently that my interest has been substantially sharpened. The re-focusing of my attention has come about through a cumulative process of people who I respect encouraging me to explore her work further, to recognise fully an artist capable of recalibrating modalities so that they resonate with a coherent pulse. This harmonising allows her curations, installations, performances, writing (including a book-length monograph) and visually-attuned material to establish consistent (if unexpected) relations with the diversity of audio media for which Chavez is responsible. In terms of these audio media, a sample from the last couple of years would include a composition for a Biennale, a broadcast on a hip radio station, a track on an even hipper cassette compilation, a collaboration on lathe-cut 7", and a CD release of her remixes of another artist's locked grooves.

An echo of those (unexpected) relations can also be heard in the ways that Chavez's projects acknowledge a constellation of historical affinities from a spectrum of sources whose connections had previously gone unnoticed: land art, feminist composition, sound art, West Coast minimalism, pop art collage and hip hop / avant-garde turntablism.

Chavez is recovering from an operation to remedy a serious medical condition, difficult circumstances which have led to her having to stop performing. As she says, her own recovery meant that she was in isolation long before the Coronavirus outbreak struck and confined so many others. Her Instagram account combines inspirationally open updates on her health with news of her creative practice and her responses to contemporary politics: a mixture of dismay with hope for enduring change.

How are you?

It's just bizarre that you're all stuck at home with me now, because I was all by myself for such a long time.

Is the recovery going as well as the doctors want? Are they pleased with your progress?

Yes. Every day is like walking on eggshells, but so far so good. My symptoms went away last May so I have just passed my one-year mark; I have a year still to go, but if things stay the same then I can officially be declared cured on February 27th, 2021. Then it will be more a question of how comfortable I feel in settings with large PAs.

My fingers are crossed. I'd like to begin by asking you about your performance for The Kitchen in New York earlier this week: one thing that excited me was the rapport that developed between you and the online listeners.

I could not do the livestream so instead I pre-recorded the video, and The Kitchen asked if I could be available on the chat for people to interact. I don't know if you've been to one of my live performances but they are not really the formal recitals that they once were, instead they have become these large exchanges of ideas where the audience can sit right next to me at the table. With that intimacy I can then open things up and say: "if in the middle of this piece there's something you don't like, if there's something you have a question about, just ask me; if you want to take a video or use a flash, just do it: don't worry about me, I'm so focused that you can just get in my face so you can get the good shot you want". And this intimacy really disarms everybody, it makes them feel "this isn't precious to her: we can have access to this, too". And that accessibility is what creates a deeper listening, which is something that I learned from Pauline Oliveros, but which I think I have translated more in terms of a social act.

My practice is inclusive because I invite everyone in and allow them to imagine that they can be in my position, too. Perhaps their chances of getting here are not high but for those who have succeeded and made their careers from my book *Of Technique: Chance Procedures on Turntable*, to me that is a trade. Because I already have this emphasis on social interaction, when The Kitchen asked me to participate in the online chat it was like second nature to me. Even if no one had been interacting, I would still have been writing online because I knew that this was going to be a document of a really important time and, in twenty to fifty years from now, this era will be reflected on the basis of what was first shown on these platforms.

I was glad to be invited to provide some content at this time, and that is why I wanted to make a new piece rather than revive an old one. I thought even if no one talks to me during the stream, I should just break down the sonic choices. After all, I write about my work all the time, it is one of the ways through which it is communicated—and the audience already have that language of the way that I speak in their heads. I'm so open, because I know that the more open I am, the more opportunities there are for people to have a more intimate listening experience with the work.

It is almost as if the work doesn't exist without the exchange: the exchange is needed in order for the work to progress.

And does that exchange become part of a process of democratisation or, at least, a destabilisation of the conventional approach to the artist and the audience?

Absolutely. One can almost see it as a naturally occurring set of events that is organic to human nature. If you create a safe space in which the public can interact, with their safety provided, then they will naturally create a transformational dialogue that goes beyond the basic stage performance expectations. I see that part of my work as being influenced by both Joseph Beuys and Pauline Oliveros. Beuys with his early attempts at 'social sculpture', Pauline Oliveros with her instructions for everyone: that approach is not yet the norm for the general public. Given that I'm a naturally warm person who can speak to almost anyone, it felt very natural for me to adapt what I understood from the results of this type of presentation practice. And when I started opening up the room, there would be a hush of surprise in the audience: "Wait, is she talking to us? We can go up there?" and then the organic process of the exchange begins to deepen.

A question which moves on from what you're saying would be one about radical openness. I think it was in 2015 when you did a mix on NTS radio in London. You started with a Steve Reich track and ended with a Steve Reich track yet in between there were all kinds of things—an Italian folksong, a Junior Boys tune, Beatrice Dillon. What I really enjoyed was imagining the listening culture that you created and its articulation of openness.

I'm glad that it translated in that way to you because I'm always curious about people's impressions. When I was DJing in Australia on my goodbye tour there was this one kid who followed all of my shows, he had been to a workshop and bought books for his sisters (there's always a few of those types of fans, so sweet). He asked me something similar to what you just said: "If you heard the songs you played separately, you wouldn't think to put them all together. But when you mixed them somehow it made sense. How did you do that?" My response was that I had been working as a DJ since I was sixteen, and by the time I was twenty I had already dealt with those stringent boundaries. Back in the late '90s DJing, talk about rules! You couldn't mix drum and bass with techno, you had to beat match, every little detail had to be perfect or you were out. And it was all vinyl. Which is hard to control! And mistakes happen! But as a woman, you made one mistake and you were kicked off. All the guys were waiting for you to mess up so they could take your spot, so I already grew up within this patrolled and managed genre environment.

When I was getting back into DJing in 2010, I had PTSD from all the bullying as a teenager because I wasn't sure if the way I wanted to sequence these tracks would be acceptable. Thankfully, the first official DJ gig was in a museum, at the Haus der elektronischen Künste Basel, so the expectation to play only techno was not the case. It was a *huge* relief when I lifted my head up and could see people enjoying the music. Normally, I'm always DJing at home—I'm always making a DJ mix, but when I was in my most profound healing phase, I couldn't listen to music or even look forward to listening to music, and that persisted until, maybe, January of 2020. As soon as I was able and willing, I went right back to making new mixes.

The validation from the people and museum staff afterwards was what made me realise that the times have changed, and the ridiculous "no genre blending" policing was over. And the bullies were gone. Or, I should say, they had taken on a different form. From 2010 onwards, I just began to DJ whatever I was listening to at the time. So now I'm in a cool place where I have so much music that most of the time my mixes become genre-less. I've realised that what people want to hear is how I listen to music and actually that NTS show you mention was pretty much what I was listening to on my phone, including the sequence of tracks, it's just that I edited it into an hour's playing time. I was really surprised by how popular the mix became.

You can manipulate the turntable in lots of different ways, you have accrued a vast repertoire of techniques, some of which you offer in your book. In the NTS mix you are playing the Junior Boys track at the 'wrong' speed. Is it the turntable that offers you that freedom? That lets you leave the right tempo behind: slow techno to dub, speed something else up.

A multi-instrumentalist sees an instrument and they can just pick it up and play because they have an understanding of the concrete and theoretical basis of what constitutes the musical. I see myself in a similar way but not in terms of being musical: with recorded sound I see it all, I know how to manipulate it in certain ways because I don't want to hear it for what it was supposed to be. This is just something that has happened over time. And you need to factor in that I grew up in Houston, Texas, the *home* of DJ Screw! So messing with pitch has always been a part of how I listen to songs, because I grew up listening to Screw tracks on the radio and learning that this type of manipulation was not only popular, it was acceptable to a larger audience.

So now even if I really like a song the way it was produced, I'm going listen to it backwards, slow it down, speed it up so I can hear all the different ways it can sound, and from there I can pick the best version (in my opinion) and share that with the audience. I love listening to tracks that are sped up so fast they only last a few seconds. Have you ever done that?

No.

If you change the pitch so that it is not so chipmunk-y, the whole song itself, when it has been sped up to just three or five seconds long it becomes its own 'sample' almost. Like a tone key, its own idea. If you place a number of the sped-up songs together to take up a two-minute sequence then you have just made a song. So instead of listening to the song as a full idea, you're listening to it as a point or note or sample in a song. But you need to change the pitch so it is not at an annoying frequency due to the fast playback rate. And another strategy is reversing the 'note' to see if THAT is even better than the original.

With the Junior Boys track you asked about, I had the record, it was forty-five rpm, I accidentally played it at thirty-three and I just loved how they sounded like big black gay gospel singers, the voice took on more meaning, the pace of it took on more meaning. That same track I listen to backwards, too. The version backwards is even more intense though, I love it because I can handle it, but some people don't like to mess with their listening in that way. Did that make sense?

Absolutely. We'll talk more about the turntable in a little bit but before then I want to pick up something that struck me after reading different interviews with you, Maria. A word that I was surprised to encounter as much as I did in those interviews was "sculpture". I know that you have an installation practice and there is that incredible piece you made for the Getty Museum, Crumbling & Responding, *which is a more literal sculpture, with the expected physicality, shape and formal qualities. I'm interested in those installations but also in your wider language of sculpture: you talk about your book as an interactive sculpture, elsewhere you refer to your performances as sound sculptures. Is that word "etching" you just used part of your definition of sculptural?*

I was already getting into a fine art terminology for the word sculpture in 2004, but I think the sculptural aspect of it really became more apparent as I started to look at the vinyl surface area as terrain and to realise the affinities I have with earthworks / land art. My hero is Robert Irwin—

<interrupting> *Irwin? Oh, cool!*

—yes, *Seeing Is Forgetting the Name of the Thing One Sees* is my bible. I feel like the way that he evolved as an artist has so many parallels to the way that I see my work. And I feel that I'm still too young to be able to fully contextualise and understand how to explain it, but conversations like the ones we are having and being in books like this are really helpful. Seeing Irwin's arc from starting with a flat surface and white paint, to light fixtures, to the curve of the horizon and the different angles with the sun in relation to the Earth's orbit. And then utilising architecture as the meeting point of the two by placing white scrim within the architecture to further highlight the sunlight's relation to the meeting point, that simplicity of the white scrim as the 'artistic material' is the type of artistic arc that any artist would be so lucky to get to have. Talk about 'bird's eye view'! You see that simplicity in the earthworks of Nancy Holt and Robert Smithson as well as in Donald Judd's work. Of course, because I'm from Texas and I grew up with Judd's sculptures and installations, so the simplicity has always been something I was intrigued by.

I feel an affinity towards those who moved away from an original fine arts practice into an embodiment of a more visceral sense of perspective, of a phenomenology of perspective in the mind: that's something that I've always been interested in but with sound or with objects.

So when you start to think about Earth, topography and terrain, the parallels between the turntablism surface area and the needle aggressively oscillating between audio grooves, so much so that it chips away at the material, that essentially amounts to a live sculpture session, right? Kind of like trying to paint a name onto a grain of rice, the chiselling is miniscule, on a microscopic scale that it is not possible for anyone to see the work, you can only hear the chiselling and result of the action. And the sculpture evolves. Not just through my own interactions, but also because time itself subtracts from the sculpture since the surface area is so fragile. This is what I like to call "The Language of Time".

Nice.

So my live performances are really subtractive sculpture sessions; subtractive because the needle is chiselling away at the audio, the vinyl is the material that is being subtracted (or added to, if I decide to place some smashed vinyl shards on top of themselves). Considered like this, there is less of a musical relationship and more clearly a sculptural practice. The difference is that it can only be experienced through live watching and listening in process. One can almost look at it like a pottery wheel but I'm not pulling up clay to make a bowl, I'm pulling up sounds.

There is one Charlemagne Palestine record I've been ruining for ten years; you can never put a needle on it and hear it the way it was originally meant to be, it's now almost complete white noise. The sounds that are recorded into the record are incredibly glitchy and it is awesome, it is so ruined, you wouldn't even know it was him. I've been deconstructing that record for so long that the combined results of my performing it, of it living with me and touring with me for all that time, mean that the scars of time it bears cause the needle to just jump up and down and dance around on its own. I love to listen to it. It's all about time, time as an organic process that teaches me.

I like what you're saying here about Robert Irwin, about the material qualities of what you're doing, about the potter's wheel. I am reminded of the performance Llafeci *in 2012. I don't know how to pronounce the title of the work—but I do know that* Llafeci *is the 'Icefall' of Nobukazu Takemura's track title read backwards!*

Ah! You figured it out! Yes, it's a form of composing I call "Sonic Scoring" where I produce a short 'sonic idea' through those manipulation tactics such as speeding, slowing, pitch-shifting, editing and reversing, then have an acoustic instrumentalist listen to the piece for a time, before I take the score away and the performer has to perform the piece from memory. For *Llafeci*, I invited Audrey Chen to listen to my three-minute manipulation of Takemura's original 'Icefall', which is chopped and screwed (edited and pitched down a lot) and reversed. I then spoke to Audrey about the WAV file once she had finished listening to it and began messing with her memory, talking about different parts of the piece that I would like to hear more of when we performed later. I didn't want her to play the piece back exactly how I had manipulated it because our performance needed to be longer than three minutes and that's not the point of the track. It's just a mental seed in their heads that then mingles with their experiences and other memories and then blooms when they're put on the spot in front of an audience. Then I found sound sources around the venue area which I then activated in the space itself, creating a percussive element that transformed the performance into improvised, site specific work.

A different sonic score I created for the Orchestra of St. Luke's had a ten-minute duration as a seed for them to internalise. I anticipated that because they were professional musicians, their methods for memorising would be expected to be really good, and I wanted to challenge that. The first time the Orchestra played the piece, it ended up being eight minutes long, so they must have been nervous. By the third performance, their rendition had stretched to thirteen minutes: to watch the piece change like that without having any control over it was the whole point of the compositional form. It was satisfying to see that not only had the idea worked, but equally encouraging to have the strong impression that had the orchestra been given still more time, it would probably have gotten even cooler.

I was thinking that one aspect of your work that is prominent is its engagement with a visuality of sound. In your book Of Technique *there are the diagrams such as the one for the "typewriter technique"; and then there is your exhibition in Richmond, Virginia,* The Topography of Sound, *where these incredible paintings become that terrain you have been talking about this evening, become the geographical.*

I feel my work going toward a land art route, for sure. I am also interested in making installations that use renewable energy sources like solar power, so should my work need sonic emission I have the option of showing it outside in real topographical terrain. That's where the work is going now. For my latest album Maria Chavez *Plays (Stefan Goldmann's 'Ghost Hemiola')*, I take one- to two-second samples of physical vinyl glitches that I created from Goldmann's original locked grooves, then stretch them between twenty minutes and sixty minutes in length. I then layered the original glitch samples with the expanded version so as to juxtapose these two distinct approaches from the same source. Each sequence of these stretched out glitches, in my mind, can be seen as the equivalent to a non-linear audio walk, where you're just walking through sound waves. The album is also non-linear as a playback technology, so while there is a track listing you don't need to listen to it in numerical order, you just pick your adventure and take a walk through a sound canyon. So as you listen you can envision yourself walking through this canyon of sound which is actually just a three second glitch.

The next phase will be to start working with the National Park Service and propose to do a literal audio hike in a canyon with solar powered speakers lined along the hike, so as you walk along the trail the sound walks with you, so then you become the needle that is playing the glitch. I want to make it as accessible as possible, not just able-bodied persons, so I'll need to work with the government or Park Service to ensure the idea can be experienced by everyone.

It's funny, this whole approach started in 2007 as an idea for cutting poorly EQ'd frequencies onto a blank vinyl record and calling it a sculpture due to the 'topography' I had cut into it. Now it has evolved from a painting exhibition to a land art installation. That's the kind of arc I like to see in my work over time.

One of the things that you said earlier related to the emotional intentions involved in you thinking about being part of this audience-performer exchange. I was listening to the piece you created for Documenta 14 called Between A Gunshot and a Whisper. *And I don't know if you've ever looked at the file on Soundcloud, but the listener comments are incredible, very attentive. I think those responses are interesting because the material you are working with in that composition is library music, Foley records, sound effects records, which become a kind of cultural memory because we hear them so often. You were just talking about canyons and I was thinking about how that same environment has been scored through Western films so that the High Plains become associated with a particular bird song or the reverberant ricochet of the bullet.*

Yeah, each culture has their own sounds, don't they, even their own media sounds? I wanted to make a piece that focused on these sounds but at the same time wasn't limited to being 'about' these sounds. I sourced sound effects records from all around the world and I saw that process of collecting as a means to learn the 'normal' sounds these different cultures were listening to when vinyl was the only available playback technology. I really enjoyed the playfulness of using samples of an Italian baby crying from the 1960s or a Greek family watching TV in the 1970s for this high art Biennale. That baby crying was used in radio plays, adverts. I chose the title *Between A Gunshot and a Whisper* to evoke a sweeping through of social sound; those sound effects records once existed out of necessity but now they're just waste, people don't find them useful at all. It's an archaeological dig that I'm then accentuating with my own sonic practice. I found these media ghosts and thought about the memory and energy in them and then blended them with elements from the archive of my own previous soundwork: what I like to call "sonic vignettes". So, it is an archaeological dig in a lot of ways; to me it was the sonic equivalent of a museum, with different exhibitions in different rooms but in sonic form, a relic with new contemporary work layered on top.

Does what you are saying relate to field recording at all?

Yes, I don't know if you have noticed this with my installation work but the common leading line is field recording and, although I've not spoken publicly about it, I've been developing this over many years and I am writing about it at the moment. The whole idea is a form of field recording practice that I'm calling Hyper Memory Installations—abbreviation 'HMI'.

Hyper Memory Installations involve taking the audio of a field recording file, such as a WAV file, importing it into your Digital Audio Workstation—I use Reaper—and then duplicating, editing and layering until you create a memory of a moment that never existed, a sonic photograph of time, manipulated to no longer look like the original. Sound familiar?

In 2018, I created an HMI called *The Centre and Periphery* for the *SoundScapes* exhibition at the Moss Arts Centre, Virginia Tech. I compounded five days of field recording that I made during my time as a Rauschenberg Fellow at the Robert Rauschenberg estate and turned those 'sonic memories' into a 5.1 multichannel installation. The Rauschenberg estate is on Captiva Island on the Gulf Coast of Florida; it's a microclimate where there are a lot of unique birds and vegetation, where sea turtles lay eggs. Originally, I wanted to record that time for personal documentation because it was so important, creatively, for me, but when the gallery got in touch, I decided to create a Hyper Memory Installation of my time on the island. The work is called *The Centre and Periphery* to represent the position of the microphone at the centre that is recording the periphery. It's also a nod to Robert Smithson and his writings about the *Spiral Jetty*. When you start to utilise the field recordings within the HMI parameters, then you are offering participants a new environment that they will never know. They will only know the HMI and walk away with *that* as *their* memory. So, in my opinion, the HMI process is a creative approach presenting field recording as an artwork, rather than just having the recordings as documentation or as an academic discipline.

If you had told me in November that you were doing field recording, I would have rolled my eyes because there seemed to be so many people doing it. Now, however, we are in the virus era and I am going to eat my words: I am so grateful that everybody was field recording when they were because now we have a document of a time that no other society had the ability to document. And I think it is really important that we all, in our diverse ways, try to create an archive and collect the sounds of our world pre-virus.

When are you going to publish your thoughts on this?

Probably in 2021, probably with me self-publishing again.

Great. I read an interview with you on the Canadian Electroacoustic Community website where you used the expression, "The turntable just happened to be there". The connection to chance and the accident feels important in your work.

As I said before, the turntable is an implement to help further advise my relationship with chance—I call it a never-ending staircase of manifesting. The turntable is chance, it all started with chance and because chance created this for me, I'm very loyal in return. Yeah, she's brutal but she's so sweet: "she", because I think chances are female energies.

Everything is chance, but it's not chaos?

Controlled chaos? Kind of like sitting in the Colosseum of Roma, the chaos is in the centre and we are all sitting outside of the circle looking in and watching. So, there is chaos—but I don't try to correct the chaos. I don't see chaos as something to avoid but something to watch in order to get a handle of it.

How do you feel about the word glitch? Do you feel like it is something that describes a part of your practice?

Technically speaking, it is not a glitch because that is a term reserved for a digital malfunction. But a skip on a record is a physical glitch. In a way it's the precursor to the digital glitch. The skip is a nick in time that left its mark and since I see my work in topographical terms I do feel that glitch is the result of the chiselling and that is a major sonic component in my work.

You've been quite open about your health condition. And you have talked previously about other health conditions and I think it has been very inspiring to a lot of people who live differently with different bodies and different minds. The way you introduced your Kitchen performance was powerful and poignant at the same time.

I'm grateful that you saw it that way, thank you. When I decided to have brain surgery, I had to understand that it would involve completely postponing two years of my life in order to ensure that the operation was a success and I would never have to undergo it again. As a consequence, I had to be open about my health for the very practical reasons that my professional artistic diary was booked through 2021 and I was having to turn opportunities down, to cancel tours. It was so painful. I also had to be public about the situation because my condition was deteriorating, and people kept asking if I was having a stroke. It had got to the point that I couldn't sleep as the spasms were happening 24/7, every second of every day, no way to stop them so I also just needed to tell people because it was so obvious. So my openness was practical, initially, but afterwards I saw that it also gave a lot of people who were dealing with chronic disorders and disabilities themselves a sense of relief in knowing that someone they admire was also suffering like them. In a way, I was coming out as being disabled to my community. And through that I was able to connect with those who were themselves disabled in different ways, and to provide a safe space for them to feel validated in their own frustrations. While I was in recovery, I was still maintaining my Instagram and I got so many messages. Sometimes it was just people checking in on me, but there were also comments from followers who were healing from various surgeries. That experience allowed me to appreciate that I had healing sisters and brothers all over the world, and to recognise that I am part of the disabled community through my brain disorder; that made me want to ensure that all of my work can be inclusive and safe for all bodies.

Do you think that there's sexism, too, in the way that—

—there's nothing that white-skinned artists, especially women, hate more than a brown-skinned woman that's better than them at everything! Just look at how jealous Kate Middleton is of Meghan Markle. The bullying Meghan has endured is so relatable it's honestly a little uncanny. If you walk into these music and art communities with more talent than the white-skinned people they will see you as an enemy or someone they must befriend in order to control. Technically, women that look like me are not supposed to have this kind of knowledge about conceptual sound art, let alone have access to the equipment for it. But my work is so relevant that it stands on its own and is supported via my fans and many amazing curators that see through the BS and understand the depth of the oeuvre of my work, not just the turntablism part of it. But it's important for white-skinned artists to devalue Black, POC and non-black artists' work, forcing them to only make relevant works about their traumas, not about contemporary art discourse. Just look at how Hip Hop has been treated. It's a global phenomenon and yet is devalued left and right by the art and music industries because the white bias cannot allow the public to realise the importance that it has or else they will lose their positions of power. So when I came into the scene with all of the good ideas and great performance practice, the NYC white-skinned artists (I say white-skinned because some of my bullies are of South American or Asian descents, but have white complexions) saw my enthusiasm and talent as a reflection of their own lack and began to slander and financially interfere.

With the brain surgery, they really were not sure how to twist that to make me look bad, but they're def figuring it out. Here I am, so much more capable and active than they are and yet they are more successful than me. That's not a coincidence or mistake, that is what slander and intimidation does to people like me in this world. It holds us in a position where we just watch them thrive while we struggle alone with no support. Thankfully, my fans and supporters have given me so many vehicles to share the practice in more underground ways, and that's the only thing that's helped me get through all of this without any support that the white-skinned artists receive.

When I was on my last tour, a regular day would involve landing in a city and immediately going to a university to teach a workshop, change in my hotel room and perform turntablism in a museum in the evening, then DJ later that night in a club, then head to the next city the next morning. No one else in my scene has the ability to do all of those things in one day because they are only known in terms of the one thing that they do. I'm not restricted like that because I am so multi-faceted, I do it all and I'm amazing at it and they know it. I think the fact that I haven't let the lack of support get to me is why I can still stay here after fifteen years in New York. Even during a medical sabbatical I still have a career that is doing the work on its own, and that is not always the case for other people in my age group. It makes me angry and I will stand up for myself when the time is right. But my tormentors get away with this behaviour because of white supremacy / white bias. If one complains then it gets scoffed at, dismissed, avoided, then you become trouble for them because you are talking back, which makes you lose even more opportunities. And that is financial interference. This is a lot more serious than people want to admit, the inequalities of the situation create devastating mental and financial costs, some are pushed towards suicide.

So every creative act, every release of a new track, every time I am interacting with my audience, regardless of the medium, is a political act: it is a collective statement that says "I belong here. I deserve to be here and you will never get to decide that—no matter how much slander you spread around about me". Because I have my loyal fanbase now, I'm written about in history books. The support of my fans and of institutions are acts of allyship towards the movement for inclusivity, they constitute the solidarity of lovely people who enjoy the output and believe in my humanity.

Mark Peter Wright

In my memory, Mark Peter Wright's contribution to the 2008 *Audio Forensics* exhibition provided headphones for visitors to listen through, but also furnished his part of the IMT gallery with objects in vitrines, black and white photographs, and a book to leaf through. I'm looking at a later edition of that book now, reading Mark's field notes and poems; looking at two adjacent images depicting string that has been passed through a gap in a ruined wall before being wrapped around an eroded brick; spotting quotes from Jacques Derrida and, most winningly for me, from Annie Dillard. I have forgotten doing this—and it is unlike me—but twelve years ago I must have folded the IMT exhibition floor plan and placed it in the book, alongside the pale, odourless, feather that the author had inserted there.

In his discussion for this book, Mark—who went on to become a doctoral student at CRiSAP and with whom I collaborated on the *Decoys* project—subtly distances himself from this period of his work. However much he has moved on from *A Quiet Reverie* and the expectations it subsequently generated, I think it made audible—in fainter form—some of the concerns he would later magnify and complexify: the oscillation between site and non-site, the theoretical pitch, the migration between media, the attentiveness to the unheard as a vibrant constituent of sound, the account of the material as sensorial and pedagogic, the blurring of processes of research, production and exhibition.

These are very strange times. How are you coping?

Well apart from just trying to cope emotionally, physically and in relation to friends and family, I have been thinking about how Covid-19 reaffirms that planetary health is undoubtedly linked to human health, and you can't really isolate one from the other. Nothing is a separate issue and this moment seems to have heightened that point. Almost 60% of all disease is zoonotic in that viruses originate from wildlife. But it is the disruption caused by humans through processes such deforestation, farming, and animal markets that is actually unlocking and bringing those relations closer to humans than ever before. Scientists now talk about an 'ecology of disease' but I would add 'political' to that phrase. This virus is a political issue at the level of racial and social justice as well as the environment.

Those two things don't have much historical pairing in the environmental humanities but they need to be linked up for sure.

While looking at your work in advance of talking this afternoon, one of the terms that recurs in your writing, in the titles of your projects and in your research statements, is that of listening. I would like to start by asking you how early listening contributes to your practice, particularly, initially at least, in terms of when it comes into the process of your work?

I would say that an interest in sound has nurtured a longer-seeded inquiry into listening. The two are difficult to disentangle. Sound, for me, is a kind of material political agent connected to power and to issues of causality, and I work with this context always in mind. What intrigues me is that sound doesn't necessarily give up these things in definite knowing ways, it acts as an inference. I often talk about sound as an itinerant actor but also as an obstinate medium that doesn't fully disclose itself. So, I think my listening grew from those experiences and has become a search for the disclosed and the undisclosed in the sonic.

I comprehend listening as an apophenia of sorts, also called audio pareidolia, where patterns of meaning are made as a necessary process of interpretation. Listening emerges from a space where knowledge can be as lost as easily as it can be found, and this has shaped my interests as a practitioner. The contexts I deal with such as ecology and climate mirror this tension, as issues of cause and effect are often obfuscated and not always revealed in full visibility or audibility.

Given what we know of listening as a modality that has apparently been less extensively embraced than other senses, does engaging with listening mean having to simultaneously engage others in listening? Does that involve a kind of pedagogy?

Yes, I actually think this is where my listening has been more and more located in the last few years. Listening-with with others, for example with students in the context of teaching and learning, is to think about the imaginative and interpretive powers of audition and analysis. Listening in the classroom is a collective 'stress testing' of sound and the ways in which we can decode and recode some of sound's open and locked information. I think of listening being connected literally to the word research, to continually be searching and researching, to be finding and re-finding without ever a completeness or an absolute truth. When I listen to something, whether in the field, the editing suite or classroom, the gaps that I hear are the missing links that often send me elsewhere: they send me to research again and again, to listen again and again, and to find things, including other sites of audition such as the archive. So, it's a listening pedagogy that's partial and co-constructed, and comes from following flows of information, perspectives and senses that are not always easy to apprehend.

Does that collective listening that you have just sketched point to a participatory dimension to your work? Was that part of your Leverhulme Trust-funded project in Manchester?

To some extent yes, but participatory is a very big word. The subjects of my own work—humans-animals-technology—are not things that can be effortlessly dealt with as an individual, you often need to crowdsource minds, bodies, ears, and tools. I think participation comes from a crosshatch of practice and of listening-with environments and species, as it does from human-orientated methods as well. Perhaps the word that I am thinking in the back of my head is actually collaboration. It feels necessary in these times to work with other people, other beings, other forms of knowledge and that, by contrast, the idea of the artist-researcher as a self-isolated genius seems long gone. Instead, the necessity right now is to join up across disciplines and, when I'm thinking optimistically, listening can be an interesting portal for those connections. The Leverhulme residency at Manchester Metropolitan University located some of this thinking as I worked with geography and educational practitioners to investigate the potential for a 'sensational pedagogy', where bodies, technologies and affective relations participate and disrupt conventional forms of linguistic transmission and representation.

One of the things that you have said relates the listening in which you are interested—whether it's co-creational, or co-productive, or something that's more connected to you as an individual—to these qualities of the critical, the imaginative and the interpretative. I wonder whether those are qualities that you associate with listening as it is conducted within a sound arts context, or whether those qualities pertain to listening itself and, as such, find themselves replicated in other contexts such as the ones that you encounter in your postdoctoral research work for the Listening Across Disciplines *project?*

Approaching listening in both imaginative and critical ways is something I try to hold on to constantly with my own work: to think of practice as serious play, to be critically and ethically provocative whilst also having a point of access for another discipline or for a public that is not entrenched in sound arts. Things like humour and play can help with that, I think. I do not know if sound or listening always affords both the imaginative and critical, but for me the creative side of listening needs to be 'tethered' to realities, so that there is a genuine friction that can spark praxis and debate.

When you were talking about serious play just then, one of the dimensions you addressed was about how you can engage a public who are not entrenched in sound arts practices, discourses and histories. That leads me to ask a question about listening as a virtuosic space. On the one hand, the pattern-discerning aspects of listening that you talked about involve high-level skills in filtering, processing, discriminating, which sounds positive. On the other hand, in my experience, the virtuosic can become alienating. Is that a dilemma that you consider?

I don't consider myself a virtuosic person at all. I'm sure I have some ingrained knowledge and methods of listening but as a practitioner I want to remain open to the hi and the lo. Working across media is a very pragmatic example of this, it shifts the focus away from a sound-centric ear and asks whether a sculpture might take some of that sensory hierarchy away? I've thought about this for years by exhibiting in public spaces, writing grant applications, thinking about the aural diversity of audiences that might come into a show.

Going back to what I said about serious play, I do think play and humour constitute points of access which have helped my work reach different types of disciplines and different types of audiences. I've been thinking about hope as well, in pedagogy and practice, as a similar tool or strategy. Climate journalism has identified a perceived phenomenon called the hope gap, the apparently ever-increasing discrepancy between what needs to be done and what can be done. I think hope is important, not necessarily in a utopian definition, but as a device for access, for crossing disciplines, for embracing different expertise, building communities and practices of affirmation. Humour, play or hope then are sort of keys I can give to the audience so that they can unlock what might be otherwise deemed hermetically-sealed sound art.

OK. I want to move on to a next set of questions which engage with process in your work. Is it possible for you to divide up a project into stages that have labels such as 'research', 'production', 'installation'? Or are these just arbitrary categories that get applied retrospectively?

That's an interesting question. As you know, each project is so different according to the funding, the context, the support, and as a result it is hard to specify any universal processes. I know that when a project goes really well, those stages you referred to dissolve into each other, they start to affect one another at all times. Having said that, I can learn a lot from analysing the phases afterwards. Thinking about those three divisions of research, production, installation, the sequence might actually be reversed. If I'm lucky enough to know that a work is going to be installed in a certain gallery, I will work backwards from there to the start, with aesthetic and spatial decisions around form and audience being at the front of my thinking. Research is always ongoing and production might be a little more 'stop start' depending on resources and practical considerations such as space.

If it is difficult to divide a project into successive steps and if the project radiates outwards in different ways, does that mean that it is equally hard to tell when you've started on a project?

Absolutely! 100%! Often the lag is phenomenal, it could be literally five years. Or longer! Earlier today, I was working on the 'protocols' part of the Listening Across Disciplines project on which I'm a post-doctoral researcher, and I suddenly turned to Salomé Voegelin who is leading the project and said "I've just remembered an exhibition I had in 2012 where I effectively made a protocol for entering and leaving the field". I often have these lagged, staggered revelations of when a process or a piece of work actually started and, conversely, when it might have ended. These are very useful moments for a kind of self-learning. Reflecting on these processes, I would say that I come back to questions that function as 'memory triggers', the biggest of which relates to "What am I not hearing?" If I get stuck, it helps to remember that question and shift my ear towards it. Whatever step I'm working on, whether I am recording a space or place outdoors, whether I am in an editing suite putting sounds together, or in the classroom teaching, I try to remember the margins, issues of authorship, the voices often left out, of noise and the acoustic life-worlds above and around anything that I can perceive as a human.

Following on from what you said about these 'memory triggers', I am interested to hear if you are conscious of there being an overall contour that is described by the individual shapes formed from each of your projects? If you do have such a sense, is it sufficiently resolved that it informs the choices you make about pursuing commissions, responding to opportunities, materialising those opportunities?

That is a really difficult question for me, it is challenging. To rewind, I used to think about what it meant to make a consistent body of work and I can clearly remember that when I received the British Composer of the Year in Sonic Arts Award in 2009, things came towards me in terms of public perception and commissions. I could a feel pigeon-holing taking place around my practice and the expectation of having an identifiable body of work—that was actually quite restrictive. In response, I wanted to escape the identity of being a soundscape composer and so started to shapeshift. As a result, I no longer have a sense of that overall contour you referred to.

Was there not a point when the shape of your work related to questions of site?

I'm thinking out loud here, but I feel that much is wrapped up with a concept I have used in my work called the Noisy-Nonself, which relates to a prototypical field recording character, part-recordist, part-microphone, a monstrous assemblage of human-animal-technological. Over the years 'site' has become 'sites' for me, plural. Media as a site, listening as a site always tied to an elsewhere, the body, technology and so on.

Practice is built in this mosaic. The field is a patchwork and I'm part of its tapestry. So, if there is a shape, it is monstrous, and I'm learning to notice that.

In a strange—monstrous?—way, this discussion segues into what you might initially consider a different tangent but which I hope you will recognise as connected. You are currently writing a book for Bloomsbury, you have a PhD, you speak in academic contexts, you are fluent in theoretical discourse—and more than that I think you enjoy that theory. Is the theoretical encounter a site for you?

Yes, it feels like that. I do enjoy theory, but not unless it is connected to practice. I'm not a philosopher, and reading theory within its own lineage is beyond my ability. What I can do is think with theory through my practice and, hopefully, through the practice of others. What has been interesting for me in terms of writing my book is the realization that a number of the conceptual devices that I'm now developing and deploying in the book come directly from my practice. The Noisy-Nonself character is one I have written up in the first chapter, and it has been important to recognise that this practice is one which has come from trying to listen to the margins, in my work, and in the history of field-recording and anthropological fieldwork. Now that I understand that persona as a conceptual figuration, I can test it with the work of others, not just in an interpretative mode but also in my work with students as a tool for debate.

The way you have just responded promotes a question which had been previously been relegated further down my list, a question about whether sound arts needs its own theoretical discourse. Is it necessary?

It would be nice for it to have such a discourse, but I don't think it's necessary. This might unravel as I speak, but what interests me about sound arts discourse is when it connects up to other disciplines, other theories and other histories. Its ability to be 'more-than' excites me—I enjoy it. I like setting sound within an ecology of the senses or within an ecology of discourse, disciplines, and expertise. If we think of sound arts as an organism within a set of relations, for sure it has its own niche, its world-making, its texts and discourse. I don't personally feel I can write those texts because I don't feel that committed to the exclusive sensory or linguistic lure of sound as a more exceptional medium than any other. I prefer the meshwork that sound sits in and with, that includes other senses and other discourses.

Is there something about the way the sound operates or the way that sound art operates that lends itself to this kind of plurality, this multiplicity, this openness?

Perhaps. As you know, sound is full of power, violence and erasures. Sound can operate as promise and threat and, for me, that is always something to remember. However, what I think sound does do is lead you elsewhere, if you follow it. Sound leads to questions, more sounds and more listening. Again, this connects back into iterative research-ing through the to and fro of theory and practice. So perhaps there is something multiple in sound's partial and generative status.

If there is a conventional understanding of sound art as being that which attaches to the sounded, if we are to follow it, as you suggest, how will we be able to address the inaudible or the silenced?

The inaudible is really key, which is why I keep returning to focus on the question of "What am I not hearing?" That question is a trigger for new methods and new practices, and it surfaces responsibilities as an artist.

Does that then lead us towards a consideration of sound and sound arts through the filter of what you have been calling the 'post-natural'?

My idea of a post-natural sound arts is an attempt to locate practice within conditions of anthropogenic entanglement and devastation, where the illusion of a rarefied nature no longer exists. As a framing device it veers more towards waste than water, to noise as opposed to pristine signal. These are things we might say are inaudible, the hidden or overlooked. Using a post-natural frame allows an unpicking of the colonial contexts around ethnomusicology and technological resource extraction. Gripping a microphone is never neutral, there's a whole web of cause and effect embroiled in a supply chain of sites, minerals and labour. These are the inaudible and silenced signals we must endeavour to hear. That's the curious thing about sound, again: that the signal is always broad whether audible or not. Even with a contact mic you are pulling in all these other frequencies that are joined to histories, cultures and practices of listening, whether you hear them or not. The geophone, for example, is connected to listening to enemies in trenches; the contact microphone came out of the throat microphone that was attached to fighter pilots' necks. I really believe that those histories, those practices and technological resources, are in the lineage of the signal whether you can hear them or not.

This question is about the more-than-human. Going back to the pilot and the subterranean trench warfare which announce military and colonial contexts for recording technologies, are there other contexts—audible or not—around animality, such as the Common Sharma that I know you have written about in terms of its 'capture' by Ludwig Koch?

The first chapter of the book I am writing involves locating the field in the midst of its nebulous definitions. There are so many precedents where the field is either a cage or an internment camp or is produced through servitude, both of the human and the more-than-human. Another dimension relates to eco-sonic media, Jacob Smith's term which draws evidence from how actual media embroil cultural and historical practices as well as the bodies and labour of animals. One example that was historically prevalent was the shellac disk where the material was derived from insect carapaces. In the last chapter of my book, I am trying to perform a geology of the microphone by tracing the neodymium magnets that allow it to work along with copper and other processed resources. That geology is another kind of more-than-human, another kind of inaudible, I think.

Through your works The Thing About Microphones *or the ongoing series* Unsiting Sound, *you remind us that we are somehow still within the force field created around recording by Ludwig Koch and others at the end of the nineteenth century. You've talked about the inaudible, but another aspect of the microphone is its invisibility, how attempts are made to hide it from the TV viewer or cinema audience. Like the flesh-coloured microphone or the boom pole held aloft, they are kept out of the picture, hidden.*

How we try to locate inaudible content differs, I think, depending on whether we are talking about analogue or digital media. With analogue, you can read more, you can literally decipher more since there is more signal there, whether it is noise or not, there is more to get your ears around than the digital. Noise provides a huge amount of context in terms of media archaeology, allowing you to hear when something was made, what type of recording material was involved. There are losses and hidden elements imbued in digital formats too, but perhaps the process of auditioning them is a little different. Noise is not so apparent, so it becomes more a case of listening for the positioning of a microphone in the field, or the cut of an edit in the work suite. One of my favourite things on TV is just catching a glimpse of a microphone accidently popping into view. Suddenly it'll get pulled back out of the picture or the editor will switch shots. There's a feeling of shame almost in that moment, like the microphone is the most abject thing imaginable. That's where I like my listening to go. I want to try and reclaim those para-sites as material that's valid and worthy of creative and critical audition.

Are things different, then, in your Matterlurgy guise, the creative collaboration with Helena Hunter?

My collaborative work with Helena Hunter [Matterlurgy] explores the intersections of art, science and technology in relation to environmental change. Our approach is interdisciplinary as we work with so many different fields, media, expertise, communities and ages. It is quite a tentacular process when you work with lots of people but again, it feels right given the current interlacing of humans and nonhumans, and not wanting to work in a top-down transmission way. Our projects have dealt with air pollution, waste and flooding. I guess you could say these are sort of invisible and obscure processes that can be difficult to directly point at. These subjects can also lead to apocalyptic, end-of-the-world tropes very quickly. It's something we always want to steer away from. We try to deal with the context we are working in and the urgency/agency of a given environment or community. A recent project in Norway for example, called *Flom Sang (Flood Song)*, was made with students, a brass band, local community members as well as our own practice of sound and experimental writing. The work is centred around a four-channel sound installation, installed in a former hydropower station, that brings together these elements into one shared sonic space. Thinking back to the inaudible, we made this work by combining our own practice with the imagination and creativity of people invested in the community. Importantly, we listened to voices that often go unheard and which fall outside the conventional idea of the expert (children and amateur musicians). This allowed us to steer clear of grand narratives around flooding, and instead focus on the lived and imagined experience of being with water, in all its confluences, impacts and complexity.

Mikel R. Nieto

When introducing the other artists in this book, I took care to establish how it was an identified and named range of work which created a context for my engagement. Mikel R. Nieto does have such a range and a lot of it is familiar to me; it is a range that has been stretched further in the time since we spoke with, in a relatively short number of months, a bewildering number of workshops, compositions for dance and performance, essays, print works, and separate releases as vinyl, flexidisc, cassette, SD card, and a data folder containing two hundred secrets that was deleted with no possibility of recovery. Although I acknowledge this range, and am much impressed by it, the work of Nieto's that I keep returning to is his *Dark Sound* project, constituted by a black CD in a black book with texts in three languages printed in black ink that is only visible in sunlight. To acquire the *Dark Sound* book involves paying a price which is pegged to the current barrel cost of Brent Crude, a gesture to connect hydrocarbon extraction with territorial appropriation and other violence to indigenous inhabitants, and to amplify Western consumers' (and artists'?) complicities in the these processes.

I connected through Skype to Nieto who was sat in San Sebastián at the outdoor table of what sounded like a boisterously crowded café close by a well-used road junction. Somehow it felt fully appropriate that our conversation—never itself particularly clearly audible to my ears—was interrupted both by repeated (occasionally protracted) signal drop-outs and by Nieto having to break off to organise a future project.

Maybe there will be a chance for us to have a second meeting where we manage to meet up in flesh too?

For sure, that would be cool.

I'd like that, too. At the moment, I guess one of the things that's interesting is the difference between flesh and not flesh, between being together present in the same space and being together at a geographical distance with technology as some makeshift bridge between the two. Inspired by these circumstances in which we are communicating remotely and by some themes I can hear in your work, one of the questions I have focuses on the question of listening and the specific role this listening adopts in your projects. I know you have worked on many projects, all with their own energies and thematic concerns, and I know we have already spoken about whether you have to use sound to think through sound but, for now, tell me about listening.

In *Dark Sound*, this question is the main subject. The book is mostly an attempt to think through how those from oral cultures such as, for example, the Huaorani people, listen to us. So it's a kind of an effort to investigate how the 'Other' listens to us. That is the idea, anyway; it involves blending reality and fiction in what I think is, for me, one of the most difficult exercises, that of imagining how it is that the Other listens and how it is that the Other's listening can be listened to, can be recorded. In that project there is the more obvious dimension, where we move from the sounds of nature to the sounds of machines, but at the same time, what I am considering is the possibility of listening to the Other.

Maybe one of the ways of approaching this subject would be to connect to the work About Listening *which you created for the publisher Errant Bodies' project space in Berlin? As I understand it you listened to other people's forms of listening practice—you listened to other listeners. Did that ultimately also involve paying attention to the differences between how you yourself listen and how the people you engaged with listened?*

OK. But what do you want to ask me about that?

Well, I think there's an active criticality to your work that differentiates it from some alternative listening perspectives. Perhaps we could start again with another, very specific example: your work, 233 Hours of Listening?

Can you repeat that again? The connection is not so good.

You know the piece of yours called 233 Hours of Listening? *It embodies this notion of eschewing the active, conscious, self-reflexive and always accurate listening agent. That sounds to me like a corrective criticality, one that trips up some of the more sauntering accounts of listening's powers.*

Yeah, for me, sometimes it is the audience that is the listener, the recorder, but I guess I understand what you are asking. My approach to the listening act is somewhat influenced by the books of the French writer Pascal Quignard. I love his work, which is itself quite different because he explores the bad side, the difficult side of sound, music and listening.
   That is his purpose. He is aware of that. I don't have too much commitment to forms of representation that just describe the good parts of things. We all know that whenever there is light there will also be some shadow but we tend to shy away from it. In that sense, in this work, I had realised how unstoppable listening was and because of this, the condition of the listening act could make us, I don't know, less able to enjoy. This

is not about agency, this is not a matter of choice, not something we can decide or decline—we are listening all the time and we cannot escape from that. We are open all the time, and it makes us more vulnerable and it makes the world more fragile. So from that perspective, my approach is closer to Pascal Quignard's in the sense that I want to pay attention to the shadows, to the dark part of the sound—like in the title of my Amazon project you asked about earlier—to the difficult aspects of the listening act. Instead of always celebrating the beautiful, such as in the social, musical listening of a concert, my approach to listening is more dark, is more close—we just can't deny that part of things, we can try but we will fail anyway.

And when you brought up the question of listening in the concert as a celebratory, a social experience, does that mean that if you acknowledge the more difficult side of listening…

Sorry, I'm losing you. I'm going to shut the mic down.

Hold on a minute, should I close the video down?

Can you hear me now?

Yes, I can. Following on from what I was just asking, inspired by you contrasting your orientation from that of the concert as a social celebration, a togethering of listeners, I was wondering whether if one talks about the entangled side of listening, whether it is still possible to evoke a collective listening experience? Or does listening become fragmented into each individual's listening approach? So, when your own body was sleeping for the 233 Hours of Listening *residency, it was a very particular listening that maybe didn't allow for a collective encounter?*

I guess it's difficult. Most importantly, that difficulty attaches to where to establish the limits, the borders for the individual, for where they are coming from, for their listening stance. And this issue of listening borders applies even when people are not aware of it. I was recently sharing a flat with a woman in a building where four families were also living. So even if these other people are not aware of the fact that they are listeners, that they are listening, it doesn't matter: the borders—and the connections—between the individual and the common listening were still active and these are what interest me. I can also illustrate the phenomenon through the voice: in the situation of a choir, even if you are the soloist, singing alone, with everyone else still and unsinging, you should always be listening to those silent others who accompany you. You have your musical score that you have to follow, you have your own voice that you have to pay attention to, but simultaneously you have to be listening to Others, in order to be in the group. So, I guess this is a beautiful example.

Ultimately, it seems difficult to believe in these fixed limits, limits that reveal themselves unambiguously to everyone. At the same time, we like to think about them, we need them somehow, sometimes to explain reality, but I'm not sure that there are these clear, fixed limits to listening that can be identified around us all the time.

Does that mean that if we were to think about a kind of manifesto for listening, a programme for listening, that would be a mistake? To be clear, I'm not being critical of such enterprises, rather I'm just interested to explore what you think.

I don't know if we need a manifesto. There are times when, in general, the manifesto becomes a more popular form and we must be living through one of those periods since I recognise, of course, that there are many alternative manifestos for listening out there. One of the problems with the manifesto connects to that question about fixed limits: when you publish a manifesto, it lists some ideas, some approaches, some conditions, but how can it endure, since it derives from a specific time? Maybe there are some useful examples, but I think a manifesto for listening is likely to be a mistake. However, if the manifesto is offered in consciousness of its own liability to be mistaken, then it is more than welcome.

Even though it is not explicitly a manifesto, nor a programme, what you do in Dark Sound *does constitute a kind of template. At the very least it is an inspiration, and I've used it as such with my First Year students several times. It is an inspiration to consider different listening strategies, to pluralise and multiply, even when the results may be contradictory. So many historical sound projects have been associated with programmes of imperial conquest, forms of ethnographic practice focused on fixing the other as other, and so many of the technologies we deploy find other genealogies in military R&D, it is hard to think of waves to move forward.*

Thanks for your comments about *Dark Sound*, Angus. The truth is, again, I'm not sure. I think we are back with those limits, in a sense. In *Dark Sound*, there is a negotiation, it is like a collective listening between three communities, all of them are Others, for each other, all of the time.

We can adopt the attentiveness that is usually applied to musical instruments and all this social approach to music. But you can also listen to how we listen. I should perhaps mention one example which I included in the book that accompanies the *Dark Sound* project—this example is about how the Huaorani people describe the white people who have come to their territory to extract oil. How can the white people be described, how can what they do be described? The white people's listening is imperial. The indigenous people have been listening since the first contact, they have been listening, and they understand that the places where we reside are best described as the places where the devil sounds. So, in a way, the listening of the white person is comprehended as the listening of a devil.

If we think about the earliest contacts, such as the encounter with Christopher Columbus, we imagine that these took place some five hundred years ago. However, that chronology takes its time perception from a Western idea. For the indigenous peoples, it was not so far back in time, not so long ago, indeed the contact, for them, happens all the time. More than this, it continually rehappens. And yet, they are more than capable of understanding our ecology, and they are applying that understanding. So, it is impossible to set those limits, when it comes to the listening act. We should remember that when we are describing, we are using one set of words, we create and recreate history through words, History is not fixed in that sense. History is dynamic. Facts don't exist in that uncomplicated way and we should try, ourselves, however difficult it is to achieve, to think more in this unfixed way. With *Dark Sound* I wanted to think about a community which was refusing any contact with the Other, and how different listenings can describe different encounters, how each other understands their Other.

Does this connect to your idea of sonic situations?

Yeah, it was difficult for me to find a simple expression to account for what, for me, is fundamental: space plus time. So whatever you are doing—it could be a lecture or workshop or a concert, it could be an installation, it could involve different formats, different media—there is always going to be an arrangement in sound of those two elements—space plus time—there is always going to be a sonic situation, in which the listening act evolves.

Your answer there about formats and sonic situations leads me to ask you about working across media. Maybe a point of departure would be your work Silence Kills, *from 2018, which was in the Tinta Invisible show in Barcelona and was a detournement of the warnings on cigarette packaging.*

Ah, that is a good illustration of my contention that sound does not belong to an exclusive technology. In the past, there were many books about sound and these predated the technological possibilities of audio recording. The discourse about sound and listening that existed long in advance of the historical inventions of sound technologies means we have to accept that we were listening for a long time before we noticed we were holding a microphone in our hands. We were listening and we were aware of sounds. Technology alters relationships, technology opens some possibilities, but technology doesn't make the sound work all on its own. Sounds were there before than any technology. If we think about sound art, we can say that it didn't start with technology and we can certainly say that it is not exhausted by the technological. So even without technology, it is possible to create a piece like *Silence Kills*, to show people that there is another way of listening, or that there are other sonic situations, other possibilities to think about the world, about reality, through sound. I am not always using sound in order to work with the sound itself, but rather to reveal the listening act, the sonic situation; sound is a medium—a connection between things—that doesn't itself demand a sonorous representation: it doesn't need to be manifest in a conventionally audible format. I know this might appear contradictory but sound art doesn't need sound, you can work your way through its presence and its absence.

And does this position that you adopt create difficulties when you work collaboratively with choreographers or other artists? How much do you have to negotiate your listening perspective when you are working with someone from a different practice?

With choreographers and with dancers I have sometimes found it quite difficult to collaborate with them. First of all, with dancers, they are working with the body so that means all the knowledge resides within the body, even the memory of the pieces, the instructions, everything is located within their body. With philosophers, by contrast and by convention, their knowledge is outside, not within, and I can relate this to a quote from Nietzsche who said something like the body of the philosopher is a cage, implying that their bodies are strangers to knowledge. I have found it a challenge to talk to someone whose knowledge is focused on the body because they understand their world in a very different way, a way that accounts for feelings, for how they felt they were in a particular moment.

This type of negotiation between different knowledges is very relevant. I would say that in the last two generations there have been a lot of developments in terms of the creation of musical situations for dancers. Luc Ferrari might be thought of as a good instance of this, at least in terms of how to develop the framework. It is a fascinating area, one in which there are not so many people working experimentally on the dancing body who do not also relent and offer the audience an easier situation through incorporating popular or at least recognisable music.

It is really interesting when you are working to connect the sonic situation to the body—when you connect space, time, the body and sounds simultaneously from scratch. This integrated approach is very different from having a song in the background which becomes an instruction to the dancer—the latter is literally a very laboured situation, where the body is forced to follow the music. And we know that the realities of the situation are that things do not work like this.

The main difference between dance and music is gravity: dancers have to deal with the mechanics of that universal force of attraction as it asserts itself it through their bodies, while music does not, it floats free. How many times have you ever seen a sound plunge? How many times a dancer fall? Examined from this angle, the weakest point of a dancer could be their susceptibility to the force of gravity and their vulnerability to falling. But it is not. The more common weakest point for dancers is sound, more specifically the listening act and their voices. In that sense, the less used part of their body is their own voice. Most of the time, dancers don't know how to use it and enjoy it on the stage.

Music in dance is usually understood in a dichotomy, either as a trigger for movements or as a background noise or soundscape. Both approaches constitute reduced ways to understand the relationship between dancers and composers. Ask yourself: what is dance without music? Can silence be danced?

Sometimes your collaborations work in less orthodox ways, perhaps in more problematic ways. I am thinking particularly of a relatively recent work that you created called The Dungeon, *which involved a collaboration with sex workers.*

Ha! You've been doing your research! Well, as you know, one of my motivations is to explore those parts of society that we tend not to look at, the aural equivalent of blind spots, those that we don't like to listen to. The first time that I went to Cologne, I was totally surprised to discover a brothel of considerable size, a building of seven floors high. That is a lot of men visiting sex workers—I'll keep for myself my opinion about these places, especially because I'm not entirely comfortable with what these places and their situation represents. As I said, this might be one of those parts of society we prefer to ignore, and yet the very size of the place made it difficult to ignore. It turned out that a friend of mine went there and they told me that it resembles a circus, that it was very cheap to enter—something like five euros—and then you get access to the seven floors, off which lead corridors and the women sex workers invite the clients into their rooms. Music is used throughout and I thought that could constitute a way in—exploring which music would be used to designate a particular space. It is the biggest brothel in Europe. So, in collaboration with one of the sex workers, I organised recordings of the general space—we hear the songs 'Somebody to Love', 'Para La Bailar La Bamba', 'Blue Moon', and the commentary on a football match from the TV at the bar—and also we listen in on one of the rooms where clients are taken and the transaction takes place.

I wonder if there are connections between the sonic situation of the brothel in Cologne and the project that I believe you did around the street distribution of cocaine? I know that you had documentation on your website and then password-protected it.

Yeah, I was thinking about that, I thought you were probably going to ask me about that. This is another example of an area of life that we don't like to talk about but which nonetheless constitutes a lived experience in Berlin or in other big cities; I don't know what London is like but I am convinced it is probably going to be relatively easy to access drugs.

As with that other work we discussed, *The Dungeon*, this project started through listening, listening to another friend describe how it was that people usually bought drugs. I was totally surprised at what I heard. The dealers have business cards now, the drugs arrive by car, like a delivery, everything smoothed out by such technologies as smartphones. The point is, whether you like what is happening or not, we should be thinking about these changes; if there are opportunities to use technologies in particular ways then people are going to take them. But these kinds of use of technology are… another blind point in our society, an unheard space, something to pay attention to and learn from.

So, I thought it was quite interesting to develop an exercise, where I could propose access to that transactional situation as a listener, to focus on the listening act. Even if they are not themselves buying the drugs, through this exercise they can connect as a listener, enter the situation as a listener.

<the line goes dead for four minutes>

Sorry about that, it was a phone call from a flexi-disc manufacturer I am working with, he is unsure about the recording I've sent because it is not 'musical'. To him it sounds more like a white noise. For me the technology of the flexi-disc itself sounds good enough. Yesterday we had a meeting at the same printers who worked on *Dark Sound*, the design is for white text on white paper, we were selecting the paper, we were selecting the ink and all the time during the discussions the printers were worried that it would not be functional as a book. It is an experiment and for them it is not easy to predict how it will be in the finished form. Yesterday I had to answer their question, "Do you want the book to be read? To be readable?" My reply was that we just have to be confident in the process, we have to make a test, to experiment. We should fail more and fail in bigger ways. The publisher for this new project—*A Soft Hiss of This World*—is Gruenrekorder, who had previously published my *Dark Sound*; having the same publisher is important because I want the two projects to work in tandem. With *Dark Sound*, the cost depends on the barrel cost of Brent Crude Oil, at current prices that makes it really expensive for someone to buy.

And what do we hear in the A Soft Hiss of This World? Is it actually white noise?

Well, it is somewhat close to that. I went on the Saari Residency that the Kone Foundation organise, which is located in a small place, Mynämäki, Southwest Finland. The point is I went there to record snowflakes. After the residency I made a successful application to a Basque government organisation for the publication itself.

When I was in Paris, I lost all the recordings I'd made because my hard drive died and ate three years' worth of recordings—all because of a friend's laptop charger. At this moment, I had to pause, you know, to take a breath and to try to find a solution to my predicament. Luckily, I had been uploading some images and sounds to Tumblr so I was able to recover a few of those and the recording that I use is a hydrophone recording of ice melting. With the flexi-disc, already a 'noisy' format—every time it gets played it will become noisier.

Talking about Gruenrekorder, this is another dimension of collaboration that interests me: the networks that exist for performance, for recording, for distribution, for those kinds of connections. Do you perceive these important to you? These kinds of collaborations, these kinds of networks?

Yes, they can be, but we should define what is meant by networks. In the case of Gruenrekorder, that is simultaneously a place to find things but also to publish things—it represents a kind of node. Networks are important, because in our artistic practices, we are concerned with the same questions, and this is especially so when we are working with sound—both the general questions and the very specific. In a sense, mostly all humans are preoccupied with similar questions, the same doubts, the same problematics, the same efforts to struggle and deal with them. So, in that way, we are all working together, as sound artists, as experimental musicians.

With collaboration I think the difficulties arise around taking a common decision, making a common decision. That said, there are different approaches to collaboration. For me, it is not only the creation of a community itself that is important but the need, also, to ensure that we are not creating limits that determine, say, if you are a sound artist or not, if you are allowed into this part of the network or not. For me it is very clear—it is about listening. We are all working in relation to listening, even deaf people, perhaps especially them.

You don't like the word network, preferring nodes and constellations?

I prefer to talk about nodes. The word network contains another set of possibilities and although we cannot be totally isolated, even if we try, we do remain connected.

Do you not like network because of its theoretical and historical associations? Theoretical in terms of Manuel Castells's work, historical in terms of labels like net art?

Of course, there are some things that are different but for me these differences are not the most important ones, after all, I don't use Twitter, Instagram. I wonder if we are largely doing the same things—going to work, eating, buying things. Obviously the access to information is faster but if you think about the international cassette network that existed in the 1980s, I wonder if we are necessarily seeing something different than what is there for sound art and experimental music today. Essentially they were sending works, perhaps we are using new channels not just to send but to sell, like Soundcloud; the fact is that more is circulating and maybe the general public can access this more easily?

I want to zoom in on Dark Sound, *which feels a little unfair since there are so many other potential works of yours that could have been subject to more detailed discussion. Nevertheless,* Dark Sound *is my favourite of yours. One of the things I like about the work is that it possesses a density, a density that revealed itself to me at a point when I deliberately shied away from more information about the project, about you. I'm interested in the process through which that density is revealed. Did you know, before you turned a microphone on, that you were doing a project called* Dark Sound?

No, not at all. But I think this is very common, the experience when we are working on something, we have an idea, but are unsure how it will resolve, we are changing some things, we are unsure: this is the beautiful part of the process, you are gathering information, changing your mind. With *Dark Sound* that happened a lot—changing my mind, I mean. With the first application for funding, what I was proposing was something more 'innocent', shall we say. After a while and moving from the research phase to actually writing the book that is part of the project, I realised that I had to change everything about that innocence and that was when I decided to print black on black. Everything is about decisions, decisions that demand your whole attention. It is difficult, because the subject itself is so complicit since all of us use oil, we all make *that* decision, to destroy the Other which means to destroy ourselves, to destroy the Huaorani people, the Taromenane people; we are consumers, we are part of the big decision, whether we like it or not. It was difficult to write this—that is the density you are talking about. The truth is, though, *Dark Sound* is only one chapter. For when I was writing, I was writing more fluently, more easily, and there are another ten chapters.

Ten?

Yes, ten.

Ten, really?

Yes, I was thinking about whether it was a good idea to publish all of the chapters—it would end up being a big book in three languages. Ultimately, it was my choice to publish just one chapter which narrowed to focus on how we listen to the Other; that chapter becomes the key, the key to everything. The other chapters constitute a kind of fictional reality that journeys from the beginning, through our arrival in the Amazon, how they perceived us, how we perceived them (and although we like to think we are the first, a Columbus, obviously that is not the case). The truth is, I have more texts. With all the books I was reading, I realised that they were all talking about history, facts, dates, and some of the chronologies didn't match. It is good to put these discrepancies in a book, to challenge the idea that we can talk about history in a simple way; we need to think about how we change histories, how they are dynamic, how they contain contradictions and this is why the chronology is there.

You have told us about how the text was constructed but what was your approach to the sound, how did you know how to present the sound that appears on the CD?

Mostly what I did was to send a selection of my recordings to Slavek Kwi, the mastering engineer, recordings which went from more natural to more industrial sounds. He, Slavek, made the mix for the CD, so the audio that appears with the book is not mine, it's his, it's Slavek's. I appreciate this approach a lot—an experimental way of doing mastering. I didn't tell him anything before, but strangely he ended up with something close to what I would have done. It was very easy to work with him, I like his work a lot.

Can you imagine a work that goes beyond even this strategy—not just the responsibility for the mix going to someone else but the responsibility for the recording itself?

Well, for *The Dungeon*, only the ambient recordings of the floors and corridors were mine, the sex worker I collaborated with was the person who recorded the interior space with the client. But this is happening anyway—if you look at what is made possible through new business communication platforms, and through things like WhatsApp, the world is filling up with recordings. As an artist, it is about identifying themes, spaces, about pointing your finger. If there are already recordings where I am pointing, why not use those? For me it doesn't matter who made the recordings, or even what quality they are. Quality is just another concept, a useful concept if you are trying to buy expensive microphones and expensive speakers.

Mikhail Karikis

In the interview, I diligently trace my first face-to-face meeting with Mikhail Karikis's work back to an installation of *Seawomen* at an arts festival in Portugal. What I did not divulge—for fear, of course, of what such an admission would reveal about my character—is how his film provoked silent envy as much as it did my out-loud appreciation. Years before our Skype conversation, I was in the midst of a collaboration with two friends, an anthropologist and an acoustic scientist, and we were seeking a sound-inflected approach to documentary that could tell a complex story without capitulating either to voice-over or to subtitles. That our project also involved a focus on a Pacific Asian community of agricultural labourers—albeit a farming family in Japan rather than Karikis's Korean fisherwomen—only sharpened my jealousy.

In the years since, my admiration for Karikis's work has only increased (and any residual resentment has diminished to an appropriately professional level). As we discuss, Karikis has continued to operate in that zone between artistic techniques and documentary truths, and has retained that early emphasis on labour and its audible cultures. However, just as he has extended and complexified both of these aspects in the intervening period, so, too, have other dimensions of his practice taken more powerful hold: for example, I discern an inclusive opening out that simultaneously attaches to who is represented and to how those who are represented can be attributed agency.

I'm just setting up the recorder. You said that you have been running around a lot. What are you doing?

At the moment I'm engaged in a number of different things and some of those involve quite a bit of travelling, which contradicts—in many respects—the themes of two projects in particular that have an environmental focus. So, flying all the way to Germany several times to talk about reducing our carbon emissions doesn't really help <laughs>. I think that once what I am working on at the moment has finished, I will really have to reconsider my own practice and how I work. When I look at the exhibition histories of older artists who died in the 1980s or 1990s, I realise that in the last five years I have had as many exhibitions as they had in their entire lives. The context for that is that the arts have entered the same cycle of cultural consumption and overproduction, and the artists have gone along with this. We all know that this is unsustainable and that it has to completely change.

Yes.

As you probably know, I was recently appointed to a part-time position at the Middlesbrough Institute of Modern Art. No longer being a freelancer, having more of a regular income, means that I can be more selective with how much work I take on, how much I travel. Maybe it is a question of reducing things. I mean, what's the point of having fifty exhibitions a year? What am I getting out of it?

I think this is a really interesting question. After all, it's not as if your exhibitions happen and they extend no value to the world. I would have thought that there are many people who are expending carbon miles in the pursuit of more wasteful things than you.

I'm not located in a given place that is always the same which I can walk to or take the train to—I don't have that kind of studio practice. My work involves developing relationships, sometimes quite far from where I live, relationships which might have to be sustained over longer periods of time, with me returning again and again. I think it is also the nature of the practice which forces me to reach this plateau. It is impossible to do ten projects a year, because it is me who has to physically be present, I can't delegate that presence or that emotional investment. Did you go to the De La Warr Pavilion for my *I Hear You* exhibition?

Yes, I did and I want to ask you about it at the end of our interview, if you don't mind. I really enjoyed it. It felt incredible to be given such intimate access to relationships that I have no personal familiarity with, other than as an indirect observer. I've been to that gallery space in Bexhill-on-Sea quite a lot and I liked the care that had evidently been invested in such apparently very simple things as the carpeting, the position of the screens, how the diagonal partition and the interpretation text lead the audience in. There were a lot of people there at the time, so there was something of a hubbub which worked well, making the voices a part of a larger conversation. But let's leave I Hear You *till later; instead, what I wanted to ask you about was the first film of yours I saw which was* Seawomen *which I think is going right back to 2012.*

When did you see it? Was it the single screen version that was exhibited at Invisible Places in Viseu, Portugal?

I think it was.

So you haven't seen the multichannel version? Or the audio installation?

No. What I wanted to ask was whether Seawomen *was a pivotal work in terms of your development, or is that significance one that I'm attaching as an outsider looking in? Did* Seawomen *happen at the same time as your exploded opera* Xenon?

No, that was a year earlier.

Although Seawomen *and* Xenon *feel very different, there are things that work between the two, aren't there?*

I hadn't really thought of the similarities before. One of the significant elements of the opera involved working with a choir of coal miners, for whom I created *Sounds from Beneath*. Fifty former coal miners on top of the coal mine where they used to work imitating the sounds of their industrial lives. That was the first occasion, after a long period of collaborating with other performers, that I worked with non-artists, non-performers so to speak, people who don't have a background in contemporary arts and music, but for whom sound has an everyday function. Sound remains a very important part of their lives, but instead of relating to their profession, it is, like the former coal miners in *Sounds from Beneath*, something that connects to the landscape, to their identity, to labour or to a local culture. It was the first time I went outside of my familiar circuit of peers and engaged with a very different community. The experience allowed me to really think of sound in a very different way.

Seawomen came about as a direct consequence of *Xenon*. After working with this group of old men, where I was very much the director, with the piece being performative and composed, I threw myself into the *Seawomen* project. At first, there was no funding involved, it came purely from intuition. A friend of mine had invited me for a residency in Seoul, Korea, and afterwards it was she who said, "You have to go to the Isle of Jeju. I think you will like it because it has 380 dormant volcanoes". It was a complete coincidence that I came across these women who dived to fish for abalone and other sea creatures, another community who related through sound. I was really intrigued by their sound practices and these allowed me to tap into different forms of creativity, where I was no longer identified as being the director or as orchestrating anything or even as composing using the language of performance. Instead, my role was complexified, if I can say that, in the sense that I also became something of an anthropologist, something of an ethnomusicologist. As a result, I started reading a very different literature, started listening to the recordings of Alan Lomax; I was observing a phenomenon from a very specific perspective, the sonic perspective. Without *Sounds from Beneath*, the work with the coalminers, that perspective in *Seawomen* would not have been possible. So, yeah, to answer your question, it was a pivotal moment.

One of the things that is poignant about documentation of Xenon *online is seeing Monica Ross performing. I hadn't realised before that when the audience hear Monica reciting the Universal Declaration of Human Rights into the space occupied by you and other performers like Elaine Michener, they are hearing a sensitivity to the labouring individual (since that is the concern of several articles of the Universal Declaration). Does that connection to rights of the worker and related themes, become another possible way to connect* Xenon *and* Seawomen *and beyond?*

In some ways, I feel that I am still doing the same project but in different settings. From today's perspective, there is more appreciation of how sound and the voice—with the voice addressed as a kind of artistic material—can be combined with visual arts. But at the point we are talking about—around 2010, 2011, 2012—that was not the case in the London scene. I was performing myself, as a singer and as a vocalist; I knew Monica Ross as an artist; there was Juice Vocal Ensemble and Elaine Michener, of course. Elaine is now so much more present in visual arts and in sound arts but she came from jazz and improv and we met through the salons that she organised in a basement bar next to Leicester Square Underground Station—something that would be quite unimaginable now! It just wouldn't be possible in the London of our current time simply for financial reasons. I felt that I was connecting with people from the visual arts and people from music, but I wondered why those two groups were not themselves meeting each other. I thought, "Let's put everybody on stage to see what happens". A lot of those connections that were made at that time—Elaine Michener, Sam Belinfante, David Toop— are the ones that have since helped transform the context into what it is today, where things are a lot more fluid.

Returning to the question about themes though, yes, you are right, there are continuities between *Xenon* and *Seawomen*. Those works share my interest in labour, my interest in the coexistence between language and what is beyond it. I used to imagine that language and what lay beyond were in conflict, now I have come to consider how they can inhabit an equal space. Those same themes have affinities with my latest work *I Hear You*, which I only realised at the very end, after we had installed the work and I was stood on my own in the exhibition space at the De La Warr Pavilion. From the speakers I heard both the extralingual sounds and the sounds that we call language and then I thought to myself, "Oh my God, this really is what I've always wanted to do". Except now, I'm not orchestrating it or artificially bringing these elements together: it's already there and I'm just finding ways to capture these very intimate exchanges.

And then the next question is, why isn't the world or the city like this? What would it take for the soundscape of the city and our everyday spaces to be more inclusive, to enable people who are nonverbal and verbal to coexist? In a way, I feel that the *I Hear You* installation connects with the themes of Salomé Voegelin's book, *Sonic Possible Worlds*, that the work is trying to speculate a world which is inclusive.

It feels that utopian projections overcoming obstacles through processes of listening and sound is also a recurrent thread. In something like Children of Unquiet, *there are the modernist industrial villages in Italy where the young people embody an openness to different registers of speech, non-speech, musicality. With the work located in the Isle of Grain in the Thames Estuary that you made for the 2016 Whistable Biennale that, too, speaks of all these different ways that bodies can be rearranged in space with sound. How comfortable are you with the term documentary?*

My methodology might use documentary techniques, but I am not sure that I aim to produce documentary truths. That is because I am always intervening, even when that intervention takes the form of relationships. In the last decade, my works have developed through relationships with people, where I am trying to produce the right conditions in which there can be a collaboration for people to create representations of themselves. Most of the time, I hold the camera, but often the collaborators will hold the camera for a while making them equally in charge of how they are represented—and when they are represented. The ethical question for me is: how I can make representations of people who are unrepresented, underrepresented or misrepresented. As artists, we have the burden of power to represent others and that, for me, constitutes a very strong ethical dilemma. It's not about how I see the other, it's about how they see themselves, but obviously how they see themselves is a reflection of how I see them in our relationship, and that is the reason why my filming is always at the end of this process. With *I Hear You*, I first met my collaborators in July 2018, yet only started to record at the end of May 2019. It was the same with *No Ordinary Protest*: hundreds of hours together before I took the camera out because I wanted the children in that work to feel that they are *seen* by me. How—when they realise I'm not a teacher, nor a parent, nor one of them—can I become the catalyst for them to feel empowered to create a presentation of themselves?

One of the incredible things about *No Ordinary Protest*, in which the situation was orchestrated but everything was unscripted, is that the school children never, ever look at the cameras—and there were two people in there filming, I was also filming and there was a sound person, too.

In the film for the Whitstable Biennale called Ain't Got No Fear, *the teenagers are very conscious of the camera though?*

Yes, in that project, they do address the camera. They felt confident enough to share with the world what they wanted to articulate about themselves and about where they live. After many months working on that particular project, I decided to give up control and ask them to tell me how they wanted to be filmed, what they wanted to wear. They grabbed the microphone and the camera and we just walked around their village and they were my guides, talking. We also spent several hours on

YouTube with them showing me music videos to get a sense of what it would be that they and their friends wanted to watch—once they had decided on the format of a song for what they wanted to communicate, I helped them with the structure, with thinking about a recurrent refrain. We see them performing to camera with bravado and then snapping out of that mode to become children again; the video constantly oscillates between two forms, the observational and the highly performative, all within a music video genre.

I noticed that at one point in I Hear You, you were addressed directly by Andrew Kötting, one of the men in the caring relationships, and then you were referred to, I think, as "the Greek person". I thought that was a nice audible announcement of your presence.

That was filmed around midnight in their living room. I had spent more or less the whole day filming. Did you have a question?

I was interested—in terms of the process of editing—as to why you left that sequence in. Do you expect the audience to hear your name at that point, to recognise that you are being addressed?

I thought it was important in the same way that a moment in *Seawomen* is important—a moment which most people probably do not notice. In Korea, I was with an assistant who was a translator, and although the women divers had said that they might bring a wetsuit for me, I hadn't expected them actually to do it. We were in the middle of filming when they invited me into the water. I asked the translator, "Please take the camera and film what happens whilst I change and go to join them". In the final film, there is one short sequence, maybe a few seconds long, in which we see a woman diver and me on a rock really laughing. Laughing because in my wetsuit, I look like them, but because I am so much taller than them the top of the swimming costume just popped leaving a hole on the top, which the sea women found so funny! It was a very intimate moment, seeing us at a distance on that rock, laughing.

In these more documentary or observational kinds of filmmaking projects, I feel that it is quite important to make the viewers aware of the fact that I am there and implicated and changing the dynamic of what is going on. And I also want to make the viewers aware that the people who I am filming have a relationship with me. With *I Hear You*, especially, when I was editing some sections I was in tears watching the footage again. I asked myself how it was possible that I had been given permission to film such intimate interactions when it can also feel intrusive, uncomfortable. That sequence you referred to is one where Andrew Kötting is interacting with his daughter Eden who has the disability Joubert syndrome; that sequence could be uncomfortable, with an adult woman sitting on a man's lap, so close it looks as if she's licking his face.

I felt that by acknowledging my presence it somehow takes some of that tension away.

I understand what you are saying and I think it leads to another question that I wanted to ask which relates to ethics and listening. We tend to imagine that ethics project outwards to involve us in issues relating to how we represent someone else in sound, but I wondered whether there's also an ethical dimension that involves the artist's own vulnerability and any measures of care that have to be directed inwards? In parallel to the external acoustic sensitivity you have to extend towards your collaborators, is there an internal component devoted to self-protection?

There is a very big internal component because these are relationships that I am developing with people and they really affect me. Sometimes the emotional impact of such interactions can be burdensome as well as joyous. It is a privilege that I am able to engage different faculties of myself—the intellectual, the technical and the emotional—but sometimes the emotional impact can be very difficult. On occasion, I have addressed this issue with the organisations who have commissioned me, proposing that a professional such as a therapist or sociologist comes on board the project so I can have a few meetings to process feelings, so I can have an emotional buffer.

In general, there is a trend to send artists who employ socially-engaged methodologies to areas where circumstances are very difficult, to areas that the Arts Council might define as displaying lower cultural engagement. And yet there is always culture; it is often more a question of what is defined as culture. I wouldn't want my projects or methodologies to be instrumentalised. On the Isle of Grain, for example, the children I worked with there were so enthusiastic, they often asked "When are you coming back?" or "Can you come back tomorrow?" That reaction is amazing and encouraging and made me want to return, but in terms of the economics of the project and in terms of what else I need to do in order to finance myself, that becomes difficult.

This is fascinating to me but if you don't want me to include this…

We never talk about this to art students. When I was taught art, I was never told that what I was going to do could be emotionally difficult at times, I was never given any tools to cope with such a reaction. What skills can we give to our students to deal with such things? What references? This is very important.

Do you think that there is something related to your exploration of the voice that gives you access to the intimacy of meaning in a negotiated relationship between making something heard and listening?

Absolutely. I always talk about the voice as, on the one hand, an emotional barometer and, on the other hand, a more cerebral communication through language. If it weren't for all the work that I had done with the voice as a performer and working with other performers, I would not have been able to do this. The voice paradoxically allows you to access parts that are unspoken or unspeakable.

Yes. And is that something that is particularly revealed in your projects that cut across languages?

I think what helps is being able to decipher the emotional content of speech without needing to understand everything that is said. In *Seawomen*, there is a section at the very end where we mainly observe the foot of a woman stepping on and off a colourful mat with floral patterns. The audience hear quite an agitated vocal soundscape, during which the translator began interpreting to tell me that the conversation concerned underwater fishing rights and pensions (during one of the periods I was there, some of the female fishing communities were on strike to improve their pensions). The translator was giving a word-for-word version but I said, "I don't really need to understand absolutely every specific detail". The sonic composition of the debate and the grain of the women's voices was enough to communicate the passion, the friction.

That aspect of speech connects to something I read later in Adriana Cavarero's *For More Than One Voice* in which she talks about the concept of vocality, the implications of which I am still working through.

If we return to the De La Warr Pavilion installation I Hear You, *there is the huge commitment of time and emotional labour involved in creating a piece like that, parallel to the significant investments you make in other works. Perhaps something else that is active in* I Hear You *but is not discussed enough with art students are the processes through which we negotiate access? Are these always specific to each of your projects?*

I always have to be sensitive to the context and I always have to reduce my own ego (I have found that practices of meditation and mindfulness have been beneficial with the latter). At the beginning of my work as an artist, I would have had an intention and would have sought to direct the group dynamics towards realising that intention. I now understand that I am an outsider entering existing dynamics with, as you said earlier, people who may be quite vulnerable. Throughout this, I always have to self-reflect. If I'm feeling a bit anxious, feeling that I'm running out of time, that I should be doing something else, I always ask myself, why should this be different from what it already is? If the teenagers want to have a fight, or a sandwich, or focus on something different than what we had agreed, rather than impose my ego or my will onto the dynamic, I have learned to allow the situation to be what it wants to be. What ultimately matters is how the creative process enriches and empowers the people who are participating in the project. They don't care about the final art installation—and they shouldn't.

The long periods involved in your projects, periods where you may not switch a camera on, as you have said, are evidently vital but can be processes that are invisible to the gallery-goers. With I Hear You, *there was a glossary of terms distributed that gave us our own way to enter the world you had inhabited long before the exhibition opened.*

The glossary was there because the world of care in the show was one that we are very unfamiliar with, simply because we are not educated about that context. Our education should be more inclusive and should inform us of those terms. For each project, I do a lot of research: reading, talking to specialists, and if I find interesting information I like to share it with people who visit the installation. The time investment you talked about in my projects is not experienced quantitively by the visitors, it is experienced by them qualitatively in the way that the degree of closeness and intimacy, the interactions of the subjects, the sincerity and directness in front of the camera, these would not be possible without that prior period of time developing the relationships. So, my hope is that people will see that investment in a qualitative way.

Samson Young

I first came across Samson's work as part of Frieze projects, the non-profit programme of artists' commissions realised annually, at Frieze London in 2016. No sooner had I heard of him than suddenly I saw his name everywhere. Sadly in the mayhem of Frieze London, I didn't get the chance to listen to *When I have fears that I may cease to be, what would you give in exchange for your soul*, but months later I found the small pamphlet that accompanied the work and was intrigued by the use of archival images. I have still never heard this work, but I was fortunate enough to be able to experience *Songs for Disaster Relief* at the 2017 Venice Biennale. I was struck by its richness—the varied forms of expression, frames of reference and production. I felt these to be relatively unusual for someone known as a sound artist.

In 2018, I was invited by CMHK, the organisation founded by Samson Young, to perform at their Multichannel festival in Hong Kong. *Songs for Disaster Relief* was installed at M+ which gave me the very unusual experience of being able to re-visit an installation in a different form. Once again, I was struck by the sumptuousness of the work, right down to the booklet and the merchandise on sale. Over the course of our conversation, which moved from a noisy workers' café to the calm space of his studio, I was impressed and put at ease by his modesty, 'hands-on' work ethos, and down to earth attitude to making and presenting both his work and that of others.

You've got a huge body of work: you're very prolific.

Yeah, I work very fast!

I was interested in the fact that you've had three very different educational experiences. Your first degree was in Sydney in music, philosophy and gender studies, and then you did an MA here in Hong Kong, didn't you?

Yeah, an M.Phil in composition—strict composition.

Then you went to Princeton where you studied for a PhD with Paul Lansky. What do you feel that those three different experiences have given you in terms of the artist you are today?

Well, I've really received a really good education in each of those three places… the way that I learn is always by reacting a little bit against what I'm taught. So, at each of these places, I have been taught different things and then they have ended up being the things that I react against.

Were you brought up here in Hong Kong?

I was brought up in Hong Kong but I did most of my high schooling and my undergraduate studies in Sydney, so I spent my teenage years there. I went to high school and started playing music there as well.

Did you learn to draw as a kid?

Yeah, I learned to draw a little bit as a kid—in the summer, we'd be sent to summer courses, like summer drawing classes, not exactly art camp, but classes for kids at the district centres, to keep them occupied during the summer. But I didn't start formally learning an instrument until I was in Australia in Year 8 when I was twelve or thirteen years old. I started with the piano, but I went to another school in Year 9 and I wanted to play in the orchestra, I was not good enough on the piano to get into the orchestra, so I picked up the viola and the double bass, because that's what they needed. I started playing in the string orchestra, then slowly, I gave up the viola and started to focus on the double bass instead—that's what I consider to be my main instrument.

Do you still play that?

Not in public really! There are much better players than I. But I play in a band, not bass—laptop, synthesiser and sensor instruments.

What about the gender studies?

I wanted to do music as a part of my BA, and at Sydney University you didn't really have to declare your major, you just accumulate credit points. So I just did the things that I was interested in and by the time I graduated, I'd accumulated enough points to get the concentration in music, gender studies and philosophy.

So you came back to Hong Kong to do your MPhil?

I actually didn't plan to come back to study. After I finished my undergraduate degree, I started looking for a job and came back to Hong Kong. I saw that there was a job opening for a concert manager at the University of Hong Kong's music department. I didn't really know much about arts administration but I had organised a music festival as an undergraduate at Sydney University, so I had some experience and thought I could handle the job.

What sort of music festival was that?

It was a new music festival, featuring musicians and composers that I knew and their friends. It was run on the main campus at Sydney

University in this old building called the Old Darlington School. We got some student union funding and ran it for two years with that money.

Are you the person who says "Wouldn't it be great if we did this?"

Yeah I am. So I came back to Hong Kong, saw that job posting at HKU, and thought "I could do that!". Shortly after I started the concert manager job, I saw that they were calling for applications for MPhil students, so I applied to that too, got accepted and stopped working as a concert manager. I only worked for about half a year in 2004.

What was the scene in sound art, new music and experimental music in Hong Kong at that time?

There were small pockets of activity. I don't think I had a very good sense of "Oh, I wish more of this would happen or more of that would happen", at that point. But those couple of years in Hong Kong were very important for me, not because of the new music scene, but actually because I met a whole bunch of new media artists. I met a really good friend of mine through this organisation called Videotage, which started out as a video art organisation, and had by then expanded into presenting new media art. They ran the Microwave Festival every year. The leap from the world of composition to the new media art world was really big, and I felt like my head just kind of exploded!

At that time, I formed an artists' collective with people who I met through Videotage, video artist Christopher Lau and poet Ron Lam, who both graduated from the new media art programme at the City University, where I ended up teaching for a couple of years. Ron and Christopher had very different training from mine, and the three of us started making things together. At first, we would work together and I would play the role of a composer, making music, then, soon, we started swapping roles. At the time it was becoming easier to make videos with iMovie and a hand-held camera, and also learning things off the Internet had become possible. So that's how I started making video, and by the time I left Hong Kong, I was still writing notated music but video had become something that I did regularly.

The collaboration sounds like good fun. Did you feel that there were things that video offered that you were unable to do compositionally?

Not really. I don't think I thought about it too much. It was more like, "Ooh, a video in the background, wouldn't that be cool?" It also came from witnessing what new media artists were doing. I was inspired by how a lot of choreographers used multimedia and new technologies in their productions, treating the performance space as a sort of expanded canvas. Chris was involved in a lot of those kind of productions, which made me think that if a choreographer could do that, then a composer could do it too. I observed how choreographers, when they worked, think of themselves as the director of the space, and I don't think composers necessarily think like that?

Are there any particular choreographers?

Daniel Yeung is a Hong Kong choreographer who Chris worked with a lot, he uses a lot of video and interactive elements in his productions. A lot of folks working in new media were making things that were basically installation art, but realised in a theatre setting, and vice versa, so there were performative things involving technologies that were being produced in the galleries as well. Maybe without thinking about it too much, all those things seemed normal to me, there was more sense of fluidity than in the classical music world.

So at that time you were making and showing work with Chris and Ron?

Yeah, and we continued until the first year that I was in Princeton. Chris and I won this grant called the Bloomberg Emerging Artist Award. You submit a proposal and say what would you like to do with the pot of money, but the venue where you would be showing your work has already been decided for you. So we submitted a proposal and then had the problem of having to realise an exhibition! That was the first time that Chris and I did things independently. There were five different individual little spaces so we decided to do one piece together and then split the rest between us. Before that we had made a piece, called *Ritual Machine*, for the Microwave Festival, the new media festival. The audience send prayers as a text message string and they get turned into sound and visuals. There are some key words connected with spirituality that produce a lotus flower on the video. It's very naïve.

Did you program that?

No, Chris did. I only did the sound. I hadn't learnt programming at that point, that was 2003. The Bloomberg show was titled *The Happiest Hour*. A lot of the pieces had to do with childhood. We did an open call asking people to give us their old Game Boys, and then we repurposed them and made little pieces. I'm not so happy with that show, but that's what we did. After that, I started feeling that I could make visuals as well, although it was not such a frequent occurrence.

What made you think that you wanted to go back and do a PhD? It sounds like you were having quite a good time and actually being quite successful.

Well, I was kind of buying time I think. It was the beginning of a transition for me. I wasn't really established in composition yet, or in the gallery world, so I felt like doing a PhD would buy me some time to figure out where I wanted to go, and to build my career. I was interested in the topic and I had fun doing it too of course.

I'm a great admirer of Paul Lansky, I can understand why anyone would go to him for many reasons, but, as far as I know, he hasn't done much work that isn't purely sonic. He is very much a composer. Why did you choose him?

Well, he's a good composer and he does computer music stuff, which I already liked before I applied. But I had also heard about the reputation of the graduate programme there. People have this impression that Princeton is very composerly, but actually it's not. They take in four graduate students every year and have quite a mixture of people. The year before I went into the graduate programme, I did the Bang on a Can summer camp. Bang on a Can is this downtown New York music organisation founded by David Lang, Julia Wolfe and Michael Gordon, three downtown New York composers. The summer camp is at MASS MoCA, Massachusetts Museum of Contemporary Art, every year, it's like a contemporary music camp—they call it Banglewood, the antithesis to Tanglewood! I met some interesting people and made a lot of my New York musical connections there.

What was the subject for your PhD at Princeton?

I can't remember initially what I proposed, but eventually, I ended up doing cultural politics in the music by the new wave generation of Chinese composers, who came after the Cultural Revolution. But I read things that were quite multimedia, so I did a close reading of, for example, Tan Dun's *The Map: Concerto for Cello, Video and Orchestra*, and the first edition of FM3's Buddha Machine, which is basically a sound art machine in the form of a circuit. I also did an analysis of the 2008 Beijing Olympics as multimedia.

That sounds like a theoretical PhD. Did you do practice as well?

It's composition, but at Princeton, you have to do both.

You write a thesis but it doesn't have to be about the practice?

In fact, it's highly encouraged that you do not write about yourself. Because then it gives you like a real thesis, but then you also have to do a portfolio of work and your art work statement, which is good.

That sounds brilliant. You spent a large part of your teenage years outside Hong Kong, do you think you needed or wanted to re-connect with any kind of Chinese heritage, or is that too crass?... sorry!

No… I feel like maybe at some point—these things, they come in stages, right? I was very critical of what they call the new wave generation of Chinese composers who really self-orientalised themselves and I tried very hard to not do that. So that's the first thing. But also, I can't rule out the possibility that, at some point in the future, I might be into tea or something and begin to explore that as a topic! But I'm interested in things like video games and those things reflect my upbringing.

However, that was the subject of your written thesis. What was your motive? Was there an agenda?

I think I was reacting against something. When I was in Sydney, I felt like there was an expectation for me to perform culture or perform identity through my musical work. So I wanted to look at people who actually sort of did that: what was the impulse, what were the external pressures that made it maybe necessary for a certain generation of composers to do that, and what does it do to the audience? There's been lots of advocates and theorists who came to the defence of this generation of composers wanting to be considered as cosmopolitan individuals as opposed to being just 'Chinese' composers. But I was wondering where the desire for composers to continue to perform culture comes from? If you look at composers like Tan Dun, Chen Yi, Zhou Long or Bright Sheng, the Chinese composers who are the most prominent, they are still writing the kind of music that alerts people to their cultural origins. I don't think that situation applies to my generation anymore, it's specific to their generation.

What's it all about? I'm aware of some non-Western artists who have re-packaged their cultural traditions into something more contemporary, which somehow manages to insert criticism at the same time. It seems very self-conscious, and the West loves it. Is this part of a bid for acceptance by the global North?

Well, that's the thing. It's very obvious when one is 'performing' an identity, and of course you can criticise it, but we also need to look at why that continues to happen. Maybe for composers on the margins, there are only certain strategies that would give them access to institutions, and in the world music industry, there is a yearning for cultural authenticity and it continues to sell, despite the fact that we know the claim to truth there is questionable. All of these things can exert pressure on a composer. So in a way it's a structural problem. Of course, the essentialising goes both ways, right? The West essentialises the East, but at the same time, the East also essentialises the West. I guess what I was trying to present in the thesis was not a straight-up critique of cultural appropriation, but leaning more towards saying that while performing identity is not helpful, it is also important to look at why it continues to happen, and tune into the dynamics which are out of these composers' control that sustain these practices. For composers or artists of my generation though, I don't think the barriers are as great as the ones that the previous generations faced.

I've noticed that people often do some education in their home country or the country they grew up in, and then they access education in the States or Europe. Did the generation of composers that you are talking about study abroad?

They all went back to the Central Conservatory in Beijing as soon as it re-opened after the Cultural Revolution, and then, through composer Chou Wen-chung they did their PhDs at Columbia. Maybe that also speaks to the conditions still, and things haven't changed as much as we think. But also, very practically speaking, being educated overseas exposes you to an international network, so these things are all very entangled.

I'm going to have to read your PhD.

It's quite dry. It's not that long, it's about this thick.

I wouldn't have expected that to be a subject which Paul Lansky would know much about at all—what did he do with it?

He was totally hands-off with me. He was always very encouraging, and he helped me with my programming skills, but I had other people who I could rely on theoretically at Princeton.

You've never been attracted to an academic career?

I have been attracted to it, and I did try to make an academic career, and then realised that I wanted to make art more.

Did your thesis give you a 'list' of things you didn't want to do in your artwork?

No, I don't think of it that way. It was rather that I wanted to look into something that I thought was problematic. My thesis is not really a conclusion, but it bears witness to the fact that I have thought about these things and not just adopted a view. Although I don't consider myself an academic, I actually enjoy writing and sometimes I think that when I make artwork the density of my argument is very much like writing an essay, except that I try not to come to any sense of a conclusion.

I can see that in the work that I know. The first work of yours that I came across was When I have fears that I may cease to be, what would you give in exchange for your soul, *the multimedia walk at Frieze, London in 2016, but I've also seen* Songs for Disaster Relief, *in Venice and here in Hong Kong. I can feel what you have just said in that work. There's a sense that you have a theme and you are going to approach it in this way, this way and this way and that the audience can make of it what they will. I found it very different each time. What do you feel the differences are between the Venice and the Kowloon stagings of the work?*

Well, it's different in so many ways. The context is certainly very different, but that's almost self-evident. In the Venice version the space has a very domestic character and you can use it to your advantage to make certain spaces look surreal, to give it that eerie quality that one needs to make it flow a little bit. In Hong Kong I'm basically dealing with a white wall space, so I needed to give each of the spaces more character than I had done in Venice, and the spatial treatment needed to be more theatrical and more heavy-handed.

How have you developed that theatricality that you've talked a little bit about? You already had the art and the composition backgrounds and you've developed a new media practice with other people, but what about that theatrical staging?

I have also done some theatrical pieces. Two pieces, *God Save the Queen* in 2008 and *Circus In Spectacles* in 2010 have been important to me. I have stopped making music theatre for now, but I might go back to it. When I first started working in the gallery context, I was thinking too much about how to make a show—whether I needed to make drawings or put things on the wall—but the year before Venice, the music theatre thing started coming back to me again, and I realised that maybe it's the thing that I can do best. I wanted to throw all these things together in the way that music theatre structures the experience. So with the Venice show, especially the curtain room, there's very much a music theatre setting.

Presumably you worked with a curator for that show—and you've worked quite closely with a curator on other exhibitions—do you feel that this has really made a difference or helped you in some way?

It's always good to have a sounding board. The role of the curator is very absent in the concert world, you have a producer, but they don't intervene creatively or not to the same degree as a curator does. But I'm mostly pretty strong-headed so I tend to just do my thing, and sometimes people telling me that something doesn't work becomes like an affirmation that it's the right thing to do!

How long was that show in the making?

About a year. Well, I've had the idea of wanting to do something with charity singles for a while, but I was just waiting for the right opportunity.

And did you know what you were going to do at that point?

I just knew that I wanted to do charity singles, then the serious research started after they had announced that we were going to Venice. When Kwok Ying and I first came together to talk about the show, we threw around a few themes and ideas but quite soon, we started coming to the conclusion that this was the best one.

Everyone that writes about you mentions that you do lots of research. What form does that take?

It's different for every piece. Sometimes it's a lot of reading, sometimes, it's actually field work. It depends on the project.

How do you manage your production process? Have you become the producer or do you still deal with the materials?

Whenever possible, I try to let my hand not be too far from the process. I think that's the composer in me coming through—you are still measured by your craft. To make that sculpture in the middle of the room, for example, using 3D printing, means that the process stayed pretty close to my hand, because I can't sculpt things, but I can make model collages into Google SketchUp. In my own films, I don't operate the camera or do the technical work, so I don't know how to push a dolly for example, but I still insist on editing and colouring my own film—it's not like professional colouring, it's all done within Premiere! I also programmed the light in the curtain room: if you write a composition that changes with the light and the curtain, you can't not do that on your own. But these things don't come to me overnight, I've picked them up over the years. At some point, I picked up programming skills, at another 3D printing, so these skills accumulate over time. Very early on, I picked up how to make video, and I got better and these things enter my work.

You must have a team?

Well, I have one assistant who works for me full time, then with the 3D printing I have one regular guy who cleans up the model for me.

Is that the first time you'd done a 3D print?

No, I have done small 3D prints before then, but this was the first bigger print that involved a collage element. I worked with a professional vendor for the curtain, but I provided them with the MIDI signal via DMX to control the curtain's movement. I did my own lighting. For filming, I always work with a very small team, usually one person who is a sort of producer who puts together a small camera team for me. *We Are the World* was shot with four people, including me.

What proportion of making that piece would you say is you working artistically with materials, and what proportion is writing administrative emails and dealing with all those companies?

I think both are part of my work. You need to communicate to people to make things happen, even before you go into the filming, you have to clearly explain to the three camerapersons which angle you want etc., so I think it's all a part of the work, really.

But do you have to do the bit that says, "OK, we'll do it on that day, meet me there"?

Yeah, I have to do it, because there's only me. My assistant VV only really helps me with things like sending stuff to the framer, or finding stuff in the archive.

Does she do your website or anything like that?

No, I do my own website. I design the website and do all the text, but VV updates the press cuttings. She also helps me with production aspects that don't really need decision-making on my part. For example, with 3D printing, I will make the model, but VV will send it to the machine, trigger the print, and babysit the machine.

So you are basically the producer, director, composer, designer, programmer and the administrator?

Right.

That's impressive.

Thank you!

Did you really do all that in a year?

Yeah, I'm really fast!

You obviously work really hard and long hours.

Yeah, I work long hours. But I enjoy my work, it's fun.

What's your studio like?

It's not that big. It's very clean and organised though. There's me and my drawing desk, some work space, a room for storage, a room for our 3D printers. On the 'studio' team, there's only VV and me. And then there is also Him Cheung and Christabel Ng, who are not working for my studio, but for Contemporary Musiking Hong Kong (cmhk.org), a sound art non-profit that I founded, which is now funded by the Arts Council. CMHK does sound art education projects, workshops for artists, and puts on an annual sound art festival. I am not very involved curatorially with CMHK anymore these days.

Is there space to make work apart from drawing?

Yeah, there are still spaces to get dirty.

Have you got a music production studio there?

Not really, when I need to record I go to somebody else's studio.

Is the forthcoming Guggenheim piece large scale?

It's pretty crazy, yeah! In terms of scale, it's like the curtain room piece, but maybe with not as many things in it, but it has a ten-channel sound installation, some sculpture on the wall, two drawings, and a video.

I feel that what you are doing goes way beyond the contemporary definition of a sound artist. I know you think of yourself primarily as a composer, but are there things that you feel that the sound artist of today needs to do, particularly in order to deal with the gallery system?

I don't have any sort of advice. It's not that I am thinking about what sound artists should and shouldn't do, but more that I do all these things because I have fun doing them.

Yang Yeung

I had heard about Yang Yeung and her activities long before I met her. Various friends and acquaintances had been lucky enough to have had residencies at soundpocket in Hong Kong and had enthused about the warm welcome, careful facilitation and opportunities to make and exhibit new work. Soundpocket has been actively promoting, educating and facilitating sound-based activities in many different forms over the last decade, and has been one of the main influences in the development of a distinctive sound arts scene in Hong Kong. It was interesting to discuss how this started and developed alongside contemporary art in HK, as well as Yang's personal motivations and thoughts. Soundpocket emphasises meaningful and publicly relevant sonic practices, and during the interview Yang revealed how her interest in sound emerged and developed, through a variety of lived experiences as well as her professional practices in radio and TV journalism. What is extraordinary is how she has used this for the benefit of others, and her adherence to the belief that sound, which is generally ignored, can teach us so much. I find Yang straightforward, without pretention, politically committed, and full of original and thoughtful insights about the local and the global situation for sound arts and Hong Kong. I am interested in her collaborative ways of working curatorially. Once again over the course of the interview, I am grateful to be introduced to artists whose work I am unfamiliar with.

You teach, don't you?

Yes, since 2009 I've taught classics full time on a general education foundation programme.

So that's about the same time that you founded soundpocket?

I founded soundpocket in 2008. The good thing about my job is that there's a lot of room for us to develop our own professional work. It's a very interdisciplinary programme. All of us on the teaching team are on the teaching track, so we are not under as much pressure to publish, but we do need to be informed about education research and we are involved in developing the curriculum—it's all good.

I'm interested in trying to get some sort of perspective on how sound art is developing outside Europe and North America; what people's primary interests are and what circumstances are feeding into it. You founded soundpocket in 2008: that's not an inconsiderable achievement, especially as now, ten years later, it's got an international reputation. What got you interested in sound in the first place?

I wasn't interested in sound as much as 'listening well'. It comes from a lot of things—I'll tell you everything but cut me short if it's too much!
I'll start from a very personal experience. I was the youngest in a family of four daughters and my sisters didn't get on with each other, so I was their ears—I would always listen to conflicting stories about this and that—the bad stuff about each other... It's partly a joke, but I have memories of not having a voice in my family. My parents told me that I wasn't very eager to speak as a child anyway, when we'd go for Sunday lunch, for instance, for dim sum, I would take a book with me and just sit at the table and eat quietly, not even running around, and I wouldn't have the urge to talk. I'm a bit nerdy in that way, so I think there's something about that sort of behaviour that made me very curious about listening to other people and the world. I already knew that I wanted to be a journalist when was in junior high school. I started professionally on a newspaper, and then I went over to radio, Metro Radio, which was the first and only commercial all-news channel in Hong Kong at the time. I learnt a lot and I enjoyed the technicalities, we were still using quarter-inch tape but we were starting to use DAT machines, this was 1993. I enjoyed that radio experience, but then moved into TV, I don't remember why, maybe because of the salary. Then I got into graduate school in the United States and so I stopped being a journalist. I gave up the PhD scholarship and came back in 1997 because I didn't feel I was in the right place at the right time.

That must have been so traumatic.

Yeah, it was, but coming back was so important for me. I went back to TV and I also started doing radio news reading as well. I really enjoyed that kind of studio environment and I always feel that this voice I have is not mine. I think everybody has the feeling when you listen to your recorded voice that it's not yours! So I have been very curious about that.
    Also in 2001, I got married (now divorced) to a mastering engineer and we had all sorts of conversations about the sound environment in Hong Kong. He engineers in his studio, records classical concerts and does sound design for theatre as well. So I started meeting people, including some musicians, and discussing how they felt that society was becoming worse at listening, to diverse forms of music for example, and that in the theatre, sound design was always inferior to everything else, and that there was not even the language to talk about it. So that's one major reason why I started soundpocket. I don't know why I wanted

to do something public but, when I look back, I realise I have always been involved in projects that have public implications. I've never been attracted to the profit-making stuff.

But I was also involved in the arts earlier than that. In 1999, I was in the TV department of Radio Television Hong Kong, the public television station, which is still running now, and I was directing documentaries. We were researching programmes on art and culture, the first place I went to was Para Site art space, which used to be in Sheung Wan. It was a community-based artist-run space then, now it's very much bigger and curator-run. They started an art criticism class and invited me to be part of it. I had to go to exhibitions and write about them and we would share our writing in monthly meetings—it was wonderful. I have to thank them for what I'm doing now. I realised there were a number of artists I really loved, for instance So Yan-kei, who did some installations with a sonic aspect at Para Site. She used water and industrial materials that evoked sound in her large-scale installations. But we didn't seem to have the vocabulary to talk about how she materialised sound and how she listened. I didn't either, but I became interested, and I think that something might have just grown in me from there.

I want to go back to that first thing you said about the sisters and your embodied experience. To move from that experience to being able to conceptualise something about listening, which has been so under-theorised and un-thought about, is really interesting I think.

Just a little thing, but it's important as well. My father died when I was twelve and in my late twenties or thirties, one day, I suddenly realised that I was losing the sound or the sense of his voice. I might still have the texture of it, but I didn't actually remember the sound and that's very intriguing to me—is it there or is it not there? The memory of that experience and the memory of that sound and the memory of losing it—what is that?

What I'm hearing is that you are someone who has a high sensitivity to sound and listening, maybe from birth, but to then move from that to actually doing something, as you say, for the public, for the greater good, is quite a big move! What were you hoping would happen, what was your aim, and how did you even know how to do it?

<laughs> That's a terrible question! Now I've got found out! OK, so the first one was what?

What did you want to happen, really?

I think I inherited something from my mum here, she thinks she is eighty-one but we all believe that she's actually older. There was a policy in Hong Kong, when we were a colony, that once you land here, illegally or not, you are a resident and people would normally lie about their age so that it would be easier to get a job. My mum came right before the Cultural Revolution, probably around 1960 or 1959—she had experienced the Mao Tse Tung labour movement and the big political turmoil—then she came here illegally to get married because my father was born in Hong Kong. She was put onto a boat at night to be transported to Hong Kong and my father arranged for someone to pick her up. She told me stories about China from that time, about her experiences as a student, and how she was the daughter of the second wife of her father, so she always felt inferior. I don't know where her moral sense came from, but I remember a lot of stories and statements about how to be a good person—you have to recognise what you hate and what you love—and it's very clear. We always joke about how we wouldn't have been here if she had gone through the Cultural Revolution, because she's so upstanding that she would have either become a follower and waved the Little Red Book or she would challenge whoever upset her, and then she would just immediately die! So then my father saved her. It's a quite typical story of that generation of people here.

When you started soundpocket, what did you want to happen?

I had this sense of sound being marginalised. I didn't use this term, but I thought, "Why do people not pay attention to it?" It was very naïve and simple but I had curiosity and my sense of injustice. So that was one major motivation. Since '97, Hong Kong has changed very quickly, politically and culturally. I grew up in this area, not exactly in Central, but this was my neighbourhood, near the University of Hong Kong. When I was young, at night, after dinner, my father and I would take a walk from home to Central and maybe to the pier, and take a bus back. So this is sort of my garden and it has changed a lot. The old buildings and the little stores are gone, the gentrification is recent, but it's become such a posh neighbourhood. I feel that listening could help us recover some of the values that we treasure in each other.

I like that, it makes me want to cry.

Me too, thanks for the question!

Let's hope that's true.

It's very basic, also.

What was the artistic landscape in Hong Kong in 2009? Did it feel like a time of possibility?

There were a number of things already. Para Site was founded in 1996, and there was also the Fringe Club from the 1980s and the Oil Street art village in a government supplies building in North Point, Hong Kong Island. The artist studios and art spaces were later relocated to Cattle Depot Artist Village in Tokwawan. Videotage is one of the art spaces currently at Cattle Depot. It was founded by Ellen Pau in 1986, they were very kind and directed me to artists with an interest in sound. So there were artist-run spaces and small collectives, the Asia Art Archive was already there, and Samson Young had already founded Contemporary Musiking Hong Kong but it was still very understated.

Was there any funding around then? Did you receive any funding?

In the first year, no. We did apply to the council —I remember in the interview, they just didn't understand what it was, and neither did I! So the first application failed. But in the beginning, there were not many costs. After we got the grant that we hired a manager, so there was just one person plus me. Before soundpocket, I did a show with Habitus, a small collective founded by designers. At the time I was writing my PhD and needed a studio space and they asked me to share the space. There were five of us at the time, so I just shared the rent and I helped out sometimes. Then we moved to an old building in the Western Market, it was a much bigger space with a rooftop and some really nice rooms, so I started to think about doing more things. I applied for my first grant from the council for a project called in *midair—sound works Hong Kong 2007* before soundpocket.

Oh, I forgot to tell you about the demolition of the clock tower. That was part of my initiation into public culture going wrong. I don't know if you've taken the ferry from Central, but now there's this really ugly clock there—this is the habit of Hong Kong these days, to pull down the old stuff and then build something new that imitates it. We used to have a Bauhaus-style clock tower and the clock was almost fifty years old but the government said, "Oh, it's not old enough to be attributed heritage status", and so people protested and this was an initiation for a lot of artists and cultural workers. Since then there have been many protests that artists have been involved in. This was around the time when the city was really changing a lot, and super-quickly, and I actually think we were slow to become aware of that. It was a very peaceful sort of protest. Every day after work, I would go to the pier and join the protestors. People just sat there and did little things, told stories to each other or read some text, and I would sometimes just sit there and read, or sometimes just sit there doing nothing. I remember one night a number of activists climbed into the clock tower and sounded the bell. That was after the pier had closed so the last sounding of the bell had already happened but then they went in to sound it out again. I was right outside the tower, on the podium. I projected a few powerpoint slides onto the clock with the help of some friends. One of them says "I am not your problem" (this was written about briefly in Frank Vigneron's 2018 book *Hong Kong Soft Power: Art Practices in the Special Administrative Region, 2005-2014*). I had been inside the tower earlier because I was invited by a magazine editor to shoot a video of the clock before it was dismantled.

And I also got the chance to go into the new clock tower. They invited an engineer from London to inspect the new installation and as we went near the new bell, the engineer pulled out a key from his pocket and swiped it on the rim of the bell, and said, "Well, this is such a new bell, it doesn't sound as good as the old one". So our old bell is now in the Museum of History but they're not bells any more, they're just stock.

You said a while ago that there were particular artists who were using sound that you admired. Who were they?

There were two works of So Yan-kei a woman artist, that struck me at Para Site. Her practice is very industrial, she uses raw industrial materials, and in one particular work she got a big rock into the gallery, I don't know how, it was lifted off the ground, and hung. It was very minimal—there were a few bamboos and a very slow, gentle stream of water that trickled onto the rock so that the gallery floor become wet—that was the installation. I experienced that as a very sonic installation—the fluidity of both the sound and the water was what made the work. I think So Yan-kei was one of the founding members of Para Site—when it was a collective. In *What kind of thing can last forever* (1998), she buried a piano in soil in the glass shop window at the front of the gallery and there was a hand that came out of the soil—this stuck with me. She had a similar series, in which a can was installed right above a chair in the shop window of the gallery. It was set in yellow-brownish lighting. It's called *hairdryer for francis bacon* (2000). It made me think about silence and sound and being silenced. A lot of her early practice comes from her dreams, it's almost like whenever she had a dream, she had to actualise the tension or the content of it in an art work.

So how much do you think that ten years of soundpocket operating has influenced the sound art scene, whatever that might be, in Hong Kong and maybe more widely. Can you see the effect it's had?

In Hong Kong, yes, there is a sense of community among young artists who share an interest in sound as a material or an idea. I remember one young artist saying that now he doesn't feel he's an orphan any more, there is this little family he can come back to. So I think we have provided a point of support—someone to talk to and to identify opportunities, and gradually, through the festival and publishing books, maybe finding a common language.

And a platform, presumably?

Hmm, not for showing, but to bring people together.

I wonder if there are more artists working with sound because soundpocket has provided a context? It strikes me that in many parts of Asia, not just in Hong Kong, there's a drive for artists to do their training, maybe at Master's or PhD level in America or Europe. Why do people do that? Is it because they can't do it here?

It's a complex question—for my generation there is a sense of the White West as superior, so it's an internalised colonial mentality. It was also a kind of careerism. This is an over-simplification, but just so we could move quickly towards the present. Now the political culture is different and, since the Umbrella Movement and more recent events, we are getting to know our history and finding our identity from within, rather than from the White West. I see a lot of artists staying in Hong Kong to study now, but that might just be to do with finances, it's very expensive to go away. If they do go away I don't think it's necessarily for the sense of superiority, they just might not be able to find the right teacher.

Are sound courses offered in art schools and universities in Hong Kong?

It's still developing.

I feel that a lot of the sound work here is very materially engaged, but also there are socio-political undertones relating the past to the present in a very engaged way with elements of history, memory and a critique of the past. This might not be only sound work—it's quite cross-media—although it relies on or is referencing sound. Could you say anything about that?

I think people are still exploring, and I see a lot of visual artists trying to introduce elements of sound into their work. For artists who work with sound there were a few people like Dennis Wong, one of our advisors, who is very well-connected and was doing a lot of gigs. We have an interview with him on our website. He doesn't really identify as an artist, but he would say he's an organiser—it's mostly live performances. He's part of the noise community in the West. I'm not so interested in live, electronic, laptop-based sort of stuff, I'm more interested in space and walking around and that was what I wanted to do from the start. I couldn't, however, find anybody who had been doing work about sound and space, except Cedric Maridet, who I worked with at Habitus and also in midair—hong kong sound works 2007. For the first Around sound art festival, we invited Akio Suzuki. We also had artists from Singapore, PRC and Rome, we also worked with John Lee, a frame drummer, and the Hong Kong New Music Ensemble. I needed inspiration myself.

Is there a network operating between South-East Asian countries?

Yes, with the Philippines, but also with art communities in Chicago in the US, Tokyo and Tango-Kyoto in Japan, Taipei in Taiwan, Kuala Lumpur in Malaysia, and I have worked with individual artists from many countries including Australia, Germany, UK, Netherlands and Italy. I didn't want to connect with the PRC just because it's the PRC, but we did work with Yan Jun, an artist working with sound based in Beijing, in

Around Sound Art Festival 2009. We also worked with Yao Dajun, who is from Taiwan but works in the PRC. There was a time when the Hong Kong institutions suddenly encouraged exchange with the Pearl River Delta region in South China, but I don't see why art should be limited by these kind of national projects. I think we need to keep alternative visions alive in our minds. The newly implemented National Security Law is making any reference to the idea of an independent Hong Kong a crime. It's suffocating and artists are responding to these things. In 2014, after the Umbrella Movement, many artists were in the protests but they made work that wasn't politically charged, but instead it opened up different layers of reality. That was also the time when teargas were thrown, it was the second day of our festival, and our invited foreign artists were curious about what was happening, so one night we went to the government headquarters, and they were very struck by how peaceful the students and young people were. We were thinking a lot about the power of art at this time—should we keep the festival going or should we just dump everything and go to the protest? I was confident that the festival should go on, because there is something inherently political about what we do, but of course my heart and mind were also elsewhere, like everyone's. But also I had to take care of our guests, which is super-important, because in a way, our sovereign state wants us to become narrower and narrower—to have a national not a cosmopolitan spirit. I just don't understand why that's attractive, I mean, for a human being. It's not attractive to me! Security, power, whatever—it's boring!

Since we originally spoke there have been mass protests triggered by the government's plans to introduce an extradition bill in Hong Kong in 2019. The bill threatened to expose Hong Kongers to unfair trials in the People's Republic of China. How has that changed the arts scene?

Thank you for asking. It means a lot to us in Hong Kong that the international community cares. We keep telling our stories to the world, and artists do, too—by keeping up their exhibition and gig schedules. These mass protests reached a climax last year in 2019, but have culminated over, I'd say, at least since 2003, when the government was proposing laws to tighten 'security' and heighten police presence in Hong Kong life.

It's perhaps another long conversation to talk about how the arts scene has changed. I would perhaps first say that the vibrancy of the current local arts scene has come a long way, from the many artist-led projects and spaces of thirty years ago, to the expansion of art fairs and large-scale institutions including Taikwun and M+ in recent years. I see an energy and diversity that are unprecedented. We also had artists democratically elected to the District Council in last year's election. They included Clara Cheung and Susi Law. Susi was actually soundpocket's first hired staff. She was, and still is, always full of ideas of how to connect people. There is an artist's union now, and they are currently trying to deliberate how to define the 'artist'.

One way artists and art practitioners have responded to society and where it is going politically is to become more united, to trust what we are good at doing more, and persist in it. It's also been about extending the humanistic value of art into other aspects of public life. Politics is more visible as a subject-matter of contemporary artists. I recently wrote about artists South Ho and Luke Ching's duo exhibition where they both presented works addressing police violence in transformative ways. I also wrote about artists Stephanie Sin and Suifong Yim and the self-care they show in their practices as a response to the turbulent times.

Has this been reflected specifically in sound art?

In 2014, soundpocket published a CD called DAY AFTER 翌日 [2014.9.29 – 12.12] after the Umbrella Movement. It collects field recordings and direct sonic actions that artists did back then, when the goal of the movement was universal suffrage. For 2019, I have been interviewing independent musicians and artists with a sonic practice. This time round, protest sites have become unsafe for audio recordings to be made—the aim was to be mobile "like water" (a main slogan in the 2019 movement), and there had been much more violence from the police and the protestors. Artists have been responding to the movement in their works. I am writing a piece for Contemporary Art Stavanger currently, and that includes independent musician Brian Chu, artist-farmer Lai-lai Lo, and independent singer-songwriter Hin-yan Wong. In a way, since their practices have been ongoingly reflective about what freedom is (and not just what kind of government our society needs), they haven't been 'changed' by the movement. But my observation is that they are even more committed to what they've been doing because making art, making music, and singing, are their sources of strength, perhaps more than ever before. A friend of mine is a curator in a museum in the US, and once said a lot of great art will come out of Hong Kong because of the movement. Perhaps 'great' is a loaded and vague term, but I do see how their 'governance of instincts' and their 'ordered enlistment of intuition', to borrow George Steiner's ideas, are leading them to succinct criticisms of life as it is lived now, in Hong Kong, and to people anywhere whose freedom is being taken away. How fortunate we are that artists are around!

I like the research interviews that soundpocket has done, it's actually quite unusual to read artists talking about their practice. There are six so far I think. How were they picked? What were the things about their practices that you felt were interesting?

In the beginning, I was involved in the research team, because I wanted to make sure that we did our homework before the interview. I'm pissed off sometimes with the way some art journalism is done, people don't research, they ask everything that does not have to be said in an interview! We wanted to bring the artist's voice out and to involve younger artists in the research, connect the generations and involve the so-called administrative staff in the team, so that we all know what each other is doing. So it was partly to bring out the under-recognised; I hope even asking for an interview shows that we appreciate that person. It was also partly for our own curiosity—we didn't know what sound practice was, so let's ask the artists! The idea of building learning communities comes from there, I guess. We don't use the term sound art except in our proposals when we might use it for convenience. We say 'sound in art' and 'sound as art' and we focus a lot on this.

You collaborated with Samson Young on curating an exhibition called Notating Beauty That Moves: Music at an Exhibition. *How did that come about?*

Samson just called me and said "the Hong Kong Sinfonietta wants to do an exhibition but they don't know how to do it". They wanted him to curate but he was already composing for the orchestra, so he told them that they needed a curator to construct a narrative and he invited me to come on board. From the very beginning, I understood it as a music project. I knew I would learn a lot so I am really grateful for their trust. I knew Samson a little already, we had organised fundraisers for our two organisations, soundpocket and CMHK (Contemporary Musiking Hong Kong). He's very good at opening up opportunities for others and I really admire that. He knew that I didn't know much about music, but he wanted this to be something different. He has been very interested in contemporary scores and notation, and I think he wanted to show beautiful objects! I loved that, that's the way I work as well—what's the point of doing things you already know? So that immediately made it possible to work together. We started talking and sharing ideas. He was always travelling, and researching a number of projects at the same time, and he would go to the libraries wherever he was and suddenly find something and send it to me. I spent a week at the New York Public Library, and did the same. He suggested a few leads but I also followed my own interests, and one thing led to another. It was wonderful to be reading and touching John Cage scores in the library. It was a whole new world for me. We would get excited about something and share it. Our tastes were quite different, but we were both like children "Ooh, can I show this? This is lovely?" and we would always say yes to each other, until there was a point where it was too much and we knew that we should stop. So it was quite easy.

Was there a decent budget for that exhibition?

Yeah, I would say so, in the beginning we proposed a budget, and the orchestra said, "Are you sure this is enough?" and it was funny because Samson and I work independently and our projects are very small and we are able to make a lot out of little money, we were very lucky.

Yashas Shetty

Yashas Shetty's wide-ranging practice encompasses experimental music, sound art, biohacking, coding and new media art. I appreciate the breadth and depth of his knowledge and interests, as well as his commitment to collaboration. He is an artist-in-residence at Srishti Institute of Art, Design and Technology, and the founder of ISRO, the Indian Sonic Research Institute, a community music lab in Bangalore for the proliferation of experimental music and sound art. He is committed to enabling people to hack, build and make, and with ISRO, is building a community through workshops, performances and residencies. Yashas was also a co-founder of Hackteria, a web platform and collection of open-source biological art projects, and runs (Art)ScienceBLR, a public laboratory also based at Srishti. I like the way that he does not see any separation between the work he does as an educator and his individual artistic practice. Yashas's individual practice includes gallery installations, sound works and interactive media art. His work often utilises everyday objects in new and magical ways. A few nights before the interview, I saw him perform with a neon tube light and assorted electronics which created more of a spectacle than 'traditional' contemporary electronic music performance. As one of the few, if not the only, sound artists (among other things) attached to an academic institution that I have come across in India, I am interested in what he anticipates might be the emerging themes, interests and areas of research now and for the future.

There seem to be a few emerging pockets of interest in sound art and experimental music in India at the moment. What do you think?

I think it's changing very fast just now. I was just looking at this site called REProduce, which is a promotion and management agency based in Delhi. The guy that started it told me that he's had all these kids coming out of the woodwork recently saying, "I do this". I also have a lot of people writing to me now saying that they are doing stuff with contact mikes and Walkmans, and asking if we have workshops, so there seems to be a lot of young people working with sound.

One area that's been ignored is Indian film sound. A lot of experimental sound and innovation happens in that world as well as with field recording for film, and that area has not been explored. For example, in the 1960s or '70s, Indian composers decided they wanted to use synthesisers, but there were no synthesisers in India, so they got people to make them. All these worlds haven't been explored very much yet. There is a book called *Taj Mahal Foxtrot* by Naresh Fernandes, have you read it? I think he's also the editor of *Scroll*, the online news magazine. It's a nice book about session musicians, which is an interesting world in itself, because all the session musicians were Goans, they had this Portuguese heritage, and they were comfortable with jazz, Western music arranging, composition and so on. So most of the Indian composers in Bombay would hire these people to arrange the film scores, yet they would not get any credit. They were the ones that were writing the scores and arranging everything for songs that became extremely popular. It's another world. Then there is the world of classical music, of course, and you have John Cage coming here in the '50s, and of course all your minimalists, everyone, Steve Reich, La Monte Young, Philip Glass...

I wonder how much of an exchange that was, because it felt like they took quite a lot.

They did take quite a lot...

I wonder how much they gave?

Er, David Tudor left his synthesiser at the National Institute of Design in Ahmedabad, and people didn't know what it was for a long time! NID and Ahmedabad was a hub because they were inviting Cage, Calder and many artists who were not yet that well known in the West.

Has anyone traced those histories?

No. If you read Cage's biography, he talks a lot about a woman called Gira Sarabhai turning him on to Zen. The whole lineage needs to be traced.

So there's an experimental culture around musical composition and arrangement and a recording culture that has some links with the European and American avant-garde. There's also a home-grown building tradition—you were saying earlier that people were building synthesisers and are building microphones. What about within an art context, is there a history of experimentation with sound?

Yes—that intersects with the experimental film world. We had an extremely interesting experimental film culture in the '60s and '70s. There were young people educated in places like Czechoslovakia and Eastern Europe where there was interesting sound for film. For example, there was Vijay Raghava Rao, again not well-known and not appreciated, but collectable, his stuff is expensive now. These are things that I'm only just discovering.

So there was never a university studio or a national radio studio?

In the 1970s, there was FSMR, Fundamental Systems and Music Research, in Bangalore, which was government funded. There is also the strange world of jazz fusion, for example L. Subramaniam who worked with loads of Western musicians including Herbie Hancock, Stanley Clark and Stéphane Grappelli. The other place to explore, from an art school perspective, is probably Shantiniketan in West Bengal, because they built bridges within Asia and had a lot of Japanese artists working there. For example, Fuku Akino was a visiting professor at the Visva-Bharati University in Shantiniketan in the early 1960s. Tagore believed that it was important for colonised countries to look to the east, not just to the west. Tagore himself was an interesting person and way ahead of his time in his pedagogical approach. He was also the first person from Asia to win the Nobel Prize. A good thing to read on that is Pankaj Mishra's book *From the Ruins of Empire: The Revolt Against the West and the Remaking of Asia*. It's about Asian intellectuals in the early part of the last century, focusing on Turkish, Indian and Chinese intellectuals questioning colonialism. Tagore was an extremely rational person, even though he was a poet and Shantiniketan was meant to be his utopia for education.

There must be a history of Indian sonic thinking—as far as you know, has anybody been looking into that?

As far as I know, no. I did look at some stuff about music from the University of Chicago or somewhere. It was more about the narrative of what sound is able to do, for example, mythologies about dancers singing and bursting into flames!

A lot of it does seem to cross between mythology, ethnomusicology, ancient classical music and language.

Most of the rituals were never written down. It was always an oral history, so everything is passed down through sound, which makes it supremely important. Writing itself was elitist. The oral tradition means that there is no one mythology or text, it has all been re-mixed, so the re-mix is also legitimate and there is no one definitive thing. That's the problem with our current politics and the current idea of what India is, we have always had our own versions of everything, but now, they're trying to standardise them and that's hugely problematic.

I'm interested in these local sonic cultures and histories, and in the differences and similarities between different traditions and, of course, the cross-overs. For example, konnakol, the South Indian tradition of playing with vowels and percussive vocal sounds in performance, has much in common with aspects of sound poetry, but I don't know whether there's been any kind of cross-pollination between them?

I don't even know who would be an expert in something like that, because there are local traditions—multiple forms of that across different places. Did you know that the first anechoic chamber in Asia is down the road, in Malleshwaram, in the first acoustics department in India, at IISc, the Indian Institute of Science, Bangalore? It was built in the late '60s.

That's interesting! I have also read that loads of ancient temples and monuments were designed with particular acoustic qualities in mind. I'm just wondering if there's any kind of tradition of anyone looking into archeo-acoustics?

Mr Umashankar Manthravadi is the pioneering Indian expert on acoustic archaeology, you can listen to his talks on YouTube. He is investigating whether early temples were actually acoustically designed as performance spaces and he has conducted research at Rani Gumpha, an ancient monastery in Odisha among other places. Whether that is true or not, the mathematical and architectural aspects of those spaces are amazing. There are also musical pillars in Hampi and other creative acoustic spaces around the country.

Everyone that I've talked to in the UK has had a circuitous route into working with sound, what about you?

So, I got my first computer when I was about ten years old, and it was a BBC Micro clone, made by an Indian company. The first thing that my friends and I were doing with computers was making sound—programming stuff to play 'Smoke on the Water'! So that's how I became aware that there was music to be made out of technology. I was also really into music and learning the violin in school. When I finished school, I went to college in California to study computer science and psychology and my mind opened up and I got into all kinds of music. I was listening to stuff on the internet which was quite new then, and hanging out at record stores. I really got into the American composers—La Monte Young and so on. When I finished, I came back to India and, around 2004, started to build a community studio in Bangalore with friends, artist and scientists, who were also returning from college. We were hanging out and sharing space and resources. A lot of my ideas for ISRO are from that time, I remember running a couple of circuit bending workshops then. When I was younger I would think about going to Ircam or some place in Paris, but now anyone can just put the tools on their computers.

Yes—one of the reasons that I did a PhD back in the early 1990s was because I needed access to a studio.

Right, and then you listened to academic computer music...

Yes, but maybe that's what's lacking—I think a lot of people haven't really caught up with the fact that they are part of a culture.

That's true. So then it doesn't matter what tools you have—and that brings up a lot of questions about what a university should be, right?

Yes—you wouldn't go to a university to learn how to do things, but you might go there to understand more about why to do things. What would you like to see happen with the Indian Sonic Research Organisation?

It's hard. I've learnt a lot of lessons, for example, we used to have free, open workshops teaching Max, Pure Data, electronics or sound and music on Saturdays, but no one would show up because it was free. When we charged a hundred rupees, tons of people showed up. You don't learn this kind of thing anywhere else—and these places like IRCAM are just dead—dinosaur institutions! Their elitism has caught up with them. A computer is now accessible and so are the tools.

I'm also conscious of gender balance within sound arts: if I look at a record made by some white guy, I'm like, "whatever!" I value people taking different approaches to technology and of just using it as a tool, for example, Bidisha Das, and Shreyasi Kar, both of who have been attached to ISRO in the past, are both into the natural world and its interface with technology. I find this super-interesting because of my earlier work with biology. I was not interested in really connecting to sound, but they're doing it, so that's great. Kids are going to be tired of their iPads and swiping stuff, they're going to want to find out about the world, this world, and this way of exploring the world, using technology, is quite new. I think that's a radical shift in art, certainly in India, in the last ten years.

People are trying to use sound and listening as an investigative tool in so many disciplines at the moment...

Yes, Lawrence Abu Hamdan and Forensic Architecture have been making ripples in the art world. I think they've gone in the same direction as design fiction where one or two people have a great idea, and they start a department of ideas, and then eighty or ninety students graduate from this department and do design fiction in the same way. In the case of forensic architecture, the trope is a map with a political narrative, of mining for instance—a map and an artefact—it's not very imaginative and then it keeps going on and on—but, in essence, the idea is great.

You talked about your earlier work with biology. Could you say a little more about some of the things that you have been involved in?

The first of my works that got shown in a gallery was *and how it rained*. It was a collaboration with a hydrologist looking at hundred years of rainfall data from Bangalore. That's how I got into working with scientists. That got shown around a bit in galleries so they figured that I was the guy that knew how to work with scientists. I was appointed artist in residence at the National Centre for Biological Sciences in Bangalore and I started working with Mukund Thattai, a synthetic biologist. At that time synthetic biology was fairly new. It was basically trying to design and program living things to do what you want. In a sense, you are playing god. From an artist's perspective, creating new forms of life was super interesting, just like creating a new composition or designing a sculpture. So one of the first works that I did was with students, and we made a bacterium that smelled like rain, which connected back to my earlier work with rainfall. That work, *Teenage Gene Poems*, won a lot of prizes in science forums, at MIT and it also got an honorary mention in the HYBRID arts category at the 2010 Ars Electronica. I continued working with biologists for a long time. I think science is a lot like cooking but there is a mystique around it. A lot of my work in that area is documented in *Hackteria* which one of the largest archives of biological tools. I put out all the instruments that I made for doing those kind of experiments there.

How do you actually show or exhibit a bacterium?

Oh well, this one you can smell! But we have put out the sequence that you would need to make that particular bacteria, the one that smells like rain, so you could make it in a lab.

Have you stopped working with biology?

Well, I'm looking for interesting projects! It takes a long time for me to get things out there, I work on projects for ten or maybe fifteen years. I still use the tools that I put together as part of my practice in previous labs and workshops.

How do you go about making the art / science collaboration truly collaborative? It seems that a lot of the time the artist is translating the scientist's work for a wider audience.

I feel there's nothing wrong in what you have just described! It's true that a lot of the work seems to be an artist illustrating an idea, certainly a lot of work that came out in the West was primarily that. It was a bit different with us because, right at the outset, we were adamant that we were not going to do that, so then you have to learn the language of the scientists. I spent three or four years learning that. If you are not speaking the same language then there is no conversation, so both the collaborators have to speak each other's language. That was a difference I felt. I see a lot of residencies where an artist parachutes into someone's lab for three months or so—it's impossible! We took the opposite approach and worked with someone for ten years.

There seems to be quite a lot of contemporary work from young artists in India that interfaces between technology and the natural world.

I don't know about that, but I do see a lot of it in South East Asia and Indonesia. I have a theory that it's to do with the idea of collaborating in communities and not being individualistic. In some sense the discourse of the individual artist has destroyed art practices around the world, and it's not conducive to something like art/science collaboration which can't just be about you, it has to be about the other person also. I have been thinking about what oriental art practices are and how much the artist stays anonymous. It's a long way from what we understand as contemporary art practices!

One of the areas that you have made work in—sonic fictions or re-creating and investigating a history—hasn't been much explored in sound art. I'm thinking, for example, of Notes from Utopia, *the work about the Jhonda tribal people and their adoption of the radio as a folk instrument. You made that for* Louder Whisper, *the online exhibition that Meena Vari curated by for CRiSAP.*

If it becomes a genre it'd be sad! It came from me reading about Richard Burton and his travels to the Middle East. It was before fake news, so I'm proud that I saw it coming! I was thinking about history and how you have to be aware what history is, especially as an Indian, where the discourse of history is so tied to power, not so much about sound.

But you realised it in sound.

Yes, but for me you need to have a good laugh when you make something—that's the primary quality of good for me—actually, it's the best.

Is that something you try and bring into your live playing as well?

It is, it turns into something like a circus. I've been looking at a lot of this Mayabazar [the 1957 Indian epic fantasy film directed by Kadiri Venkata Reddy] stuff and at this whole Indian mythology circus—where has that spectacle gone? Especially in terms of live music?

Is playing live what you are doing mainly at the moment?

Mainly. The struggle is to find a venue and all that stuff, so I'm also questioning what it means to just go and play? I think it's important. I'm wanting to explore ways that show you how you can distribute sound?

How have you been distributing it?

There are multiple ways. One is you mix a bunch of artefacts and throw it in a show! Then the other is, you create a spectacle, you perform, something happens…

In a traditional performance space?

Again, that's changed, because there are all these opportunities in Bangalore, for example in the subway stations. Also, you have this vast world of the Internet, I often wonder whether I can distribute stuff back in time—to the Jhonda tribe maybe—can it go back and mess with time that way? The means and the mechanisms of sound distribution is interesting.

What might your typical performance set-up consist of? What are you taking to Japan, for example?

The primary constraint is the electric supply voltage of the country so everything has to be reconfigured based on that! So, for example, the neon light tube that I performed with the other day works on 220 volts, but in Japan it's 110 volts so I can't take the neon tube. Also I'm an Indian guy going to Japan, playing electronic music—what do I do? Do I become the Indian guys with these Indian ragas? Am I going to be that quiet, Indian, meditative Zen guy who is not meditative or Zen at all, or is it going to be about taking the dysfunctionality and chaos of this space there? I was twelve years old when India liberalised, up to that point you couldn't get Coca-Cola in India. The India I live in now however is totally McDonaldised, a shining star of neo-liberalism, so you develop multiple identities even in India. I'm aware that everyone has multiple identities: which one you choose to present to the world is probably the artistic struggle I guess. I don't think generally it's necessary to perform my Indian identity.

Let's talk about the Nine Billion Names of God.

It's a program that downloads pornography, and looks for the point at which the person shouts out for 'God', and then collects that—in the hope of collecting nine billion instances of it. While the program is doing this, it uses artificial intelligence and machine learning to identify the word 'God' and the more it collects the better it gets.

So despite the fact it's said in different accents, different pitches, different voices, it still collects more and more as time goes on?

Yes, the gathering will make it better—or that's what the scientists who made those algorithms say! It's based on the 1953 short story by Arthur C. Clarke where once nine billion names of God are collected, the world will come to an end.

How many has it collected now?

It's collected about seven hundred names of God.

Does it collect the same voices a lot?

Well, it does. It does some crazy things, for example, it mistakes Russian words for God. It makes a lot of mistakes, it's a work in progress. Every time I tell someone about the work, they give me great ideas of what I should do next. Someone told me that people should donate money to the site and I should use it to buy computer space to store the increasing amount of things that are collected—at the moment I am doing it manually. The cutting-edge of technology has always been the porn and the sex industries, whether it's immersive environments or coming back to the idea of distribution—because they were the first ones to figure out how to distribute porn!

Outside established channels, yeah.

...and the robots, again, on the cutting edge.

How long did the programming for that take?

The programming took about three or four months, but that's only because programming itself has changed. You don't program any more. You have billions of libraries of someone else's code and you just plug it in.

Assemblage.

Yeah.

What are you interested in at the moment?

I guess my main concerns at the moment are thinking about the practicalities of performance and distribution; how you can build a community and how sound art can be political.

Locations

Adam Basanta / CL
Berlin, 2019

AM Kanngieser / AC
London, 2018

Budhaditya Chattopadhyay / CL
Kolkata & Beirut, 2018

Caroline Devine / CL
Milton Keynes, 2019

Elsa M'bala / CL
London, 2019

Evan Ifekoya / AC
London, 2020

Hanna Tuulikki / AC
Glasgow–Brighton, 2020

Hong-Kai Wang / CL
Taipei, 2018

Jau-Lan Guo / CL
Taipei, 2018

Jennifer Walshe / AC
London–Brighton, 2020

Khaled Kaddal / CL
Berlin, 2019

Lawrence Abu Hamdan / AC
Dubai–Brighton, 2020

Lina Lapelyte / CL
Vilnius–London, 2020

Maria Chavez / AC
New York–Brighton, 2020

Mark Peter Wright / AC
London–Brighton, 2020

Mikel R. Nieto / AC
San Sebastián–Brighton, 2019

Mikhail Karikis / AC
London–Brighton, 2020

Samson Young / CL
Hong Kong, 2018

Yang Yeung / CL
Hong Kong, 2018

Yashas Shetty / CL
Bangalore, 2018

After-words

Now that we've done all the interviews, what do we think? Has it been surprising?

What stands out for me, after reading back over our twenty interviews, is the diversity of what we've taken to constitute sound art: the diversity in everything from the artists' thematic concerns, the processes they adopt, the collaborations that they engage with and the ways their ideas and explorations end up meeting the world.

I agree. Each interview reflects our individual concerns and interests. I'm interested in what motivates each artist and enables them to produce their work, so I've asked questions about their background; how their practice and career has developed over time; how they work on a day-to-day basis; who commissions them; and have discussed, in some cases, whether they've got children or not—I feel that those things are important. I want to know if they are juggling work and family duties or whether they've got an income that's supporting their artistic output.

I think those things are absolutely fundamental but I admit that those dimensions are much, much, quieter in my own interviews where, instead, the thematic and theoretical sides of things become amplified. Perhaps my reticence to inquire into the textures of biographical identities could be a skewed and defensive projection on my part, one that derives from my own feelings about not having the right background, the proper musical or artistic bona fides. One consequence of the approach that I've adopted is that some of the lived lives are more occluded than they might otherwise have been.

It is possible that some of the people that I've interviewed might not have talked about their theoretical concerns as much as they had wanted to, because the time was taken discussing their biographical journey. But when I started developing an artistic practice I wanted to know how other people managed their lives and their artistic development. So our interviews are all very different, but hopefully, when you look at them as a collection, they reveal a greater scope of sound art practices than we might have imagined, and a rich variety of both thematic concerns and lived experience. Overall the things that emerge from the interviews, maybe more strongly than they might have twenty years ago, are the emphasis on listening and the growth of sound as a research tool or methodology.

I do hope that the collective scope is palpable. Within this notion of listening that you bring up—and sometimes listening appears spontaneously, sometimes in response to a direct question—there is, yet again, another diversity: even if listening practices are centralised within an engagement with sound, there are wide discrepancies in the 'hows', 'whys' and 'whats' of listening, right down to the most basic levels of meaning.

Yes, people are not just talking about their own listening practices, but also about discovering other contemporary and historical cultures of listening. Some people are trying to manifest their own listening practices in their work: for example, Maria Chavez talks about DJing her listening; Lawrence Abu Hamdan and Mikhail Karikis are trying to listening out for other people's listenings; Mikel R. Nieto talks about how others listen to us; Mark Peter Wright about 'listening-with', Hanna Tuulikki, listening to the 'more-than-human'; Caroline Devine recounts learning to listen at the BBC and triggering other people's memories of listening: listening seems to be at the centre of the practices discussed and the membrane that holds these interviews together.

On the one hand, listening is presented as a medium or modality, a genre or a discipline in itself; on the other hand, maybe it is the exact opposite, with listening becoming subsumed, becoming a reflexive part and parcel of what a critical practitioner does? As it is understood in these interviews, listening enables access to such apparently divergent aspects of the world as an artificially intelligent process for extracting data; an archive of visual material; the lifeworlds of a bird in a tree or a cage; and the perspectives of communities threatened by deforestation or by the rising sea levels in AM Kanngieser's Pasifika projects. I wonder if listening is something that has become enriched, developed, and complexified even since our edited book *On Listening*? What emerges from these discussions seems to have gone beyond what, when we finished that book in 2013, was already being felt as a great opening-up of the parameters. Now, in 2020, we're looking at people who are not just theorising listening in breadth and depth, but people who are practising it in ways that would have seemed unimaginable to me when we began working together on developing a sounds arts curriculum back twenty-two years ago.

There seems to have been a seismic shift. In On Listening, *it was fundamental to what people did but instrumentalised within their discipline. Now, it feels like a core practice with its own disciplinary subsets.*

I think a measure of that shift is the way that the commitment to the idea of listening as exclusively positive is much less prevalent. There is much more recognition that listening experiences can be dense and difficult and painful, can be repositories of injustices. Alongside that, there are departures from the idea of listening as an exceptional event and different approaches to how it might codify the experience of the everyday. Lina Lapelyte's interview is really good here...

... there is also Caroline's everyday socially engaged, local listening. There often seems to be a tendency for people to focus on big overarching issues like ecological change or government policy that mean that people often overlook the small and the everyday...

Yes.

Do you think there's a historical lineage for either of those positions? I was just thinking how much Pauline Oliveros's development of Deep Listening derives and focuses on everyday experiences of listening, whereas maybe sound as a methodology has often extracted listening from the everyday and expanded those ideas... is this true? Anyway, I welcome that elasticity and the pushing at the edges of what listening could be, what it could tell us and where it could lead us within the idea of sound as a research tool.

That notion of elasticity really resonates. It reminds me of other conversations we have had, which themselves shadow some of these interviews, where we have discussed the potential for both sound arts practices and listening methodologies to each become instrumentalised for other purposes and find themselves slipping away from iterative artistic processes. The elasticity might enable innovation, but I worry whether something gets lost if those methods become extracted from the care and attention involved in the practices of their original contexts?

There are few, among the people that we've interviewed, who produce work that we would have considered to be sound art twenty years ago. At that time we were at pains to try and define what sound art—as opposed to what music, experimental music or music technology—could be, and we probably would have partially defined it as the artistic manipulation, production and exhibition of sound. However, of the artists we've interviewed, few are concerned with that: Caroline might be the only one who has got a primarily sound-based practice. Everybody else has many different elements.

Over that time there has been a shift from what can sound be and what can it do as a means of dissemination, to how can sound be used. Sound, or listening, is still central to all the practices, but the work produced doesn't necessarily end up being sound, or sound alone. On the one hand, that feels really interesting, and on the other, it seems that we have moved beyond exploring the artistic possibilities of sound. I don't want to see that exploration totally left behind.

Have these shifts in sound arts happened through an inevitable breaking up of what might previously have been a narrower commonality of prior histories, experiences and identities?

Many of the people that we have interviewed have lived or grown up in a number of different countries so maybe it's surprising how many early formative influences they have in common. There's a significant amount of people—including Khaled Kaddal in Egypt, Caroline Devine in the UK, Elsa M'bala in Germany and Adam Basanta in Canada—who have talked about progressing from playing the guitar to experimenting with it, and then their need to expand out of that format. Certain bands have been influential in that, so maybe it's generational as well. Others, particularly those outside Europe, have expressed an interest in Western avant garde music or film and become interested in experimentation through that. I often wonder whether there's some sort of psychological fault <laughs> in people that are drawn to this style of unpopular experimentalism. Why are some people drawn to that, when others are happy to just listen to U2 for their whole lives?

Obviously there's a big question about the kinds of agency that operate behind such decisions <laughs>! Choosing the more experimental over the popular is not just a matter of converting the currency of your classical music training, or your popular music performance within a band. It might also be about determining the access you have in the future to a stable income, to opportunities for dissemination, to engagement with different networks, to a sense of prestige and even to how you describe yourself to someone you meet in a taxi, as Jennifer describes. Whether choice is the right word for what happens, I don't know.

As one of our interviewees said, it's a mixture of luck and effort. People have had different paths and starting points—some have come from music, some from a media or journalistic background, some from a training in new media art, or as an instrumentalist or performer, but often, although there might not be a sound arts 'scene' in the country that they're in, there is often a significant gallery or organisation which has acted as a focus for them. In some countries, for example in Taiwan, there seems to be active support for young artists to exhibit internationally. So there are many levels of support ranging from your friends and family, to a local gallery or organisation, to national support, or, in the case of Egypt and India, input from European organisations like the British Council or the Goethe Institute.

I didn't anticipate how the presence of academic institutions would become very tangible for some people and negligible for others. Of course, education is not simply a matter of going to a prestigious university, and a number of these artists engage with sound arts practices in ways that themselves sound pedagogic: we heard of workshops, learning spaces, co-learning, co-production, critiques of canons and proposals instead, for other approaches, sometimes decolonial, sometimes anti-patriarchal, sometimes queer, and sometimes there was the acknowledgement that these alternatives are yet to materialise (I'm thinking about what Evan Ifekoya said). Listening, yet again, becomes central to some of these definitions of the pedagogic; these processes occur in the context of concrete and digital infrastructures but are, excitingly, also about building new constituencies, communities, and collaborative opportunities.

It makes me realise that a lot of these things are contingent on a particular moment in time, and maybe also a wider political initiative. I'm thinking back to the 1980s, when I was involved in not one, but two, government-funded community recording studios in London, one of which was women-only. That would never happen now for a variety of reasons, but so many people benefited from that access. I think what Yashas Shetty is doing in India, and I'm sure others elsewhere, to open up opportunities for people in places where there's virtually no way of getting any education in sound art as we know it, is incredible. I am also engaged by the thought of people, at home, deconstructing a Steve Reich piece, and playing it on the guitar. That offers another kind of education, one that maybe motivates you to go somewhere else to find out more.

Maybe there is also an equivalent time-jump back into the '60s and '70s and to a sense of collective possibility outside established structures, one that can now be more pluralised and fair. Is this one of the many reasons why Pauline Oliveros appears again and again as an influence?

That's exciting, and I do hope that there is! Our interviewees are a pretty educated selection of people, actually, and through their educational backgrounds they bring a welcome pluralism. Some have studied computer engineering or computer science, others, classics, geography, fine arts, political science, music, electrical engineering, new media art: and they are all threads that feed into sound arts practice. Many have gone on to postgraduate studies at MA level and I would say at least half have got PhDs.

That brings us to the question of whether sound art is essentially, as has sometimes been said, an academic subject? It's interesting that various people are setting up spaces for sharing learning, exchange, collaboration and experience as part of their practice—is some of that concerned with funding? In the '80s, people did not necessarily see that as part of their practice, or, if they did, they might call themselves community artists, at least in the UK. However if you go back to the '60s and '70s, Oliveros and others would be more likely to see setting up those spaces and groupings as an important part of their artistic work. At this moment, many people seem to be moving between having a singular, individual practice, a collaborative practice and a participatory practice. It's as if people are trying to expand what being an artist and particularly a sound artist—or an artist that works with sound—actually is.

Maybe that is why, at least in these interviews, the issue of a canon is less prominent? Both you and I asked questions that could have been responded to with references to a kind of family tree of sound arts practices (though obviously the hetero-normative idea of families and lineage needs to be problematised). Maybe that is less of a touchstone because of the disparate educational and other formations which you identified? Perhaps because this is a wider-scoped selection of interviewees than you might normally encounter, the focus on Western art music genealogies is not so insistent.

I think you identified that Oliveros had been mentioned by the most people in the interviews. If we'd done this book eight years ago, there wouldn't have been so many people mentioning her. Her work has only come to widespread prominence in the last decade and particularly since she passed away in 2016. When you investigate the range of other influences mentioned, they are often quite extraordinary and random, including in the cases of Budhaditya Chattopadhyay and Elsa M'bala, their families, so the idea of a canon at this moment in time seems to have been exploded.

I wonder if a theoretical canon is coalescing in place of an artistic one <laughs>! After Oliveros, probably the next-most-referred-to person in the interviews would be Donna Haraway. Perhaps that relates to what Jennifer Walshe said about the sound arts students that she has encountered being people who are incredibly philosophically articulate, but paradoxically less sensitive to their sonic materials!

And it's interesting what Jau-Lan Guo says about whether an exhibition "pleases the ear". There is this separation between something being sound and something sounding good. Adam expresses it well, when he says that many people with a background in music or electroacoustic music think that sound art sounds awful in comparison with the practice of refining your sounds in the studio.

Yes.

But coming back to the theoretical, as we have mentioned in the introduction, we've interviewed people who speak English, because that's what we speak, but I'm aware of how differently equipped people who don't speak English are in terms of being able to access those theoretical underpinnings that so many people refer to from the western canon. For example, the latest Donna Haraway book came out in 2019 or 2018, and I don't know how many languages it's been translated into yet, but you can guarantee that significant writers from Western elite universities will eventually be quite widely translated. Conversely, how long do we have to wait for the books written in Arabic, Farsi, Japanese or Hindi to be translated into English?

Yes, you are right, and we have to acknowledge the kinds of exclusions that language (among many other things) imposes. Very early on in this long process of researching and then writing this book, we realised that what it most immediately invited was a sequel. Even if there is the welcome absence of the canonical, nonetheless, each of the interviewees calls out a set of relations to people who they see as colleagues, friends, rivals, and to scenes which they identify with (or have historically identified with). At the same time, it is obviously very difficult to hear what Evan was saying about the lack of opportunities to make meaningful connections to people in whom they could identify a historical antecedent for what they do. And that is probably something that other people who we interviewed would share.

Totally, and I think that will be one of the things to be addressed in the future through the work and theoretically.

One of the other things that really strikes me about everybody that we've interviewed is that their work has significantly developed over a relatively short period of time. Often their thematic concerns remain the same, but the method or the way that the work manifests has, for most artists, changed. The themes that have emerged from the interviews are very varied. There are intersections, or nodes concerning labour, language and voice; the unheard—whether that's to do with place or people or ecology; concerns with the local and the specific; the act of listening; and maybe also with the relationship between art and science; but there's very little work that is concerned with the condition of sound itself. Maybe this reflects our choices, most of those people are quite thematically engaged.

It may even reveal how people perform for an interview that's destined for an ink-and-paper publication. Though there is a pronounced sense of there being an active thematic sensibility, and though sound is, naturally, fundamental for everyone we talked to, nonetheless, sound in its materialities as sound feels much less represented.

What feels amplified, and maybe it's to do with the moment that we live in, is the political: the connection between art and political protest or people's experience of protest or sound art as a tool for political intervention as well as the politics of nation, labour, colonialism, gender, queer and black politics. In general our interviewees are all politically engaged, and that manifests in the work in many different ways.

Eight years ago, we finished a book with a similar scope that focused on field recording practices. We did adopt a different approach, one we discuss a little in this book's Forewords; however, it is interesting to weigh up the extent to which this is a more political collection of responses than what we had in *In the Field*. After all, we are both the same people, we have the same political sensibilities and affinities. Or was *In the Field* differently political?

I don't think we are the same people—we have gone through eight years of political turmoil nationally and internationally—

—Yeah, that's true.

—Along with everybody else, we've encountered things that have forced us to question everything about the world around us, and so have all those artists.

In our own small way, over the last two decades we've done our bit to try and tease out the politics in sound art and also, in the last year or two, more books and essays have been published that engage with the political in sound arts' practices. I anticipate that there will be an increasing amount of these books being published in the next few years and particularly in other languages.

There is a political turn and, in this current Covid moment, when everybody's questioning the point of even making any art, for many people there is absolutely no point if it doesn't engage with some sort of politics.

I think you're right. The definitions of politics at work mirror similar diversities that we talked about earlier in terms of both backgrounds and sound practices. Here, politics can be a collaboration with an NGO to support a specific court case through a mechanism of evidential truth; it can be the creation of a space where previously marginalised voices are given opportunities to be heard differently; it can be the development of utopian sonorities; it can be the attribution of a critical audibility to something that had not been fully registered: such as the operations of machine learning, women working on the decryption of enemy communications during World War Two, relations of intimate care and all manner of environmental stresses and their impacts. So this politics is incredibly complicated, spanning advocacy, direct interventions, forms of documentary, dreams of alternative futures.

I want to add re-framing popular culture to reveal misogyny and sexism to that list. But what struck me when you were just speaking, and this again relates back to In the Field, *is that a lot of people have mentioned the politics of recording. Again it varies from situations where it's actually dangerous or illegal to make a sound recording, so much so that by doing so you risk arrest, to thinking about the repatriation of historic field recordings, to considering the power relationships within the recording and the ethics of recording. I was also interested in Budhaditya's idea of a national consciousness being resistant to recording because they feel that it fixes a tradition that's essentially improvisatory, and the links that he made between that and the current political climate in India, where there is a drive to standardise things that have always been fluid. So sound recording itself becomes a reflection of the wider political climate.*

As an extension of what you're saying, a number of people we interviewed are working to create a politics of animality, with widened constituencies that embrace the more-than-human, that reconceive the ethics around that encounter.

A further dimension might also be the way that the national past of some of our interviewees finds repercussions and resonances in their work and how they express the expectation to perform identity in order to be accepted in certain spheres. Some have also talked about their inability to find a 'lineage' or a heritage in sound that reflects them. It's important, as Yashas says, there was such a big cultural exchange between the West and for example, India, and we know what the West gained from India but are less informed about how India benefited. Similarly there's a lot of talk about going abroad for your education and what that gives you, but maybe not so much about what it takes away and diminishes.

There is a wider international context for sound art that is informed by and is interrogating many manifestations of colonialism and postcolonialism and is more accessible to a wider selection of people. Whether those making the work are called, or call themselves, sound artists is interesting! In the future the means of production will be further democratised and made accessible, and the idea that sound art is a Western art form will be debunked, because actually there's loads of interesting stuff happening with sound in every country in the world.

I think another question emerging from a number of interviews is whether sound art itself constitutes an elite art form—and whether this accusation might differ slightly from it being critiqued as a Western art form. I liked hearing how definitions of sound art shuttled between ones imbued with the apparent unapproachability of High Art and others that explicitly engage with the more widely familiar forms of vernacular and colloquial culture. Boundaries that might previously have been quite dominant can become disrupted and blurred. Everything doesn't instantly become easy nor does everyone immediately get access to all the toys—those systems of power retain their potency—but the more definitions of sound arts can be broader, rather than narrower, more unstable, rather than more firmly fixed, the better.

When you look at how people's practices develop, and how they navigate realising their work in different formats and distributing it through different means, although some of our subjects have some assistance some of the time, everybody is pretty hands-on. They might regard themselves more as a producer or a director on some projects, but they all pitch in and learn what they need to learn. So Adam learns about big concrete blocks, Samson Young about 3D printing, Jennifer about AI and Caroline about transducers on glass—everybody has to be a polymath and to be adaptable.

And then there is Mikel as a counter-example, where he describes delivering up the sounds to a sound engineer who he respects, and seeing what emerges from that. His anti-authorial approach certainly seems distinct from those people who, even when presenting at the Venice Biennale, are having to equip themselves with new skills to finish work for exhibition.

Everybody we've talked to is into collaboration in some way.

Definitely.

Some of the people that we've interviewed have been collaborating with the same people for years, they are socially connected and there's an element of play. I like the fact that Hong-Kai Wang, after being in America, goes back to Taiwan, and works with her old friends, as well as what Samson was saying about working with those two artists and each swapping roles and art forms. So there's different forms of collaborative relationships going on.

You get a sense of the relational aspects of collaborations extending towards curators, funders, residencies, artistic networks. I thought the detailed discussion Lina offers of how her work developed through processes of broader interactions was very interesting, including her articulation of the importance of securing a residency where she and her collaborators could work on the opera together—

Absolutely.

—and then, later, having developed Sun & Sea, how they made a commitment to stay with the same performers for the duration of the show. There is a palpable sense that if you eschew isolated autonomy, you open yourself up to all these different kinds of relationships. Perhaps the emphasis on networks and the different people who can be involved in them is yet another explanation for why the 'canonical' is quieter in these interviews: you don't need a genealogy if you can be inspired by speculative, imaginative, friendship-based, professional, educational and all kinds of different relationships!

Yes, that's great. Most people don't talk so much about their relationships with curators that much, but with Jau-Lan and Yang Yeung, speaking as curators working with sound, we are offered an insight into how they think, and their concerns are actually quite different from the concerns of the artists. In the next volume, we need more interviews with curators who are primarily concerned with sound!

Alongside the curators, would it be interesting in the future to hear more from critics, commentators, the magazine writers, bloggers, and from users of social media channels? We hear about the artists, of course, and their different collaborations, and there is amplification of the organisations those artists and their collaborators work with, festivals, residencies, but perhaps there is more to learn about the importance of a kind of public sphere?

It's true, but I feel that in the economy of the art world or academia or even life, those people that you have mentioned get heard! This is obviously debatable but often I feel that it's the artists that don't get heard apart from through other's interpretations of their work.

On the one hand, during the period you and I have been collaborating on projects, the articulation of sound arts as an 'an emerging discipline' has gone from a familiar refrain to an expression that feels more and more awkward to keep repeating. On the other hand, some of what our interviewees—very successful interviewees—have said suggests that there is still a way to go before sound achieves a parity with certain other fine arts practices. The negotiation of disparities between opportunities, spaces, networks, becomes a preamble to thinking about how sound arts might constitute a career, which goes back to what we talked about at the start of our discussion today in terms of how artistic practices are conducted amidst the living of a life that might include caring responsibilities, other relationships, unrelated waged and unwaged labour. However much we can see commonalities, there are also big disparities between the different routes that people have taken and the different stages that people find themselves on their journeys.

I wonder what the pinnacle of success for somebody working in sound is? Surely winning the Golden Lion at the Venice Biennale is up there; although, in her interview, Lina talks about how, when they were in Venice, and performing every day having won the prize, they could barely afford to pay for child care.

Yes, and by the same token, you have someone else winning the Turner Prize in a collective gesture of solidarity who registers scepticism about the very term sound art. So there are contradictory narratives surrounding measures of success, the solidity of disciplinary definitions, and relative opportunities to contribute to livelihood, well-being, security.

For the last two decades we have always framed sound art as 'emerging' but I'm wondering what has emerged and whether it could be said to have developed from emerging to disparate—'the disparate field of sound art' and, thinking further into the future, whether it will become the 'disappearing' or 'disappeared' field of sound art . I'm not sure whether sound art is going to continue to be a separate disciplinary area. I think it might have emerged into something else: a myriad of possibilities and all these pluralities we've been talking about.

So it's very difficult for people to trace where their career could go, although most of the people that we've interviewed do seem to have a sense that they are building a career.

I agree. From almost all of the interviews there emerges a sense of career at least in terms of the chronology of an artist's work, a progression in which people can step back and declare "Oh, I didn't like that project", or "In retrospect…" or "I don't put it on my CV".

Yes, and many of them refer to a pivotal or a break-through project.

That's true, it could be productive to conduct a focused analysis of what it was that made that project pivotal: was there a significant and previously unanticipated amount of funding; was a particular skill finally realised; did it accompany a specific collaboration; or did it connect back to what we talked about earlier as a coincidence of a number of different factors, role of a curator, emergence of a network, access to technology, or an alignment of the stars?

It's difficult to identify a pivotal work until quite a long time after it's made and you gain some distance from it. It is something that puts distance between your past and your future and you don't necessarily recognise that until much later.

Following on from that, we didn't talk to people so much about whether they would call themselves a sound artist or not. But they all signed up to a big element of sonic engagement. So sound and listening are identified as a central method, inspiration or way of working in every case, and that's interesting about what it means for the definition of a sound artist, because twenty years ago, we probably would have thought it was someone who worked with sound, or whose work produced sound, and now I think we understand it in a different way?

This might sound boring, but I remember from a very long time ago conversations that we all had around curriculum design where there was an aspiration to deliver sets of skills, technical resources and professional aptitude that could then prepare a student to choose from a variety of different possibilities, some of which would be in the recognisable domain of fine arts practice, and some would be in the allegedly more commercial worlds of sound design, music for screen.

I think that's true because there wasn't such a long lineage to draw on and we were trying to open things out to a variety of approaches. What has also happened over that time is that certain aspects have developed, certainly among the kind of people that we've interviewed, and one of those is the theoretical aspect. That comes back full circle I think, to our earlier discussion of people studying for PhDs and investigating things, other than sound itself, through their work. Because when you think about it, when we started out with that curriculum, there was very little research or reading at our disposal, and the publications that were available were predominantly historical mappings, you know? At that stage, it felt like they were trying to establish what it was, "OK, this is sound art, and this is sound art, and this is sound art, and this is as well: actually, they're all a bit experimental music, too, but, you know, we're kind of conflating the two". Then at some point, beyond that, as people started to work with sound more, the possibilities became apparent and then the theory followed that—so it's back to that iterative process again.

There is maybe now an additional part of this discussion to unpack, which is around the splitting off of what might be termed the artistically-inspired theoretical resources from another tendency that has since coalesced into what is called sound studies. Sound studies could have been the thing that we were looking for twenty years ago, could have been perfect for our students, but now what has arrived feels a little bit too much in the hands of the researchers who are not also practitioners (though I know that separating those two is already problematic!).

It felt like pushing at the edges of practice allowed us all to build up the theory, so the theoretical and contextual framework was, to some extent, practice-led. But the rise of sound studies doesn't feel practice-led, or if it is then it's not artistic practice as we understand it, and actually, what's happened is that the voice of the artists has become obscured and unheard.

Sound studies is a big field, of course, but the little corner of it that I've explored seems to be as you've described it, with less sense of how the artistic might constitute a research process in itself, or how the artist might have something interesting to say through their creative practice.

I think that a lot of artists feel they have to be sound studies experts as well, or maybe some of them already are, but there's definitely a tension.

That is a really interesting phenomenon and could be said to be reflected in a number of our interviewees who balance artistic practices with developing sound arts discourse or sound studies. As just one example, Budhaditya is very active in terms of his scholarship, he has recently published work on film theory and film history, environmental aesthetics, listening.

I wonder whether this is why sound arts are sometimes seen as an academic practice? Is the implication that they are situated in academia, or that many sound artists think, or are forced to think, academically about their work and become a sound studies scholar as well? I don't know.

So where does that leave us? From these interviews, at this moment in time, if we had to say what sound art was... <laughs>...I really don't know whether we could... it would need a long list. In the past, we used to be able to say—and used to have to say—what it wasn't. I don't know whether I can say what it isn't any more. It's almost like there's nothing I could say it isn't.

I agree! On the basis of our conversations in this book, it is very hard to say what sound art is not. In terms of what thematic concerns are excluded; what compositional, performative, aesthetic or technical processes are outside its remit; what kinds of collaborations, partnerships, intentions, and approaches to 'exhibition' are impossible.

I think what we can say is that it's constantly shape-shifting. There's this big emphasis on listening, an increasing breakdown of disciplinary borders, and work that might be sound-led but not necessarily sound-realised, and in general it has a tendency to be politically engaged.

Search index

Activism 123, 210
  See also: Protest
Alexandria (Egypt) 122–123
Alexievich, Svetlana 119
All India Radio 40
Afrofuturism 75
Anderson, Laurie 48, 119, 149
Archive 56, 72, 75, 77, 85, 105, 130
  Asia Art Archive 206
  Becoming audible 105, 163
  Berlin Phonogram Archive 39
  British Library 28
  Contemporary 158
  Her Noise Archive (whiteness of) 79
  Imaginary 113
  Personal 123, 157
  The Travelling Archive (Bhowmik) 40
Art world 92, 112
Audible 42, 72, 92, 94, 105, 135, 163, 168, 176
Audience 18, 87–88, 106, 126–127, 139, 165, 189, 194, 217
  Online 16, 151, 157
  Proximity 152
Aural diversity 137, 147, 151, 165, 179
  See also: Listening

Band 12, 15, 47, 82, 121–122, 192, 225
  Church band 60
  Marching band 144
  See also: Le Tigre, Nirvana
BBC (British Broadcasting Corporation) 36, 49, 111, 117, 215
Beirut 45, 124
Bell Labs 137
Bells 31, 54, 206
Berlin 6, 11, 40, 59
  Berlinale 39
  Errant Bodies project space 172
  SAVVY project space 68
  "Weirdo vibe" 65
Birdsong 55, 83, 88, 158, 223
  Away With The Birds (Tuulikki) 83–84
Bodies 33, 71, 86, 94, 118, 123–124, 171, 176
  Embodied 25, 82, 87, 155
  Health 65, 146, 159, 162
  See also: Breath, Listening, Sensory, Sleep
Breath 83, 123
Butler, Octavia E. 75, 78

Cameroon 61–64
Canon, see Sound Arts
Care (as solicitude) 139, 188, 190
  Self-Care 78, 188, 210
Chance 159
  Of Technique: Chance Procedures on Turntable (Chavez) 151
  See also: Luck
Cities 54, 55, 185, 206
  City of Things (Devine) 53
  See also: Alexandria, Beirut, Berlin, Milton Keynes, Mumbai, New York, Taipei
Climate Crisis 28, 34, 82, 84, 90, 120, 162–163, 178, 180, 182
  See also: Ecology, Flooding
  See also: *Sun & Sea* (Lapelyte)
Collaboration 67, 85, 100, 142–143, 169, 193
  Compared to participatory 164
Colonialism 33, 97, 106, 125, 168
  Anti-colonial 100, 214
  Legacies 113
  White West 208
Commissions 15–16, 53, 57, 86, 94, 97, 99, 111, 127, 147, 166
  See also: Finance, Residency
Community 98, 123, 179, 207
  Creating 220
  See also: Friends, Networks
Coney Island 94
Curation 45, 102, 104, 198, 204, 211
  Relationships with 16, 40, 86–87, 94, 198

Dance 33, 37, 82, 87, 122, 144, 193–194, 214
  Dance drama 137
  Gravity and 177
DIY 14, 53, 56, 74, 105, 123, 199
DJ 79, 107, 152–153
Documentary 187, 204
  Alternative 120
  Methodology 186
Drawing 21, 87–88, 192, 200

Early influences 76, 82, 111, 149, 192, 203, 215
Eastman, Julius 79
Echo, as affective encounter 79
Ecology 29, 81, 89, 162–163, 175
  Acoustic ecology 12, 55
  Ecology of senses 167

Education 5, 111, 190
    Art classes 192
    Art school 82–83, 111, 208, 214
    Film school 37, 39, 111
    Musical training 118, 121, 141
    Need for inclusivity 190
    PhD 3, 12, 41, 98, 195, 197, 203, 226, 233
       Achievement of 46
       Dry 197
    Postgraduate degree (MA, MPhil) 12, 123, 141
    Undergraduate degree (BA), 12, 50, 78, 109, 141, 192
Emotion 29, 70, 157, 183, 188
    Anger 34, 62
    Grief 34, 89
    Humour 70, 91, 113, 165, 218
    See also: Care, Laughter
Everyday 82–83, 94, 106, 129, 184–185, 224
ALL THE MANY PEOPLS (Walshe) 115–116
Exhibition 105, 107, 117, 127, 185, 194, 211
    Soundings (MoMA, 2013) 14
    See also: Curation, Museum
Exile 43
Exoticism 108

Family 33, 60–61, 97, 125, 129, 142, 146, 203, 205
    Influence 111
    Combining with art 148
    Support 62
Feminist approaches 5, 25, 57, 75, 77, 112, 143, 216
    Gender Studies 192
    See also: Haraway, Lorde, Oliveros
Festivals 16, 110, 192, 209
    Berlinale 39
    Documenta 101, 157
    Film 37, 50
    Huddersfield Contemporary Music Festival 110
    Instal 82
    Liminaria 99
    Microwave 193
    Venice Biennale 97, 105, 108, 146–147, 148, 191, 197
Fiction 114, 172, 180, 216
    Science Fiction 75, 77, 114, 117, 118
       See also: Octavia E. Butler
    Sonic fiction 218
Field recording 11, 13, 38, 55, 94
    Ethics of 27, 168
Film 183, 187, 199
    Film Sound 37–38, 41, 48, 49, 121, 213
    Sound effects 136, 157
    See also: Education, Film school
Finance 62, 124, 204, 211
    Art market 18, 76, 107, 109
    Fairness and 31, 112, 161
    Grants 96, 102, 114, 124, 165, 194, 206

Arts Council 188, 200
British Council 124, 130
Canada Council 18
Government Funding 109, 214
Self-financing 127–128, 146
See also: DIY, Family Support
See also: Commission, Residency
Flooding 38, 169
    See also: *Flom Sang* (Matterlurgy) 170
    See also: Sea
Food 93, 100, 148, 203
Friends 15, 33, 43, 56, 102, 111, 143, 163, 187, 192, 206, 227
    See also: Family

Gaelic (Irish) 117
Gaelic (Scots) 83, 89
Gallery 52, 103, 125, 132, 143, 165, 198
    Compared to nightclub 69
    White cube 103, 104, 197
    See also: Curation, Museum
Gender, 64–65, 72, 88–89, 216
    See also: Feminist Approaches
Global South 45
Google 21, 33, 51, 119, 199
    See also: Internet
Guitar, see Instruments

Haraway, Donna 86, 88, 116, 227
Histories 45, 51, 100, 105, 113, 175, 181, 208, 218
    Historical present, the 77, 81–82, 118, 147, 150, 162, 171, 229
    History books 161, 214
    Museum of History (Hong Kong) 207
    Oral, 27, 51, 57, 100, 110, 172, 214
Holy Grail (of electro-acoustic world) 22
Human rights 132–133
    Universal Declaration of 185
Humanities 163
    Anthropology 184
    Geography 25, 89, 156, 164
    "sonic turn" in 24
    See also: Histories

Improvisation 11, 42, 74, 82, 114, 119, 121, 144, 185
Indigenous cultures 36, 67, 175
Installation 53, 70–71, 87, 92–93, 103, 125–127, 135–136, 158, 194, 207
    See also: Site-specific
Institutions 33, 43–44, 62, 103, 130, 161, 196, 209
    Elitism and 216
Instruments (musical) 49, 63, 121
    Bengali instruments 36
    Guitar 11, 47, 61, 121
    Synthesiser 62–63, 74, 192, 213
    Violin 122, 141, 145, 215
    See also: Band, Music

236 SOUND ARTS NOW

Instruments (scientific) 51, 217
Internet 76, 123, 129, 218
  See also: Google
Interviews 6, 31, 51, 92, 107, 119, 147, 208, 210-211, 222

Kim, Christine Sun 11, 79

Labour 31, 93, 97, 115, 168, 185
  Reproductive labour 97
Language and Languages 119, 132, 185, 217
  Accent test 133, 138
  Alienation 96
  Mimesis and 86, 115, 134, 184
  Six languages 60
  Translation 96, 146, 189, 227
  See also: Voice
Laughter 30, 39, 40, 46, 59, 61, 90, 92, 107, 182, 187, 204, 225
  See also: Voice, Emotion
Le Tigre 70
Listener 52, 116, 135, 178
  Audience as 172
  Essentialist category 140
  Nomadic Listener, The (Chattopadhay) 44
  Primacy of 69
  Reliable 133
Listening 13, 25, 172-173, 223, 228
  Cultures of 129
  Deep 33, 82, 151, 224
  Differences in 30
  Difficult 172-173
  Ethics 27-29
    'Listening well' 136, 164-165, 203
  Investigative 216
  Multisensory 87
  No definition of 25
  Non-linguistic 96
  Other 172, 186
  Politics 132-133, 139
  Sessions 124, 129
  Shared 163, 173
  To music 141, 153, 174
  Tradition and 82, 205
  See also: Audible, Radio
Live, see Performance
Loop, Looping 21, 64, 73
  Feedback loop 15, 17, 48, 112, 124
Loudspeakers 52-54, 92, 126, 151, 157
  Multichannel 50, 105, 126, 145, 158, 200
  Ready-mades 18
  She Was A Full Body Speaker (Ifekoya) 72
Lorde, Audre 77, 138
Luck 16, 40, 79, 93, 95, 210, 225

MA (postgraduate degree), see Education
Manifesto 41, 174
  Recovered Manifesto of Wissam [inaudible] (Abu Hamdan) 139-140

Map 25, 71, 89, 105
  Countermap 138
  Sound map 30, 55
Materials 13, 20, 26, 106, 204
  3D printing 199
  Concrete 21
  Cultural 115
  Feedback 17
  Glass 54
  Metals 19, 128, 134
  Real world 13
  Sonic 25, 48
  Text as 119
  Tradition 84
  Voice as 52, 77
  "working with" 24
  See also: Archive
Memory 36, 48, 57, 100, 134, 204
  Hyper Memory 158
  Media as memory 66, 85, 136, 157
  Mnemonic topographies 89
  "Memory triggers" 166
  Sonic memories 97, 158
Mentor 88, 91, 96, 112
  Guru 39
Microphone 17, 21, 158, 166, 168-169, 175, 186
Migration 59, 63, 91, 95, 195, 204-205
  See also: Exile, Network
Mix 68, 70, 152-153, 181
Monk, Meredith 87, 119, 149
More-than-human 27, 82-83, 85, 167, 168-169
Mumbai 41
Museum 93, 98, 103, 106-107, 120, 132, 158
  Victoria and Albert 56
Music 122, 213
  Art and 69-70
  Genres
    Arabic classical 129
    Contemporary classical 39, 112
    Folk 82, 88
    Hip hop 143, 160
    Indian classical 37, 56
    Jazz 11, 60, 92, 185, 213
    Metal 39, 121
    Opera 96, 124, 142, 184
    Rock 11, 39
    Techno 75, 153
    Western classical 36, 121, 194, 213
    See also: DJing, Instruments
  Harmony 122, 145
  Scores 155, 173, 211, 213
    Sonic Scores 155-156
    See also: Improvisation

Names 106, 135
  Gaelic Place Names 89
  Nine Billion Names of God (Shetty) 219
  On grain of rice 155

SEARCH INDEX 237

Nature 28-29, 57, 181, 216-217
   Post-natural 168
Network 33, 40-41, 179, 207-208, 231
   International 197, 208
   Neural 114
   Online 31, 76, 151
   Personal 16, 96, 184
   See also: Friends
   Voice as 138, 185
New York 14, 91, 93, 104, 112, 151, 161, 195, 211
New York Times 115
Nirvana 11
Noise 168
Noise artist 103, 208
Noisy media 155, 179

Oliveros, Pauline 82, 83, 119, 143, 151, 226-227
Orgonite 71

PhD, see Education
Performance 15, 21, 42, 63, 84, 118, 127, 144-145, 184
   Campaign truck 95
   Cultural expectation and 67, 151, 196, 219
   Energy and 89
   Field recording and 40
   Karaoke 105
   Performance space 48, 145, 185, 193, 215
   See also: Audience, Improvisation
Place 25, 27, 35, 39, 55, 85, 89
   of Abundance 75
   History of 85, 100, 184
   Place names 89
   See also: Site-specific, soundscape
Poetry 31-32, 56, 60, 126
Process 20-21, 51, 84, 165, 180
   See also: Research
Protest 65, 107, 122-123, 136, 210, 228
   Greenham Common 57
   No Ordinary Protest (Karikis) 186
   Protest song 100
   Umbrella Movement 209
   See also: Activism

Queer 72-73, 77, 89, 112

Racism 43-44, 67, 79, 160-161, 162
Radio 49-50, 67, 75, 98, 107, 203, 214
   Radio listening 23, 36, 129, 153,
   Radio play 77, 157
   Radio waves 25, 51
   See also: All India Radio, BBC
Rain 216-217
Recording 28, 50
   Binaural 55
   History of 42, 45, 168
   Recording of performance 11, 52, 203, 213

Technologies 37, 39, 52, 114, 175
   See also: Field Recording, Microphone
Remixing 70, 214
   See also: Mix
Research 13, 19, 29, 43, 51, 57, 73, 75, 84, 100, 106, 115, 121, 129, 132, 163, 190, 198, 204
   Artist-researcher, idea of 164
   Evaluation of 32, 33
   Potential inequalities in 31
   Sound arts now 6, 227
   See also: Education, Process
Residencies 44, 65, 98, 112, 142, 173, 178, 184
   Leverhulme Residency 57, 164
   Schloss Solitude Residency 112, 146
Rhythm 70, 128

Science 29, 129, 169, 215, 217, 228
Sea 71, 83, 158
   Seawomen (Karikis) 184, 187
   See also: *Sun & Sea* (Lapelyte)
Senses, Sensorial 122
   "sensorial politics of experience" 132
Silence 23, 48, 129, 177, 207
   Inaudible 168-169
   Listening in 124
   Of absence 42, 135
   Silence Kills (Nieto) 175
Silenced 34, 168, 207
Singing 60, 66, 83, 85, 100, 114, 173, 210
   Harsh singing 105
   Have A Good Day (Lapelyte) 142
   Singing Revolution, The 149
   Traditions 36, 40, 83, 106, 122, 129, 148, 185
Site-specific 42, 48, 54, 92-93, 147
   Idea of site 166
Sleep 89, 145, 159, 173
Software 20, 21, 40, 44, 74, 94, 105, 114
   Coding 22, 65, 194
   Processing 44
   Pro Tools 47
   SketchUp 21, 199
Song, see Singing
Sonification 33, 57
Sound 26, 34, 107
   Acoustics 25, 135-136, 215
   Body 176
   See also: Breathing
   Condition of resonance, as 133
   Eavesdropping 27, 119
   Medium and method, as 104
   Sculpture, as 16, 155, 217
   Sonic image 138
   Soundscape 92, 130, 137, 185
Sound art 106, 112
   As art of listening 99, 123, 140, 163, 179
   Canon 6, 39, 226-227
   Deconstructing 122, 225, 231

Inequalities in 45, 79, 216
Theoretical 227
Exclusionary 29, 78-79, 160-161
Local and global definitions 7, 104, 108, 129, 230, 233
African sound art 65, 129
Indian sound art 43, 212
Interdisciplinary 103
Political 112
Sound artist 106, 128
Career 23, 29, 62, 79, 132, 161, 182-183, 194, 208, 232
As academic 197
Defining oneself as 14, 66, 78, 127-129, 133-134, 179, 200, 226, 233
Sound map, see Map
Soundpocket 202
Sound systems 74-75
Soundwalking 30, 33, 157
Speaker, see Loudspeaker
Studio 47, 74, 93, 114, 124, 200, 215
Music Studio 38, 50, 55, 123
Radio Studio 203
Studio Space 20, 206
No studio 95, 183
Sun, emissions from 57
Sun & Sea (Lapelyte) 142, 145-147, 231

Taipei 93, 103, 208
Teaching 6, 83, 109, 161, 163, 186, 193, 197, 202, 225
See also: Education, Mentor
Technology 175
Access 29, 31, 76, 123, 129, 160, 179, 215
Early introduction to 11, 35, 48, 215
See also: Microphone, Recording, Software
Temporality 45, 73, 89, 103, 115-116, 120, 126-127, 155, 175, 218
Timelessness 124
Texture 37

Very Low Frequency (VLF) 57
Video 12, 43, 67, 70, 100, 114, 144, 151, 173, 186, 199
Music video 187
Video art 106, 193
Visual
Dominance of 25
Visibility as trap 72
Visual art in relation to sound 17, 72-73, 128, 148
Visual score 87, 105, 110, 122
See also: Music, Scores
Voice 49, 51, 63, 188-189
As emotional barometer 188
As network 138
Grain of 189
Radio voice 67
Whisper 66
See also: Breath, Language, Singing

Weather 74, 117, 178
See also: Flooding, Rain
White supremacy 31, 45, 161
See also: Racism
Workshop (as method) 82, 98, 100, 144, 146, 161, 163, 175
Writing 46, 55, 60, 118, 151, 167, 170, 180, 197
Elitist, as 214
Geography as 26
See also: Fiction, Language, Poetry
Wysing 115

Years
1960s 125, 213, 214
1970s 20, 54, 157, 214
1980s 57, 105-106, 179, 182, 205
1990s 75, 121, 152
YouTube 63, 119, 187, 215